Ann,

3

V

GW00836387

Three Sons

Mary Turner

Bloomington, IN Milton Keynes, UK

authorHOUSE®

AuthorHouse™
1663 Liberty Drive, Suite 200
Bloomington, IN 47403
www.authorhouse.com
Phone: 1-800-839-8640

AuthorHouse™ UK Ltd.
500 Avebury Boulevard
Central Milton Keynes, MK9 2BE
www.authorhouse.co.uk
Phone: 08001974150

First published by AuthorHouse 4/19/2007

ISBN: 978-1-4259-9242-2 (sc)

Printed in the United States of America
Bloomington, Indiana

This book is printed on acid-free paper.

Chapter One

Her long blond hair stuck to the pale bewildered face as rivulets of sweat ran freely from every pore. Encouraging voices sounded distant, although they came from directly above. Her body rested and was free from the searing pain that had taken over and tortured her for the last fourteen hours, but she waited for its return. It only gave her a minute and it was there again, tearing her apart like a hungry beast as it rose to a peak before tapering off.

"Come on girl, you're doing fine." The nurse wiped her young patient's head with a wet flannel. "You're nearly there," she encouraged her with a knowing smile.

The face that looked up from the pillow was that of a girl just turned sixteen. She was just a child herself and here she was about to become a mother. She lay in the downstairs bedroom of her mother's house, in the mining town of Prestonpans, on the East Coast of Scotland, defying them all by refusing to go into hospital.

Her mother had only learned of her daughter's condition six weeks ago and had barely recovered from the shock.

"Oooh A-ah! OH GOD Ma-a-a!!" She arched her back as she screamed.

The nurse was now urging her young patient to push on the pain, as the baby's head was now visible. As she bore down hard, she gave another agonising cry.

"That's it lass, go on, it's almost there." Nurse Marshal's encouraging words and skilful hands brought the bawling child into the world.

"You have a bonny wee lad Mary," the nurse informed the young lass who had now lain back on the pillow totally and utterly exhausted.

Mary's mother looked down on the child who was being wiped over by the small bustling nurse and remarked, "He is a wee beefy right enough."

"Yes Mrs Fairly, he is that. Can I ask you to make a pot of tea? I think Mary could do with one. She's had a long tiring labour." Her words tinged with slight sharpness.

"Aye, but it will make her think twice afore she gets into trouble again, so it will," Lizzie remarked back rather bluntly.

Lizzie Fairley was a good mother, but she could be described as being overpowering. Her word was law and no one dared defy her, but recently, her daughter was getting away with things that would usually earn her the back of Lizzie's hand. It was Mary's condition alone that saved her from Lizzie's wrath.

The shame that Mary had brought upon the family was hard enough to deal with, but keeping it from them for so long made Lizzie look so foolish.

Mary's father Charlie sat down and cried openly when he was told of his precious daughter's condition. She had let him down and it hurt him so much. He thought his daughter was above such things, especially being so young. She was his pride and joy and very special, as she was born twelve years after the boys. He looked on her as a gift from God. His two boys had often felt the weight of his trouser belt, but at no time had he laid a hand on Mary, he left that to his wife.

"A man should never strike a woman, if he does, he ceases to be a man," he would say. Often he would cover up for his Daughter, all to the fury of Lizzie.

"You spoil that girl Charlie Fairley so you do, and you'll live to regret it," his wife constantly chided.

Although Lizzie loved her daughter, she very seldom displayed physical affection, nor did she at any time tell her she loved her, although she was constantly buying things for her keeping her going with all the usual teenage fads.

The only one who seemed to light up his mother's eyes was Billy. He had always been special to Lizzie. Mary's brothers, being a good deal older than her, had both left home. The eldest boy Joe, had married and moved down south to Corby, where the job prospects were much better than they were in Scotland. Billy, who was a year younger than Joe, was in the merchant navy and very seldom at home. Leaving school at fifteen, Mary had gone straight into the cotton mill. She worked on the bobbins and loved every minute of it. She didn't leave school because of failed exams, it was purely and simply because she hated it. She had always been impatient, longing to grow up and earn her own money. Her father tried to persuade her to give school another year, but being headstrong she would not listen. Lizzie did not mind one way or another if her daughter left school, as long as she found herself a job she could do as she pleased, so Mary started work. Her friends changed as well. Work mates were more interesting than her school pals, most of who had stayed on for further education and became boring. Saturday nights were now spent in the neighbouring town's dance hall were she met up with the girls from the mill. This was where the teddy boys gathered, dressed in their drain-pipe trousers and long velvet collared jackets, fluorescent coloured socks under their winkle picker shoes. They looked exciting and far more interesting than the clean-shaven fresh-faced young lads in her neighbourhood.

During their breaks at the mill, the women taught Mary how to jive, putting it into practice on the dance floor where the music stirred her blood, making her feel alive. It was there she met him. She saw him watch as she danced with some spotty faced youth she wasn't the slightest bit interested in. The first half of the dance was over and as she and her partner waited for the band to strike up once more, he stepped onto the floor beside her and tapping the insipid looking lad on the shoulder said, "Move" and the lad did just that. Without a word, Mary started to dance with her new partner. He was handsome, tall and slender while his dark side burns and thick black hair made him look foreign. When he smiled, his mouth turned up slightly at one side, showing the most beautiful pearly white teeth Mary had ever seen. This guy that now held her was the kind she often daydreamed about, and here he was dancing with her, embracing her, breathing on her neck. Although she felt weak at the knees, there was no way she was going to sit down. His cheek lay against Mary's as they swayed back and forward to the gentle romantic music that filled their ears. Instinctively her arms tightened around his neck as she felt his warm hands move slowly over her back and down to her bottom. With his hands spread out on each side of her buttocks, he gently pressed against Mary and as their bodies moved to the slow rhythm of the music, Mary felt the burning desires of intimacy for the first time in her life.

She went with him that night and being so young and naive she fell for his bewitching charms. Her secret romance lasted a short while, but when Mary told him she was pregnant, he discreetly disappeared. All she knew of him was he was from Edinburgh and he called himself Ali. That and a small passport photo, secretly hidden behind the lining of her handbag was hers alone to know. She kept her worries to herself, afraid of what her mother might do if she found out. Now, nine months from that magical night, the consequence lay in the little wooden cradle beside Mary Fairley's bed.

"What are you going to call him my dear?" the nurse asked buttoning up her Burberry raincoat.

Mary, still very weak, looked over at her mother. Lizzie waited to hear, hoping it would give her some clue as to who the father was. As Mary refused to name the father of her child, every one assumed he must be a married man. "I don't have a name for him just yet. I'll have to think about it." She sounded so tired.

"Why don't you call him after your grandfather Mary? He was very good to you when he was alive, so he was," Lizzie suggested. Mary closed her eyes to stop the tears. She was now at her mother's mercy as having no money of her own, she would have to depend on her for everything. How was she ever going to break free now? Every day Lizzie would remind her daughter how grateful she should feel.

"All right Mother. Frank will do. I suppose one name's as good as another," Mary answered weakly.

The nurse bent over Mary and whispered, "I'll see you later. Get some sleep and think of a name you want for your baby. You'll feel better after a good sleep." She patted her young patient's arm and left, giving Lizzie a nod and a grunt as she passed.

Going to the window, Lizzie pulled the lace net curtains to one side and watched the nurse push her bicycle along the front path.

"She went to school with me she did. Always thought she was better than anybody else. Snotty bitch. What she needs is a man. Aye, then she would understand what life was about, so she would. Forty- six and still single," she tutted.

Mary listened to her mother miscalling the nurse and thought how utterly stupid her remarks were. Jenny Marshal knew all too well what life was all about. She had deprived herself of any private life, as night and day, seven days a week she tended not only to the new mothers and their offspring's but also the elderly and infirmed including her own ageing mother. Poverty and abuse was also no stranger to this woman, as she came across it every day of her life. The nurse certainly knew what life was about and the last thing she needed to complicate her way of life was a man.

"Ma-Ma," Mary called.

Lizzie let the curtains fall back into place and walking away from the window walked towards her daughter. "Aye what is it?" "Can you lift the baby up and give him to me?" she asked as she pushed herself gingerly up onto the pillows.

"Now Mary, you should be resting when he's asleep. You'll have plenty of time to hold him when he's bawling his head off. You heard the nurse...sleep she said. Anyway, you don't lift a bairn up when he's sleeping. He'll get to know and want lifting all the time, so he will."

"For goodness sake Ma, he's just born. He'll not know any difference." Lizzie went forward and gently laid her daughter back on the pillows. Arranging her bed covers she chide, "Take a telling. I know what's best, so get some sleep and I'll look after young Frankie."

Mary thought, perhaps her mother was right. She certainly needed to sleep, but couldn't quite settle down as her head was full of troubled thoughts. She had turned her life up side down and would now have to leave the rest to providence. Staying under her mother's roof wasn't going to be easy, but there was nothing else she could do.

Just as Mary thought, her mother had completely taken over. Lizzie decided what was best for the baby and Mary had to comply, and no matter what Mary did, Lizzie found fault.

"I know what's best," Lizzie used as the final word.

Problems also occurred when Mary arranged an evening out as Lizzie had to know where she was going and with whom before considering whether to allow her out for the evening, then if she approved, she would set the time her Daughter had to be home. Fighting back was useless as Lizzie had the upper hand; after all, it was she who had to look after the baby. Mary found herself in a no-win situation.

"You should have thought about all those things before you got landed my lady!" Lizzie constantly snapped.

"Aye ma, and you like to use the bairn to manipulate me. Don't you?" would be her refutation.

Lizzie would then played her trump card. "If you don't like the rules of my house...*GET OUT*, but mind, you take the bairn with you."

It was during such a row, Charlie returned home from working a hard shift down the coalmine. He was on the early shift, six in the morning until two in the afternoon. He walked into the house as Lizzie screamed. "You damned ungrateful wee bugger, so you are!!!"

"Well Ma, its Mary you'll do this, Mary you'll do that. I'm sick of it. Can't you ask me to do things instead of demanding all the time?" Mary sobbed though her words.

"Oh for heavens sake you two, can't you get through the day without screaming at each other?" Charlie laid his piece tin on the sink top and turned to face his wife. "Can't you give it a rest woman? She's right enough. You do go on a bit and you have her working like a blooming slave at times."

This infuriated Lizzie. The veins on her neck stood out like roads on a map and her face turned bright purple with rage. Lizzie was a fine looking woman but the anger within her distorted her features and made her look almost ugly. She turned her wrath on her husband as he walked over and stood by his daughter's side.

"Oh now it's me that's always at fault. You don't know half Charlie Fairley. You only see what you want to see. You'd have me working night and day in this house while madam here sits reading in her room. It's the cheek she gives me as well! She's so ungrateful."

"No I'm not Ma, but you never let up. I've just brushed the stairs down and done the top windows. I only sat down with my book for ten minutes, then you were on at me."

"LOOK!" waving his hands in the air and shouting with frustration Charlie continued, "I've just done a hard shift and I'm not coming home to this, something will have to be done."

"Like what?" snapped Lizzie? "You try talking to her as I get nowhere with her these days. I watched the bairn this morning while she went to the chemist. She was out for two hours...Two hours to go to the chemist! Now I ask you, is that not taking a complete rise out of me?" With questioning eyes, Charlie looked at his daughter who flopped wearily into a kitchen chair. Her huge green eyes met her father's stare and shrugging her weary shoulders she said in a dejected tone.

"I met Suzie McKenzie and I had a cup of tea with her in the cafe".

"Well that's not so bad Lizzie. She's very seldom out without the bairn." Smiling down at his daughter he gave her a sly wink.

"For God sake Charlie, I didn't know where she was and the bairn had to be fed. I'm not here to be used." Anger was still very much in her voice.

"Well forget it. I want some tea," Charlie said, showing signs of frustration.

Mary made some tea for her father while Lizzie prepared the vegetables for the evening meal. Both women worked in silence. The spoon clattered on the side of the cup as Charlie stirred his tea. He looked at the two women in his life and shook his head sadly.

"Do you know what I think Lizzie? Mary should find herself a job. Two women in the house don't agree."

"Well, if she wants to work there's no one stopping her. The bairn's no bother, it's just when I'm watching him she's gallivanting, that's what gets me fair rattled, so it does."

"Ma, I don't gallivant!" Mary stood up quickly causing the chair legs to scrape across the floor.

"Don't start again. Please," pleaded Charlie.

A cry came from within the pram that stood in the hall. "There, you'll both be pleased now. That's the bairn wakened." He glared at the two women.

"He's been sleeping a while. He'll want changed and fed." Mary left her parents in the kitchen and disappeared into the down-stairs bedroom with her young infant.

Charlie lifted his mug of tea and walked along the hall and into the living room. A blazing fire raged in the black cast-iron range and the brass rail and fittings shone like a new penny, reflecting the warm glow from the leaping flames back into the room. He sat back in his chair and lifting his pipe from the rack that hung by his side, started to fill the silver bowl from the pouch that he pulled from his pocket. Puffing rhythmically he soon got the tobacco glowing, sending a rich wooden aroma through out the room in swirls of smoke. Lifting his paper, he now settled down in comfort, far away from the bowels of the earth from where he had just come. He was a hard workingman, a good father and loving husband.

His face was still extraordinarily handsome. His tall well-built frame towered above his wife, as she was barely five feet tall. Her once slim figure was long gone and she was now round and plump, constantly going on diets and buying all sorts of rubber gadgets to wear or exercise with. All to no avail as she didn't lost an ounce in fact she usually ended up gaining more weight. Although her hair was now silvery grey, it had been as lovely and as blonde as her daughter Mary's was now. Charlie was still puffing his pipe and studying the racing section when Lizzie came into the room.

Muttering under her breath she walked over to the highly polished table and covered its surface with a thick felt matting before throwing the crisp white linen cloth on top, then, walking round the table, she straightened the cloth, making sure it was evenly spread, wiping her hand over the surface as if brushing away invisible crumbs and removing offending folds.

Charlie looked over the top of his paper, shaking his head slightly, he continued reading without comment. With muted muttering, she opened the dresser doors where she kept the dinner plates and crockery. Cutlery clattered onto the table, and spoons rattled as they were thrown into the saucers. It became almost too much to bear. Charlie threw the paper to one side and glared across at his wife. "For goodness sake woman do you want a bloody hammer? What's getting at you now? I've not had as much as a minute's peace since I came home. What the hell's up with you?"

Lizzie stopped and glared over at her irate husband. Wagging the spoon she was holding, she complained bitterly. "Charlie, you think I'm hard on her, don't you?" She waited a few moments for an answer, but none came. He just continued to stare hard at her. Despairingly she drew a large intake of breath then slowly sighed "Oh! Charlie. If I'm going to help her, she'll have to take life more seriously. She's playing at dolls with that child. She still hasn't realised she's got responsibilities, and you, you always take her side."

Charlie rose and going to his wife's side, gently took hold of her arm and led her to the chair directly opposite his own. Without protest, she let him ease her into the chair, then patting her hand, he stepped back and sat down on the edge of his cushion. Leaning towards her, he spoke softly. "Lizzie, now listen. You still haven't got over the shock of the bairn and I don't blame your actions at times, but listen to me for a while. Mary is young and hasn't come to terms with motherhood yet, but it will come. Give her time. She's doing her best round the house, granted she can't work like you, but she only had to keep her room tidy before, now she's doing windows and jobs she never had to do. Think back to when you had Joe."

Lizzie straightened her back and sounded indignant. "Don't compare me with our Mary. I never had our Joe when I was sixteen. I was going on eighteen and *married*!" She emphasised the latter part of her statement.

Exasperation crept into Charlie's voice as he tried to reason with his wife. "Lizzie, will you let me finish? I meant that you too had to learn how to cope with a baby and keep a house, and as you rightly said, you were older. It wasn't easy for you at first, so it's just the same for Mary. And think. You had me and felt settled, while she is missing out on her youth. She's bound to feel trapped. Don't treat her like a child, that's another thing. She'll respond if you talk to her and treat her as an adult."

"Listen to you now," Lizzie snapped. "First of all you say she's only a child then in the next breath your telling me to treat her like an adult. You don't know what your saying." Rising quickly, she disappeared once more into the kitchen.

Charlie muttered to him-self while sucking on his pipe, "I give up, I really do. Women!"

Pulling the pram up two steps and trying to hold on to an umbrella was no easy task but Mary managed it with a struggle. Pushing the door open and yelling at the top of her voice caused her mother to come running along the lobby.

"Wheesht lassie, what are you yelling at? Your Da's having a sleep." Looking down at the small pools of water and the mucky pram wheels on her lino, Lizzie displayed great annoyance. "Look at the mess on the floor. I should have had papers down when it's so wet out-side so I should." Waving her hands about frantically, Lizzie ran with short steps towards the cupboard under the stair, where she stored old newspapers and various household items.

"Ma will you stand still and listen. I've got a job!" Filled with excitement, Mary tore back the waterproof cover and the woollen blankets and lifted her cooing child into her arms.

"A job. Where about?" Lizzie asked, turning away from the task in hand and holding her arms out to receive the precious bundle.

"Miss Smith's paper shop. I've to work with her and Pearl as Miss Smith's cutting her hours down now that she's getting on a bit." Removing her wet coat she followed Lizzie into the living room, and as her mother removed the baby's outer garments, she stood over her and prattled on about her new job.

"Do you realise you have to be up very early in the morning when you work in a newsagent's?" Lizzie asked, as Mary hadn't mentioned her working hours.

"No Ma, I don't have to go early. Pearl does the early morning papers; Miss Smith is doing the late ones so I work in between, see? I start at nine o'clock and finish at five and I can be home for an hour at dinner time."

Becoming aware of her father's empty chair, Mary stopped talking about the job and asked with concern where her father was. Without looking up at Mary, Lizzie kept her concentration on the job she was doing, changing the baby's nappy. Every thing she needed for that job was kept altogether in the brass box that stood along side the fire- place.

"I told you when you were making that unholy din that your Dad was having a sleep."

"In the bed?" Mary voiced surprise.

"Of course in bed. Where else would he go?" she answered.

Mary gave the empty chair another quick glance, as if she had missed something. "But he always sleeps on the chair before the fire. Why has he gone to bed?"

"He just felt like a lie down, that's all. Now what about this job?"

Unknown to her daughter, Lizzie too was worried about Charlie. In all their thirty years of marriage, he had never gone to bed during the day. Charlie had a routine that hardly ever changed which consisted of his mug of tea, a smoke of his pipe and a read at his paper, followed by an hour's sleep in the chair before his evening meal.

Chapter Two

Mary hurried home from work, as the black clouds above grew nearer. As it had been quite bright when she left home at lunchtime, she wore a thin jacket that would soon get soaked through, once the skies opened up. The house just became visible when she felt the large spots of rain thud against her head. Running up the path she kept her head down until she reached the front door. On removing her jacket in the hall, it occurred to her that the house was very quiet.

"Mum!" She called, but there was no answer. This silence was strange, as both her parents and the baby were always in at this time of night. Mary crept through and looked into the kitchen. The pots were boiling on the stove but there was no sign of her mother. She then doubled back and opened the sitting room door. Mary's mouth gaped open as she yelled in surprise. "Billy!" She ran over to her brother almost knocking him over with excitement. "I wondered why the house was so quiet."

"It was difficult Sis, but we managed to stick a plaster over the bairn's mouth."

"You never!" Mary gave a quick glance over to where the child sat filling his mouth with biscuit, caring nothing for the goings on around him.

"When did you get here? How long are you staying? When do you go back?" she quizzed without pausing for breath.

"That's typical," laughed Billy, "I've just arrived and you want to know when I'm leaving." He gave her a gentle shove and winked over at their parents, who sat laughing at the antics of their children.

After Billy had released his elated sister from a long hug, he looked her intently in the eyes and keeping his hands firmly on her shoulders said seriously. "I want to have a word with you my girl. It'll keep for now but we must talk."

She felt the joy in her heart fade, as she knew what Billy wanted to talk about. This was her first encounter with him since she gave birth to Frank. Her mother had written to him about it, but he had never commented or asked questions, as he preferred to leave it until he arrived home. Being so very close to his sister, the news from his mother had upset him very much.

Lizzie saw the change in Mary's face and as she wanted to keep the evening pleasant, she interrupted by standing in front of them, giving a shove like a referee separating two boxers, saying light-heartedly, "Get yourselves seated or the meal won't be worth eating."

"Aye Ma," Billy mocked, "I only came home for your cooking."

Charlie added to the banter. "The food you get in the navy must be really bad when it makes your Ma's cooking taste good."

"Cheeky bugger," Lizzie said as she walked out of the room. She could still be heard talking to herself as she dished the evening meal on to the plates.

Charlie thumbed in the direction of the kitchen. "If there's any burned bits, you know who's going to get them."

Mary looked towards her brother and smiled affectionately. "It's great to have you home Billy."

The meal over and young Frank in bed, the family gathered round the fire while Billy told them fascinating stories of his long voyage that had taken him to Singapore and China, and then excusing himself, he disappeared into his bedroom only to return minutes later laden with gifts for the family.

"Ma, I hope you like these," he said handing Lizzie a brown paper parcel. All eyes were on her as she picked meticulously at the string.

"Pull it off Ma," Mary said impatiently.

"No! You'll learn to save things as well," Lizzie snapped at the over curious lass.

"But, string Ma?"

"Aye string." Lizzie mimicked Mary.

This peculiar ritual when coming across string really annoyed Mary. After straightening the string out, Lizzie wound it around two fingers, then, taking the end piece, wrapped it round the middle, forming a neat little bow. This would then find its way into an old toffee tin beside many others.

The paper was now removed with extreme care, as that too would be folded and saved. The contents of the parcel now lay before Lizzie. Picking one of the items up, she gasped. The rich blue silk square fell from its fold as Lizzie held it up. Fingering the delicate embroidery that adorned the centre, she could only utter.

"My, my!" Gold and silver threads entwined with rich colours formed the flowers in the centre of the scarf. Laying it down carefully, she lifted the second parcel. A white silk square with the same delicate embroidery, but this time it was birds that formed the centre pattern. "Oh Son, these are really something. I couldn't wear them, they're far to special, so they are."

"As long as you like them Ma."

"Oh aye son I really do."

"Mary, these are yours," he said, handing her two brown parcels. Both were long shaped, one large and the other quite small. Much to the annoyance of her mother, Mary tore at the paper.

"A *FAN*," she squealed. "It's absolutely gorgeous Billy," she gasped as she flicked it open. The colours were stunning as was the geisha girl that smiled out at her. Opening the second parcel brought a similar reaction. It was a parasol. Quickly she had it opened, and then resting it on her shoulder, she made it spin.

"That's all we need now our Mary", Lizzie sighed deeply, "bad luck."

"Don't be daft woman," Charlie laughed. "It's an umbrella that brings bad luck."

"Well," she said, "what's that then, it's just the same."

"No it's not Ma. This is for the sun and anything as lovely as this can't possibly bring bad luck."

"Now Da'," Billy grinned, "I've brought you back your usual tipple. No doubt you're a bit short by now, but before I give you it, have you been looking after my you know what?" Billy was referring to his motorbike.

This was a sore subject as his mother hated motorbikes and worried herself stiff every time he got on it. "Aye he has been looking after it and I'll be grateful if you'd get rid of it, so I will. I never get peace of mind when you get on that contraption."

"Not that old argument again Ma," Billy pleaded. "I'm safe on it. I don't go fast."

"I don't say you do Billy, but you worry me to death when you take it out."

"Well you'll just have to worry because I'm having it on the road tomorrow."

Mary's attention was now on her brother as she begged. "Can I come too Billy?" "You'll be working," he reminded her.

"Not tomorrow. I'm off tomorrow. Can I come? Please Billy?" grabbing at his arm she pleaded.

Lizzie was not amused, as Mary knew full well what her mother thought about motorbikes. She hated them with a passion. Billy bought the bike a few years back and his father polished and looked after it while he was at sea.

Lizzie wagged her finger at her daughter.

"You'll not be sitting your hint end on that bike tomorrow or any other day my lass, and that's final."

"But Ma!"

"No buts about it lady, you'll stay off that bike!"

Mary looked pleadingly at her brother, who mouthed, "Shush" giving her an impish smile that said, 'Leave it to me.'

The following morning Billy had a lie in. Mary had risen early to tend to her infant, and as it was her day off, she usually gave her mother a hand with the housework. The morning went well. The two women chatted happily and Mary did her best to stay on the right side of her mother.

Around eleven o'clock, Billy emerged yawning and rubbing his tousled hair.

"Well!" remarked Mary, "the sailor has surfaced from the deep."

Giving his sister a warm smile he answered, "Aye and it was deep. Lovely deep, sleep. I don't know when I've had such a good night's rest, certainly not since I left these shores."

"Come away and get some breakfast", Lizzie beckoned. "I'm going along to old Mrs. Millians to do a bit of cleaning and ironing for the poor soul. She's expecting her son and his wife this weekend, so I washed her windows and changed her curtains. I have to make up the spare bed for her and do bits and pieces. It's a shame when old folk don't get the help they deserve, so it is." Lizzie shook her head in despair.

"Aye, so it is Ma," agreed Mary, then she asked sweetly, "Are you taking the bairn? You know Mrs. Millian likes to see him."

"I suppose I could. I'll only be gone an hour or so, and besides the air will make him sleep."

Mary glanced quickly over at Billy who stared back with questioning eyes and a stupid expression on his face. Mary signalled back by mimicking a driver holding on to the handlebars of a bike.

He quickly got her meaning and nearly choked on the food that he had just spooned into his mouth. Lizzie turned round and hurried towards her son who coughed and spluttered. Thumping his back with great gusto, she sent the food from his mouth flying. "MA!" he gulped, "you can stop battering me to death."

"If he doesn't choke to death, you'll finish him off," laughed Mary.

"You all right now son?" she enquired, looking into his face with motherly concern.

"Aye Ma, I said I was." His cheeks were wet with tear. "You never know the minute. I read, just the other day, a wife in Glasgow choked to death just tasting the tatties. She didn't know if she salted them or not, so she tasted one and choked. See the heat of the tattie made her take an intake of breath, and the tattie slid o'er her throat".

"And had she?" Mary asked with tongue in cheek.

"Had she what?" her mother frowned.

"Salted the tatties?" Mary giggled.

"That's not funny. Really Mary, sometimes I wonder about you," she snapped, giving her daughter a dark look.

Billy sat with his hand over his mouth, trying to suppress his laughter, but he failed miserably. Shoulders shaking he let out one big belly roar.

"Not you an' all." Lizzie looked at him and shook her head in despair."Ah Ma. I'm sorry, but it's just the things you say at times." Billy fibbed. It was Mary that had caused his laughter.

The two of them watched through the net curtains until Lizzie disappeared out of sight. "Right Billy, get the bike. We've only got an hour, so hurry up." She pushed her brother towards the door.

"If she finds out, she'll bloody kill me. I'm worse than daft listening to you," he said as he hurried along the lobby. He made his way towards the shed that stood at the bottom of the back garden. Opening the door, he stopped for a few seconds and beheld the sight before him giving a low whistle. Rubbing his hands together, he spoke lovingly. "Hallo my wee beauty." Pulling off the oilskin hap, he gazed upon his pride and joy. It sparkled as the light fell on the highly polished chrome. Not a bit of rust had dared to appear, his father had seen to that. Billy wasted no time in getting the Enfield up the garden, along the path and out into the street. Giving the starter a few kicks, he soon had it roaring. Turning the engine off, Billy returned to the house and called up stairs to Mary. "Come on then. It's ready to go."

She hurried down quickly and laughed at him as he fixed his goggles and helmet. "You look like Biggles," she sniggered.

"Where's my big black coat?" he asked.

"Under the stair cupboard beside all the rest," she pointed along to the door at the other end of the hall. "Hurry Billy, we've only got an hour."

Billy moved smartly and opening the cupboard door he could just see the pile of coats hanging on the hooks, as it was quite dark under the stair. He rummaged through them barely recognising his own heavy Black coat. It was a long cupboard stretching all the way under the stair and it badly needed a light. Throwing the coat over his shoulder, he ran along the lobby and out the door after Mary, who was standing waiting by the machine. "Right, on the back and hold on."

Billy was now seated on the front and wriggling into his coat. He had a bit trouble getting it buttoned, but he finally managed. Starting up once more the bike engine roared. Billy moved the throttle back and forth, causing the bike to act like a wild animal straining on a lead. "Right Sis," he shouted to be heard.

"Take her away our Billy," Mary giggled as she pointed ahead. They took off. Mary's hair blew around her face while the cold air battered against her cheeks causing them to tingle. She loved the bike and often dreamed of taking off on it by herself, but she knew that could never happen.

They reached the edge of the town and now approached the country. Fields whizzed passed, hedge rows and dry stane dykes appeared and disappeared like magic. It was late autumn and the trees were almost bare, their branches looking like knobble fingers. A few rustic leaves still clung to the neatly trimmed hedgerows. They passed by the birched woodland with young oaks and sycamore, surrounded in a carpet of bracken. The smell of decaying leaves and fungus filled Mary's nostrils as she inhaled air, inflating her lungs to their limits.

"Don't hold me so tight Mary," yelled Billy.

"What?" she shouted, straining to hear above the roar of the engine.

"Don't hold me so tight. You're stopping my circulation."

"I'm not holding on tight. I'm hardly touching you", she yelled in his ear.

A mile or so further on, Billy shouted back again. "I feel funny. I have to stop. I haven't any feeling in my arms. I'm bloody paralysed about the arms."

The bike came to a halt and Mary jumped off quickly. Going to the front of the bike she faced her brother, who by now had somehow managed to remove his gauntlet type gloves, and was staring down at his hands. They were purple. "Don't tell me I'm taking a stroke. My arms have no feeling." He really looked worried.

Mary gaped vacantly at him before going into hysterical laughter.

"For goodness sake Mary, what are you laughing at? This is serious."

"Billy," she said between short breaths, "och Billy, no wonder your arms are numb. You've only gone and put Ma's winter coat on. The sleeves are far too tight and you've stopped your blood circulation."

"Shit Sis, I thought I was a goner." He struggled with the sleeves until he was free from their vice-like grip.

Mary danced up and down in pain, the kind that usually follows hearty laughter. Billy joined her as he collapsed against her for support. Tears ran down their cheeks as they clung together. "I should have known when I was buttoning it up. I thought I had put on a hell of a weight." Again they fell into uncontrollable laughter.

"I'll not be able to control myself when I see Ma putting on that coat. She'll wonder what I'm laughing at and I'll not be able to tell her." Doubled up, she held her side and gasped for breath.

Pulling himself together Billy wiped the tears from his eyes, "You'll need no explanation if we don't get back before her. Come on, get back on the bike and let's be off." He threw his leg over the machine before holding it steady for Mary to scramble on.

"Billy!"

"Aye, what now."

"Why don't they put springs under the seats of motor bikes? My arse is red raw."

"I'll take the matter up with the makers and order you a padded seat when I get back. Come on, get on or you'll have a sorer arse if Ma puts her foot on it; and by the way, less of that language," he scolded her lightly.

They arrived back before Lizzie, but only just. The bike was put back into the shed and the pair of them looked as if they had never ventured out. When Charlie arrived home from work, he was surprised to see his son at home.

"I expected you to be off on that bike of yours instead of sitting around here." He thought it unusual, as Billy was always eager to be out and about when he came home from sea.

"Tonight Da', I'm going over to see Fred and Sandy." He was referring to a couple of his mates.

"You'll have trouble getting a hold of Sandy as he's seeing a lassie and I hear it's real serious," Charlie informed him. "He's even dropped his darts for her."

Eyebrows raised, Billy looked surprised, "Dropped the darts? Really? Must be love. Do I know her?"

"No, I don't think so. She's a townie I'm told." His father laughed. "How long she'll keep him from his darts is debatable."

"I'll soon have no pals left," he remarked.

Listening to their conversation Mary added. "Well Billy, you'll just have to find yourself a wife."

"I'm not so stupid our Mary, and talking about stupidity, we have still some talking to do."

"What have you both been doing all afternoon, I thought you would have talked each others heads off." Lizzie looked at them suspiciously. She looked as if she knew they had been up to something.

"Well, Billy did talk till he was blue in the face." Mary smirked as Billy looked on with a knowing grin.

The Royal Enfield bike was taken out of the shed regardless to what Lizzie said. Charlie felt the bite of his wife's tongue as she accused him of encouraging her son, but Mary was never on it again as Lizzie had created the devil of a row at the very mention of it.

The next few weeks passed and Mary saw very little of her brother as he had caught up with a few of his friends. During the week, he would spend his time in the Railway Tavern playing darts or dominoes with the lads, and at weekends, like most single guys, a couple of pints would be swilled down before heading for the local dance halls.

Lizzie had gone over the road to visit a neighbour and Tom was out at a union meeting leaving Mary alone in the house with Billy. This was the first time they had been alone since the bike episode. It was while she fed her child, she looked up and caught her brother looking thoughtfully at the baby's face. As their eyes met his questioning gaze betrayed his thoughts. Mary's face flushed and although she felt quite disturbed she had to answer the question that was running through her brother's mind. "It's bound to come out Billy so say what's on your mind."

"I don't know what to say Mary. I was so angry when Ma told me in the letter, but I'm left with nothing but pity for that bairn."

"How? He's all right. We manage," Mary answered indignantly.

"Who's the father?" he asked looking her straight in the eyes.

"You don't know him Billy; and before you ask---*NO*! I'm not saying. Anyway, I don't know where he went to," her voice faltered as she looked away, "as a matter of fact, I never knew where he came from."

He shook his head in despair as he said, "You're a silly bugger. You've gone and burdened yourself for life now. Sixteen and tied down with a bairn!"

She knew Billy was right. She was beginning to feel trapped of late, but still he had no right to tell her what she already knew, still, she hit back. "It's no better than you. Your life is not all that great! Twenty-eight and left on the shelf! You should..."

"What?" he interrupted. "I should what??" His voice raised slightly in anger. "Get married for the sake of it? Is that what your trying to say? You must be flaming joking."

A silence fell between them and all that could be heard was the crackling of the coal in the grate and the sucking noise from the sleepy child who drained the milk from his bottle as if his thirst could not be quenched.

His gaze still focused on Mary and her child. He broke the silence by giving a slight cough.

Looking back into his face, Mary smiled weakly and said, "Don't worry about us Billy, we're fine. My job's not the best for wages, but we get by."

"Aye so you do, but you've no rent or electricity to pay. What would happen if it weren't for our folk? You'd be in deep shit then."

Her lips quivered, "You've made your point. You're just like Ma. She's never done telling me how grateful I should be.

I can't rub the past out. The bairn's here now and I love him. I thought you would understand." Her eyes filled with tears, and as she looked upon her child, a teardrop fell from her eye splashing on to the small chubby fist that gripped the feeding bottle.

Billy sat down on the arm of Mary's chair then slipping his arm round her neck he gently kissed her hair. "I'm sorry pet. I've no business interfering but it's only natural that your favourite brother should worry about you, now isn't it."

Mary's reply was a nod of the head and a sniff. "Well then," Billy continued, "If ever you need help, you tell me. OK?" He gave her a tight squeeze. She nodded her head as he rose and walked to the kitchen door. "I'll make us a cup of cocoa before the pair of them get in."

The following evening, Billy arrived back with word of his next sea voyage. He was leaving within the week and had to make his way by train to Liverpool. As usual, Lizzie cried her eyes out when she was told the news. Her favourite child was leaving once more.

"Come on Ma, I've still got a few days left. There's plenty time for all this when you wave me off." Giving his mother a brief hug, he tried humouring her.

"She's practising Son," his father quipped from behind his newspaper.

Mary too was on the verge off tears as she asked, "will you be gone long?"

"I don't think so, at least not as long as the last time. Canada this time, but when we arrive there, goodness knows what will happen."

Sitting himself down on the couch, he groaned aloud as he removed his shoes. My feet are absolutely killing me in these shoes. I think I'll give them a steep in hot water."

"Put some washing soda in the water. It helps to soothe them," Lizzie sniffed, still feeling down at the knowledge of her son's departure. "But do it in the kitchen and not in here. If there's anything I can't bear to look at, that's feet!" She could still reprimand him even in her distress.

Billy was now in his bare feet and heading for the kitchen calling to his mother, "Where will I find it?"

"Washing soda? It's under the stair in the cupboard on the top shelf. It's in the brown paper bag." Lizzie informed him.

Billy called to her from under the stairs, "I wish you'd get a light put in under here. I can hardly see. Where did you say it was? Never mind, I've found it!" Taking the brown bag from the shelf, Billy went into the kitchen and filled the basin with piping hot water. Easing his feet gently into the basin he gave a few yelps as his feet came in contact with the boiling water. His feet now resting on the bottom of the basin, Billy sprinkled the contents of the bag into the water. Giving a groan of relief, he leaned back into the chair and closed his eyes, murmuring softly to himself. "Heaven, I've died and gone to heaven." He sat like this for a good few minutes before attempting to move his feet, and when he did try, they wouldn't budge. His feet were stuck firm to the bottom of the basin. Panicking he yelled, *"Ma! Ma!"*

Lizzie hurried through to the kitchen, followed closely by Mary.

"Ma! Oh Ma! *MY FEET ARE STUCK IN THE BASIN!*"

"What happened?" Mary asked, staring down at the jelly like substance that held her brother's feet fast.

"What have you done? Let me see the paper bag." Grabbing the bag from the table, Lizzie turned it upside down allowing the remaining granules to fall into the palm of her hand.

27

Charlie had joined the group in the kitchen, and removing his reading glasses, he too stood open mouthed.

Lizzie broke into rapturous laughter and all three faces looked agog.

"He's only gone and filled the basin with a pound of semolina mix. The hot water has jelled it all together." The rest of the family now joined Lizzie, roaring with laughter. Tears ran down her face as she held her side. Her laughter was causing her pain. "Oh my God Billy, you're a bloody star turn, so you are," she howled.

"I've told you before to get a light put under the stair," Billy chuckled.

"Why on earth do you keep those things in there anyway Lizzie?" Charlie asked between his laughter.

"Because that cupboard keeps packet stuff nice and dry, so now you know!"

The morning Billy left for sea was like every other goodbye he had said. It never did get any better. Lizzie cried her eyes out while Charlie gave his son the usual fatherly advice. "Don't get into bad company, write to your mother regularly and keep clear of bad women."

The latter Billy did think very funny although he refrained from making any comments. Here he was nearly thirty and his family regarded him as celibate.

They said their goodbyes at the gate, as the lad hated the embarrassing scenes Lizzie had caused in the past. Once she had held the bus up for five minutes as she hugged and patted him, bawling her eyes out as the passengers looked on. Some grinned and some were near to tears themselves.

Her brother leaving made Mary feel so down. The house seemed empty without him, but his home was on the high seas.

Hanging her jacket in the cupboard beneath the stairs, Mary caught sight of her mother's black winter coat. She laughed quietly as the vision of Billy flashed through her mind.

"What's so funny?" her father asked as he passed the door.

"I'll tell you some night Da'. Some night around the fire when we're telling tales."

"I'll hold you to that," Charlie said, clipping her playfully across the head.

Chapter Three

"How old is the lad now?" asked Mrs.Younger as she waited for her change.

"Eighteen months," Mary answered dropping a few pennies into the inquisitive customers outstretched hand.

"And who is he like?" she inquired.

Mary, keeping her composure, smiled thinly at the inquisitive woman and answered curtly, "He's like his-self Mrs. Younger. Just like his-self."

Pearl, who was counting out magazines at the other end of the shop, stopped what she was doing and looking along at Mary, signalled to her to ignore the busybody.

Mrs. Younger was one of the town's gossips and a regular know-all, and it would be a feather in her cap if she were to find out who fathered Mary's bairn.

"I saw your mother with him the other day, and I thought, 'now, what a handsome child'. Brown eyes and such lovely dark hair, and you being very blonde," she grinned.

"A throw back Mrs. Younger...Now is there anything more I can get you?" Mary's smile had turned into a hard glare.

"No, no I think not. Good day to you Mary."

As she spoke, a young man in working clothes opened the shop door. Holding it ajar he allowed the interfering woman to pass through. Without waiting to be told, Mary turned to the shelf, took down a packet of Woodbine and lifting up the Evening News, she handed them both to the approaching man.

"Your late tonight Pat," Mary commented.

"Aye. I am a bit." He automatically took the paper and cigarettes from Mary, giving her the right money.

Pat Sweeny had come through from the west of Scotland to work in the mines, and had found lodgings with an elderly couple who treated him like one of there own family. He was a tall, dark, handsome bloke, rugged to the point of being slightly coarse. He worked hard all week and played hard at weekends. He liked his drink and could be seen staggering home on a Saturday night as if his two legs wanted to go in different directions. He never bothered very much about women that were until Mary started working in the paper shop. "Well Mary, when will you come away out with me?" He asked the same question nearly every night.

"When you sign the pledge and turn tea-total Pat Sweeny," she teased, "and there's fat chance of that."

He stood for a minute eyeing her up before replying.

"I think, you think I'm kidding. I really would like to take you out. How about it?" Spreading his hand across his chest he said, "I'll be the perfect gentleman. Honest!"

"I'll think about it, but don't hold your breath," she said laughing.

Taken quite unaware by her answer he asked, "You'll think about it? Really!"

"I said I would. Now get out of here before I change my mind!"

"I'll see you tomorrow then," he replied. He looked over towards the figure lurking in the corner and called, "Bye Pearl."

"Aye Pat; bye," she shouted back, knowing he called out only to let her know he was aware of her eavesdropping.

Going along the counter to where Mary stood, Pearl looked into her eyes. "You're not thinking about going out with him Mary?"

Jumping to his defence, Mary answered quite abruptly,

"And why not? There's nothing wrong with Pat, except he likes a drink on a Saturday night. If that's a crime then the whole of the town wants locking up. Besides, there's not much else he can do him being single an all. Perhaps if he had a regular girl he wouldn't drink so much." Pausing for a second, as if it suddenly struck her she said, "Yes Pearl, I like him. He's good looking and he makes me laugh." She straightened up the papers that lay on the counter in front of her, deliberately avoiding Pearls gaze.

Pearl continued to scrutinise her, then giving a sigh and a quick shake of the head she said, "Well maybe so Mary, but he's worth watching. He's a right dark horse is that one!"

Mary did take Pat's offer up and that first date led to many others. Pat cut his drinking drastically, although not altogether.

Eventually the time came for Pat to meet Mary's parents. Lizzie wasn't keen on him at all. She thought he was forward and too self- assured. She had been informed by, 'well meaning' individuals of Pat's devotion to the evil drink. The fact that the men in her family liked a good skin-full now and again was neither here nor there. Pat Sweeny was, in her eyes, a drunkard. Charlie on the other hand knew Pat from work and was aware of the lad's eagerness for hard graft. He liked a man who wasn't work shy so needless to say, they had a lot in common.

The women were in the kitchen preparing tea and Charlie and Pat sat talking in the living room. Charlie rose and going forward to the cabinet where his wife stored her best dishes he asked, "Would you like a dram?"

"Well I'll not say no, Mr.Fairley. A small one though."

Opening up the door on the right side of the cabinet he grinned and said, "I always manage to find a wee corner in here for a bottle, although if Lizzie had her way, it would be down the sink." Charlie poured out a couple of whiskies and handed one to his guest. "And by the way, the name's Charlie."

"Oh aye then Charlie, cheers!" Pat raised his glass as if he were about to give a toast.

"I'm quite serious about Mary Mr. Fai.... I mean Charlie," Pat stammered.

Mary's father looked long and hard at him. He never expected such a statement, not at this early stage. Pat continued after clearing his throat. "I love Mary and I hope some day she will be my wife." He waited nervously on Charlie's reply.

Charlie walked towards the fireplace and stood with his back towards Patrick staring hard into the burning coals. He stood like this for what seemed ages to Patrick, when at last he turned and faced him. "Have you told her how you feel?" he enquired, taking a gulp from the glass he held in his hand, but never taking his eyes of Patrick.

"No. I'm not a soppy person, in fact, I'm surprised at coming out with such a thing, but I do want Mary to be mine; and the kid of course. I'll look after them both. They would not go short."

Finishing the remains in his glass, Charlie, still weighing up his daughter's suitor said, "Well son, I don't doubt you at all, but it should be Mary you're talking to not me, mind you, I take it your plans are a while away yet?"

The conversation came to an abrupt halt as Lizzie, pushing a tea trolley through from the kitchen entered the living room. Mary, carrying the teapot with the freshly brewed tea, followed on behind. Catching a glance of the glass in Charlie's hand, Lizzie threw her husband a long dirty look. She had warned him not to offer the lad a drink, as she didn't want him encouraged any more than he already was. Charlie, seeing Lizzie's scowl, made light of the situation, as he knew only to well that his wife could spoil the evening for Mary by opening her mouth and speaking her mind.

"Just having one to welcome the lad into our home," he said to Lizzie, who gave a grunt and proceeded to pour the tea.

Mary sat down on the sofa beside Pat and as their eyes met, he gave her a cheeky wink. Handing Pat his tea, Lizzie enquired in a matter of fact fashion, "Where are you originally from Patrick?" Mary felt sick, as she knew this was the start of the interrogation. Her mother had started her twenty questions.

Helping himself from the sugar bowl that Lizzie held out to him, Patrick took his time in answering. He stirred his tea with the spoon from the bowl rather than from the one sitting in his saucer, causing Lizzie to turn her nose up slightly in disgust. Replacing the wet spoon back in the bowl he answered her question. "I come from the west."

Not being content with his answer she continued, "but where about in the west?"

"Oh, here and there Mrs. Fairley, here and there. I moved around a lot."

No! She definitely didn't like this man, but forcing a smile she went on. "And why have you settled here."

"Work! Simply that. I was offered a good job so I took it." He was beginning to feel uneasy, and Lizzie alone sensed this, much to her delight.

"And what about your folks? Don't you miss them?"

Patrick looked sideways at Mary who realised he was feeling uncomfortable, so she interrupted her mother in a light- hearted manner.

"You know mother, you should have been a detective. You're not happy until you give folk the third degree."

Resenting Mary's remarks she answered back abruptly. "Well! I'm sorry. I'm only showing interest." It was Lizzie who now looked uncomfortable. She rose, and going over to the fire, she lifted the poker and set about the well-lit coals with vigour.

Charlie defused the situation by quickly changing the subject.

"What do you think of that lad of our Mary's then Patrick? By...he's some kid! Never seems to get cross."

Glad of the interruption Patrick smiled "He's a nice bairn. What I've seen of him. Still he has a good looking Mother." Mary blushed as she nudged him playfully.

The rest of the evening was somewhat strained, as Lizzie made her feelings towards Patrick quite obvious. She didn't like him at all. Her remarks were few, but when one was made it bordered on sarcasm.

Charlie watched the pair of them as they stood at the gate saying their goodnights. He said nothing, but he was feeling vexed at his wife's behaviour.

Mary slammed the door shut as she came back into the house.

"Are you trying to waken the bairn?" Lizzie remarked.

"No Mother I am not, but I'm blazing mad at you! Couldn't you have been nicer? Had you to make things awkward?"

Lizzie, knowing she had spoiled the evening, remarked defensively. "*Me?*" she said, "*I* never said anything!"

"That's the point mother, you ignored us all evening, and the few times you did speak it was to make sarcastic remarks. Tell me, what's wrong with him?"

"He's too old for you for a start, and he's been around! I can tell so I can." Lizzie dashed around the room frantically puffing up the cushions that had been flattened.

Not prepared to let things drop, Mary spat her words out.

"He's not too old! He's only ten years ahead of me, and I can hardly talk about anyone being around, as you put it. *Me!* With a *bairn*."

Charlie watched the two of them face each other up like fighting cocks until he could stand it no longer. "Enough!" he shouted. Both women turned sharply and looked towards him.

He was on his feet and looked furiously at Lizzie. "You Lizzie, you are too quick to judge. I can't see anything wrong with the lad, and besides, it's no concern of yours. Mary isn't daft. If she wants to go on seeing Pat it's nothing to do with you or I."

Lizzie took a few steps over to where her husband stood and stopping directly in front of him, she placed her hands firmly on both her hips in a defiant manner. "That's where you're wrong now," she growled, "but you are right on one thing. What Mary wants is not my concern, but what happens to that bit bairn is. If she wants to take up with anybody, I will make bloody sure it's a decent fellow who'll look after that wee soul." She wrung her hands anxiously as she continued to say her piece. "And as for that statement ' Mary's not daft', I would have thought twice about coming to that conclusion. If she had any sense she wouldn't have landed herself with a bairn in the first place."

Her last remark caused tears to well up in Mary's eyes and she struggled to keep control of her emotions.

"To hear you go on Ma, you'd think he was about to ask me to marry him."

"Mary." Charlie said her name tenderly, causing her to look round. "He is!"

"What?" She wasn't sure if she understood him. Charlie, not looking at Lizzie but directly at his daughter spoke again. "He is lass, he's going to ask you to marry him."

Mary's mouth gaped open. She was speechless.

"Now then, I knew it." Lizzie snapped. "He'll get sent away with a flea in his ear if he comes back here again, so he will."

"LIZZIE!!" Charlie yelled. It's not you Patrick wants, it's our Mary, so shut up woman."

She would not give in. "Over my dead body will she marry him." Her face turned crimson with rage.

"Shut up Ma, just shut up. If I want to marry Patrick Sweeny I will, in fact the way you go on I'll be glad to marry and get out of here." Mary could hold her tears back no longer. She ran from the living room taking the stairs two at a time. In her bedroom, she threw herself down on the bed and sobbed uncontrollably. The small child lay peacefully sleeping in the cot beside the bed unaware of his mother's distress.

Three weeks later, Pat proposed. They left the cinema early that night and took a walk along the shore, as it was such a beautiful evening. The sky was clear and heavy with bright sparkling stars. The tide was well in, but not a ripple was on the still water as it lapped gently against the rocks. The heavy scent of seaweed filled their nostrils and only the occasional cry from a far off sea gull broke the silence.

Mary and Patrick strolled hand in hand content in each other's company. A couple of men walking their dogs passed by and as they did so, one of them looked at Patrick acknowledging him by saying, "Yip."

Giggling, Mary looked up at Patrick. "Why do they do that?"

"Do what?"

"Yip! Why do men say that? It sounds daft."

"It's a lazy way of saying hallo I suppose," he laughed. "You don't half ask some daft questions."

"It's the only way you get answers," she replied.

"Well then, I'll ask you a question for a change."

"Go on then smarty pants, ask me a question!" she jested.

His voice was low, but distinct. "Will you marry me?"

Mary had waited every day for Patrick to ask her that question. Every day since her father had let it be known. She gave no hint to Patrick that she knew of his conversation with Charlie. Now he had finally asked, she was taken aback.

"Well then Miss, what do you say to that? Will you or won't you?" He waited.

"What about the bairn?" was all she could say?

"What about the bairn? I take you I also take the bairn. What's the problem?"

"Aye well, aye Pat, but where are we going to live?"

He gave a laugh as he punched the air with his fist. Putting his arms around her waist, he danced her round and round.

"Mary, I only wanted to hear you say you'll marry me. Leave the rest to me," he said. "Oh. You've made me a happy man." The smile left his face as he thought of Lizzie, and with a frown, he asked, "Do you want me to be there when you tell your mother?"

"Oh! For heavens sake, no Pat." Casting her eyes up to the sky she said, "God help me when I tell her though. She'll do her nut!"

Putting his arm around her waist, they continued to walk on. Looking down at his feet while he walked, Pat asked, "Why does she hate me Mary?"

She felt sadness within. She would liked to have said that things would change but she knew they would not, as once Lizzie took a dislike to a person, that was it. Mary too looked down at the ground as she answered, "I don't know. I honestly don't know. I think its because you drink."

"I've hardly touched a drop since I started going out with you. I only went out for company. There's not much to do on your own around here except for the dance halls, and I don't dance, so it was either the pub or sit in my lodgings on a Saturday night."

Giving him a reassuring squeeze, she said, "I know that, besides, if I had to wait on my mother's approval I'd end up an old maid."

Grabbing her playfully by the arm and giving her a tug, he teased, "Come on then, I better walk you home before she sends the police after me for kidnapping."

Pat left Mary at the top of the street and watched until he was sure she was safely inside.

"You're late the night!" Lizzie remarked when Mary entered the living room.

"Aye a' know. We went for a walk," Mary said gingerly. "How's the bairn been?"

Lizzie, who was engrossed in a book looked towards Mary. "He's slept all night. My, you've got a good bairn so you have. He never says a word when he's put in his cot. Some howl there head's off when being put down. If my memory serves me well, you and our Joe were girning (fretful) bairns, so you were. Your Da' walked the floor at night shushing you to sleep, so he did. Billy was more like your wee fellow. Aye, he was a grand bairn an all, so he was." Lizzie smiled at the memory.

Mary cringed. Although she loved her brother Billy dearly, she thought, "You would have to be the best, our Billy."

Both woman looked towards the door as Charlie came in. He removed his cap and jacket, then as he always did, much to his wife's annoyance, hung the jacket on the back of a dinning-room chair. Lizzie put her book down sharply and as if catapulted from her chair, shot to her feet and pulled the jacket and cap from the chair giving Charlie a mouthful as she did so.

"If I wanted coats in the living room, I would have put a wardrobe through here. Can you no' hang your jacket under the stair like every one else does man? It's just as easy! How many years have I been telling you?"

"Too many!" Charlie smirked as he looked over at his daughter. "Good picture?" he asked ignoring his wife as she briskly swiped her hand over the offending jacket as if holding an imaginary brush.

"Naw Da, it was rubbish, so we came out early. Went for a walk though!" She waited until her mother had gone from the room before whispering across to him.

"He asked me tonight," she beamed, keeping her voice low.

Charlie whispered back, "Don't tell her tonight. Wait till tomorrow, wheest! Here she's coming."

Both conspirators smiled at each other knowing full well what would happen once Lizzie heard Mary's news. All hell would be let loose. As it was late in the evening, Charlie was in no mood to cope with his wife's outburst. It could wait till tomorrow.

Mary's mother had been busy with the laundry all morning, and as the weather had turned nasty, she was forced to dry the clothes indoors. The wooden clotheshorse and the twin roped pulley that stretched along the full length of the kitchen, hung with the damp garments. No room was left, not even for a solitary hankie. Taking her husband's working clothes into the living room, she laid them carefully along the hearth.

Charlie watched her arrange his navy blue singlets (vests) along the brass rail of the fireplace. She hated when she had to do that. It made the place so untidy.

He puffed at his pipe as he studied her well-rounded face. It was still beautiful. Ignoring the lines that the family and the years had put there, he could still see her fresh pink cheeks and that cute little button nose. Her snowy white hair only enhanced her beauty. She was still a fine looking woman. If only she would learn to keep her mouth shut more Charlie thought. She caught him staring and with a frown she asked what was wrong. Without hesitation he said smiling, "I don't know what your going to do when the council takes the fireplace out and puts the new tiled one in."

"Neither do I, still they're modern and a lot less work."

The clothes started to steam as the heat from the hot coals set about the damp material.

"It's like a Chinese laundry in here to-day. It's a wonder we don't all come down with pneumonia," Charlie remarked.

"If you want the pit clothes dry for the morning you have to put up with this," Lizzie chided.

Shaking his head he remarked, "Lizzie, it was nice yesterday. The washing could have been outside."

"Aye now, so it was; but I wasn't here to do it, was I? And if it bothered you that much, you could have had it washed and out instead of standing in a betting shop all afternoon, so don't tell me when to do my work and I'll not bother you," she snapped.

She was now sitting on her knees at Charlie's feet arranging small items on the hearth. Pulling himself up and sitting on the edge of the chair, Charlie bent down and laid his hand on Lizzie's arm. "What's up now Lizzie? I can hardly talk to you these days but you shoot me down in flames."

Lizzie, aware of the concern in his voice felt guilty for the way she had spoken. Looking up into his eyes, she saw the warm kind man that had stood by her all those years, looking so tired, and yet he never complained. She looked at him for

41

a few seconds, and then diverted her attention once more to the job she was doing, answering him as she continued her chore.

"I'm sorry Charlie, but I just feel things get on top of me at times. I don't mean to get at you."

"You do far too much at once Lizzie. You should take things a bit slower; and I had no right to remark about the washing. You were right to go away out yesterday."

Young Frank came running in, and going straight to his grandfather he began to climb up onto his lap. Mary followed him through carrying a mug of hot tea. "Fancy a cup Da?" she asked warmly. "There's one poured out for you Ma, but I didn't know if you wanted it here or in he kitchen."

"Frank!" Lizzie said firmly, "You mind your granddad's tea and not go knocking it over on yourself." Looking at her daughter, she nodded her thanks; "I'll take it through the kitchen as I'll have to peel the tatties."

"I'll do them Ma," she said cheerily. "I'll do them after I finish washing up the dishes. You sit down beside Dad and drink your tea. I'll bring it through." Leaving the living room, Mary made her way towards the kitchen.

"Well I must say, she's in a pleasant mood today. She's worked like a beaver all morning so she has." Lizzie, looking a lot brighter, sank into the armchair opposite Charlie and waited for Mary to return with her tea.

"That's more like it lass," Charlie said smiling, looking content with his grandson on his knee, "take the weight off your feet. The work will get done just the same."

Later that evening, Mary decided it was time to break the news to her mother. She couldn't keep her intentions to marry a secret any longer.

As Mary had been particularly careful not to upset her all morning, she had her mother in a contented mood. Reasoning with Lizzie was difficult at the best of times, so it was vital to Mary that her mother should be approached when in a placid state.

Charlie was reading the Sunday paper and Lizzie sat darning a working sock. Mary, sitting on the end of the sofa, caught her father's attention. Glancing over to where her mother sat, then looking back at her father, she made a sign with her eyes; as asking, "Shall I tell her now?"

Charlie, lowering his eyebrows tried to signal back, when Lizzie, without looking up from her darning spoke, "What are you two up to?" she asked lifting her head up slowly and fixing her attention on Mary.

"Well, what are you hiding? I can always tell when you're up to something," she smiled warmly.

Mary felt the blood drain from her body, and the tips of her fingers suddenly felt numb. Heart thumping against her ribs and her stomach churning violently, she struggled to keep her composure. The roof of her mouth turned so dry, she swallowed a few times before making a feeble attempt to speak.

"Well then! Has the cat got your tongue?" Lizzie pried before Mary could answer.

Almost in a whisper, Mary made her announcement. "Patrick has asked me to marry him!" She had said it! Now she waited for her mother's reaction.

Lizzie, returning her attention to the task she was doing, pondered for a few seconds before asking, "And what did you tell him?" Her voice was gentle.

Mary didn't like this. Her mother was too calm. "I said...I said.... I would. I would marry him," she stammered.

Knowing full well she had unnerved Mary, Lizzie kept her voice very controlled. Laying the darned sock down on her lap, she smiled warmly, and calmly replied. "Well now, I suggest you tell him you've changed your mind. Your Father and I don't want his sort."

Mary looked at her father, then at Lizzie.

Taking his pipe from his mouth, Charlie knocks it gently against the fireplace, causing the grey ash to fall into the fire. Looking over at his wife, he too spoke in a calm manner. "Lizzie. I wish you would speak for yourself. I have nothing against Patrick. He seems a nice enough lad to me." He stared at Lizzie, who was by now losing her composure.

"There's nothing wrong with Patrick Ma!" Mary pleaded. "He's a nice decent bloke and I couldn't do any better."

"You what!" There was no trace of softness in her voice now. "You couldn't... *do* any better than *that*... *that* drunken sod. Oh Mary! You don't think much of yourself when you say things like that...Look at you. You're a *bonny* lassie. You could have *anybody* if you tried, so you could."

"Oh aye Ma, *me* with a two year old bairn...sure! The fellows are queuing up out side. Don't you see them?" Mary's courage had returned... "I'm going to marry Patrick and that's that!"

Rising to her feet, Lizzie pointed her finger fiercely at her daughter and almost growled. "*It'll be over my dead body!*"

"Lizzie! For heaven's sake! You can't stop her, so you might as well help her." Charlie tried to calm his wife down, but he only succeeded in making matters worse. She scowled while looking him over, as if it were the first time she had laid eyes on him, and then hissed.

"I thought you would have supported me in this. She doesn't know what she's letting herself in for. She's only eighteen for God's sake! She's not ready for marriage let alone marrying a no-user." Moving towards her husband, she bent over him and spoke through her teeth, "You knew all about this Charlie, didn't you? You knew and didn't let on! Well! So much for loyalty!" Straightening up and with hands on her hips, she turned round and faced her daughter, who was now reduced to tears. Looking hard at her she spat angrily, "If you are determined to go ahead with this marriage, you can leave this house! Think about it Mary, think hard, either stop this nonsense... or get out! It's up to you. Your crying now, but you'll have a lot more to cry about if you take up with him, mark my words!" Turning from her daughter, she walked out of the room.

Charlie went to Mary, put his arms round her and drew her to him. Her soft cries were muffled by her father's broad shoulder. "Never listen to her Mary, her bark's worse than her bite. She needs you as much as you need her, now wipe your eyes and let her cool down. She'll change her mind. Give her a bit more time."

Mary listened to her father, but knew only too well that he knew as well as she did, once Lizzie took a dislike to anyone; she never ever changed her mind.

The following morning, the two women passed each other in the house without uttering a word to each other. Young Frank stayed with Lizzie as usual while Mary went to work. Mary's solemn mood stayed with her all through the day. She hadn't the usual cheery conversation with the customers as she felt worn out from the night before. She had had practically no sleep and what little she did have, was filled with tormenting dreams. Her mother was a stubborn woman and Mary knew she would have to make a choice. Taking her lunch break at one o'clock, she arrived home to be greeted by the usual hug and kisses from Frank, but Lizzie spoke still not a word.

Thinking the situation through carefully she came to the conclusion, the only thing to do was to move in with Patrick.

They both sat in silence, Mary's hands wrapped round the mug of tea that lay before her on the grey Formica table.

Patrick sat opposite with elbows bent resting his head between his hands in deep thought. Now and again he looked up at Mary, who watched and waited for his reply. They sat in the cosy kitchen of Mrs Watt's house that had been home to Patrick for quite a few years. The smell of freshly baked scones lingered in the air, as the old lady had not long removed them from the oven.

"Well Patrick? Have I to wait all day? You said you would figure something out, didn't you?"

Giving his bottom lip a bite, he gave a blow from the side of his mouth. "I did, I did, but hell Mary! I didn't expect things to move so quickly. Sure you can stay here. I know the old lady would like to rent another room, but the bairn. I would have to ask her."

Getting mad with his dithering, Mary shot to her feet causing the chair she had been sitting on to fall over. Patrick rose up and hurried round to where the chair lay on its side. Lifting it up with one hand, he caught Mary's shoulder with the other.

"Now Mary, you're taking the wrong meaning out of that. I know what you're thinking and you're very much mistaken."

With eyes full of tears, she turned her face from his gaze. "I'm thinking you don't want us, that's what I'm thinking!"

Placing both hands firmly on each side of her distressed face, he kissed her gently on the tip of her nose, and then pulling back he cocked his own handsome face to the side. That bewitching grin appeared on his mouth and she smiled weakly back at him.

"Now then," he said softly, "leave it to me. Stay with your parents a few more weeks and don't upset your mother. If she mentions us being wed, tell her we've not come to a final decision about it... Now do you think you can handle that?"

She gave a couple of sobs. "But Patrick, I thought you..."
He held his finger against her mouth. "Now Mary, leave it to
me. I don't want to start life with you in lodgings; besides, it
would be involving the Watts. Now let it be, and I promise
you that I'll have a place for us real soon. Now can you be
patient?"

"Yes, but it's going to be awful at home. She wasn't going
to let me out tonight, imagine that!"

Drawing her near, he hugged her tightly, and as they stood
motionless he felt the warmth of her body penetrate through
his thin shirt. His emotions were deeply stirred and he longed
to fill his desires but the time and place was wrong. Drawing
away, he placed his fingers under her chin. Gently lifting her
head he gazed into her wet eyes. "Oh Mary! We'll be all right,"
he murmured before placing his lips on hers and kissing her
tenderly.

It was almost two weeks since she had asked Patrick to let
her stay with him, and as he had said no more about it, Mary
assumed he wasn't trying to find a place. Becoming downcast
and sullen, she moped around the house, causing Lizzie to
think the relationship with Patrick Sweeny was coming to
an end. This made her ease up a bit on her daughter as she
watched and waited for the whole sordid episode to finish. She
was to be greatly disappointed.

That Friday evening, Mary left the shop ten minutes later
than she normally did as she waited to see if Patrick would show
up since he hadn't called in for his evening paper. Naturally
she was very worried.

The weather was atrocious, as a blizzard had raged all
day. Hail stung Mary's eyes and drove hard against her head,
the cold air making her gasp. Lowering her head, she pushed
against the wind while hurrying towards the bus stop as she
had decided to take the bus to the bottom of her street. It

was only three stops away, but the weather had forced her to seek transport. A shop doorway provided her with shelter as she waited for the bus; fortunately, she had not long to wait. Stepping forward, she waited for the passengers to alight.

Looking up she saw Patrick. He was last to get off.

"Where have you been Patrick?" She was relieved to see him.

Standing aside, Mary allowed the rest of the soaking wet passengers to board the bus. Giving her a non-to-gentle push towards the waiting vehicle, Patrick said briskly, "Get on Mary. I'll come along with you. I've got some news." Traces of a cheeky grin showed on his rugged face.

Sitting at the front of the bus, Patrick paid the fares before telling her his news. " I didn't want to tell you in case it came to nothing, but I've been away sorting things out."

"Sorting what out?" she asked anxiously, as she shook her head allowing the water to fly from her soaking wet hair.

"I've got us a house!" he laughed.

Forgetting where she was, Mary squealed aloud. "Oh Patrick! That's bloody great!" She bounced on the seat like an excited child. "When can I move in? When can I see it?"

"Don't you want to know where it is first?"

"I don't care. I don't care, as long as I can get away from my Mother!" She could not contain her eagerness.

Patrick tugged firmly at her coat sleeve as he realised all eyes were on them. "Mary, if you don't calm yourself down, I'll tell you no more, anyhow, I wonder if you're moving in with me for the right reasons? Is it just to get away from your Mother, or do you want to be with me?"

She looked at him with her large blue eyes; pouting her generous lips she scowled, "Don't be daft. It's because of you I'm getting all the agro; where is it then.... this house?"

"Crown Square. I get the keys next week...Come on Mary, it's your stop. I'll tell you about it later."

Leaving the shelter of the bus, they once again exposed themselves to the wild night. With heads bowed down, they battled their way against the raging wind. Patrick left Mary at the gate of her house before leaving to struggle on against the storm.

Crown Square was located next to the coalmine. The houses, known as 'miners raws' (rows), being the property of the coal board were rented out exclusively to the mining community. Four rows of houses formed the square and there were eight houses in a row. Their living room windows faced into the square as did the back doors. The front doors were very rarely used as they led into the one and only bedroom. Outside toilets were still the only sanitation, although a good many families had gone to the trouble of bricking up the outside door, and entering from inside the house. The new entrances were knocked through from the scullery wall.

Each living room had two huge recess beds, where very often all the children of the family slept in one, while the parents occupied the other. Some tenants rented their front bedroom out to young married couples, while some made front parlours out of the rooms. They were considered by the majority to be 'uppish.'

Black cast-iron ranges still dominated the centre of the living room wall and as they were miners' dwellings, fires roared up the chimneys summer and winter.

The huge square was divided up and each household was allocated two clothes poles. On washday, the square was turned into one gigantic washing green as the washings from thirty-two households hung together and danced in the wind.

Mary kept quiet about the house. She was terrified of the confrontation that had to come.

She had gone with Patrick to view the property and was excited at the idea of setting up home. It was common practice to enter by the kitchen door as family life revolved around the back of the house. Every one knew the comings and goings of their neighbours due to the women sitting at their windows looking out into the square, watching their offspring at play.

Mary entered the kitchen of eight Crown Square and looking around in silence she observed every detail. Fortunately, the previous tenant had made the alterations to the house, thus doing away with the outside door to the toilet. A large stone boiler stood in the corner to the right of the kitchen and two huge sinks stood alongside. Although the rest of the house had wooden floors, the kitchen floor consisted of large flagstones. The walls were painted dark green and a narrow yellow border ran along the top. Mary walked in silence, moving into the sitting room. She observed the floor. It was covered in yellow linoleum, which was bare in places due to the constant tramping of feet. Huge chrysanthemums screamed out from the walls.

"Yuk! How could any one live with that paper?"

Patrick made no comment as he led her through to the front room.

Walking on the bare floorboards made a hollow empty sound and their footsteps echoed through the house. Facing the room wall, Mary smiled.

"I could live with that paper for a wee while." The pattern was made up with silver stripes on a white background as small bunches of forget-me- knots tied with blue bows scattered between the stripes.

Patrick satisfied that Mary had done her viewing asked, "Well then, what do you think?"

Clasping her hands together, as if in prayer, she smiled broadly,

"I can't believe this is ours. Once we change that awful paper in the other room, it will be lovely. I'll say this, the last tenant has left it nice and clean."

"We can't paper until we move in. I'm getting bits and pieces at the weekend, so if everything goes well, we should be able to move in soon."

"My Mother will probably hear that I've been here. Someone must have seen us come in."

Patrick led her back through to the other room.

"I don't want you to say anything until we are ready; and stay away from here until then. We'll just have to hope that she doesn't hear before things are finalised."

Mary gave a groan, "If she does, I'll be out on my ear."

Going behind her mother's back didn't worry Mary but she was troubled when thinking of her father. Twice she had been on the verge of telling him but changed her mind at the last minute. Her father was going to be greatly missed but she hoped he would understand, and, maybe; once the dust had settled, he would come and visit. On the other hand, she knew never to expect her mother, as she was not the kind of person to forgive and forget.

All weekend, the tension in Mary grew, causing a terrible nausea to creep in, as she visualised her mother's reaction if told the news by 'a concerned outsider'. The chances of that had now increased since Patrick was moving in furniture and working on the house.

Arriving home from work, Mary entered the house very apprehensively, but she knew immediately that Lizzie hadn't heard any gossip. She was very relieved and if her mother was to stay indoors all day, the chances were she would never know.

Saturday went without a hitch. Sunday came and she went through the same agony, but nothing was mentioned yet again. Things were going as planned. Patrick would soon be seeing her and giving her the go ahead.

The newsagent was quite busy that Monday morning. A few ladies browsed through the magazines while Pearl was at the top counter with a customer settling her paper account. Mary was up the ladder retrieving something from the top shelf for the woman she was serving, when she caught sight of her mother passing by the window. Her heart rate increased with fear as she watched Lizzie approach the door.

"Ma!" Mary exclaimed, giving nervous a laugh. Lizzie's eyes darted around the shop eyeing up the customers before looking up at her frightened daughter. Having been attended to, Pearl's customer walked past Lizzie, giving her a sideward glance as she passed on her way out.

With lips tightly drawn and arms folded securely under her well-inflated breasts, Lizzie stood in silence, breathing deeply as if to keep her composure. She watched and waited till Mary was free.

Walking over to the counter where her daughter stood, Lizzie spoke quietly but venomously. "What's this I'm hearing this morning?" With narrowing eyes, she studied Mary's shocked expression. "Well then lady! Did you think I wouldn't hear?" Her voice had grown louder.

Embarrassed and very agitated, Mary looked quickly towards the women that were still in the shop. She pleaded with Lizzie, "Ma! Not here. We'll talk about it when I get home."

Lizzie's face was now full of rage, "Oh! So you'll talk about it now will you! I had to hear from outsiders that my Daughter has a house."

"I've not got a house, it's Patrick's house," Mary corrected her.

"But your set in going to stay so you are. Now don't deny it our Mary!" She peered into her eyes. "Do you think I don't know? I can read you like a book, an' a dirty one at that!"

Mary gritted her teeth, and although very frightened she faced her irate mother up. She hissed at Lizzie "I've had enough of this Mother, get home and we'll talk later. You'll get me the sack behaving like this, so go home."

Pearl came and stood beside Lizzie and diplomatically she smiled and spoke softly, casting her eyes over to the couple still at the magazine stand, "Lizzie, it's not like you to let everyone know your business, besides, don't you think you're jumping the gun a bit? Mary's not said a thing about leaving home now, so wait till she gets in and have a good talk. Anyway, where's the bairn?"

Without looking at Pearl she answered, "He's with Mrs. Millian." Still glowering at her daughter she snapped, "You get home sharp Mary! Do you hear?"

She now glanced briefly at Pearl before saying, "I'll away then. See you later."

The two magazine browsers followed Lizzie out glancing over at Mary as they left. They had heard all they wanted to hear, now it was with great enjoyment that the latest scandal would be told to everyone they met.

Pearl and Mary stared at each other. Shaking her head, Pearl remarked with concern,

"I hope you know what you're doing. There are a lot nicer fellows around without..."

"Pearl!" Mary said angrily, "It's none of your business. It's my choice, and I don't need your advice either. I get enough from her without you starting."

"Well," Pearl shrugged her shoulder, "don't say you weren't warned."

"Alright, I won't," Mary answered abruptly.

Back home in the kitchen of her home, Lizzie prepared a few nice sandwiches for lunch. She sorely regretted her words with Mary, and as she waited for her to come home, she did a lot of thinking. She had decided to approach the subject differently. She was going to keep calm and reason with her, after all, it was like Mary said,' it was Patrick's house not hers'. Maybe she was wrong about Mary moving in. She was seen viewing the house sure, but that didn't mean anything.

Mary entered the house quite prepared for a confrontation, but yet again her mother's mood had changed. She was pouring the tea when Mary entered the kitchen. The baby was in his high chair feeding himself although there was more food on the tray in front than in his mouth.

"See to him Mary lass, whilst I pour this tea," she said warmly, as if nothing had happened earlier on in the morning. It was so typical of her. Knowing how to manipulate people was one of her many talents. Here was Mary prepared for battle and the tempo had suddenly changed.

"Well!" thought Mary, "you're not getting away with it this time. After all, it's got to come out sometime." Ignoring her mother's change of heart, Mary challenged her.

"How dare you embarrass me in front of people" she hissed through her teeth. "You wanted me home to have a go, *WELL HERE I AM!*"

Lizzie continued preparing the lunch. Keeping her head lowered and deliberately avoiding Mary's gaze, she said untroubled, "Sit down and eat something, you'll only upset the bairn carrying on like that, so you will."

Shaking her head violently, Mary gasped, "I don't believe this. You couldn't wait this morning, now you have nothing to say!"

Her mother finally looked at her and still ignoring her outburst, quite calmly explained, "I jumped to conclusions, and I'm sorry. I thought you were moving in with him."

"His name is *Patrick* mother, or can't you say it? And you're right for once; because that's what I fully intend doing. Aye.... Do you hear? I am moving in with *Patrick*!"

Lizzie walked round the table, and standing close to her daughter, who was now visibly shaken, she too spat out her words. "You go to him, and I swear, you'll never set foot in this house again!! He's bad news and you will not listen. Drunkards like his lot can't stay away from it for long. You'll see my lady! No one knows a thing about him, and I think that's very strange. Don't you?"

Her mother was standing too close for comfort, so she took two steps backwards before answering back. "If the people in this town know nothing about you, does that make you a bad person? Is that what you're trying to have me believe! Oh Mother! Hasn't it crossed your mind that there's maybe... just maybe... nothing to know!! He keeps himself to himself and in your eyes that's wrong? You just will not give him a chance. It's as pure and simple as that! Well, I intend to!"

Standing at the kitchen doorway, Lizzie pointed towards the front door at the other end of the lobby. "You can get out now lady if that's your intention, and you better mind that you have a bairn, so, if Mr. wants you, he'll have a ready made family. Your Dad and I have already been humiliated with your actions and I don't intend to go through all that again! Staying with a man and not wed!!. It may not bother you but it certainly bothers me!"

Tears started to roll down Mary's cheeks as she lifted the baby from his chair, "It doesn't have to be like that Ma, we want to be wed but..."

"I will never agree. I've told you and I'll not go back on what I've said! He's not welcome in this family."

"Well it means I do it my way Ma, and I hope you're proud."

"*PROUD! PROUD*! You don't know the meaning of the word our Mary, or you wouldn't be doing what you're about to do, so don't say *PROUD* to me!!"

Desperate to get away from her mother, Mary's voice softened. "Can I have some of Frank's things?" Her chest moved in small sudden jerks as she sobbed quietly.

"Get what you need and go!!" was her mother's cold reply.

Lizzie closed the door to the kitchen and going over to the chair at the table, she sat down and waited, hoping that the door to the kitchen would be flung open at any minute by Mary, telling her she was sorry and that she would never go. She listened to the feet walking back and forward on the lino-covered floor, as her girl, her wee girl, filled the pram with clothes. 'She would change her mind. Mary always did', thought Lizzie. The front door banged and silence filled the house. Nothing but the slow drip, drip from the tap in the corner was heard as the droplets landed onto the pots that waited to be washed.

Springing to her feet, Lizzie threw open the door and ran to the living room window. She peered through the net curtains only to see the distant figure of Mary pushing the pram filled to the top with clothes.

Somewhere under that bundle was Frank, the baby she would hold no more. Tears weld up in Lizzie's eyes thinking that Patrick Sweeny was chosen before her.

Making her way to Patrick's lodgings, she waited until he arrived home. He knew something was wrong when Mary had not turned up in the afternoon for work. Pearl told him about the scene created by Lizzie and she too was worried about Mary. Seeing her there waiting for him did not come as a surprise, in fact, he too was amazed at Lizzie not hearing sooner.

Later that evening, they bundled the clothes into the small van that had been borrowed. It was making its final run with odds and ends, as all the main furniture had been transported down that weekend. The baby's pram and a few bags of coal were last to be lifted in before Mary, Patrick, and the baby, crammed themselves into the front beside the driver.

Mixed emotions filled Mary's heart; sadness, regret at her mother's attitude, hurt, and worry as well as excited nervousness and anticipation.

"Well now Mary," Patrick noticed she was in deep thought, "Looks like you and I are about to embark on a new life together and I promise to do whatever's best for you."

She felt his fingers give her knee a tight squeeze as they huddled together on the passenger's seat, the baby on her lap. For some odd reason, a cold shiver ran through her body, as if giving her a warning.

Chapter Four

Frank had been washed, fed, and now lay asleep. Mary felt uneasy, the child sleeping all night cramped up as he was. She would have to try and get his cot from her mother's house.

They both ate a fish and chip carry out and after Patrick had smoked a cigarette, they set to work arranging the room and emptying boxes. He had managed to acquire a couple of old utility armchairs, a table, and three wooden straight-backed chairs. A large square rug covered most of the hideous looking lino. His landlady had kindly contributed a sideboard, two small tables and various kitchen utensils. One thing they didn't need to worry about was a bed as a large recess still was very much a part of the fittings. As they had only enough furniture to fill the living room, the bedroom would remain unused until such times as they could afford to furnish it. The huge cupboard in the bedroom would be used to store their clothes, and two orange crates laid side by side provided an ideal cabinet to hold the baby's garments. Mary intended to cover them with material when they were settled.

It was now past midnight and the fire roared in the grate sending it's warm glow round the room. Mary cast her eyes round the room, and although it could be described as being very sparsely furnished, she liked what she saw. She felt content. "We'll soon get it looking grand. Given time we'll get what we need. I'll call into Burns' junk yard and pick up bits of knick knacks, things that make a home."

Patrick sat in the armchair watching, as she planned out what was needed. He stretched out and catching her arm, pulled her towards him. Toppling over, she landed heavily onto his lap.

"We'll get back to these things later, but in the meantime Mary, we're together at last. You've worked all night and never given me as much as a cuddle, but being a patient man, I decided to wait. Now it's my turn to demand attention."

Her heart pounded but not with desire. She had secretly dreaded going to bed. He had never pressurised her into anything before, but she wasn't that naive to think he wouldn't now. It would be expected of her. There was only the recess bed in the living room and it was all made up with brand new bedclothes, in fact, they were the only things Patrick had bought, as everything else was second hand, even the curtains were given to them by their new neighbour, who had offered to help in any way.

"Come on Mary, let's get to bed," he whispered as he hugged her.

Springing to her feet, she gave a nervous laugh, "You get ready then I'll join you shortly." Gathering up the dirty cups, she took them through to the sink and rinsed them before returning.

Stripping off his clothes Patrick leapt into bed, while Mary, averting her eyes from his naked body, did some last minute tidying up then, having a look into the pram, she made sure Frank was all right before switching off the light. She had left her mother's house with few clothes of her own, and in her haste gave no thought to nightclothes.

Undressing by the light of the fire, Patrick watched as she slowly stripped off her clothes. The dancing flames cast shadows across her pink flesh like demented demons as her nakedness glowed in the firelight. Her back was still turned to him and he waited anxiously for her to turn round. When she did, her loveliness was almost breathtaking.

Mary felt his eyes burn into her back, and as she turned, she ran towards the bed not because she was eager to be with him, but simply because she wanted out of his gaze. Recess beds were quite high, so she had to climb onto the chair before reaching the bed. Once under the covers, she felt better, as the blankets gave her the feeling of being clothed. Patrick turned and gazed into her face. Lifting his arm from out under the covers, he twirled his fingers through her blonde hair. "You're not shy Mary are you?" he asked.

She gave a slight shiver. "Aye Patrick, I am. I would have liked to have married first," she said rather coyly.

He gave a hollow laugh, "That's funny coming from you. You're a bit late for that Mary. It's me your going to marry, and I've got to wait while some other bugger's had you first!"

She was shocked. He had never spoken to her like that before. Her mouth gaped open as she looked at him in the firelight.

Before she could answer, he removed his hand from her hair and cupping her face with both hands, he groaned. "Oh Mary, I'm sorry! I don't know what made me say such a thing. I'm sorry, honest I am. It's just that I am so frustrated. You look so damn good." Wriggling slowly towards her, their naked flesh touched, causing an electrifying sensation to run down Mary's spine. Patrick took her in his arms and kissing her hungrily, he ran his hands down her body, exploring the warm crevasses he had lusted over for so long, when his concentration was shattered by the loud wailing that erupted from the pram.

Frank had wakened. Pulling himself up, he did not recognise his surroundings, causing the child to be instantly terrified.

Jumping down from the bed, Mary threw Patrick's shirt on, and going over to the screaming child, she lifted him up and hugged him to her.

"I'm bringing him in beside us Patrick. He'll not settle in that pram. I'll have to get his cot from my mother tomorrow. He can hardly turn in that pram now. He's too big."

Patrick rested his elbow on the pillow, and although he felt angry at being disturbed, he did not let it show. "OK. You're right. Put him at the back of the bed. We'd best get some sleep, it's late and I'll soon be rising for work."

Mary lay down at the far side of the bed with Frank between her and the wall. For the second time in so short a time, Mary was full of mixed emotions, but this time it was a mixture of disappointment as well as relief.

Her mother had said she wasn't old enough to know her own mind and she secretly wondered if she could be right.

Six pounds lay on the table with a scribbled note from Patrick. 'You slept so soundly. Didn't want to waken you. Money is for food and what ever. See you at 3pm.'

It was shortly after nine and both she and Frank were washed and dressed. Mary had only to put a match to the fire as Patrick had it cleaned and set, ready for her to light. This surprised her but it also set her thoughts on her father as he did the same every morning before leaving for work. Kneeling down in front of the fire, she watched as the paper was set alight, catching the sticks and causing them to crackle. Watching the flames leap up, she felt the warm glow as the heat radiated out and touched her cheeks. The vision of her father was very much in her mind when the sudden knocking on the door brought her back to the present.

Going to the window she looked out before answering the door.

Her heart leapt with joy and she gave a cry of delight. The depression that had overcome her minutes before had suddenly lifted. "Da!" she called.

Running through into the kitchen, she hurriedly opened the door and threw herself into her father's arms.

"Come on now! Come on. Let me get in." Breaking free, she pulled at his arm until he was over the threshold. Filled with emotion, Mary fought to hold back tears. "Oh Da', I'm sorry, I really am. I didn't want to hurt anyone, really Da'. Oh! I'm so glad to see you."

Without answering, he walked into the living room and looked around. Frank ran to him with open arms. Lifting the toddler up he hugged him tight. "Well then wee man, missing your Granddad already are you?" The child's chubby arms were wrapped round Charlie's neck so tight, he pretended to choke, causing the infant to laugh heartily.

"New house Pa-Pa", he said excitedly. "New house!"

"Aye son, so it is." Looking now at Mary, he asked with sadness in his voice, "Why in the name of heavens did you do it like this? You could have at least told me your intentions."

"Da', before you start, it was forced on me." She took the infant from her father's arms and put him down on the floor. "Mother wouldn't give in and you know that, she said she would never give her permission."

Charlie sat down heavily on one of the wooden chairs, causing it to groan under his weight. "You didn't even tell me Mary. I could have worked on her, but staying with someone like this is... is, a terrible thing to do. It's just not right."

"Da'. We are going to get married as soon as we can, and I'm not coming home!"

Realising his daughter's determination, he sighed wearily, "Well I suspected that... so I came to see that you and the boy were all right and to see if you needed anything."

She sat down beside him. Smiling, she took the opportunity to ask for the baby's cot and high chair. He stayed and talked for more than an hour, and as he was leaving, he slipped a long brown envelope into her hand.

"Take care sweetheart. This is from me so don't let on." Kissing her on the cheek, he left, turning round a few times and waving before disappearing round the corner.

Mary watched him until he was out of sight, only then did she close the door. She stood for a few moments with her back against the door, looking down at the brown envelope. Opening it, she drew out the contents. Her mouth gaped open as she stared in disbelief at the bundle of notes she now held in her hand. Taking them through into the living room, she sat down at the table and counted out one hundred and fifty pounds. Three times she counted the notes. Oh how she loved her father. He had always been around when she needed him and not once had he let her down, not even when it caused trouble between her mother and him. She could imagine the row that took place that morning when he took the day off work to check her out.

Returning home from her morning shopping, Mary set about filling the large pantry with the supplies she had bought. Once again the pram came in handy as Frank could hardly be seen for the brown parcels that were piled up on top of him. Groceries now put away, she lifted Frank from the pram before unwrapping her purchases. The child tugged anxiously at her skirt until Mary handed him down a wooden train that pulled along a flat cart full of coloured bricks. "That's what you've been waiting for, there now, you busy yourself until mummy finishes unwrapping the rest of the parcels."

The child chuckled and laughed as he pulled the engine back and forward. Almost as excited as the child, Mary admired the items she had bought before arranging them in there prospective places. Tables were covered with fresh new day clothes and cushions were placed on the chairs. Plastic flowers were arranged in a pink mother of pearl vase and tiny ornaments were placed here and there on the mantle shelf. Opening the final parcel she pushed the paper to one side revealing a round gilt-edged mirror. This she hung carefully on the wall over the sideboard.

The house was beginning to take shape and Mary felt as if she was now part of it. She had just put her stamp on the living room, and no matter how small the contribution, it was a start.

Patrick noticed the homely touches as soon as he came in the door. Mary had changed the day cloth and replaced it for a white linen one, and although very little of the dishes matched, the table was nicely set.

The three of them sat down to eat. Frank reached the table by sitting on the cushions that were piled on top of one another. Mary looked round the cosy little scene and convinced herself that her decision was right.

She told Patrick of her father's surprise visit, and although her father had significantly asked her to keep quiet about the money, she had to tell Patrick, as he asked where she had acquired the money for the bits and pieces she had bought.

"I'm going to buy a second hand washing machine and new pots, dishes, and some more bedding...."

"Hold on, hold on a minute... Don't be going daft. Keep something for a rainy day." Then he said, "After all; you'll not be going back to work, so hold on to a bob or two."

Mary's smile left her face. She knew she couldn't go back to work, as Frank had to be looked after, and since Lizzie had turned her back on them, she had no one else to help her. Once again she was dependent on someone else keeping her. She felt terribly uneasy at the thought of asking Patrick for money, but how else could she manage? Still, didn't married men give their wives their pay packets? Her father did. Then, a sudden thought struck her, 'If her father handed over his wages, like her mother maintained he did, how on earth had he all that money to give away?' This she pondered on, and laughing to herself she thought, "Good for you Da". You're a fly old devil after all. It's hard to get one up on Mother but you certainly have."

Her thoughts were interrupted by the knock on the door. Patrick answered it and entered the living room with a cheery whistle.

"No more crying bairn, that's the cot arrived, and all your clothes. Your Da' has sent Jock Murray down with his pick up."

She gave a quick glance towards the recess and groaned quietly to herself. She had no excuse tonight. None whatsoever.

What was once the old Kirk manse had now been converted into the Town Council offices. The interior of the building with its dark green walls was as drab and dismal as the dark grey stone from which the exterior was built. The long corridor within, led to different divisions of council business. Members of the general public used the offices daily to pay their rent and rates, or just to lodge complaints, usually about their poor housing conditions. Further up the corridor, a wooden bench was positioned outside the council chambers, which served as both court room and Registrar Office, and the smaller room to the right had black painted lettering stencilled across the glass panelled door 'ADMINISTRATION OFFICE.'

It was outside this sombre looking building the small wedding party arranged to meet. Patrick, leaning against the wall of the building casually smoked a cigarette. He waited with his best man, a pal of his from work, when the taxi carrying Mary arrived. Dressed in a deep blue woollen suit trimmed with black velvet piping round the lapels, pale blue silk blouse, and wearing a neat little black velvet hat, she looked radiant. Her long blonde shiny hair hung loose, allowing the cold watery sun to pick up the high lights making them glow. A single red rose pinned to her jacket was the only flower she had.

Pearl followed Mary out of the cab, and holding young Frank's hand, she allowed him to jump onto the pavement.

Patrick nodded his approval and, without taking his eyes from her, threw down his cigarette, stubbing it out under his shoe. As she approached, he joined her without saying a word.

A small group of housewives stood along the corridor waiting to pay their rents. Respecting each others privacy, they entered the payment office one at a time, as many who had rent arrears wished to keep their business to themselves, therefore a queue was often formed in the passage way.

Passing through the line of woman, Mary knew she was the topic of their conversation. Heads nodded together in low whispers as they conversed with their hand over their mouths making it unmistakably obvious.

At the front of the queue, an elderly woman stood by herself. She wore an old brown coat held together at the top with a large safety pin. Steel curlers peeped from beneath the woollen scarf that was wrapped round her head. Clutching an old battered shopping bag to her swelling breast, she seemed to distance herself from the others. "Good luck dearie," she said with conviction as Mary passed by. Smiling back at the well-wisher Mary noticed the woman had only two front teeth on her upper denture plate and when she grinned broadly she revealed a bare bottom gum.

Having pushed their way through, the wedding party arrived at the bench and sat down.

Mary's thoughts were now on her father. She had sent them word about the marriage, but as she expected, no reply was received.

A few minutes went by before they were ushered into the chambers by the Registrar. The room was slightly better than the rest of the building but it still could not be described as being warm and friendly. A large highly polished table separated them from the gentleman who was about to perform the marriage ceremony.

Red, being the dominant colour of the decor was obviously chosen to try and put warmth into the room. The long narrow windows were draped with badly faded curtains that matched the red velvet on the chairs. Thick red carpet covered most of the varnished floorboards, but failed miserably to bring warmth to the room. The damp musty smell that embeds itself into old buildings filled the nostrils. Light from the window filtered in, casting its rays upon the table. Mary watched the dust particles as they danced wildly in the strip of light, and once more her thoughts had turned to her father.

Five minutes into the marriage service, the opening of the door disturbed the registrar. A familiar voice apologised causing Mary's heart to leap for joy. Turning her head, her eyes met his. Tears of happiness filled her large blue eyes. Once more her Dad had stood by her. He was the best in the whole wide world.

Frank broke free from Pearl's charge, running to his grandfather, he looked up and placed his chubby hand in his. "See Pa-Pa, Mummy's bonny!"

"Aye, I know son. I know." Charlie looked over at his daughter and winked.

Chapter Five

1960

Being the last day of the year, Mary worked non-stop in her small house as it was considered extremely unlucky to bring in the New Year with as much as a tiny speck of dust left over from the past. In some cases it was the only real clean the house had endured from the last Hogmanay.

The square was alive from early morning, with the women washing every dirty article in sight. Washing of every kind, from sheets to pit clothes blew vigorously in the cold biting wind of December.

Nine months had passed since that day she came to stay at Crown Square and in so short a time she had transformed the once sparse rooms into a home to be proud of. She painted, papered, and did the odd joinery job on her own, as she had learned very early in her short married life that Patrick was not in the least bit domesticated.

Although the front room was now furnished, they preferred to sleep in the recess during the winter months, it being a lot warmer, although young Frank's cot remained in the front room and was only brought through if the weather was severe.

The one ringed gas burner had been replaced with a proper cooker and a second hand washing machine stood in the corner of the scullery beside the double sink. The huge stone floor had been covered with linoleum and a few small rugs scattered here and there added some warmth to the cold draughty back kitchen.

The house looked cosy and shone like a new pin. The smell of home baking still lingered in the air, as two freshly baked shortbread rounds lay cooling on a wire tray.

One more task, had to be done, but she would have to wait until near midnight to do it. The task consisted of emptying the ashes from the fire into the tin pail that lay outside. Her mother did that every year, following on the tradition from past generations. The reason behind this was ridding the house of every last bit of the old year's dirt.

Patrick had gone out after tea, his excuse being that he was getting out of Mary's way. Going to the pub for a few drinks was quite the done thing for the man to escape the 'big clean'.

It was now ten thirty and Mary began to feel slightly concerned, as he should have been home an hour ago. He had said nine thirty at the very latest.

Hearing footsteps outside, she jumped up, patted her hair and freshened her lipstick in double quick time, but the footsteps trailed off into the distance. Going to the door, she opened it and looked out into the square. Laughter could be heard coming from a nearby house and further up the square a small group of merry men tried to sing in harmony as they swayed back and forward trying to keep their balance. They had obviously started to celebrate early. In the distance, a dog barked voicing its disapproval of the 'Barber Shop Singers'.

Leaving the doorway, Mary walked round the outside of the house and looked towards the main road, but there was still no sign of Patrick.

The cold night air made her shiver so she hurried back to the warmth of her home.

The bells rang out the old year and in the new. The square came alive with neighbours as they gathered together wishing each other the best for the brand new year ahead forgetting their differences and squabbles for at least a few days. Parties continued on all round her until the early morning. People laughed and danced with their loved ones as they ate their fill and drank to one another's health over and over again.

Pouring herself a sherry and sitting in the quietness of her living room, she sobbed gently. Never in her whole life had she felt this lonely. Her thoughts drifted back to previous New Year celebrations when her mother forgot her hatred of drink and held parties for family and neighbours. The door of the house was left open and all were welcome. Once the men had a few drinks, they found their singing voices and tried to outdo each other for the centre of the floor. This carried on till early morning or until her father started singing Danny Boy, this seemed to be the signal that the party was over, as it never failed to clear the house.

The loud banging on the door made her jump to her feet. Opening it apprehensively, she gasped as she saw Patrick being held up by two men (who found difficulty standing themselves), one at each side propping him up under the arms. "Del-iver-rin' one Pat-Pat-ri-rick Swee-eeny," one managed to mutter.

"Oh my God!" groaned Mary. Taking Patrick's full weight onto her shoulders, she led him into the house. Getting him to lift his feet up the single step into the living room was very difficult, but she eventually managed. At one stage, she had an overwhelming desire to drop him and leave him lying in a crumpled heap on the floor. He could lie all night on the floor as far as she was concerned. Getting him over to an armchair, she pushed him down none too gently. Lifting his head and forcing his eyes open, he tried focusing, then, as he tried to speak, saliva ran out the corner of his mouth trickling down his chin. Moaning, he dropped his head once more. Now snoring and grunting, he was beyond help.

Tears stung Mary's eyes as she watched her husband puff and blow. He looked bloated and his contorted face was ugly. Feeling very sorry for herself, she went over and put the light out to discourage any first-footers. The excitement of having company had gone, and she just wanted to be alone.

Lying in bed with tears streaming down her face, she sobbed, "Happy bloody new year to you Mary Sweeny."

It was almost five o'clock when Patrick awoke. His body was cramped and sore and his neck was rigid and very painful. A sledgehammer pounded away mercilessly inside his head and he had become as cold as ice. Throwing off his clothes, he let them drop onto the floor before staggering to the side of the bed. Pulling himself up onto the bed, he landed heavily down beside Mary. As he was so cold, he tried to wrap himself round her warm body, but she lashed out at him with all the strength her arms and legs could muster.

"Come on! Come on, I'm bloody frozen. Don't be rotten Mary!" he pleaded.

Spitting her words out she hissed, "Don't talk to me about being rotten. In fact, just don't talk to me at all!"

"Awe, come on Mary!" As he tightened his grip round her, she lashed out again with her feet, catching him on the shinbone with her heel.

"You bitch, you bloody bitch," he called out angrily.

Her back was to him; therefore she was quite unprepared for what was to follow.

Taking his clenched fist and using great force behind the blow, he punched his unsuspecting wife once in the kidney area, causing her to lose her breath and gasp frantically for air. Apart from the severity of the pain, Mary's head reeled with shock. Turning round, she lashed out at her drunken bedfellow like some demented demon, but it was sadly to her disadvantage. She felt the bone in her nose crack, as he took a swing at her tear stained face. Mary fell back onto her pillow as blood spouted like a fountain from her nostrils.

Crawling from the bed, she staggered towards the kitchen door as the blood ran freely down onto her nightshirt and onto the floor. She stood in the kitchen thinking that he would rise and follow her through, begging her forgiveness and apologising profoundly, but all she heard were deep snores and satisfied grunts as he had fallen into another drunken slumber.

Mary knew that night the honeymoon was over. Her husband was now flying his true colours. Her mother had been right all along, but no matter how she felt, Mary would never give her the satisfaction of knowing, besides there was another reason for staying where she was, she was now carrying his child. Her plan had been to tell him after their first kiss of the year, now that appeared to Mary like some far off dream.

She spent a sleepless night huddled on one of the armchairs, her legs pulled up underneath her. Staring into the newly lit fire that had struggled to catch alight, she went over the horrifying events that took place a few hours ago and, looking across at the sleeping figure that lay in the recess, she knew that the love she had for him had died. What he wanted from her now he would have to take, as she vowed never to give her self to him freely again.

The child's chatter and the familiar noises around the house woke Patrick around ten o'clock. He sat up in the bed and holding his head in his hands he groaned loudly.

Mary paid no heed.

Swinging his legs over the bed, and still with a slight stagger, he made his way into the back kitchen. Once there, he disappeared into the toilet.

The kettle stood on the hob beside the fire and, as it was constantly filled with hot water, Mary proceeded to make a pot of fresh tea. She had just poured out a cup for herself, when Patrick made his appearance in the room. With head bowed low, he sat himself down at the table.

Without looking at Mary, he began speaking softly, his voice full of remorse.

"I'm sorry Mary. I got involved with a few mates last night and I can't remember coming home."

Still she remained silent.

"I'll make it up to you. I promise."

Mary's back was turned towards him, and as she turned to face him, he looked up into her face and gasped. "What-on-earth?" he jerked his head back with shock. Both her eyes were black and so puffy, only small slits allowed Mary to see the bridge of her nose as well as being severely bruised, had an open gash which was now congealed with hard black blood. Breaking her silence, she confronted him with hate in her voice. Pointing vigorously to her injuries and peering at him through eyes that were almost shut she hissed, "Don't tell me you can't remember doing *THIS*!"

Rising to his feet, Patrick rushed over to where she now stood, and with outstretched arms, he made to hold her. In a low distinct voice, Mary emphasised ever word, "Don't- you- dare- touch me, Patrick Sweeny, or - so help me, I'll do you in!!" Her fear of him had gone, as he now looked half the man he was.

"Oh! Mary!" he stammered, "I can't remember. I...I. thought it was all a bad dream. I can't remember doing that to you. Not you! I'm so ashamed."

She now paced back and forward, looking down at him, as he was now slumped helplessly in the armchair. "I'm sorry, I'm sorry Mary," he whined, "I don't know what happened, but you would never deserve that..."

She watched as tears ran down his face. She almost felt sorry for him, but the pain she was feeling prevented her from weakening. "It will take a long time, a very long time Patrick, that is if I can ever forgive you, but there's one thing for sure, I will never forget."

Chapter Six

Wrapped loosely in his shawl, his small cherub face peeping from under the white knitted helmet, the new baby was carried out carefully to the awaiting world by the matron. It was the done thing at the small cottage maternity hospital, for the matron to carry all the new babies out into God's fresh air (as she put it.)

Mary had said her goodbyes to the patients and staff and followed on behind the tall slim woman who had dominated the small cottage hospital that had accommodated her and her infant son for the last eight days.

There were only two wards in the hospital, one providing beds for eight patients, while the smaller one held four. The delivery room, TV lounge, kitchen, bathrooms and the visitors' waiting room were at the front of the 'house'. The wards and staff rooms were at the rear beside the baby nursery and the admittance room. Matron's house was the first building as you entered the grounds and the nurses' quarters were located at the back of the main building. They grew their own vegetables in the huge gardens maintained by an elderly gardener, whom matron privately employed.

The patient's own family doctor was informed by the hospital on arrival, and except for the few babies that were anxious to be born and couldn't wait for the doctor, were brought into the world by the resident midwife.

Mary's home had no running hot water; as the water was heated by lighting the fire under the old stone boiler, drawing the water from there, or by using the old washing machine; so as the thought of a home confinement was out of the question, the doctor booked her into the local maternity. The only thing that worried Mary was Frank, but Cissie, who lived next door, took good care of him. She had turned out to be a very valuable friend as well as a good neighbour.

Patrick stood outside by the waiting taxicab and as the two woman approached, he opened the rear door to the cab allowing Mary to enter. Once seated, Matron gently handed her the sleeping infant as if it were a parting gift. Patrick slipped in beside his wife and child and after a final good-bye; the car sped off down the gravel drive, heading for home.

The birth of Mary's second son had been quick and somewhat easy, as was the whole nine months of pregnancy. Home life since that dreadful night had been relatively peaceful, except for the odd quarrel that is familiar with most married couples. One thing had changed though; Patrick left Mary alone every Saturday night, as he had resumed his old habit of having a few drinks at his local. Although he never came home as bad as he was the night he broke Mary's nose, he was often near to becoming legless. Handling him had become an art as she learned very quickly when it was best to say nothing and let him sleep it off.

Entering the house with her baby son felt strange. Looking round, she was surprised to see the place gleaming. The bedroom door was open, and catching sight of the baby's cot, Mary walked through into the room. The cot was freshly made up and waiting for the infant. Frank, now four, had a small bed of his own in the far corner of the room. A cheery fire, encaged by a fine mesh fireguard, burned brightly in the grate.

"You've been busy Pat," she said surprised and proud.

She felt disappointed as he confessed, "It wasn't me. Cissie did all the work for you."

'I might have known,' she thought.

The outside door was thrown open, and young Frank rushed in full of excitement. Cissie followed him in.

"Mummy! Mummy!" he called, as he rushed over and encircled her legs with his small chubby arms.

"Careful Frank! Mind the bairn," Cissie chided. Cissie lifted the boy up, enabling him to see his baby brother, and as they cooed and fussed over the boys, Patrick made his way into the kitchen and filled the kettle for tea.

"There's cairds; weel a think they're cairds. Oan the mantle shelf!" Cissie informed Mary.

Laying the baby down in the cot, Mary walked over to the mantle shelf and lifted the envelopes down. She studied the envelopes before opening them as if looking for clues as to who had sent each one. Cissie guessed right. They were indeed cards. There was one from Pearl and Mrs. Smith and one from a neighbour. The last one she opened was from her father. The short note written inside simply said 'See you soon, Love Dad / Granddad.

Cissie watched her young friend's face brighten as she read the card from her father. Looking up, she smiled and said happily, "It's from Dad. He never forgets." She handed her neighbour the card and Cissie studied it.

"Did he manage intae the hospital?" Cissie asked curiously.

"No Cissie, and I feel there's something wrong, as he's never let me down before." Sadness filtered through Mary's reply.

Mary Turner

"Dinnae be daft. The caird says, ' see you soon', so how kin there be onything wrong?" Handing the card back to Mary, Cissie nodded in the direction of the back kitchen and whispered, "Noo there's somethin' very wrong, Patrick Sweeny makin the tea."

Mary's worried expression changed to laughter, as she agreed wholeheartedly with her friend.

Charlie Fairly hadn't felt well for the past few days, but he struggled on, not letting a soul know how he felt, in fact, he didn't know himself. He couldn't pin point the trouble, except he felt unusually tired. His idea of a cure was to work what ailed him off, but this time, whatever was wrong, he knew it wasn't going to go away so easily. He felt drained of energy and in need of a rest, so he made up his mind to visit the doctor if he didn't pick up over the next few days.

Word had reached him about Mary's baby and he knew she was due home that afternoon, and, as it was Sunday, he decided to pay her a visit. He had visited as often as he could, but not as often as he would have liked. Most of his visits were behind Lizzie's back, as he couldn't stand the fuss she made whenever Mary's name was mentioned. Once again he tried to persuade Lizzie to forgive and forget, but just like all the other times, Lizzie was adamant, she wanted nothing to do with her daughter.

"You're only depriving yourself of your Grandchildren woman!" He pleaded with her to change her mind.

"No child of his is welcome here!" she said.

"You're a hard bitch Lizzie. The bairn's your flesh and blood an all, besides, you surly would like to see Frank again, wouldn't you?"

"I've learned to do without and I'll not turn back now," she replied stiffly.

He shook his head in despair. "Well, I'm going, she's still my Daughter and as far as I'm concerned, she'll always be my Daughter no matter what she does."

"Your Daughter! She's all you think about. You never gave the boys half the love you showed her. Look where it's got her. Living with a no good drunk!"

It generally took a great deal of pressure and persecution to make Charlie lose his temper and Lizzie had managed to do just that. The veins in his neck swelled out as if ready to burst, and his jawbones moved back and forward in anger. His eyes grew large and stared hard into Lizzie's astonished face. Words clear, loud, and meaningful filled her ears. "WHAT WAS THAT WORD YOU USED JUST NOW? LOVE! LOVE! When did that word creep into your vocabulary? You use words that you know nothing about!! LOVE! LOVE! You are incapable of loving anyone. So don't you tell me I showed no love to the boys? You on the other hand, have never uttered a kind word to our Mary. You've forced her to seek love from anywhere or anybody willing to give her affection, so you just think on..." Charlie banged his fist on the table causing Lizzie to jump with fright. She had never driven Charlie this far in a long time and she was scared, so scared that she did not utter another word.

He walked away from her and mounted the stairs two at a time. Reaching the bathroom, he went in and slammed the door shut. Once inside, Charlie felt the most awful pain shoot across his chest. He doubled up momentarily and held himself until it passed. Feeling it ease away, he straightened up slowly, then, looking at himself in the mirror, he saw the reflection of a grey, ill-looking face stare back. Taking a deep breath, he held the air in his lungs for a few seconds before slowly letting it out. It gripped him again, stabbing at him like some invisible demented demon, taking revenge on his distorted vulnerable

79

body. This time it refused to ease up. Stronger and stronger it came, causing Charlie to gasp desperately for air. Grabbing hold of the towel rail with one hand, and clutching his chest with the other, he tried to overcome his torture. Knocking against the glass shelf that sat above the towel rail, he sent bottles of all shapes and sizes flying across the floor. The towel slid from the rail under Charlie's grasp like a film reel played in slow motion. Slowly it slipped with Charlie, until the big man hit the floor. Lying motionless, the towel still clutched in his hand, Charlie gave a long slow agonising groan.

Lizzie heard the smashing of glass, as the bottles hit the lino, and hesitated for a few seconds at the foot of the stairs. The thud that followed alarmed her and instinctively she dashed up the stairs, calling Charlie's name. She called again when she reached the door, but was met with an eerie silence. "Charlie!! Are you all right?" No answer. She became filled with sheer terror. Hammering frantically on the door with both fists she screamed his name. The house filled with her piercing screams, as she realised something dreadful had happened.

If he had been all right, he would have yelled back. Especially in the mood he was in. Putting her weight against the door made no impression on the solid lump of wood. She stood paralysed with emotion, then, she suddenly took hold of the situation. Running downstairs, she opened the door and flew along the path towards the front gate. She caught sight of two neighbours walking on the other side of the road and called frantically. Seeing she was greatly distressed, both men ran to her and without a word, they followed her beckoning gestures. They soon understood the situation as Lizzie sobbed and pleaded for their help.

Putting their weight against the solid door, the lock burst open throwing them both in.

Charlie lay still, and while one of the men stooped over his body, lifting his limp head gently, the other tried to keep Lizzie from entering the small room. "Best stay here love and let Geordie see to him."

"No!" screamed Lizzie as she battered onto the man's chest with both fists. She pushed past and threw herself down on the floor, and as she did so, a piece of broken glass sunk into her knee. Ignoring the pain, she hugged Charlie's still lifeless body. George looked up at his mate and shook his head.

Lizzie went into hysterics, as she pulled frantically at her own hair. Her screams were like that of a wild animal caught in a hunter's snare. She started clawing at her distressed face making it bleed, deep vesicles, made by her nails, became embedded in her skin.

Both men fought with her and eventually managed to move her downstairs.

The doctor arrived and soon Charlie's body was taken to the mortuary. Lizzie had been given a strong sedative and lay on the bed, staring silently at the ceiling. Lizzie's neighbour, a very old friend, stayed and offered her help. She was an unobtrusive woman who showed great kindness. Although she had heard Lizzie and Charlie argue a short while ago, it would never be disclosed to anyone outside Lizzie's family. Mrs. Wallace knew of the rift between Mary and her mother, but she was wise enough to know the lass would have to be told before she heard it from a gossip, so she sent her husband down to Crown Square to break the news.

"Lizzie, Lizzie," Susie Wallace spoke quietly. Lizzie opened her eyes and looked into the face of her trusted neighbour.

"Lizzie, I've sent my Eddie down to let Mary know."

Lizzie, greatly disturbed, thrashed about the bed.

"Now Lizzie, she's got to be told."

"Don't let her near me Susie. I don't want to talk to her. She has no place here. Not now. Her Father's gone, and it's all her fault."

Taking her gently by the hand, Susie Wallace comforted her and patting her softly she tried to calm her.

"All right All right Lizzie. If you want Mary to stay out, I'll see to it. But it wasn't Mary's fault Charlie had an attack Lizzie. You surely don't blame her for that!"

Struggling to sit up, Lizzie's voice was almost panic like, "It was her. She caused us to row. Charlie has...had never spoken to me like that in all our married life. She left us for trash and caused us to row!!"

Pushing her back on the pillow and stroking her weary head, Susie once more tried to calm her neighbour, "Wheesht now Lizzie, try and rest."

Lizzie now grabbed Susie's hand, "What about my boys?"

"Don't worry, Eddie is going to phone Corby when he gets back, and he's also calling the Ben Line for Billy. Joe won't take long to get here Lizzie, and as he can't do much today, it being Sunday, things will get done tomorrow, anyway, you have to wait on the post-mortem before arrangements can be made."

Tears filled Lizzie's red swollen eyes once more and her mouth quivered violently as the wailing sound came from within her very soul.

"Oh my God! Oh my God! Why had you to take my Charlie? He was so good." She turned her face into the pillow and lost herself in uncontrollable sobs.

Patrick relaxed in the armchair reading the Sunday paper. Mary had just finished feeding and changing the infant and was about to tidy up. Young Frank had gone into Cissie's house, as the new baby hadn't really impressed him at all. He had his mind set on a baby that could play with him, not some sleepy uninteresting doll, besides, Cissie's big lads carried on with him and made him scream with laughter. He had great fun next door.

The wee red mini stopped outside Mary's window and she recognised it immediately. For a moment she thought his neighbour had given her father a lift down but, when Mary saw that only Eddie Wallace appeared from the car, she was filled with curiosity.

"Eddie Wallace is at our door Patrick!"

Looking over his paper, he glanced momentarily towards the window, and then back at Mary, "Well you'll find out what he wants if you open the door!"

Feeling stupid, Mary walked into the back kitchen and opened the door. She knew instantly that something was wrong, as Eddie wasn't very good at hiding his feelings. His eyes welled up with tears and without waiting to be asked in, pushed gently passed Mary going straight into the living room. Standing in the middle of the floor clutching his cap in his hands, he looked so uncomfortable. All eyes were on him, and then Patrick broke the silence.

"Well man, what is it that you find hard to say?"

Still Eddie stood dumb struck, as no sound come from his gapping mouth. He just stood there like a man in shock. He couldn't find the words. He faced Mary and stammered, but his words were incoherent.

Mary felt the vibes from the man who stood motionless in front of her.

"It's my Dad! My Dad's sick!" Her hand darted up and covered her mouth as she gasped aloud.

The man's voice cracked. He cleared his throat a couple of times before moving over to where Mary stood. "Sit down Mary," he finally managed said.

Mary sat down on the chair without taking her eyes from her old neighbour.

"Your Dad died a short while ago Mary."

She stared hard at him and her mouth fell open. In a daze she looked blankly round the room, as if seeing it for the first time. Her hand went to her heart, feeling it to make sure it was still beating. This was a dream. She would wake at any minute. No! She wasn't going to cry out, not her; this is a dream, a terrible nightmare, and if she sits still, she will eventually wake up. There! Just sit and wait.

"Mary!" The voice came from the other end of the tunnel. "Mary!!"

There it was again! She felt at peace, warm and distant, and she never wanted to return to that place again.

"Give her a bit o' brandy Patrick!" Cissie bent over her friend and wet her lips with the strong liquid, causing her to cough and splutter. She was choking. Something was swelling up in her throat. Opening her mouth wide, Mary set the obstacle free.

Ear-piercing screams filled the house while she shook violently as if in some sort of fit.

Her body, now totally exhausted, Mary sobbed broken-heartedly into the cushion that rested on her lap.

"What's she to do?" Patrick addressed Eddie who was disturbed at Mary's show of grief. He shuffled his feet nervously and not taking his eyes of the distraught lass he answered. "I don't know. I was only sent to let her know. If she's up to it, later on that is; maybe she should go to her Mother." Eddie shrugged his shoulders, not knowing what to suggest.

"No! She'll not go there. Not until she's asked," Patrick said adamantly.

Cissie, who was now comforting Mary, looked up at Patrick, "A think you aught tae send fir the doctor. If ye ask me, she'll no' be goin' oanywhere, the state she's in."

"I want no-no do- doctor," Mary managed to say between her sobs, "I'll be ok."

"Weel, go an' have a wee lie doon an' I'll mind the bairns," Cissie kindly suggested.

Mary did as Cisssie said, and as she drifted into an exhausted sleep, her father came to her. He stood over her, and with his usual warm grin, he looked down on her and winked. Softly he spoke, "Couldn't go before seeing wee Allan now, could I? I love you Mary. See you again!!"

On his last word, he faded slowly into the shadows.

She had not decided on a name for the baby, but she now knew her father had chosen the name Allan. Another thing crossed her mind as she lay in the darkened room. His card had said 'See you soon'. Even in death he had not let her down. He had come and said good-bye. He would come to her again. He said he would, and he never went back on his word.

Lizzie sat by the window, her eyes fixed rigidly on the road outside. Billy had arrived home from sea the night before, and was sitting talking quietly to his brother Joe who had come up from Corby with his wife. The house was filled with friends and relations, quietly talking in low murmurs. Joe's wife Pauline, walked over to where Lizzie sat and, gently patting her mother-in- law's arm, she tried to get her over beside her sons.

"Come away from the window Mum and sit beside your boys."

Looking up into Pauline's face, Lizzie smiled faintly, "I'm all right here hen."

Pauline looked towards her husband and shrugged her shoulders. She had tried. Joe rose up and carried his chair over to where his mother sat, placed the chair next to hers and sat down. "It'll be another half hour before the car comes Mother. It would be better if you sat away from the window."

Looking at her son, she shook her head, "I'm not watching for the hearse Joe, I'm watching out for our Mary, for if she dares set foot in this house, there'll be need of another hearse, so there will."

"Mother!" Joe spoke quietly; casting his eyes towards the people gathered in the room, "You don't want to let that lot know about the family business, now do you?"

Lizzie looked away from her son and continued to scan the road. Joe continued. "If Mary's at the cemetery, you can't say anything there now. Do you hear me Mother?"

Lizzie gave no answer. "Mother! Will you listen to what I am saying?"

"I'm listening to you. I know perfectly well that I can't stop her from going to the cemetery, as long as she doesn't come here-- her and that drunken sod of a husband!!" She spat the last part of the sentence out of her mouth, as if something bitter was on her tongue.

Shaking his head sadly, Joe left his mother's side as more of his father's friends had entered the room.

The cemetery where Charlie was to be laid to rest was situated two hundred yards from his home, so no cars were needed. It was purely a walking funeral. The immediate family walked behind the hearse, the strong afternoon sun beating down on them as they made their way towards the group of people who stood along the pavement's edge waiting to join the end of the cortege. Mary stood among them, clutching on to her husband's arm.

Her eyes filled with tears and her heart ached as she gazed upon the coffin that carried her beloved father. It was barely visible under the blaze of colour from the vast amount of wreaths. It passed her by very slowly. She watched as her mother walked on behind, supported by her two brothers. They walked with bowed heads, unaware of Mary's presence.

Pauline spotted Mary and nodded in quiet acknowledgement.

It wasn't until the burial was over; Lizzie noticed Mary and Patrick standing near. She walked over towards her distraught daughter stopping directly in front of her. Softly, but venomously she hissed, "He'd still be here if it wasn't for you. You killed him, so you did. You caused the row that led to his death- you- you." She struggled to keep from raising her hand. Now setting her sight on Patrick she hissed, "You both deserve each other. You're nothing but a drunken sod." Pointing frantically at Mary, she growled, "and you're nothing but a wee whore, so you are."

Feeling herself being pulled, Lizzie tried shrugging off the hands that tugged her arm. "Your no Daughter of mine! DO YOU HEAR?"

"Mother!" Joe pleaded. "Come on Mother, people are listening. Come now before you say too much."

Lizzie looked hard at Mary with hatred in her eyes, before she allowed her son to lead her away.

Mary stood as if in shock. She watched as her family disappeared into the street. A few of the crowd lingered on, some making their way to other parts of the cemetery where loved ones of their own lay. Mary stood with Patrick and watched as the gravediggers laid boards over the grave. She wasn't really taking in the goings-on of the workers; she was just standing staring through tear filled eyes. Staring at nothing in particular. Her vision was oblivious to everything round her.

"Come on Mary," Patrick urged with growing aggravation, "she's not worth upsetting yourself over. Come on home."

"Our Billy never even spoke," her voice was only a whisper.

"Give him time. He'll come before he goes back to sea."

"I don't think he will Pat. She'll see to that."

"If he's anything like your Da', he'll not be stopped. Now dry your eyes and hold your head up. "Your Mother will regret what she has just said through time. You wait and see." He gave her a gentle squeeze as he took her arm in his.

"It's obvious you don't know my Mother very well. She'll never come round now. She even blames me for my Dad's death. You heard her. No Patrick! She hates me."

He made no further comment, as he knew she was right. Lizzie was a stubborn, mean woman, who would never give her daughter the time of day.

Chapter Seven

Patrick had been right. Billy did come and visit that very night. It was quite late, around ten o'clock, when they heard a small tapping on the window. Patrick opened the door, and there stood Billy looking cautiously at Patrick, not knowing how his unknown brother-in-law would welcome him. The picture his mother had painted of Patrick was not in evidence, as this man before him stood sober and upright. He was led to believe he drank himself stupid every night.

"You'll be Billy I suppose!" Patrick looked the caller over from head to foot.

"I wasn't sure if I had the right house. Is Mary still up?" He made no move to enter the house, as he was very unsure of the obstruction barring his way.

Patrick gave a grunt and stood to one side indicating with a nod in the direction of the living-room door. He walked passed Patrick and into the living room where Mary stood waiting. She had heard his voice and as he entered the room, Mary ran to him and threw herself into his arms.

"Oh Billy, I thought you too had turned against me. I thought..."

"Now, now! I couldn't go away without seeing you again, could I?"

After Mary had calmed down, she sat on the sofa holding hands with Billy, looking at him with all the affection of an adoring lover. They talked of their lives for some time, although Mary spoke of only the good things in her marriage.

They avoided talking about their mother for as long as possible, but Billy had to give her the latest piece of news from home.

"Joe and Pauline are taking Mum back to Corby with them. She's talking about giving the house up and staying down there with them"

"But Mum doesn't like Pauline that much. It will never work out!" Mary sat open mouthed at the news.

Billy shook his head wearily, "I told her that, but 'Pauline has changed,' she told me."

"Aye, I can imagine she has. She's looking for a built in baby-sitter if you ask me, and what about you, in all this Billy? If she gives up the house, where will you go when you're on leave?"

"Don't worry about me Sis. I've been thinking about buying a flat. I'm getting on in years you know, Thirty- two this year. It's time I had a place of my own," he said, smiling his teasing smile. Mary smiled back at him in a half- hearted manner before resuming a sombre look.

"What did she mean at the cemetery Billy? She said I killed Dad."

Billy's faced flushed as he rubbed the palms of his hands on his trousers making it obvious he felt embarrassed. He looked towards Patrick, who sat listening without adding to the conversation.

He watched Billy with inward amusement. At last he spoke, "It's all right Billy. Say what's on your mind! You wouldn't be saying anything I haven't heard before."

Billy cleared his throat and nodded to Patrick. Looking directly at Mary he said sadly.

"Dad was coming to see you and the bairns, and was trying to coax her to forget everything and come with him. They had a terrible row. She didn't say what was actually said, but I gather from next door that Dad had lost his temper and was yelling back at her. He was in the bathroom getting ready to come to you, when ...It happened."

Mary sat in silence. Billy watched her momentarily before going on.

"That wasn't all Mary. She got hold of the bankbook after Dad died, and she noticed a withdrawal of one hundred and fifty pounds. It was taken out at the time you left home. She knows you got it from Dad, and she's saying that you borrowed from them."

She shot up from the chair with rage, "I never borrowed anything," she cried.

Patrick's voice, now filled with anger, added swiftly to his wife's denial. "Anything Mary was given from her Father was given of his own free will. We asked nothing from no one."

"How dare she say that!" Mary added.

Billy's hands shot up in the air and he waved them about frantically, "I'm only telling you what she's saying Mary. I don't care about the money."

"No!!" Patrick bellowed. "Then what the hell did you mention it for?"

"I only..." Billy stammered.

"Get out of here, and tell your bastard of a Mother to clear off to Corby and to stay there. She's nothing but an interfering old bag and the sooner we are rid of her the better."

"Patrick," Mary pleaded, "It's not Billy's fault. Don't talk like that to him."

"It's all right," Billy replied, not taking his eyes from this man who had suddenly turned very nasty.

"Look Mary," Patrick said angrily, "I've had enough of your bloody family. Let the witch go to Corby or to hell as far as I'm concerned, for as long as you're in contact with any of them, you'll have no bloody peace."

"Not our Billy," screamed Mary.

Patrick grabbed his coat and walked to the door. He stopped and looking once more at his brother-in-law and growled, "Sort it out between you, but I'll tell you this, be out before I get back. We are not welcome by you lot; so don't come into my house, as none of you are welcome here.... You Billy! You didn't let on this afternoon. Were you so scared of your Mother?" Pointing vigorously at Mary while scowling at Billy, he continued, "You didn't stop and think how she felt, DID YOU!" With that, he turned and marched out into the still summer night.

"Where will he go?" Billy asked.

"A walk most likely. He'll not get a drink at this time." She wrung her hands in agitation.

"It's true then, he does take a good drink?"

Mary shook her head wearily. "What do you want me to say Billy? Do you want me to tell you my Mother's right? No Billy, I'll not do that. Aye he takes a drink like most men, but he's nothing like Ma says. He never sees me short. What he drinks is his own."

"Are you happy?" he asked.

She longed to tell him that she had made a dreadful mistake and that she was just going through the motions of life, but she couldn't. Her problems were hers and no one else could solve them. It had been her own doing. At the time, she couldn't wait to leave home but she soon discovered her mother's words rang true. Patrick did have a drink problem and it was now her problem too. "I have two lovely wee boys sleeping through there and a place of my own. What else could I want?"

"Right. Well! I must be going. I'm going back in a couple of days."

Looking at Mary, he was overcome with emotion. He drew her into an embrace and held her tightly as the tears welled up in both their eyes.

"Mary, your husband is wrong. I couldn't speak to anyone at the cemetery, and if I had, I would have just made matters worse. I felt like I feel now, awkward. Nothing in the world prepares you for death and I only realised Dad was gone when I helped lower him into the ground. I couldn't speak to anyone... especially you...and I know dad gave you the money, because it was in a way, right to do so. He loved you very much, just as I do, but I can't come here until your husband says it's all right, after all, it is his house."

"Mine too remember. I shall be putting that right." She sniffed and wiped her eyes.

"Will you write to me?" He pulled a folded envelope from his jacket pocket. "This is the address. The company will forward your letters."

She took the envelope and threw her arms round him once more. They hugged for a few more seconds, then forcing back the tears, Billy released his hold, and taking his young sister's hands in his, he smiled that familiar smile and asked, "Well! Are you going to let me have a peep at the boys before I go?"

Drying her eyes once more, she too forced a smile as she led Billy through to where the boys lay sleeping soundly.

Some fifteen minutes later, Mary stood at the corner of the house and waved goodbye to the brother she loved dearly. Clutched in her hand was the envelope Billy had given her with the address where he could be reached. She watched him until he had faded into the night. Returning to the house, she sat down in the armchair. She felt tired and very weary. Staring into the smouldering remains of the fire, the events of the day came rushing back to her. The fire with its dying embers was like a powerful crystal ball demanding that she stare into it. Mary did stare hard, till her eyes burned, not with the heat from the fire, as that had long gone, but from the burning tears that now flowed steadily from her very tearstained eyes. She did not sob. The tears just trickled down her cheeks quietly on their own. The only sound that was heard was the steady ticking from the clock. The volume of the ticking exaggerated by the stillness of the room.

It was there in the armchair; Mary finally let go of her torment, and drifted off into the depth of welcome sleep. The baby's cry woke her around five in the morning, as the hungry infant demanded feeding.

Patrick had not come home. This was not the first time he had stayed out all night, but she was far from caring.

After she had attended to the needs of her infant, Mary then slipped into bed, knowing that her husband would soon return to change into his working clothes. He had never been known to miss a shift at the pit, even when he was suffering from the effects of a heavy weekend's drinking.

Chapter Eight

1967

Liverpool docks were alive as ever with the hustle and bustle of early morning loading and unloading of cargo ships. Great cranes loomed upwards, silhouetted against the barely lit sky. Pallets of cargo waiting to be lifted aboard the moored vessels and great metal containers stood in line, ready to be hoisted aboard and stowed in the huge holds.

Overcoat collar turned up and hands in his pocket, Billy walked with reluctance towards his ship, dodging the Dockers as they hurriedly went about their business. He watched his step, as coils of rope and wire lay on the quayside awaiting loading by the scurrying movements of the forklifts.

Billy felt awful. He dearly wanted to sleep as he had been on the hard stuff the night before and his head was retaliating.

The Ben Line had been his employer for many years and now he had signed up with Richard Blake Shipping Company. He had been on two voyages already with them, taking him around European ports, but this voyage was to take him further a field. He wasn't altogether happy with the company and was intending to make this his last voyage with them.

In front of him now sat the 'M V. Windsmoor'. Billy stood for a moment looking up at her. He could never say she was a grand looking vessel; in fact, he wasn't at all pleased with the way she looked. He began to wish he had never agreed to sail in her.

Blinking his eyes a few times and giving his head a quick shake from side to side, he hitched his holdall further up on his shoulder and walked briskly up the gangplank.

After reporting to the first mate and signing on, Billy made his way towards his cabin, which was located at the aft of the ship. The sailor whose bunk was beneath Billy's, stood in the narrow alleyway between the bunks and the long narrow seat that was attached to the bulkhead and, as Billy approached him, the sailor eased himself to one side enabling Billy to pass.

"Sorry mate" he said, as Billy threw his holdall on top of his bunk.

"No harm done," Billy replied, forcing a half smile. "You sailed in her before?" Billy enquired.

"Man aye. This is me second trip," he answered easing himself onto the top of his bunk, before lying with his arms behind his head.

"It's not the greatest of ships, but I've been on a lot worse."

Billy gave a sarcastic laugh, "Oh aye, the' Vital Spark?" he asked, referring to the old Glasgow puffer that appeared in the television comedy of the same name.

"Vital Spark?" asked the sailor.

Being in no mood to explain, Billy shook his head, "Never mind. I'm only joking."

"By the way, Terry Manley's the name."

"Oh aye." Turning round and looking down at his new friend he introduced himself, "Billy. Billy Fairley."

The crew on the 'Windsmoor' were as usual, a mixed bunch of lads, although Billy found himself to be the only Scot. Which was rather unusual. A good few of the crew were from Newcastle, a couple from Portsmouth, but the majority of them came from the Liverpool area.

Loaded up with its cargo, the ship put to sea later that evening and her first port of call was Gibraltar. They reached there three days later and took on board a further shipment of goods and set sail down and round the straits, into the Mediterranean sea on route to Port Said. There they remained for a few days while some cargo was discharged and other great containers were loaded. Billy became concerned when checking the bilges. He noticed the cargo in the hold had moved from its lashings. In his opinion, it hadn't been loaded on board properly, but it wasn't his job to complain. During the weeks he had been on board, he had learned that the Captain of the 'M.V.'Windsmoor' was more concerned in profit than on safety, and this worried Billy tremendously. Word had it that the shipment loaded on board at Gibraltar was the captain's private dealings.

While sailing on down through the Suez Canal, passing Aden and Socorro and into the Indian Ocean, unrest grew amongst the crew as the ship began to list slightly on the port side. This was shrugged off as being nothing to be concerned about by the Captain. He had sailed on many occasions with much more of a list, so his experience was to keep going and get to the port of call as soon as possible.

The noise in the engine room was deafening, but Billy was well used to it. He cut the din out by drifting into thought. His job was second nature to him and his hands seemed to work automatically. He was thinking of his sister, and wondering how life was treating her. She had stopped writing away back years ago, and he could only contribute that to her husband. He waited for nearly a month after sending his last letter, and as there was no reply, he knew that her husband had succeeded in breaking their relationship. The letters he had received from her always asked why he never wrote. Billy realised then, her husband was keeping his letters from her. His mind drifted to the day they rode the bike, and he smiled as he recalled his mother's coat.

Terry, whose swearing rang in his ears, brought him back to the present. "Fucking nutters. That's what they are. Fucking nutters."

"What's the matter mate? Who's nutters?" Billy asked.

Terry swore a bit, but very seldom did he curse, unlike the majority of the crew.

"The bloody first officer and his like. That's who."

"What's happened?"

The men, who were nearby, crowded in to hear what was amiss.

"There's only a fuckin' hull plate leaking. I goes to do a check on the bilges an' I sees it and the bloody first mate tells me to ignore it. 'It's not much,' says he. 'It'll not give us trouble,' says he. Not fuckin' much it won't."

"You've got to be joking? They can't ignore that," one of the sailors remarked knowingly.

"They can, and they are," Terry informed him.

"Where exactly is it Terry?" asked Billy

"Under the bilge plate in the cargo hold, and another thing," Terry added, "the water level down there is higher than it should be."

"How bad is it Terry?" Billy rubbed his chin taking in every word.

"Bad enough," came his anxious reply.

His face now red with anger, Billy threw down the spanner he had been using.

"Where are you going Billy?" Terry asked as he watched Billy push the surprised sailors aside.

"I'm going up to have a word with that mad bastard of a Captain. I never signed up to become fish bait."

Billy and Terry led the procession of men towards the bridge, and as they went, Terry filled him in with the details.

The first mate and the captain saw the men advancing. The captain himself stood abreast the door of the bridge as if guarding the entrance. He was a stocky built man, ruddy faced, who seemed to be minus his neck. His head looked as if it sat directly on his shoulders. A canopy of thick bushy eyebrows, shielded his small grey beady eyes from the glare of the afternoon sun.

"Well!" he bellowed. "What's this in aid off? A delegation Eh!"

"Captain, Sir. We want a word," Billy demanded.

The captain threw back his head in mocking laughter. He then came down and stood facing Billy, legs apart his hands on his great hips. "It's a long time since there was a mutiny on the high seas".

"Captain," Billy proceeded, "There's some concern over the hull plate that's leaking and.."

"And," he bellowed, "And. So there's more?"

"Aye Sir. There is more."

"Well Greaser?" He bent down and glowered at Billy, his eyes disappeared behind the narrow slits.

"Greaser Fairley Sir," He showed no fear as he faced this overpowering hulk.

"Well Greaser Fairley, you'd better come into my office where we can discuss these matters of concern in comfort." The sarcasm in the Captain's voice alerted the men who knew there was going to be trouble. He now looked at the rest of the crew and yelled, "You lot...Get back to your duties or I'll have you all logged and dock your wages. Go on!" He roared. "Move your bloody selves!"

The men hesitated, and then one by one they turned and headed back along towards the aft accommodation of the ship and disappeared below deck.

Billy followed the Captain into his office and stood watching as he poured a drink out of a bottle from a drawer. He waited for the great man to turn and face him.

"Well now seaman Fairley, you don't agree with your captain's judgement," he said obnoxiously. "You seem to think you have reason for complaint." He stared hard at Billy.

"Yes Sir I do," Billy said courageously.

"You do what?" he asked, knowing perfectly well what Billy meant.

"Agree with me do you."

"No Sir, I mean I have reason for complaint."

"Oh you do, do you. Well maybe I should listen to your complaint. Maybe I, a Captain for many years, can learn a thing or two from a greaser."

"Sir," Billy, aware of the captain's arrogance, wanted to get straight to the point without the play-acting. "Sir, the ship is listing and the crew and I are concerned about that, and the fact that one of the hull plates in the bilges has sprung a leak."

"Is that your complaint in full Fairley?"

"No Sir."

"Go on then, have your say."

"Well Sir," Billy went on, "We are patching up parts of the engine that should have been renewed long ago. Some parts are beyond repair Sir."

"And you can't patch up. Is that what you're saying?"

"Yes sir."

"You're not so bloody clever then. Are you Fairley? A good greaser can get on with things without whinging."

"Sir. There's also concern about the level of water that's been taken in below the bilge plating," Billy said ignoring what had just been said.

"Have you been down below Fairley? Have you seen the water level?" the captain asked.

Billy had to be honest and replied, "No sir, but motorman Manley has just checked the bilges and has reported his findings."

"To you?" the Captain roared, and before Billy could answer, the great hulking body of the captain came lunging forward. Billy felt his shoulders being pierced by the Captain's thick finger. "So the crew think you're the first officer, or maybe the Captain himself that they go running to you, so I'll tell you this boy, I happened to have knowledge of the slight list, and it's nothing to be concerned with. I happen to know of the trickle of water coming from the hull plate, which is a mere detail. And I happen to think that the level of water in the hold is at an acceptable level. So what do you think of that?"

Billy felt his anger grow, as the Captains finger prodded repeatedly into his flesh on every word. "Sir. The lives of all the men are at stake here. There is reason for concern." He stepped back a few paces to avoid the captain's finger.

The captain thrust his face forward, allowing his hot whisky breath to be felt against Billy's cheek. "You boy. You are a troublemaker. I've met your likes before, and I can tell you, when I had finished with them, they couldn't even get a job on the Irish ferry." As he spoke, he pushed Billy roughly on the shoulder with the flat of his hand. Billy's rage erupted and he retaliated by pushing the captain forcibly to one side, but the man's great weight saved him from toppling over.

Furiously, he lifted Billy by the boiler suit collar, shook him like a rag doll and threw him into the air. Billy felt his head crack on impact as he hit the bulkhead. A searing pain shot through his head and he felt the trickle of warm blood flow down his cheek. Running his hand down the side of his face, Billy looked down at the blood that ran through his fingers.

"You mad bastard," he hissed, "Do you think we don't know your game. You're making money by overloading the hold with cargo the company doesn't know about. That's why you're ignoring the listing. It's in your interest to keep going. The first mate should know about this, or is he in the racket an all?"

"You couldn't let it go; could you? You had to make trouble. Well boy, you'll be kept out the way until the cargo is offloaded, and you'll rue the day you opened your mouth."

The Captain opened the door of his office and yelled out to his officers to come and escort Greaser Fairley to the rope locker where he was to remain locked up for the duration of the trip.

The rope locker was located in the bow of the ship and as Billy was thrown in, the steel door clattered shut behind him. There was no porthole to shed light in the small room, but Billy felt round in the dark for the light switch. Finding it, he flicked the switch but nothing happened. He tried it a couple of times in succession, and swore as he stood in the darkness. "Shit!" he fumed, realising that the bulb had gone. Feeling his way carefully, he managed to trace the outline of coiled rope. He sat down cautiously in case the coil would tumble, but it was well secured. He felt his head throb and his back was now giving him trouble. How he wished there was a light in the place. He couldn't see a thing but the total darkness made his hearing acute. He sat and listened to the familiar creaks and groans as the ship swayed with the swell of the waves. She sounded as if she was dying. She called out for help, but her calls were unheeded. The sound echoed in Billy's ears. His sense of smell was alerted too. Rope had a smell of its own and it now filled his nostrils.

Later on that night, the door opened, and after blinking a few times, Billy was relieved to see one of the cooks standing holding a tray of food. "There you go pal," said he, handing the tray into Billy.

"You couldn't get a bulb down here? I can't eat anything in the dark."

The cook looked round as if making sure they were alone. "I'll have to go up and get you one. Can I trust you to sit there and eat this with the door open."

"Of course. Where am I going to get a taxi at this time o' night?" Billy said trying to joke.

"You hear anybody comin', you get in and shut the door. I'll whistle when I come down," the cook warned him. "Mind, if you get me into trouble you'll have to sing for your supper!"

He wasn't away long until he was back with a bulb. Billy fixed it into the socket and tried the switch. It worked.

Before the cook left, he thrust a note into Billy's hand. "Here. It's from your fan club."

Leaving him behind locked door, Billy finished his meal and read the note. It was from Terry. The ship was to pass the coast of Sri Lanka the following afternoon and he planned to jump ship and head for the shore. As there were plenty of fishing boats in the area, he felt sure that he would be picked up. He wanted Billy to go with him, as he knew the Captain was mad enough to keep him locked up until they reached a British Protectorate. He would more than likely be charged with all manner of things on returning home.

Billy knew this to be true. He would be charged with assault for a start, although it was the Captain who did the assaulting. He had nothing to lose, so he made up his mind to go for it.

The plan was carried through. Terry followed the cook down as he carried Billy's meal. As he reached the door of the rope locker, Terry waited until he had opened it. Once he handed Billy his tray, Terry pounced. Billy pulled him into the locker while Terry pushed from behind. Once the cook was inside, the two deserters locked the door and fled. No matter how much the cook shouted for help, his cries would not be heard as he was down in the bowels of the ship. He would have to wait there until he was missed. Terry laughed as they ran.

"The crew will thank us. Locking him up will give their stomachs a rest."

Terry was right. After launching a life raft, they were sighted and picked up by a fishing boat manned by a crew of Sri Lankans.

Chapter Nine

The houses at Crown Square were earmarked for demolition, and as tenants were re-housed, the dwelling places were boarded up and left to decay. The Square, once alive with children playing, screaming and fighting, now stood in eerie silence, as if in mourning for the families that had gone. No more would it see the blazing colours dancing gaily in the wind as housewives bantered with one another on washdays.

The weeds were already pushing up through the cracks on the concrete slabs that were once scrubbed and bleached by the over zealous housewives who took pleasure in making the outside of their homes clean and presentable. The neighbours were apt to judge the cleanliness of the house by the windows, doorstep and front knocker. If your face didn't reflect back off the shiny brass, then you were judged as being ' a clart', however, a few of them were scrupulously clean on the outside, while the inside of the houses left a lot to be desired, but the biggest majority kept exceptionally clean homes, in spite of the lack of modern conveniences.

The hive of activity had slowly died as one by one the tenants were re-housed. The buildings now stood like ghostly figures, remnants of the past, awaiting their fate. There could be no reprieve as they had been condemned and the coal board had other plans for the area. If only walls could talk! What tales they could tell! Tales of poverty and hardship, but in spite of it all, they were happy days, when doors were never locked and what few luxuries acquired were shared with one another.

Mary was among the last tenants to leave, and although she was glad of a house that had a bath and running hot water, she felt sadness when leaving the Square. The neighbours there had become her friends. Eight years she had spent there, and, although she had many a heartache, she also had many happy memories. Often the neighbours gathered together for a singsong and a few laughs. On fine summer evenings, the womenfolk normally gathered outside to have a good gossip, keeping a wary eye on the youngsters playing with their skipping ropes, while others played peevvers with an old shoe polish tin filled with earth, while the boys wanted to tie the girls up, pretending they were cowboys with imaginary guns, skelping themselves on their hip as they galloped into Indian country.

Now she was in a housing scheme, where the neighbours strived to be better than one another. Children were chased from the front of the houses and the girls weren't allowed to chalk the pavements. Footballs were definitely banned and it was hopeless playing ball in your own back garden, as it would inevitably land in the neighbour's gardens never to be seen again. Mary had only been in the new house a week before her neighbour tackled her over the boys. 'They were too noisy' she said. Mary chose to ignore her and go about her own business. One good thing was, her old neighbour Cissie had been housed directly opposite, so that was a great consolation for Mary, as they had become each other's confidantes, and Mary needed a friend to talk to as her marriage was anything but happy. It had gone from bad to worse since the birth of her third child Tony. He was a puny child, who seemed to prefer his own company rather than joining in with the other boys. The least bit of boisterous play had him screaming for his mother. He was only two years of age when they moved into the new house. Frank by that time was eleven, and Allan had just turned seven. Apart from the usual squabbles among brothers, the two eldest got on fairly well; in fact, Frank became very protective towards Allan and was always there to defend him whenever he felt threatened at school.

Mary's marriage had never been a happy one, but there was the odd time of laughter with Patrick. Things were bearable until he started keeping her short of money. He lied about it at first, telling Mary that the job he was doing didn't pay very well, then, he made the excuse that the pay office had made a mistake with the wages, but Mary knew that he was lying from the start. He had a good position down the mine and earned more than the average miner. Overcome with curiosity, she searched through his pockets one Saturday while he was in the bath, and found that her suspicions were not unfounded. He certainly made sure he had plenty.

The only way Mary could increase her income was to look for a part time job, but it seemed impossible with the boys being so young. Then there was Patrick. He had always objected to her working. At first he would tell her that it was his place to look after her, but that was in the beginning of their marriage. The real reason became very clear to Mary shortly after their marriage; Patrick Sweeny liked her to be there at all times to do his bidding. She wasn't allowed to have a life of her own. She had to ask him for every thing. He liked to be in complete command.

Mary had gone over to her friend Cissie's for her morning cuppa, as this had become a habit over the years. They took it in turn. The only time the habit was broken was if for some reason or other Patrick was around, but that never happened very often as Patrick Sweeny very rarely missed a shift.

Cissie's home had always felt like a refuge to Mary, as there was so much warmth and love radiating from this fat, jovial woman. She had been a seamstress in her younger days and did a bit of sewing for friends and neighbours for a pittance. She wasn't very tidy about the house so, to get a seat in a chair meant removing piles of clothing or newspapers. Dust was part of the furniture and the top of the chest of drawers in the living room was never seen for the array of bits and pieces of material and threads that she constantly used. An old Singer sewing machine was her pride and joy. She always referred to it as her salvation as many a time it helped feed her hungry boys.

"The kettle's oan the boil Mary," she called out as Mary opened the back door. "I'll be through in a second love. I'm jist finishin' Mrs. Telford's curtains oaf."

Mary walked over to the cooker, lifted the kettle off the gas ring and poured the boiling water into the teapot that stood on the sink top. Cissie had already cleared the table in the back kitchen and had the cups out waiting to receive the hot tea along with a plate of biscuits.

"Ah! Guid lass," she said when she joined Mary at the table. "Where's the bairn?"

"I left him outside. He's fallen asleep in the go-chair, and am I no' glad of that. He's clung to my skirt all morning. I don't know what to do with him Cissie. He's driving me mad."

Tapping Mary's hand affectionately, Cissie gave a chuckle, "He'll grow oot o' that, dinnae you fear. My Alex wis the very same at his age. A used tae dae me washin' in the sink, scrubbin' the board wi' yin hand an' him held under the either airm screamin' like a banshee. Honest Mary, mony time a wis sorely tempted to stick his heid in the sink along wi' the dirty washin'. But see him noo. A nicer nature ye couldnae find." Cissie's eyes lit up when thinking of her eldest son. Her chest swelled with pride, for somehow out of the poverty she endured, she managed to keep him at school and see him through college. He was now a schoolteacher and lived with his young wife in Edinburgh.

Mary gave a sigh and staring into her cup she sat silent for a few moments before looking up into the older woman's face.

"What's wrong lass?"

Mary shrugged her shoulders and gave another sigh.

"I'm sick to death of having no money Cissie. He's still keeping me short."

Fixing her eyes firmly on Mary, Cissie's voice became very serious. "I've teld you before no' tae dae withoot. I've no' got a lot, bit I'll help you oot."

She smiled weakly at her dear friend. "Cissie, It's not that simple. I manage, but just and no more. It's not having anything of my own that bothers me. I have to depend on what he gives me. It's like when I depended on my Mother." Eyes filled with tears, Mary fumbled in her skirt pocket for a handkerchief. When none could be found, Cissie thrust the dishtowel into Mary's hand. Mary wiped her eyes and Cissie had by this time moved over and was comforting her.

"There, there noo. Dinnae let that big rotten bugger git you doon. By, if he wis mine, a'd shake the livin' shit oot o' him so I would."

Mary looked up at Cissie and amid her tears, managed to give a faint smile. "I bet you would an all Cissie. Oh look at me," she sniffed with a forced laugh, "I'm using the towel to wipe my eyes," and as if she had found sudden strength she joked, "I'd be much better employed drying up your dishes."

"You leave them alane. There's mare important things tae dae than dishes. Fir a start, it's high time you stood up tae that big ape o' yours. An' ither thing! There's nothin' tae stop you comin' oot wi' me oan Saturday nichts waiting oan tables. There's no' much money tae be made in wages, bit the tips are no' bad."

"I'd love to come with you Cissie, but even if I could, there's no one to watch the bairns. He would never stand for it either."

Cissie rested her elbow on the table and stroked her chin in thought. Smiling broadly she said. "You leave it tae auld Cissie. An' dinnae worry aboot the bairns. Oor Daniel will baby-sit. He an' Elizabeth are savin' fer their weddin' an' never go oot much. And, as fer your Patrick, I'll ask him." She shook her great fat finger at Mary, causing the flab on her large strong arms to wobble. "And a'll no' take no fer an answer."

Mary wasn't at all sure that she relished the idea of facing Patrick, and felt uncomfortable about the whole idea. "You're awful sure that I'll get a start with you anyhow Cissie?"

"Aye you will. The boss is always lookin' fer workers. He gits a lot o' contract work caterin' at ootside functions. A'll ask him this weekend, an' you micht git a start next Saturday. How's that fer plannin'?" Lifting the plate of digestives biscuits, she held them out to Mary. "Would Madam like a wee biscuit tae dip in her tea?"

"E' don't mind if I do," replied Mary plucking a biscuit gracefully from the plate before they both fell about laughing.

The following week, Cissie kept her word and called over in the evening to have a word with Mary and Patrick about the job she had secured for Mary. Both women had arranged to play it by ear and Mary was to pretend that she had just been approached. It was all very devious but to beat Patrick it had to be that way.

Mary had just finished washing up the tea dishes when Cissie popped her head round the door.

"Somebody's busy," Cissie remarked. "Would you like tae come ower an' dae ma dishes fer me?"

"Not on your life. I've seen the dishes that's left in your sink!" Teased Mary. "Go through to the living room and I'll be with you in a minute. The boys are up in their room supposed to be doing homework, but by the sound of them, they're doing demolishing work. Go on through. Patrick's in," she said giving her friend a sly wink.

Cissie walked in the room and Patrick greeted her with a nod and a grunt.

"Hard shift the day?" Cissie enquired, although her question bordered on sarcasm.

Patrick hardly looked at Cissie when answering. His attention was on the television blaring in the corner. "No harder than any other," said he.

Mary came through drying her hands on the hand towel. "What's brought you over to night then Cissie?" (As if she didn't know)

"A came tae ask a favour."

"Oh! An' what's this favour?" Mary enquired with a smile.

"I'm lookin' fer an ither hand for Saturday. There's a dinner dance at the hotel an' we're raither short staffed. Could ye help oot?"

"Well I don't know Cissie. What do you think Patrick?"

Patrick looked over at the two women, who now sat side by side on the sofa. "What's that?" He heard all right, but he played his own game.

"Cissie has asked me to help out on Saturday. What do you think?"

"What do I think? You've got the bairns to think about, that's what I think!"

"That's awe richt," Cissie interrupted enthusiastically. "Oor Daniel an' Elizabeth will look efter the bairns, an' it's always a bit extra in Elizabeth's pocket."

Patrick glowered at Mary.

"She's never waited in her life. She wouldn't know what to do!" he sneered.

"She hands you yer dinner oan a plate every meal time... Doesn't she?" The big woman decided to treat the matter as a joke, as she felt it would go down better. She smiled at Patrick but got no response. "You dinnae need trainin' fer that, besides it'll dae her the world o' guid Patrick, an' she'll be wi' me. Noo where's the herm? Tell me!"

Cissie's wide eyes stared at Patrick until he was forced to look away.

He muttered. "She can do what she likes as long as the kids are looked after". He turned his attention back to the television.

Mary's mouth fell open in amazement. She thought that he would have given Cissie a run for her money, but it never happened. "Come through the kitchen Cissie and I'll make a brew."

Standing up, Cissie waved her hand in a negative gesture, "No lass. A hiv tae get ower an' tackle the ironin'. The piles so big, a dinnae ken whether tae climb it or vault it. But what a dae ken is, there's nae shirts ready fer the auld man, so a better get ma arse movin. I'll be ower tomorrow wi the details."

The door had hardly shut behind Cissie, when Patrick brought up the subject of the job. Mary didn't think that it would be that easy. Patrick would have to have more to say on the matter.

"That was a bit of fine planning if ever I saw It.," he said to Mary.

She acted surprised. "What was?"

"Come off it Mary. Cissie saw you this morning. She must think I'm stupid! 'kin ye dae me a favour'?" he mimicked. "What did you tell her? What? Eh! Do you sit an' discus our affairs? Eh!"

Mary stood up smartly. She didn't wish to hear any more, but Patrick was just as quick in getting to his feet. He grabbed her by the arm and held it tightly. "Let go of my arm Pat. You're hurting me!" she snapped.

"Just don't think you can ever outsmart me." He threw her arm to the side and sat back down and watched the news.

Cissie and Mary caught the six o'clock bus that took them via the hotel. It was situated along the coast and was an hour's journey from their town. Mary was a bit apprehensive about it all, but was assured by Cissie that it would be all right. Cissie had worked in that particular hotel for a few years, but had been in the catering trade for many years. She only worked on Saturday nights or the odd time if the manager was really stuck. She was also an excellent and efficient barmaid and gave them a few hours work in the bar after she had finished waiting on the tables. The meal was to be served at seven thirty and it was arranged that Mary would stay on until ten thirty helping to serve the drinks and collect glasses.

Entering the kitchen, Cissie took Mary through to where their coats were hung. It was a very small room off the kitchen. The women were gathered in the room and greeted Cissie warmly. She introduced Mary to them all, and set about changing her shoes and putting on her white apron and lace cap. Mary had borrowed hers from a friend of Cissie's.

"What's the dance in aid o' the nicht?" Cissie asked.

"It's something to do with the Lord Provost. Teenie here says it's silver service."

"Oh!" Cissie moaned aloud. "It never is?" She looked towards Mary and shook her head.

"What's the matter with you?" the woman asked. "You're the master of the silver service."

"Aye, maybe so, bit Mary here has never been oot before. I thought it was a plated meal."

"What's silver service? Is that where you use the fork thing to lift the meat?" Mary asked.

"Aye. Dae ye ken how it's done?" Cissie asked hopefully.

Mary bit on her bottom lip. "No."

"Awe weel, we'll stick her at the end o' the line wi' the peas. You'll be able tae dae that awe richt." Remarked Cissie.

"We better tell you the other thing Cissie,"

"What noo?" she asked impatiently.

"The chef is in one of his moods."

"Tell me somethin' new," Cissie remarked.

"I mean," the woman went on, "he's worse than normal."

"He's just a wee temperamental toad. Don't even look at him and he'll no' bother you. You'll be as richt as rain," Cissie reassured her once more.

They stood in line ready to go out into the dining room. Cissie was in front with the huge silver salver that carried the sliced up roast chicken soaked in gravy. Another woman followed on with the potatoes, and Mary was behind her carrying a plate containing three kinds of vegetables. This formation was repeated twice behind Mary. Nine waitresses in all. They were set to go, and waited for the order from the chef, who was looking them over. He suddenly spied Mary and asked who instructed her to carry the vegetables. Cissie called out. "I did chef."

The irate chef took a great intake of breath adding a bit height to his small, slight stature and marched to the front of the line. He clenched his teeth and thrust his undersized head towards Cissie. His head almost found it embedded in Cissie's well-endowed breasts. Seeing it as extremely funny, Cissie's fat wobbled as she tried to suppress her laughter. Chef's face turned red with rage and he hissed at Cissie, "I give the orders round here, so you change places with...with...the girl at the end. You take the vegetables and give her the chicken!"

Mary could have at that moment bolted for the door. Sweat poured down her back as the thought of leading the way out into the dining hall carrying the great silver dome made her feel sick. She couldn't tell chef she was inexperienced, as Cissie had lied to him bye telling him she had done waiting before. If she spoke up now, she would probably get her friend fired from the job. She wasn't caring about herself, but Cissie needed the extra income, so with trembling hands, she took the silver platter from her friend and balanced it on her shoulder. Cissie whispered, "A'll be richt behind ye. Just listen to what I say."

Chef stood at the door and waited until everyone was back in line. His lip curled up at one side as he smiled contentedly. He was now satisfied. He had shown everyone who was boss in the kitchen. Opening the swing door, he stood to one side to allow the procession of waitresses to pass.

The sudden noise of chattering people filled Mary's eardrums, and her legs now shook as much as her hands. There before her were three long broad tables The top table was the shortest of the three and around it sat the dignitaries and their partners while the other guests sat at the remaining tables that ran down each side of the room. Being the first out the door, Mary should have headed for the main table, but Cissie skilfully guided her to the side table and signalled to the other woman who carried a main platter to go to the top table.

Cissie tried to talk Mary through the art of serving but it was no good. She couldn't get the hang of lifting the chicken with the spoon and fork.

When concentrating on lifting the meat, she was inclined to lose the balance of the platter. Looking down and trying to balance the platter, Mary noticed that she had let some of the gravy run into the brim of a rather oversized hat. Panicking, she let the piece of chicken that she had managed to grip, fall back onto the platter.

The hungry man, who had been waiting patiently, noticed Mary's difficulty and jokingly remarked, "Put the plate on the table and let the chicken legs run onto the plates themselves. It would be a hellish lot quicker."

It was all too much for Mary. Relief came when Cissie grabbed the platter from her and thrust the vegetables back into her hands.

"Sod the bleedin' chef. You follow me," Cissie said with authority.

The rest of the evening went without mishap and Mary found that she actually liked waiting, especially after the meal when drinks were being ordered. That's when she began to make her money. The tips were better than the wages.

Both friends left the hotel at half past ten. As the bus was in sight, Mary started to run towards the bus stop calling on Cissie to hurry herself up. Cissie was wearing a large cape coat that made her appear much fatter than she really was. There were no sleeves in the garment, only a slit at each side to allow the wearer the use of their hands. She waddled like a duck as she tried to catch up. Mary looked back, and as she saw her friend struggle, she decided to run on and ask the conductor to hold the bus up.

As Cissie was a regular on the bus, the conductor was quite used to waiting for her, so Mary sat down on a seat and waited for her friend to board the bus. When Cissie eventually pulled herself aboard, she clumsily made her way up the aisle and flopped down heavily beside Mary causing her to jam against the side of the bus.

"Oh! God Cissie, you have to lose some weight. You're massive in that cape. You'll have to do something about it." She nudged Cissie with her shoulder, "Get over a bit. You've nearly got me out the window." She felt her own body shake as Cissie broke into hearty laughter.

"I'll dae somethin' aboot the extra wecht richt noo." Like a professional conjurer, she pulled a couple of fat chickens from her cape. "Will that dae ye lass?"

Mary gaped at her. "Oh! Cissie, you never?"

"How aboot an encore." Dropping the birds into Mary's lap, she placed her hands back inside the coat and drew out two bottles of Vodka.

"Cissie!!" Mary cried, staring in disbelief. Blinking slowly a few times, she asked, "You haven't got the hotel silver platter in there by any chance?"

The fat jovial woman filled the bus with her laughter. "No," she answered, "but a micht hiv that wee toad o' a chef!"

Rocking back and forth and with tears streaming down her face, Mary struggled with the pain in her side, caused by rapturous laughter. "OH! OH! I have enjoyed myself to- night Cissie. I really have."

"I'm gled lass, it's guid tae see ye laugh."

Patrick Sweeny had left the house an hour before his wife, and caught the bus into Edinburgh. He made his way towards the Drookit Craw the public house where he met up with his mistress every Saturday. They normally had a few drinks there before doing their usual pub-crawl. Sometimes they spent their evenings at the greyhound racing where they could drink and gamble.

He bought himself a pint and stood at the end of the bar waiting for his companion to arrive. The pub was quiet as it was still pretty early. The bar staff busied themselves in preparation for the evening rush. Patrick stood and watched as the busty bar maid wearing a low cut blouse, bent down to fill the bottom shelf with small bottles of fruit juices.

"Who's would you rather look at, hers or mine?" The seductive voice from behind him asked.

Patrick was momentarily startled, as he had not heard his lady friend creep up. "I never saw you come in darlin'. Gin and tonic for Nancy," He called to the buxom barmaid.

Nancy Butler was a divorcee, a dyed blonde with a large but shapely figure. She had no family of her own and didn't care if the men she took up with were married. In a way she preferred them to have a wife at home, as there were no demands put on her that way. She didn't have to cook or clean for them and she received little gifts from time to time in appreciation for her sexual favours. She could have been described as a slut but that wouldn't have bothered her one bit. Her marriage had been violent and she found solace in the gin bottle. Now that her husband was gone, she found other reasons for her habit. The couple lifted their drinks from the counter and made their way to the corner of the bar where they were out of sight from gazing eyes.

"You're sharp in tonight Pat! I thought I would have been here before you," she said as she settled into her seat.

"I left early. She was going out to work, so I left before her." As he gulped his beer the froth from the top left a white moustache across his upper lip. He wiped it off with the back of his hand.

"Work? When did your wife start to work? I thought you told me she didn't work!" She was always curious about Patrick's wife as he very rarely spoke of her. What little she knew had slipped out in conversation. He had once commented to Nancy that he thought women should stay at home, unless they had no man to depend on. That had given her the idea that his wife didn't work.

"Oh," Patrick replied reluctantly, "it's just a daft notion she's got into her head, encouraged by a friend of hers no doubt."

"Where's she working?" she asked with interest.

Lifting his glass, he took a long drink. She watched his Adam's apple move up and down in his thick neck. It looked like a lever opening and closing, allowing the liquid to pass through on its way to the stomach.

"Ahhh!" he exclaimed, returning the near empty glass none-too-gently onto the table. "Ready for another Nanc'?"

"I've hardly touched this one ... Oh! Go on then, it'll keep." She watched as he strode towards the bar. He was tall, well built, obviously a hard workingman. The hard toil in the mines gave him a rugged down to earth look. Just how she liked her men. He was her kind of animal. Why he wasn't with his wife only made her curious. 'Still,' Nancy thought, 'if she can't keep her man, it's hardly my fault. I only borrow him at weekends!' A wicked grin spread across her face.

Returning once more to the table, Nancy asked again, "Where's she working then?"

"*I* don't know, do I? Some hotel down the coast."

"I thought you didn't believe in women working?"

Sneering he answered, "As long as it doesn't interfere with me, she can do as she bloody likes."

"You're terrible Patrick Sweeny," she laughed.

"You drink up and stop being so nosey. Where would you like to go tonight?"

It was almost eleven o'clock when the two drunken companions walked unsteady along the road devouring fish suppers from last week's newspaper. They reached the very old tenement building where Nancy had her flat. The building smelt of dampness and decay. In fact, it was a slum. Entering the close door, they made their way along the narrow passage and started to mount the four flights of stone stairs that led to Nancy's home.

Patrick staggered a few times but regained his balance by leaning against the walls of the stairway. Nancy was used to the narrowness of the stairs and followed on behind Patrick, ready to steady him up if he happened to fall backwards. Reaching the top landing, Patrick rested momentarily against the wall and inhaled deeply, straightening himself up as he did so. Nancy pushed past and putting the key in the lock, opened the door. She switched on the light. The room was dark and dingy and reeked of cats. A huge ginger tom lay along the back of the tatty old couch that was covered with a torn tartan plaid rug. It stretched lazily showing its attenuating claws. One old armchair was occupied by a black and white cat, which lay licking her leg quite uninterested in the intruders who had just walked in. It was the grey cat in the corner that was alerted. It watched in apprehension as Patrick staggered in. Ears pricked back and body tensed it waited for the chance to bolt out of the room.

"This place smells like a piss house Nance', you should do something about them bloody moggies." He approached the black and white cat that now watched Patrick with concern. "Scat!" Patrick growled sending the animal running in terror. It near collided with the grey cat as both felines ran for the door together.

"Here!" Nancy chided, "I'll have less of that! They're doing no harm."

"Dirty flee ridden bits of vermin!!" Dropping into the chair, which the cat had vacated, Patrick muttered. "Stinkin' bits o' fur balls."

Nancy raged, "I'll have you know that they're all the family I have and I'm par-par- ticu- u laarrly fond of them. Hic."

"Ok, ok. I'm sorry Nance'. Come 'ere. Come 'ere." He patted his lap and grinned.

"Just leave my pussies alone. Right?" she said more calmly.

Still patting his knee, Patrick joked, "This knee is ready for only one pussy, so bring it over 'ere and make me happy."

She walked over towards him slowly, in a coy manner, lifting her skirt and showing her shapely legs and although she was heavy busted, and on the round side, her legs were slender and very shapely. "Why sir, I'm sure I don't know what you mean," she purred.

He dragged her roughly on to his knee and Nancy squealed with delight. He groped at her wildly and Nancy responded by pulling his head downwards, burying his face in her huge breasts. The old armchair groaned under their weight as they wrestled with one another in the throws of lust and passion.

Nancy pulled reluctantly away, and pouted. "Come on, through to the bed. I don't fancy the floor. I hate friction burns."

It was three o'clock in the morning when Patrick returned home and slid quietly into bed beside Mary. She lay motionless, pretending to be asleep. She was used to his late hours and had learned long ago to keep her questioning until morning, as he was generally aggressive if annoyed. He hid his guilt by going on the defensive, often ending with a shouting match, wakening the whole house. He had a unique knack of making Mary feel that it was she who was wrong.

His head was no sooner on the pillow, than his body heaved in deep sleep, snoring and puffing loudly. The pores of his body filled with sweat and Mary's nostrils were filled with the nauseating smell of his stale, sour body odour mingling with the foul stink of cheap perfume. She felt sickened.

Mary had had her suspicions for some time now. Keeping her short of money, coming home at all hours and reeking of perfume. Now he was happy enough to let her out to work. It was pretty obvious that he was seeing another woman. Lying awake most of the night she tried to figure out why she felt no jealousy. The only emotion that she had for him was anger; anger at being taken for a fool, anger at having to do without so that he could spend on another women. For all she knew, he could have a different one every weekend although she doubted very much that so many women used the same awful perfume.

The only good thing to come out of Patrick's affair was he left her alone. She couldn't stand him touch her. The very thought of sex with him, made her feel sick as any love she had felt for him was long-gone.

Her mother was in her thoughts too. How she would have revelled in Mary's downfall. Not once had her mother written since she moved to Corby. And Billy too, he had never answered her letters and that hurt her more than anything. She stopped writing after her third letter as Patrick had managed to convince her, Billy didn't want to know. Her father was also on her mind that night, although that was not unusual; she thought of him every day of her life, and as she lay in sleepless torment, she realised that he was the only one who ever truly cared for her. Oh! How she missed her father.

Her own death too, entered into her train of thought. Who would miss her if she were to go? Who would mourn? As far as she could make out, no one. Patrick would be free to do as he pleased!

She could not switch off. She tossed and turned, and tried to empty her mind, but she could not find repose. When sleep eventually overcame Mary, it was to set her mind swirling down into the abyss of darkness, where voices moaned and whaled, "You thought you knew it all," her mother screamed. "Murderer! You killed your Father," Billy called out. "Mary! You shouldn't have done it!" A woman laughed uncontrollably, and a child screamed. Its screams grew louder and as the child's face came nearer, she recognised her own face on the child's body. In terror, Mary cried aloud, and in doing so, she woke with a jolt, her heart pounding erratically against her chest, her flesh awash with perspiration.

Patrick gave a slight moan and turned on his side towards her. He stretched his leg over the top of hers, pinning her down. His arm was thrown across her breast and his hand spread over her face. The obnoxious smell of tobacco from his fingers made her feel physically sick. Throwing back the covers and pushing free from his legs, Mary made for the bathroom, where she retched.

Chapter Ten

Sunday morning, the heavens opened and it poured with rain. Relentlessly it battered on the windows and drummed on the rooftops. A roll of thunder could be heard rumbling down from dark hills. A few seconds passed, and the distant sky lit up with menacing flashes of lightening. Because of the foul weather, the boys were house bound. They sat on the hearthrug in front of the fire playing cards.

Mary had already tidied up in the kitchen after the breakfast, but the table was still set for Patrick, as he was yet to rise. Sitting in the armchair, Mary relaxed and read the Sunday paper while the baby played happily at her feet.

The noise of feet padding around on the lino from above, informed her that Patrick had risen and would be down shortly. She listened to his footsteps make their way to the bathroom where he would perform his usual ritual of coughing, spluttering, and clearing his lungs of foul phlegm, caused by the coal dust from the mines, aggravated more by his constant smoking.

Putting the paper down, Mary made her way into the kitchen and started to prepare her husband's breakfast. The aroma of bacon and sausages sizzling in the pan, filtered out into the staircase and into Patrick's nostrils, making him aware of his hunger. He hurried on down into the living room and noticing the boys on the mat playing, he walked over and stood looking down on them.

They were aware of his presence, but never raised their heads to look, as they were much too interested in the game they were playing. Allan studied the cards that were in his hand, while Frank scrutinised his brother's face looking for a clue as to what he was thinking. Patrick bent down and looking at Allan's hand advised, "Lift up that card and throw away the six of hearts."

Frank threw his cards down on the floor and yelled, "That's not fair! Ma!" he called to Mary. "Ma! He's cheating. He's getting help!"

"For Christ sake! He's younger than you. Any more yelling, and I'll clip your ears lad!" Patrick snapped.

Frank couldn't let it go. "What have I done? It's you! You're helping him. Leave him to play what he wants!"

"I'm warning you." Patrick thrust his finger at the protesting child. "Any more lip and you'll feel the weight of my hand!"

Mary appeared at the kitchen door, "What on earth's going on here? What's all the yelling?"

Gnashing his teeth together, Frank was determined to stand his ground, even if it meant a clout from his father. "It's me Da. He's telling Allan what to throw away. That's no' right Ma. Tell him that's no' fair."

Mary would normally have agreed with Patrick when he said 'it was only a game', but as she was in no mood to side with her husband, she took Franks part.

"They've been playing quietly all morning till you put your oar in. What did you have to do that for? Can't you bare to see them quiet?"

"Oh God's truth! He's got you in it now has he?" Looking down at Frank, Patrick lunged forward and gave the unsuspecting lad a sharp slap on the side of his head. The boy roared as Patrick's hand connected with his ear, causing a hot stinging pain to shoot against his flesh. "Now you've something to complain about boy," he snarled.

Allan sat with his mouth gaping open, taking in the scene that unfolded before him. He too threw down his cards and yelled. Leaping to the defence of his brother, he tried to put his arm round his neck, only to have it thrown to one side.

Jumping to his feet, Frank ran over to the settee where he threw himself down heavily. Burying his face in the cushion, he tried to muffle the sound of his cries.

The baby joined in the fracas by screaming at the top of his lungs and as Mary rushed to pick him up, she glowered at her husband.

"You'll be well pleased now! Big man. You've got them all screaming. Can't keep your hands to yourself. I thought it was just when you had a few, but it's starting when your sober now!" Trying to comfort Tony, Mary cuddled him into her, all the while scowling at his Allan's assailant. She felt all the bitterness she had ever felt for Patrick swell up inside. Almost bursting with contempt she gave vent to her feelings.

"Why not go and live with your whore and give us all peace." She faced him up without faltering. Although she felt herself shake, it was not out of fear, but temper.

Patrick laughed mockingly, "Your off your bloody head! You're stark raving mad!"

"I'm mad all right. I'm mad living with you! Do you think I don't know your game *Patrick Sweeny*?"

"What game is that then? What are you trying to say? Spit it out then! Spit it out!" He poked her in the shoulder as he taunted.

Realising she had said too much in front of the boys, she fell silent.

"Come on then. Where's your tongue?" Patrick goaded.

The smell of burning alerted Mary, and she suddenly remembered, - his breakfast!! Pushing past Patrick, she hurried into the kitchen where she was confronted by a burning pan. The flames licked up the sides of the pan and the smoke was belching from the burning remains of food.

Patrick followed through on the heels of Mary and pushing her aside, set about extinguishing the fire, cursing as he did so.

The two boys stood at the door and watched in amazement. Although Frank had stopped crying his young face was blotched and tear stained. They watched open mouthed at the antics of their father as he fought with the burning pan. The blackened pan with its charred contents, were finally thrown into the sink out of harms way. Contact with the cold water made it hiss and splutter, like some dying creature reluctantly giving out it's last breathe.

"That'll bloody do now!" Patrick yelled, "You can't even cook a breakfast without burning it. Look at the pan! It's burned black! Can't get that clean now, you silly bitch!"

Mary answered in a low but very distinct voice, "You've never spoken a truer word. Yes Patrick, I am a silly bitch, silly marrying you. Silly for not seeing what every body else saw, --"

He interrupted her. "You should have listened to your Mother then. Shouldn't you? No! You thought you had an easy escape. You were looking for a way out. Somewhere to run to when the going was tough. You wanted someone to bring up your bastard. A mug! A mug like me, and what did I get for my trouble, eh! a bloody cold, frigid bitch. You're like your Mother, a cold, passionless bitch. You wonder why I go elsewhere for my lovin'-Oh don't look so shocked! You're the one that brought it up. You're the one that mentioned my whore. Aye you're right---she is a whore, but there's more lovin' in her little finger than you have in your whole fuckin' body. So there you have it."

Mary was silent. Patrick's words were not what silenced her. It was Frank. He stood listening to the row. He stood in the doorway with Allan. He heard his father call him a bastard. Patrick had never said that so vehemently before and never ever in front of the boy.

Mary stood and stared hard at Patrick, then walking slowly passed him, she spoke almost in a whisper, "Go up to your rooms and play."

Getting no immediate response from the bewildered children, she spoke with more authority "Go on!" The boys hesitated slightly before moving. They walked slowly towards the door and as Frank reached the opening, he looked back at his mother with questioning eyes.

Patrick, realizing that Frank had heard what he had called him, turned away. Holding onto the sink with both hands, and bowing his head, he rocked his body to and fro'.

"Why, oh why did you make me say that? Why do you make me so flaming mad? I've always considered Frank as mine. Why did I have to say that in front of him?"

It was Mary who now stood in the doorway. Tony was still in her arms, but as she spoke, she let him down onto the floor. "It must've been on your mind or you wouldn't have said it."

Although the full length of the kitchen was between them, he turned around to face her. "I'm sorry I said that. I truly am." Their voices were no longer raised, but the bitterness was still inside Mary.

"It's too late now. You can't take it back. He heard you, and you can bet he knows what you mean. If he doesn't, he will figure it out. He's thirteen years old and no longer a bairn. And while I'm at it, your whore doesn't matter one bit to me. Just as long as you keep away from me, you can do as you please."

They spent the rest of the day in silence, speaking to one another only when necessary. Patrick tried to make it up to Frank, but he recoiled whenever his father tried to touch him. Although Frank didn't know exactly what a bastard was, he knew it wasn't a very nice thing to be called. It was a swear word that he heard regularly, but he only knew it as such. Now there was a meaning to the word and he would have to find out just what it was.

It was Mary's turn to host the morning coffee, and Cissie arrived earlier than usual. She was bursting to find out if Patrick had said any more about Mary working on the Saturday. The baby ran to greet her as she entered the kitchen. Lifting him into her arms, she kissed him on the cheek. "Hiv you been a guid laddie fer Mammy?"

The child responded by nodding, although he was more interested in Cissie's spectacles. His small chubby hand shot out and tried to grab them, but Cissie jerked her head back quickly. "You little devil. You near' had them there." Laughing, she put the child back down on the floor. "You'll hiv tae get this lad a pair o' glasses fer he's determined tae git mine." Now looking at Mary she added, "I've been wonderin' awe weekend aboot you. A wid hiv called ower yesterday, if the weather hidnae been sae bad."

"Thank heavens for the rain then." Mary would normally have said that in a jovial manner, but her tone of voice, and facial expression, alerted Cissie that all was not well.

"So he did have something to say about you working." Cissie sighed shaking her head and dropping her oversized body down heavily onto a kitchen chair. "I thought it was too good to be true."

"No Cissie. He said nothing about me working, in fact, he still hasn't mentioned it, but we had a barney first thing Sunday morning."

"Tell me somethin' new!" Cissie remarked.

Mary prepared the tea with the help of her friend, relaying to her what was said during the row with Patrick. Cissie listened without comment.

Deep in thought, Cissie stirred the spoon round and round in her cup, reflecting over what she had just been told.

"Mary," she eventually said looking into her friend's face, "you've got tae tell Frank the truth. If ye dinnae, there's always somebody willin' tae dae it fer ye. You dinnae want tae hiv him find oot himsel', dae ye?" She watched as Mary agonised over such a thought. Her bent elbow rested on the table and her hand rubbed at her brow. She looked so tired.

"An' as fer Patrick, dae ye really think he's seein' an ither woman?" Cissie asked in disbelief.

Mary stopped rubbing at her brow and bringing her head up quickly, she said without hesitation, "Oh aye! That I *am* sure of. I asked him Cissie, I asked him." She gave a nervous laugh. "He admitted it. He flaming well admitted it."

Cissie seemed to grow in height as she inflated her well-endowed breasts. "He needs his arse kicked tae hell an' back again," she said angrily. "Whit are ye gaun tae dae?"

Mary shrugged her shoulders, "I'm not going to do anything!"

Her friend looked bewildered. "Yer daein' nothing aboot it? Mary, ye canny let him play aroond. He's making a fool o' ye." Shaking her head in despair Cissie continued, "Mary, ye canny let a man intae yer bed that's philandering! Surely ye think mare o' yer sel' than that?"

"Oh Cissie. Don't worry about me there. I have it all worked out. I intend moving the lads round and I can share a room with the bairn. I have it all worked out."

"That's nae merriage Mary. You cannae live like that--"

"Oh can't I Cissie? Look, you know this has been a disaster of a marriage and there's nothing I can do. I've got three laddies for goodness sake. As long as he leaves me alone I'll get along fine, An' another thing. I will be taking that wee job on Saturday nights, if that's all right with you."

"Of course it is, but whit will---"

"What will he say?" Mary laughed defiantly. "I don't care two hoots what he thinks or says. From now on, I make my own decisions."

"Weel, guid fer you lass," Cissie remarked, wondering if Mary really had the nerve to carry her intentions through.

Mary thought long and hard about telling Frank the truth. She would have liked more time but that was one thing she had little of as Patrick had sown the seed in Frank's mind. It was obvious that the lad had been affected by his father's words as he had become very withdrawn and distant since that evening. Normally the two boys came home from school together, but Allan had arrived home by himself. He was crying and informed his mother that Frank had gone off with some other lads. It was approaching five o'clock when the boy eventually turned up. Mary was angry and sent him to his room.

The following day the same thing happened. Allan returned once more by himself. The clock on the mantle piece had struck five when Frank turned up. Patrick was sitting in his chair reading the paper when the lad entered the room. He was walking cautiously towards the door that led to the hall, when his father gave a roar that caused him to jump, stopping him in his tracks. The boy's hand was actually on the door handle. His body looked as if it had frozen in terror. Looking round at Patrick but still with his hand on the handle, the lad said softly.

"I'm going to ma room."

Mary was standing at the far corner of the room; she too had jumped at the ferociousness of Patrick's roar. Hurrying towards her son, Mary stood as a shield between Frank and his father. "I'll handle this Patrick. You sit down and let me deal with it." Mary tried to defuse the situation but Patrick wasn't giving in. He grabbed at his wife's arm and pushed her to one side. She toppled over and fell against the arm of the sofa. Regaining her composure, Mary shot back onto her feet and once more pushed herself in between the boy and his father. Frank had already received one blow across the ear and was now cowering behind his mother using his arms to protect his head from further clouts that were imminent.

"Patrick! Patrick, leave him to me. Your hand is too hard on the bairn." She tore at his arms as she screamed her plea.

"Get out my way woman," Patrick yelled impatiently as Mary darted to and fro making a frantic effort to protect her son from her husband's wrath. They swayed together as if in dance, and Frank, seeing an opportune moment, crouched down and slid through their legs. Running towards the back door, he managed to get out and away before his father could reach him.

"That little bastard" he cried. "Just wait till he gets back. I'll flay the living daylights out o' him." Turning to Mary he growled at her, "You'll deal with him! You made a fine job last night. What good did you do? Sending him to his room! I ask you Mary. What good did it do?"

"Heavens sake! He's only a boy Patrick. He's never ever come home late from school before. You did it. He's never been the same since Sunday. It's your fault."

Lifting his eyes to the ceiling, Patrick cried "For God's sake! He leaves the wee fellow to come home from school by himself while he runs off with all the strays of the day, and you blame me!"

"Aye. I blame you. Are you that blind Patrick that you can't see he's hurting? Are you that blind you don't see that he's confused? You need to think Patrick. Think before you let fly with your muckle big hands. Think before you open that great big hole under your nose; or are you incapable of thinking?"

Patrick stood and stared down at his wife and seeing her rage, he turned away muttering. "You better go and find him."

Mary came back to the house at nine o'clock. She had looked everywhere but couldn't find Frank. His school friends hadn't seen him, and he wasn't over at Cissie's. She had wandered the streets covering all his usual haunts. Cissie and her husband had joined in the search, but they too returned without a sighting. Patrick and Cissie's husband, Robbie, left the house to continue the search while Mary stayed indoors with Cissie. The men were giving him another hour, and if he wasn't found, they were calling in the police.

Cissie had made Mary a cup of tea and had given her something for the blinding headache that had come upon her. They sat opposite each other in silence. The boys were put to bed and although the baby was sound asleep. Allan lay awake listening to the comings and goings of the adults downstairs. He too was worried about Frank. He didn't understand what it was all about, but it had to be something to do with what his dad had said while arguing with his mother on Sunday. It was from that moment Frank had been bad, he knew that much. He started to cry at the thought of never seeing his brother again.

'Maybe he's been kidnapped. Maybe he's run of to London like Dick Whittington. That's an awful long way away,' he thought. His sobs grew louder.

"That's Allan. I better go and see him." Mary said lifelessly.

"I'll nip ower an' put some coal oan the fire Mary. A dinnae want tae let it dee doon. A'll only be a minute."

Cissie entered her living room and made straight for the fireplace. The coal had burned well down and the glows of dying embers were faintly visible. Kneeling down in front of the fire she lifted the poker and gave the fine ash a rake. She took some dry sticks from the side of the fireplace and laid them on top of the dying fire. Then, taking a sheet of newspaper, she held it against the fire, forcing the sticks to catch alight. The sticks sparked and crackled, and once they were well lit, she lifted over to the hearth an old battered enamel pail that contained a few small lumps of coal. Placing them carefully on top of the now blazing stick, she spoke aloud. "There Cis me lass. Now awe you need is a shovel foo o' dross an' that's the fire banked up fer the nicht." She pulled herself up and lifting the now empty pail, waddled outside the back door to the coal cellar. The coal cellar was similar to a huge walk in cupboard but built onto the outside wall. A light switch was located inside the cellar and as Cissie switched on the light, she let out an almighty gasp dropping the pail and clutching her heart. The boy sat on top of the mountain of coal looking pale and frightened. His face was black, and it was evident by the white streaks that ran down his cheeks that he had been crying. His clothes too were covered in coal dust.

"Michty me lad!" Cissie cried. "Whit in the name o'----Come away oot o' there."

As Frank scrambled down, Cissie reached in and offered him her hand. The mound of coal that he had been sitting on toppled over when he moved, causing him to stumble forward, but Cissie caught him in her huge arms.

"Whit are ye tryin' tae dae tae yer auld auntie Cis? Ye nearly gave me he'rt failure." Pushing the quivering child into the kitchen, she held him at arms length and surveyed the mess before her.

His shirt and trousers were filthy. Knee length stockings were down about his ankles, showing his skinny black legs. There were also scrapes and bruises on his knees.

"My, my Frank Sweeny, Yer as black as the earl o' hell's waistcoat. We'll hev tae get ye scrubbed up before ye go across the road."

Frank spoke for the first time. "I'm not going over there Cissie. Me Da' will kill me. I'm no goin' back there ever again." Panic filled his voice as Cissie drew the child towards her and gave him a reassuring cuddle.

"Noo, noo. There's naebody goin' tae kill ye. They're awe oot lookin' fer ye. They're worried seek (sick). Noo then, if folks are worried aboot ye, they're surely no' goin' tae hurt ye."

Pushing away from her, he spoke erratically. "Cissie, I can't go back. Not now! Not now that I'm a bastard. He said that I was a bastard and I went to the library and looked it up."

Cissie closed her eyes and drew in her breath. What she was hearing tugged at her heart. It was bound to come out, but she never expected to be the one that was faced with this.

"Frank son. Some folk swear an' use that word tae hurt ithers. It's no" tae be taken personally. It's..." What was she saying? She knew the child was right. She knew that he wasn't a baby. He had heard his father refer to him as being someone else's, and here she was trying to convince the boy that he was wrong. Wasn't she just saying to Mary the other day that

Frank should be told? "Frank. Listen tae me. You've got tae talk tae yer Mammy."

Through his tears, Frank continued as if he hadn't heard a word Cissie had said. "It's when some body his a bairn and is nae married. Gordon Livit said that it's only bad people that have bairns and aren't married."

"But yer Mammy's married. She's married tae Patrick."

Quickly he reminded her, "Aye, but he's no' ma Da'. He's the other two's Da', but he's no' mine. He took me and ma Mother on."

"Frank, you just listen here noo. Gordon Livit has nae richt tellin' you that women who hiv bairns before they wed are bad. That's no' richt."

Staring at Cissie's face with his dark doe like eyes his expression became one of curiosity. "It's all right to have a bairn before you're married then?" he asked in amazement.

"Oh dear Lord, help me wi' this yin," she asked under her breath.

"No Frank. It's no' the done thing, bit sometimes mistakes are made an,' an..." Cissie didn't know what else to say. Frank had it all worked out. If she continued with the conversation, she could easy make matters worse, so she changed the subject.

"Weel. How aboot me nipping ower the road an' lettin' yer Mother ken that you're okay. I'll try an' persuade her tae let ye bide wi' me the nicht. Mind you, a canny promise onything, but I can try."

"Cissie. Will you really let me stay here?"

She smiled broadly at the lad and ruffled his tousled hair, "I said a wid. Only if yer mother says it's awe richt mind! Noo, away an' wash them legs an' that mucky face. You're no' sleepin' in ma bed lookin' like that. Noo I'll jist get some dross oan that fire before a nip across. Hopefully I'll no find ony mare waifs or strays lurkin' aboot in the coal cellar."

Frank smiled through his tear stained face. He loved Cissie. She always made him laugh. He always felt secure and warm in her home. Not that his house was ever cold, for mining families always had plenty coal, but the warmth in Cissie's house was different. It was special warmth, one that wasn't brought about by roaring fires. He couldn't explain it. He just enjoyed it. The untidiness of living room added to the cosiness, and it just felt right.

Banking the fire up and securing the guard, Cissie ran over to let Mary know that Frank was safe.

Mary was pacing the floor when her friend arrived to give her the news of Frank's safety. Overcome with relief, Mary dropped into a chair and cried her eyes out for what seemed ages. Cissie could only watch helplessly as her young friend let out all the pent up emotions that had been stored up within her. The frustration of living in an unhappy marriage, as well as the rejection from her family was now taking its toll.

The back door opened and Patrick appeared with Robbie, a puny small man who seemed to have a constant dry spasmodic cough. No matter what time of year it was, he was wrapped up in a thick woollen muffler that crossed over his chest and tucked in round his back, no doubt by Cissie who treated him like one of their seven children, all who now were adults with wives and homes of their own, all except for one, and he was soon to be married. That would leave Robbie alone with Cissie who would eventually smother him to death, although she alleged to others that she was tough on her ailing husband.

When Patrick saw Mary in floods of tears, a sudden terror came over him. He thought for a moment that Frank had been found injured or even worse. As he walked slowly to his wife's side, he glanced at Cissie searching her face for an answer.

"It's awe richt Pat, Frank's awe richt. Mary's jist had enough, that's all. She'll be awe richt in a minute." She caught him looking round the room and as he turned to make towards the door leading to the stairs, she added, "He's no' up there. He's ower at ma hoose." Looking towards her husband she said, "Robbie, go ower a' side him. I'll be ower shortly." He acted without speaking and left Cissie with Patrick and Mary.

Patrick cautiously laid his hand on Mary's shoulder and when she didn't react he sat wearily down beside her.

Cissie watched as he rested his head in his hands, his eyes, ringed with dark circles. It was obvious that he too had been worried.

Patrick at this moment in time was not able to strike back therefore Cissie saw the opportunity to have her say. Placing her hands on her hips and shaking her head in despair she spoke in a quietly, "It's time somethin' wis done here. Yer set in driving her oot o' her mind Patrick an' I'll no' stand by an' see that happen. She's been like a daughter tae me, an' it hurts tae see her so unhappy." She waited for some comment from him but none was given.

He just sat gazing down at his hands.

Cissie continued. "An' anither thing, Frank's across there terrified tae come hame. What the hell are ye daein' tae the laddie?"

Springing to life, he looked up at Cissie, "So you think he should be left to run wild? He got a skelp for no' coming home."

"But why his he taken tae staying oot sae late? Ask yersel' that man. He thinks he's no wanted ony mare. And dae ye blame him? And by the way -- he kens all aboot bastards. His definition is spot oan, so somethin' will hiv tae be done aboot that noo."

"I'll see to it Cissie. I'll Come over and get him." Mary said.

"Naw lass, let him bide where he is the nicht an' see him in the mornin'."

"Aye then, maybe that's best," she replied wearily.

Patrick rose to his feet, and as if nothing had happened, said, "Well it's all right for some folk, I have to be up early in the morning, so I'll away up."

Cissie remarked once he had disappeared out the door, "I canny believe that man. You never ken where you are wi' him."

Sighing, Mary shrugged her shoulders and sighed, "It's a complete waste of time".

Hands on her great hips, and in her usual defiant stand, Cissie snorted, *"Ignorance*! That's what it is Mary-*IGNORANCE!"*

Chapter Eleven

Since the day Frank found out the truth of his birth, he was never the same towards Patrick. He resented being chastised by him and the more he antagonised Patrick, the more the conflict between them grew. His love for his mother somehow survived the trauma, and if anything, he was drawn even closer to her.

She had told him that his real father had gone away without any knowledge of her being with child. Mary knew that if Frank was told the whole truth, he would think that his father left because of him, and although that was true in a way, she had to spare the lad from the guilt that she knew for certain would swallow him up. His sensitivity grew very apparent to Mary as she saw the bond between Frank and his brothers weaken and fall apart. As they grew older, the closeness that once bound the boys together was no longer evident.

Now at the age of seventeen, Frank had matured and had lost all interest in Allan, he being only a lad of thirteen they no longer had anything in common. The youngest boy was now eight years of age and he still was a boy that liked to be by himself. The only time Tony joined in was if it happened to be girls that were playing. He always had the fear of being hurt. Being rather a frail looking child caused Mary to believe that was the reason the child hated boisterous games. Curiously enough, he liked to dress up in his mother's clothes. This became a bit of a joke. He would enter the room wearing an old wig and Mary's make up. The eye shadow and bright lipstick slapped on like Coco the Clown. Falling about in laughter, they were all convinced that Tony, shy though he was, was destined for the stage. He seemed to lose his shyness when hiding behind a painted face.

Mary shared a bedroom with Tony for a few years, but now that Frank had left school, he wanted a room to himself and due to the fight he had with Allan, Mary relented and moved the two younger boys in together, giving Frank the smaller room to him-self. This meant that Mary had to move back in with Patrick, but she gave the boys Patrick's double bed, and moved the singles into Patrick's room, so as to avoid sharing her husband's bed. He had a bit of a moan, but Mary ignored it.

Her life with Patrick hadn't changed much over the years, although the tension that she lived under grew easier to bear. She attributed this to adaptation; in other words, she had become accustomed to the situation. The rows that took place were now more often between Patrick and Frank.

Frank had grown up to be a handsome devil. His black shiny hair and dark eyes made him the image of his father. Mary looked at him with pride, and often shivered at the likeness. She watched him as he now stood in front of the mirror in the living room, combing his newly washed hair. He chewed the side of his mouth as he concentrated on his actions. Stripped to the waist, his broad muscular shoulders still looked tanned although it was now well into February.

"Oh my," Mary laughed, slapping him playfully across the back, leaving the impression of her hand. "Take a look at that body."

He swerved to the side in case she repeated the slap. "Watch it", he taunted, putting his fists up and taking on the stance of a boxer.

Mary laughed and waving her hand in admonishment, "Think you're George Foreman o you? More like George Formby."

Patrick looked over the paper and snarled, "I wish you'd get your bloomin' clothes on. Prancing about half naked."

The fun finished, Frank turned to Patrick and remarked, "You jealous or somethin'?"

Mary gave her son a shove and nodded towards the door, "Go on." Screwing up her face she gestured, "Go on, before you catch your death."

The situation defused, Mary followed him into the hall, returning seconds later carrying her coat.

"Where are you going Mam?" called Tony.

"You stay here. I'm only going to get a few messages."

"I want to come," Tony whimpered.

"No I said." As Mary buttoned up her coat, the door knocker rattled. "Who is it now," she muttered making her way towards the front door, Tony running along side her. On opening the door, Mary stood for a few seconds looking down at the woman standing on her doorstep. Eventually she recognised the caller to be Mrs. Wallace, her mother's old neighbour. She hadn't seen her since the day her father was buried and that was all of thirteen years. "Why! Mrs. Wallace! How nice to see you." Mary was so surprised. "Come away in." She reached out and helped the elderly wife up the few stairs that led to the house. Mary took her arm and slowly walked with her into the living room. She was amazed at how much older the woman appeared.

"I'm sorry to drop in on you like this lassie, but I had to come by and give you this letter."

"Well come over here and sit by the fire a minute and get a heat."

Giving Allan a shove out of the chair he was occupying, she then helped the old frail body into the chair. "You're not going to tell me you came all the way across town to give me a letter." She shook her head at the woman who now fumbled frantically in her shopping bag.

"It's here. It's definitely here," she mumbled, rummaging at the very bottom of her bag. At last, finding the letter in question, she thrust it into Mary's hand.

"I was saying, I hope you didn't trav..."

"No, no," she answered with a shake in her voice. "My nephew drove me over. He's waiting outside in the car for me."

"Ah well! That's not so bad."

Mary looked down at the letter she now clutched in her hand and noticed that it was not addressed. Her gaze then fell back on Mrs. Wallace who now was looking directly back at her.

"It was sent in a letter to me from your Joe. He didn't know where to find you Mary so he asked me to deliver it to you." Clearing her throat, she croaked, "I'm afraid it's not very good news."

Patrick rose and stepped forward towards his wife, "Sit down and read it and I'll make Mrs. Wallace a cup of tea." Patrick was now wearing his charming hat!

"No lad, I'll have to be on me way and I'm sorry to bring you this letter." She rose and walked to the door. Mary tore at the envelope and took no notice of her visitor who now was being escorted to the front door by Patrick. She was out in the lobby when Mary then called out, "Oh aye Mrs. Wallace. Thanks for coming." Looking at the scrawled handwriting, she read.

> *Dear Mary, I'm sorry to have to send this letter through Mrs. Wallace but I never did get your address. I am writing to let you know that we buried mother last Monday. She was never the same since Billy was drowned.*
>
> *His ship went down in the South China Sea six years ago. They had just left the Philippines and were heading for Singapore when it happened. I told mother to tell you about it, but she just refused to write. I should have written, but as I said, I didn't know where to get you and you know how mother felt about things. Mary, she had a little money but Pauline feels that we are entitled to it as we kept her here with us. Sorry Mary to tell you this. She wouldn't even let me send for you as I offered to phone the police for a trace,*
>
> *Hope you are o .k*
> *Joe.*

In disbelief, Mary stared down at the letter. She was struck dumb with shock. Patrick came back into the room and noticing Mary's bewildered expression, immediately knew there was something wrong. She looked up slowly and handed him the letter. Reading it through, he then glanced down at Mary who sat motionless. It was he who broke the silence.

"I'm amazed that he took the trouble to write and tell you." Even at this time, sarcasm was manifested in his voice. "Money, she had money and that's the only reason you have been told. They're warning you off. And your Billy was bound to have a bob or two put by."

144

Mary sprang from the chair and faced him up.

"I don't believe this. I've just been notified of my Mother and Brother's deaths, and you're going on about money. I can't believe anyone could be so cruel."

"What have I said now?" Patrick inquired insensitively.

Mary pushed passed him and ran towards her room. Throwing her-self on the bed, the floodgates opened spilling her grief out onto the pillow. Her heartbreaking wails travelled through the house.

Frank was unaware of what had taken place, as he had been in his own room during Mrs. Wallace's visit. Hearing his mother's sobs, he immediately ran into the room, and seeing her spread across the bed in such a state, the first thing that crossed his mind was she had taken a beating from Patrick. Mary lay face down with her head resting on her arm. Frank sat down on the bed beside his mother and spreading his arms round her gently lifting her up and enfolding her body into his strong arms.

"I'll bloody kill him," Frank vowed. "I'll bloody kill him."

Breaking free from her son's embrace, she shook her head as she wept. "No. No son, It's n- not him." Through her tears, she explained the reason behind her distress. All he could do was to give her the comfort her husband had failed to give.

* * *

Billy's death weighed heavily on Mary's conscience. The fact that she had stopped writing to him, even though she never received a reply, troubled her. She had to find out more, so she got herself ready and travelled to Edinburgh. Her intentions were to call in and enquire at his last known employer.

Arriving at the shipping company offices, she hesitated before entering the building. She felt very awkward and hadn't much to go on, except that Billy's ship sunk six years ago.

Pushing through the swing door, she walked towards the reception desk and stood directly in front of a smart looking young man in naval uniform. He was busy studying some important looking papers. At the far end of the desk, a woman, a little older than Mary, and also dressed in uniform, was doing likewise.

"Excuse me." Mary interrupted. "I wonder if you can help me?"

The receptionist looked up and smiled. The woman at the other end looked along at Mary, and then bending her head once more, she continued to study her papers.

"It's my brother. I wonder if you know anything about him? He sailed with your company and I want some information about him."

"What ship is he on Ma'am?" he asked.

Biting the corner of her mouth, Mary looked vague. She shook her head wearily.

"Do you know in which ship he sailed last?"

"No. No I can't remember. It was such a long time ago. It was away back in '56 see and he was with you lot for years afore that."

"Ma'am that was all of seventeen years ago. Are you sure he's still at sea?"

"Oh God," Mary called out softly. The woman, who had been standing along from them had become aware of Mary's anxiety. Leaving her studying behind, she walked out and round the desk and now stood at Mary's side.

"He went down with his ship six years ago, and I just wanted to know..." Her voice trailed away. Her mind went blank. What did she want to know? Why was she here? It would serve no purpose.

The man asked, "Where was this Ma'am. Do you know where the ship went down?"

"The South China Sea," she replied weakly.

"He sure wasn't with the Ben Line then. We haven't had a loss since I came here."

"What was his name?" the girl asked, and then aware of Mary's blank expression, she repeated. "Your brother. What was his name?"

"OH, oh sorry." Springing back to life she answered, "Billy. Billy Fairley."

"There's so many crew coming and going, it would be impossible to track him down. I suggest you contact Lloyd's of London. They keep all the records of ships that have sunk and they may be able to shed some light on it for you."

Now leaning on the counter and stroking his neatly kept beard, the man immersed from deep thought... "Jinny, go on up to the wages and ask up there." Looking now at Mary, he said sympathetically, "We may be able to give you the date of his leaving."

"That's an idea," agreed Jinny. "Now you sit down over here and I'll see what I can find out." She led Mary to a comfortable lounge area and sitting her down, made her way to the wages department.

Fifteen minutes later, she returned with another woman who looked to be in her mid thirties. She was very slim and elfin like, very attractive with eyes as blue as the ocean.

Jinny touched Mary's shoulder. "Funny thing. Your Brother used to have quite a thing for Elizabeth here."

Elizabeth sat down beside Mary and smiled warmly. "Hi. I overheard Jinny asking about Billy. I remember him well.

He used to carry on with the girls in the department. We even had a drink together once."

Mary smiled. "That would be our Billy all right."

"Jinny tells me he was lost at sea. Is that right?"

Mary felt she could talk openly to this woman, so she told her about the contents of Joe's letter.

"But why didn't you ask your Brother Joe what happened?"

"I can't ask him. I want to find out myself," Mary explained.

"Well, as far as I can remember, he bought a flat somewhere near Liverpool. That's when he left us. That was about six or seven years ago. Now, I think he signed up with somebody down there." She studied Mary's facial expression. She saw the disappointment. "I'm sorry love, but that's all I can tell you."

Thanking them all, Mary rose and walked to the door. She looked back at the woman called Elizabeth and said, "It was nice to meet you." Why she said that, she didn't know. Maybe it was because Billy liked her.

Part Two

Chapter Twelve

1977

The local coalmines were gradually disappearing as one by one they ceased production. The miners of the town were forced to travel further a-field in order to keep their jobs. Patrick was no exception. His work-mates, like himself, had been transferred to Dalkieth Pit, twelve miles from their homes. The journey was made easy as the Coal Board provided transport to and from work.

Patrick gave the all clear as the dust began to settle. The miners lifted their picks and preceded along the narrow tunnel, the only light paving the way came from the lamps secured to the front of their helmets. Further back, the main roadway was brightly lit but this section was still pitch dark. They were preparing the road into the coalface. They came to the newly blasted facing and began hacking at the rock.

Tammy Lindsay broke into song as he swung his pick at the wall of loose stone. His bare muscular arms blackened with dust, streaked with sweat.

"Yer wasted down the pit Tam, ye should be in the theatre," called his neighbour Davie Sinclair.

"Aye," cried Patrick walking back up the road- way, "A bloody operating theatre."

Tam continued his song as the others bantered with one another, their voices echoing in the blackness of the mine. They were soon drowned by Archie McLeod 's pneumatic drill as it attacked the wall of stone preparing the holes for the next shots to be fired.

At the newly blasted opening, Pete Cranston and his neighbour, Hugh Duff, prepared the girders ready to support the roof of the new section.

"Mon Hugh, a'm fair in need o' ma' break," Pete informed his mate.

"Ma belly is grumblin' fer the want o' sumthin' in it."

"Has your Bella put something nice in yer tin then?" enquired Hugh.

"Aye, she said she put a couple o' wee meat pies in along wi' ma' piece."

"Pies? Meat pies?" asked Hugh in mock amazement.

"Aye. What's wrong wi' that then?"

"An' here's me thinkin' you're a good catholic, and you're eating meat oan a Friday!" Hugh said jokingly.

"Oh but they're Thursdays pies," quipped Pete. "It's awe right if they're bought the day afore."

The two mates laughed as they eased the heavy girder into place. As they pushed the head of the steel support there came the dreaded sound of falling debris. Both men froze as thick dust encircled them like black fog, filling their lungs, setting off convulsive coughing. The thunderous noise that ensued filled them with terror as they had nowhere to run, the roof behind them crashing down entombing them in the bowels of the earth.

An eerie silence followed. Hugh dazed and shaking tried to move his legs but the very girder they had been erecting pinned them down. His body ached. Tears streamed from his grit filled eyes streaking his coal black face. Warm blood tried escaping from the gash on his head but the coal dust that covered the wound blocked the flow. He remembered Pete.

It was too silent. Looking round the veil of dust his companion was nowhere to be seen. He listened for a sound, any sound, but all he could hear was the wheezing that came from his own throat. "Pete," he called in panic, but there was no reply. The fear that took hold of him now was worse than he felt during the fall. "Pete!" Arms outstretched he searched frantically through the rubble. "Pete, for Christ sake answer man!" His ears filled with the sound of eerie silence.

The cable that led from the battery on his waist to the lamp on his hat snapped leaving him in complete darkness. He gave a curse, then raising his arms he realised that the roof above him was only inches from his head. Another tremor would be enough to bring it crashing down on top. The air too was very thin, he would either be crushed to death or suffocate. Behind him he heard faint groaning, then voices. He then realised that Tammy, Davie and Archie were trapped behind him.

"Hugh!" It was Tammy Lindsay's voice. "Are you all right Hugh?"

In spite of the situation, Hugh gave a short sarcastic laugh. "What a bloody silly question. I'm pinned by the bloody legs, I'm gaspin' fur air and the least wee movement ma bloody skull will be cracked open like a bloody walnut, but otherwise I'm ok."

"What about Pete?" the voice asked.

"Oh man, a think he's had it. I canny get an answer. What are you all like?"

"We're ok. Cuts and bruises but we're ok."

"We're goin' tae try an' clear the rubble an' pull ye through aside us."

Patrick was well up the passage when the thunderous noise of the fall and the thick back dust that followed filled his ears and lungs. He momentarily froze, then, without thinking, he ran back towards his fated colleagues. Unable to see the extent of the disaster, as the road was filled with thick coal dust, he turned and ran with trembling legs back towards the main passageway and the phone. The distance between the men and the main passage was little over half a mile. Although Patrick ran as fast as his legs could carry him, he felt he was not moving at all. Reaching the phone, his hands shook as he grabbed at the handle and turned it frantically. The seconds it took him to get an answer from the control office seemed like forever. "Come on!" he growled anxiously as the ringing filled his ears. Bent double he gasped for air, "Come on! Where the hell are you?" he repeated impatiently.

The voice at the other end sounded lackadaisical, "Control office," it said.

"There's been a fall at number six south main gate. Get the mine rescue down here now! For Christ sake hurry," Patrick ordered.

Life immediately shot into the control officer. "Right away," he said quickly. "Is it bad?"

"Of course it's bloody bad, and get the men from the next section to give me a hand."

Patrick slammed down the phone and ran back towards the fall. Reaching the mass of rubble, he clawed frantically at the stone.

"Help's on the way," he yelled, knowing that any survivors would be able to hear.

In no time at all, the noise of running feet could be heard coming along the mine. It was the miners from the next section. They tore in about the rubble with their bare hands removing what they could, knowing that it would take twenty minutes at least before the mine rescue would arrive.

The word was out. 'A disaster at Dalkeith colliery'. The pithead was soon crawling with reporters anxious to get the story as it happened. Two hours passed before the body of Alec Cranston was brought to the surface. The rescuers managed to pass an airline through to the others and a further hour passed before they rescued Hugh Duff. Wooden props had to be used to support the huge bolder that threatened to fall on top of him. The three other miners trapped beyond Hugh worked from the other side to free his legs. He was brought out unconscious, his legs so badly crushed it was unlikely he would walk again. It was one o'clock in the afternoon when the remaining miners walked into the cage, their coal black faces failing to hide their sombre mood.

Refusing to go to hospital, cuts and bruises were attended to in the first aid-room after they came from the showers. The men, shocked at the death of their colleague were in no mood to talk.

Patrick stepped out onto the pithead with his three colleagues, and was immediately bombarded with questions. The reporters were eager to hear something, anything, as long as it came from the men involved. Cameras clicked as questions were asked, but with bowed heads the men ignored the reporters and made their way to the manager's office. With sadness in their hearts they were united with their families. In the small office, Betty Cranston comforted her grief stricken mother as they waited on transport to take them home.

The pithead was swarming with locals trying to find who was involved in the accident, as they all knew someone who was on the day shift. The men from the other sections were brought to the surface and they too hung about in bewilderment. Although mining accidents were infrequent, death of a fellow worker made them more aware of their own vulnerability.

The following morning, Mary as usual, rose at seven. Being Saturday Patrick had no work to go to, but she still had the lads to see out to work. She had been glad to see daylight filter through the slits in the blind as she had lain awake, tortured with guilty thoughts and unanswered questions. Her mind would not empty and allow sleep to take over. How would she have felt if it had been Patrick's body under that blanket? Why hadn't she felt relief when told he was all right? She also knew Patrick had not slept well, although they slept in separate beds, she heard him toss and turn all night.

Entering the boys' room Mary went over to the bed and shook them both none to gently. She hated this part of the morning, as both boys were sleepy headed and hard to rouse. Frank, now twenty- one, had finished his apprenticeship and was now a fully-fledged motor mechanic, while Allan at seventeen had newly started his training as a panel beater.

"Come on you two, time to get up. Don't have me shouting at you this morning as your father's in bed."

Bleary eyed, Allan threw an arm over the covers. "What's the time?" he grunted.

"It's time you moved yourself, that's what time it is, so don't give me a hard time and have him roaring."

Frank stirred, and although his eyes had not opened yet, he heard what his mother had said. Moaning, he rubbed at his hair.

Mary left them and ran down stairs to the kitchen where she systematically prepared the breakfast, listening for the sound of movement from above. She heard the bathroom door close and sighed in relief as she was in no mood for confrontation this morning. Ten minutes later Allan entered the kitchen. "He's not up yet," he informed Mary.

With a sigh, she rolled her eyes upwards. "He's no' bloody real that laddie." Pushing passed Allen she marched up the stair. As she opened the door, Frank sprung from the bed. "Sorry ma' I'm up now."

"It's a bloody good job an' all," she said quietly, thumbing at the door opposite. "Waken him and there will be hell to pay."

Descending the stairs once more, she heard the newspaper being pushed through the letterbox. Walking along the lobby she picked it up from the floor. Without looking at it, she walked back into the kitchen where Allan was pouring the hot water into the teapot. Bacon and sliced sausage sizzled in the pan, filling the kitchen with mouth-watering smells.

"He's up then?" asked Allan.

"Aye," Mary handed him the paper. "See here, and give me that pot and you sit down."

"It's all right Ma, I'm capable of filling the tea."

With that, Mary's attention turned to the contents of the pan. Two rashers of bacon and a piece of sausage was then laid on a plate and handed to her son. Frank entered the kitchen in time to take his late from his mother.

"Ta," he said, winking at Mary.

"Sit down you cheeky bugger, you nearly had the auld man up. He listens to every thing that's going on, and you of all people know that," she said sharply, wiping her hands down the side of her pink candlewick dressing gown.

"Sorry Ma'." His mouth turned up at one side as he gave his mother the smile that never failed to melt her heart.

"Aye Frank, you suit your grief," Mary remarked with sarcasm, then turning her attention to Allan, whose head was hidden by the open newspaper, she said, "And you an' all, put that paper down and get on with your breakfast."

Ignoring what his mother had just said, Allen gave a low whistle.

"Our Dad's a hero. His bloody mug shot's in the paper."

Grabbing the paper from Allan's hands, Mary looked down at the picture of her husband. It looked as if he was unaware of it having been taking, but it was Patrick for sure. Mary read the headlines, 'Mining disaster at Dalkieth. One dead and one seriously injured' Her silence was broken as she read the piece about Patrick.

'One of their colleagues, Patrick Sweeny, bravely tore at the rubble in desperation, ignoring the fact that he too could have become engulfed at any moment.'

She continued reading the news article as both sons stood behind her peering over her shoulder at the paper.

"Would you believe that?" Allan said. "Our Da' a hero."

Mary closed the paper and turned on her sons, "Your Da's heroism won't save you both from being sacked if you're late for work, so get a move on and finish your breakfast."

Both lads gone, Mary sat down cupping a mug of tea in her hands, newspaper spread out on the table, she read about the accident once more.

As she turned the page to read the rest of the news, she heard Patrick thumping on the floor above. She knew instantly that he wanted a cup of tea, his cigarettes and the newspaper. Collecting the pages together neatly, as he hated an untidy news paper, Mary rose, poured him a mug of tea, then tucking the paper under her arm, she walked through the living-room, lifted his cigarettes and matches and ascended the stairs once more.

Handing Patrick the tea, she threw the paper, cigarettes and matches on the bed. Without a word, Mary left the room.

She hadn't reached the bottom of the stair when Patrick let out a roar. "Mary. Come here!" he bellowed. She knew he had seen the report of the accident along with his photo, and she had expected this reaction.

"Have you seen this?" he asked in anger, pointing furiously at his photo. Without waiting for an answer he raved. "The bastards have no right putting my photo in the paper without asking. That's a violation of privacy."

This phobia about his photograph being taken had always mystified Mary. In all their years of marriage, Patrick had never had his photograph taken. Many a quarrel had ensued due to Mary pestering him to get into family snaps.

Throwing the paper to one side, he jumped out of bed, grabbed his trousers from the chair pulling them on hastily.

"I don't know what all the fuss is about Patrick, it's only a photo and it's not a very great one at that."

"My bloody name's there as well!" he snapped.

Frowning Mary asked, "So what Patrick? So what? What's so terrible about that?"

Pushing past her, he made for the bathroom, "I don't like it. I just don't like it."

Mary followed him out onto the landing, giving a slight jump as he slammed the bathroom door. "Nice start to the weekend," she thought.

Over morning coffee, Mary discussed Patrick's reaction with Cissie and they both came to the same obvious conclusion, Patrick had something to hide.

"I think he must have lied to his latest floozy. Or maybe he's owe someone money," Mary concluded.

Making light of the matter, Cissie said, "Naw. He's maybe yin o' them folk who think his spirit's pinched if his pictur's taken."

"Oh Cissie, have sense, the only spirit Patrick's familiar with comes out a bottle."

"Aye lass, you're richt, he certainly his somethin' tae hide, an' mark ma' words, it'll syn come tae licht. The truth will out."

Forty miles away, someone else was staring at Patrick's photo, someone who couldn't believe his luck.

Chapter Thirteen

Women struggled to keep hold of their umbrellas, as gale force winds blew them inside out. The men, collars up, hands in pockets, stooped against the ice cold rain, constantly staggering to keep their balance.

The priest, his cassock billowing in the wind, could not be heard, as his words were carried off like the leaves from the trees. After the burial, the Cranston family moved from the graveside, making for the black limousines.

Patrick, alongside his work-mates, headed for the cemetery gates.

Battling against the storm, they made their way towards the Miners' Welfare, where a small buffet had been organised for the grieving widow, although it was not tea and sandwiches Patrick and his companions had in mind. The bar would be open it being a private function.

During the tea, condolences were expressed, and the deceased was honoured at great lengths. The fact that he had only three months before retiring, led to the shaking of heads in disbelief. And who was going to look after his pigeons?

Who was going to take his place as President of the Miners Welfare? Those matters were the topic of conversation.

Standing at the bar with his colleagues, Patrick listened to the accolades without adding to them, his eye on the clock waiting for opening time at his local. A nod of the head was the signal to move so, downing their beer, Patrick and his two cronies said their goodbyes and left.

Outside the gale still raged. The sea battered ferociously against the sea wall, causing the angry waves to rise and crash over onto the deserted street. Blinded by the cold sea spray that was carried in the gale, the three men held on tightly to each other, forcing their bent bodies forward, taking three steps forward and one step back until reaching the shelter of the high buildings. Still battling against the gale, they carried on until they reached the other end of town, where the welcoming sight of the Railway Tavern's swinging sign groaned in the wind.

Freddy Campbell, the licensee of the public house, was busy stacking small bottles of tonic water on the shelf beneath the bar, when Patrick and his mates entered. In the far corner, three regulars warmed themselves by the fire that roared angrily in the grate. Leaning on the bar, a lone drinker studied the sports section of the Daily Record.

"Three nips an' three pints Freddy; when yer ready like." Patrick ordered rubbing his hands vigorously together.

Studying the three men momentarily, Freddy lifted three small glasses and filled them from the optic on the hanging bottle of Scotch, then, pushing the glasses towards Patrick, he pulled the first pint.

"A good turn out?" he enquired.

"Eh?" Patrick asked not hearing properly.

"The funeral. Was it a good turn out?" repeated the barman.

"Oh aye, a fairly big turn out in spite o' the weather." Patrick watched the dark liquid fill the glass, the white head topping the beer just perfectly.

"Aye," added Patrick's friend Sammy. "He wis weel liked wis Pete." He shook his head in despair.

"Mind, there wid be a good few nosey buggers among the crowd, ye ken what this place is like. Nosey bloody women!" added the third friend Vince MacLeod. Lifting his whisky he threw it over in one go, thumping the glass back down on the counter.

Raising his head from the paper, the customer at the other end of the bar added his thoughts to the conversation. "He had only a few years to retire an' all, so I heard."

"A few months, no' a few years, jist a few months," Vince informed him.

"Aye right enough," the man corrected himself. "A few months, right enough."

Following their friend's action, Patrick and Sammy gulped down their whisky, then, lifting their pints, made their way over to the fire.

Acknowledging the three men already hogging the heat, they sat along side them. The conversation started with the day's events, then, after that subject had been exhausted, the topic of conversation switched to Red Rum's third National triumph to which the lone drinker viewed his expert knowledge.

A few hours later, the bar began to get busier. In the games room, the pub's darts team and their followers awaited the arrival of the challengers, the team from the next town. Freddy's barmaid had arrived and was busy polishing the glasses, while Freddy himself collected the empties from the tables.

"Mind lads," he said stretching over Patrick and retrieving the glasses.

"Aye Freddy, nae bother," remarked Patrick, swerving slightly to let the well liked man in.

"Here Pat, while I mind, there was a stranger in yesterday asking if you drank here."

"And?" Patrick asked with interest.

"Well, I asked who was asking, and he said 'a friend'." Freddy shrugged his shoulders.

"What did he look like?" Patrick asked with slight alarm.

Shrugging his shoulders once more, Freddy tried to recall. "About your height, greyish; and oh aye, he had a kind o' West Country accent I would say."

"Bloody reporter, that's who it 'ill be," Vince piped up. "Bloody nosey reporters."

"That's probably right," agreed Sammy. "Bring the same again Freddy," he pointed to the three empty pint tumblers.

"Naw. Nane for me Sammy, I'd best get hame." Getting to his feet, Patrick waved his hand in protest. "The wife's face will no doubt be tripping her."

"Now there's a lassie I would run hame tae, Patrick's Mary," Vince said sincerely. "A right bonny lassie. Completely wasted on you Sweeny."

"A well, maybe Vince, maybe." Changing the subject, Patrick added, "Sounds as if the wind's died down a bit, so I'll be on my way. See you at the pit tomorrow."

Turning up his jacket collar, Patrick stepped out into the night. The fierce gale had died down considerably but a fairly strong wind still persisted. Crossing the road, he was unaware of the figure lurking in a doorway at the opposite side of the street. With his head well down, he headed for home, staggering at times against the wind rather than the effects of alcohol as he was far from drunk him being a seasoned drinker.

Throwing his cigarette to the ground, the stranger crossed over and followed Patrick a short distance until he was sure he was the man he was after. Walking briskly, he fought against the wind until he was directly behind him. The lights of a passing car shone on the men, its wheels hitting the water logged guttering, sending a flood outwards, soaking both pedestrians. Stopping suddenly, Patrick turned, his eyes following the car. He shook his fists, cursing the driver. It was then Patrick became aware of the figure behind him. Noticing the man was equally as wet, Patrick grunted taking in the stranger's condition, however he failed to observe his face. Patrick turned to walk on, when the man spoke.

"Sweeny!" He grabbed at Patrick's upturned collar.

Turning round quickly, Patrick raised his arm to free himself from his unknown assailant's grip.

"Take a good look Sweeny!" Their eyes peered at one another, Patrick's with curiosity, the man's with hate.

"So you cannae recognise me eh! Hiv I aged that much?" he scowled.

Patrick's heart raced as he now recognised the older man. "Jock McTaggart?" The palms of his hands turned moist with sweat.

Jock McTaggart, although a good deal older than Patrick, was muscular and as strong as any man half his age.

"A've waited a long time fir this; a bloody long time. A' made a vow tae ma' lassie that a would settle her score." Seeing Patrick recoil, with hands like shovels, Jock grabbed the lapels of Patrick's coat, then as Patrick struggled, Jock managed to pull Patrick's right arm up behind his back at the same time grabbing him by the hair.

Another car passed making Jock realise he was too much in the open.

"Come wi' me Sweenie you bastard an' try an' leave me in the same state you left ma' lassie." Pushing forcibly from the back, he frog-marched Patrick, who was hopelessly immobile, across the road and down a narrow lane towards the seashore. The rough sea had ebbed, but the darkness of the water and the cloudy sky almost made the shore pitch black.

Pushing his victim down eight very wet steep steps, they both struggled to keep their feet. The crunching sound from the shale, pebbles, and numerous small shells washed up by the tide, was heard with every step they took. They now stood on the shore, the angry sea at one side, a high wall protecting and providing privacy to the High Street shops and upstairs flats, from all who walked along the little shore path.

Turning Patrick round, McTaggart punched him with the full force of his huge strong fist. The impact on Patrick's jaw, felt like a sledgehammer, knocking him to the ground. Grabbing Patrick by the lapels once more, Jock lifted him up as he would a rag doll, only to knock him back down with no less a force than he had done before.

Filled with terror, Patrick felt warm blood pour down his face and with a throbbing in his head, he almost passed out. Sensing Jock was about to repeat this action, Patrick felt a rush of adrenaline flow through his veins. As Jock made to strike again, Patrick swiftly shielded his face with one arm while grabbing at Jock's fist with his free hand. An inner strength, caused through fear, had taken over. Pushing and jostling ensued, causing both men to fall to the ground, but it was by sheer luck Jock lay beneath Patrick giving him the advantage for the first time, and being well aware of the older man's notorious reputation, he knew full well that he had to act quickly, him being no match for this powerful man. Patrick dared not let himself be overcome, so pinning Jock to the ground, he punched at his face relentlessly. Jock McTaggart still heaved his massive body upward like a wild mare being broken in. Patrick almost toppled over a few times as his blows seemed to have no effect. As Patrick's hand fell to the side in the struggle, he felt the cold wet piece of wood. Grabbing it, he swung it down onto Jock's head crashing against his skull. He cursed at Patrick, then it struck again. Feeling Jock's struggle lessen, Patrick continued beating, beating, beating until the body beneath went limp. Exhausted and relieved, he rolled off Jock's chest.

Falling back onto the shale, he lay looking up at the heavens panting erratically and heaving deeply. Feeling the cold dampness beneath him, he struggled to his feet and with bent body, he looked down on the still lifeless figure. It was then his heart quickened once more in panic. Lifting the wood, for the first time he saw the six- inch nails protruding from the end that crashed down on Jock. The wood itself was enough to do damage, as it resembled a solid table leg. Looking about in renewed terror, Patrick could not think clearly. He felt his heart thump against his chest; the hot sticky sweat he had felt earlier had turned to cold dampness causing his teeth to chatter uncontrollably.

He had to get rid of the stick. Walking briskly to the edge of the water, Patrick, staggering slightly, swung the stick with all his might. The noise from the lashing waves and the darkness of the night made it impossible to see just how far it had been thrown. Staring transfixed into the darkness, Patrick was brought back to reality by the cold spray that lashed at him through the wind. Shivering, he held himself tightly, then with a quick glance in each direction, hurried back up the beach ignoring the body that lay on the shore.

Removing his working boots in the back porch, Frank called out his usual greeting. "It's me Ma, number one Son!"

167

Entering the kitchen, the smell of stewed sausages and onions filled his nostrils. Standing in his stocking feet, rubbing his hands together vigorously, he took a deep sniff. "I'm bloody starving," he remarked.

Stabbing at the boiling potatoes with a fork, Mary gave her oldest son a dark look, cautioning him, "Less o' that talk in here me lad. Your still young enough to feel the back o' my hand. Away and wash your hands. Dinner's no' quite ready 'cause the tatties are still a bit hard."

Passing through the living room, he acknowledged Allan who warmed himself at the fire. "Aye Brother, some day this."

"Aye, so it is," replied Allan.

Meeting the youngest brother at the foot of the stair, Frank playfully ruffled his hair.

"Och oor Frank, I've just combed ma' hair. Your always the same you!" he grumbled.

"Oh my," teased his older brother, "aren't wee a sour puss." Closing the bathroom door, Frank's rendition of 'Hound dog' could be heard in the hall.

As Mary served up the meal she called her three sons.

Allan and Tony sat at the table and their mother passed them their plates. She then laid Frank's and her own down at their usual places at the table, before placing a lid over a fifth plateful of food returning it into the oven.

Sitting alongside his mother, Frank nodded in the direction of Patrick's empty chair. "Not back from the funeral then?"

"Does it look like it?" Allan answered sarcastically.

Ignoring Allan, Frank waited for his mother's answer.

"You might expect him to make a day of it knowing what he's like once he gets the taste o' drink." Looking down at her food, she avoided her son's gaze.

"I asked him for money for the pictures this mornin' and he said he wis skint," moaned Tony.

"Never mind wee brother, there's a good film on telly to-night, besides, it's too flamin' cauld tae go out."

"Your no' goin' tae the darts tournament the night then?" Allan asked with mocked amassment.

"Now, I never said that!" Frank laughed, "The show can't go on without me," he jested.

"Oh aye," added Mary, "There's no show without punch!" Standing up, she collected the empty plates, all but Tony's.

"Ma, can I leave this?" Tony asked pushing his plate to the side.

"What's wrong, aren't you hungry?"

Screwing his face up, he moaned, "I've had enough. I'm full up."

"Then you'll no' want pudding then. Apple pie!" Mary informed him.

Patting his stomach, he declared, "Well, I have a wee bit room left for my pudding."

"None for me Ma," Frank said rising from the table, "I'm off to get ready. Leave some aside an' I'll have it when I get in."

An hour later, Frank left the house making his way to the Railway Tavern. With the wind behind him, he was helped on his way along the street. Dark clouds scurried by, blocking out the light from the moon. Stopping for a moment, he pulled a cigarette from his top pocket, then, cupping his hands round a match, tried to light it. Flickering momentarily, the flame blew out. Stepping into a doorway, he went through the same ritual, this time with success. As he puffed a few times, making sure it was well lit, he saw the figure of a man running from the lane that led to the shore. As the man at the other side of the street drew nearer, Frank stepped back further into the doorway, then, to his surprise, Frank recognised the figure to be that of his father. Patrick hurried past unaware he was being watched.

The Railway Tavern by now had become very lively, the noise from the games room spilling out into the public bar.

Frank nodded to Freddie and without questioning; the proficient bar tender pulled a pint of best lager. Laying it down in front of his young customer, Frank handed him the money, "Cheers man!" Knowing that the discreet barman would never volunteer information about his regulars, Frank added. "Is ma' auld man long away Freddy?"

"A wee while noo son," he answered, before looking over towards Patrick's earlier companions. He called out, "Half an hour since Pat left, is it lads?"

"Aye it will be that," Sammy answered drunkenly, looking directly at Frank. "Come away o'er here lad and have a pint wi' auld Sammy."

Laughing, and with a shake of his head, Frank called back, "Naw, bit thanks a' the same Sammy man. If a sat doon with you lot, a would never see the darts match. You're too professional swillers for me."

"A dinnae ken if that's a' insult or a compliment." Sammy answered with a grin that showed a toothless cavern.

"Naw you wouldn't," Freddy said quietly, winking at Patrick. "He hasn't the brains he was born with".

Lifting his pint, Frank headed for the games room. Pulling a seat from the stack of chairs in the corner, he sat at the table beside his friends. His father was still very much in his thoughts as he was very curious as to what had taken him down to the shore on such a foul night, however, the event that was taking place before him and the boisterous company he sat amongst, soon wiped Patrick out of his thoughts.

The back kitchen tidied, Mary settled herself down in front of the television. The older boys both out, Tony curled up in his father's chair reading a comic book.

As the fire blasted and roared up the chimney, Mary covered her legs with a woollen plaid to stop mottled burn marks, or what is known as 'fire tartan' She had just settled back when the back door opened.

Tony look up as his father appeared in the living room, but Patrick went straight through to the bathroom without saying a word.

Mary saw bewilderment in her son's eyes. "What's the matter with you?" she asked concerned.

Wide eyed, Tony said, "He looked awful Ma."

Shaking her head in dismay, Mary explained. "He's been with his buddies Tony, you should be well used to yer Da's bedraggled look by now. You've seen it often enough."

Kneeling over the toilet pan, Patrick vomited. While violent pain hammered in his head, lights flashed relentlessly behind his closed eyelids. Never before had he felt like this. It was his worst nightmare. Staggering to his feet, he turned to the washbasin, turned on the taps and balanced himself by holding on to the sides. As his head bowed over the basin, saliva dripped from his lower lip. Cupping his dirty hands beneath the flowing water, he doused his face a few times before looking into the mirror hanging directly above. Distorted features stared through wet hair that hung limp over his eyes. His gaze then fell on the arms of his jacket. Damp shale still clung fast.

Then he looked down at his trouser legs, groaning at the sight. It was obvious he had rolled on the beach. Running his hands through his hair in panic, he tried to think clearly then, springing into action, he started to fill the bath. Stripping his clothes off, he wrapped himself in the large bath towel that hung from a hook at the back of the door, the same towel that Frank had used earlier. He cursed, as it was damp. Opening the door he called to Mary.

Although she had heard him retching, being well used to it, she sat still.

"See what he wants Tony?" she said, irritation evident in her voice.

Without his usual protest, Tony went to the fractionally opened bathroom door.

Hiding his anxiety Patrick spoke in a controlled manner, "Get me a dry towel Son, I've been soaked to the skin so I'll away and have a bath. And...and fetch me that dressing gown that's hanging at the back o' the press door."

Gaping at his father, the youngster knew there was something strange going on, his Da' in a dressing gown? He had one right enough, but never wore it. He was given it at Christmas a few years back and said it was for 'pansies.'

"Well dinnae stand there staring, git goin'," he ordered. "An' leave them here at the door."

Obeying his father's orders, the lad then returned to the living room, curling up once more in his father's chair.

Seeing the cheeky grin on her son's face, Mary frowned at him questioningly.

Now giggling, Tony cupped his hand over his mouth.

Mary, now laughing, despite being unaware of the joke, asked, "What's so funny?"

Still the boy giggled, "You'll no' laugh like that when he knocks you out o' his chair. Get out o' it before he comes through." She gave a quiet laugh.

Thumbing in the direction of the door, and between childish laughter, he blurted through his fingers. "He asked me to fetch his dressing gown. He's going to wear it Ma'."

Biting her lip, and half a smile on her face, Mary cautioned him, "That's enough now. If he sees you making fun o' him, he'll do you." Then without smiling, she asked, "Has he had much?"

"Ma, he looks all red eyed and that, but he's no' drunk, he's been drenched though."

Considerably a lot calmer, Patrick soaked in the warmth of his bath water, his mind trying to work something out. Who could link him to the body on the beach? No one had seen them together. He could have been washed up on the shore. No- there would be no water in his lungs!

His head started to hurt once more. Then he remembered Freddy.

Pulling him-self bolt up right, the water surged over the edge of the bath onto the lino Oh God! Freddy. "Bloody Freddy!" he whispered, closing his eyes in despair. He had mentioned someone had asked after him. Then he recalled how everyone assumed the man was a reporter. The relief he had just encountered as now replaced with Panic. Oh how his head hurt!

A sharp rapping at the door alarmed him. "Da, how much longer are you goin' tae be. A need in Da', a need a pee," called Tony.

"A minute. A minute. You're always the same you. No matter when a come in here, you want in. Well, you'll have to wait a minute" He called in annoyance. Rising from the water, he opened the door slightly retrieving the fresh towel and robe then drying him-self vigorously, slipped into the dressing gown. As he turned to let the water out from the bath, he had an idea. Emptying his pockets of loose change, comb and hanky, he held his badly marked clothes over the bath, dropping them in the water. Cursing loud enough to be heard, he swirled the garments round, making sure the loose shale washed completely off before rinsing them under running water. Lifting the sodden garb from the bath, he then piled them into the wash-hand basin. The bath now empty of water, wet shale settled on the bottom. A black filthy tidemark encircled the tub. Sloshing water from a handy jug, the evidence eventually disappeared down the drain.

Lifting the lid from the wicker laundry basket that stood in the corner of the room, he then deposited his shirt, undergarments, and wet towels, then with a quick check of the bathroom, Patrick ventured through into the living room and continued the next part of the deception, unaware that he had overlooked his shoes that were tucked in between the wall and the lavatory pan.

"A bloody idiot I am," he remarked, aware of Tony's stares. "I dropped ma' suit in the bloody bath water."

It was only then did Mary turn her head and look towards her husband.

"Your good suit?" she asked in disbelief. "How the blazes did you manage that?"

"A just did Mary!" Patrick jumped in defensive knowing she would not pursue the matter. "A had a bloody *accident*. It happens sometimes woman. Now, where do you keep the bloody Ajax?"

Rising, Mary followed Patrick into the back kitchen, then pushing past him, she opened the small door under the sink and lifted out the cleaning agent. Grabbing it from her hand, Patrick grumbled, "Give it here, I'll do it." Returning back to the bathroom, he found the door locked. Tony had nipped quickly through unnoticed. "Could you no' have waited?" he called to his son in annoyance.

"Naw Da'," came the reply from within. "A teld you a wis burstin'."

Patrick stood impatiently in the hall waiting until Tony appeared at the bathroom door, then, with an abrupt shove, almost knocked the inquisitive lad off balance. Hurrying through to his mother, and in a low fervent voice, he told her about the state of the tub, not forgetting the pile of clothing heaped up in the sink. "And it's his very best suit. His very, very best."

Laughing at her son's account of the situation, Mary shook her head, "Accidents happen lad. You heard him," but in her mind, she suspected her husband to be up to something as it was out of character for him to insist on washing a bath out, not to mention taking one immediately on entering the house, as normally his empty stomach was the first thing on the agenda. The sudden decision to wear the dressing gown was another strange factor. There was something very strange about the whole thing.

Completing the washing of the tub, Patrick filled a polythene bag with the sodden clothes, then washing the hand basin out, a quick check of the room, he was sure any evidence of him ever being on the beach was well gone, however, once more he failed to notice his shoes.

Returning to the kitchen, he handed Mary the bag of clothes. "And what am I supposed to do with this?" she asked quietly.

"What do you think?" he snapped impatiently. "Get them to the cleaners tomorrow." Turning, he muttered, "I'm a way up tae bed." and before Mary could ask, Patrick added, "I don't want anything tae eat, I'm no' hungry."

Sniffing every now and then, cocking his leg to cover previous scents, Barney the mongrel ran in front of his disgruntled owner, who minutes ago had been sprawled in front of his fire listening to the wildness of the night batter against the window, and would still have been there if it hadn't been for the persistence of his beloved pet.

Andy Webb's one roomed flat look out onto the shore and it was here Barney expected his walk, no matter how bad the weather.

"Come away lad, that's far enough the night," he called to Barney, and with a whistle, he stood and waited for his usually obedient dog to turn back. A last sniff and the dog half turned, only to turn his attention to the heap on the shore. Taking to its heels, the dog ignored Andy's commands and ran towards the steps leading to the water. Sniffing round the body, Barney barked repeatedly as he did when overexcited. Watching his dog's strange behaviour, the elderly man followed down the steps, then, shooing Barnie to one side, observed the still body lying curled up on the shale. His immediate thought was the body had been washed up on the tide, as that had happened not so long ago when the body of a woman had been carried down the River Esk and on to the shore.

Frank lifted the four brimming pints from the bar and placed them on the tray just as an old school chum entered the pub. Recognising Frank at the bar, the old chum gave him a playful shove, causing the beer to trickle over the brim of the glasses, leaving a pool of ale on the bottom of the tray.

"Aye my old son, where have you been hiding?" Frank greeted him warmly, and without waiting for a reply, turned to the bar man, "A pint fur Tam here Freddy."

Tam Donaldson, his elbow on the bar, waited for his pint. "What's goin' on out there then?" he asked, nodding towards the outside door.

"A wild night, right enough," remarked Freddy, his attention on the almost perfect pint.

"Naw man, I'm no' talking about the weather. It's police. If there's one, there's a hundred." He grossly exaggerated.

Frank patiently waited while his friend tasted his pint. Freddy, ignoring a customer's call for service, also waited for more information.

Wiping the froth from his mouth and knowing he had their full attention, Tam was about to continue when two more men entered the pub.

"You should see the carry on along there," one called out, catching the attention of the whole room. "A body on the shore. Andy Webb and his dog found it."

"Washed up on the tide no doubt," Freddy remarked. "Probably been swept doon from the Esk. Maist bodies come from that direction. It awe depends oan the tide."

"Naw, they've taken the poor soul away in the ambulance, and they'll no' dae that if the body's deid," informed the other new comer. "They wid carry it along tae the morgue oan a stretcher if it wis deid." The slow shake of his head and his grim expression verified his knowledge on the matter.

As the speculations as to what had transpired on the shore was passed to one and other, Frank remained silent. The thought of his father sneaking up from the shore brought sweat to his brow. The tray that he held in his now clammy hands suddenly felt very heavy. Returning it swiftly to the safety of the counter, Frank rubbed his hands together before his attention was drawn to the young man who stood in the games room doorway.

"Come away Frank with them pints. The time you've taken we thought you'd gone home."

Back in the games room, Frank had now lost all interest in the match, as he could not get Patrick out of his thoughts. Leaving his pint still half full, he rose from the table. Wrapping his scarf round his neck, he made an excuse and left.

Passing the vennel, from where a few hours earlier he had seen Patrick emerge, three police cars still stood, the occupants obviously on the shore. Frank's gut feeling told him Patrick had been involved one way or another.

Mary looked up in amazement as her older son walked in. "Well, you're early. What's wrong? The match been cancelled, or has the pub burned down?"

"Naw Ma, it's still going on".

The blank expression on her son's face alarmed her. "What's wrong Frank? You look as if you've lost a shilling and found a sixpence."

"Naw Mam, I felt tired, that's all."

"Well I've just made a fresh brew, so you'll sit and have a cup of tea and the apple pie you left at dinner time."

Seeing his young brother lying in front of the television, he growled, "You should be in bed. No wonder you get bad marks at school, you're always half sleepin' in the mornin'."

Mary glanced sideways at Frank, "It's not often he's up at this time. He's watching the film. If he had gone to the pictures he'd 'ave been later than this at coming home. What's up with you the night man? As I recall, you were the one who told him about the film."

Once the tea was poured, Mary carried it through to her son along with his slice of cold apple pie. Taking it from his mother, he laid it on the long glass table at the side of his chair. "There was somethin' going on at the shore the night Ma, police every where. A body was taken off in the ambulance."

"What has happened?" Mary gasped.

"That's all I know." Then he asked. "Where's he?" Referring to Patrick.

"In his bed. He had a bath when he came in and went straight off to bed."

At that, Tony pushed himself upright from the floor. "Oh our Frank, you should have seen him." Sniggering, the lad recalled what went on. "He was wearing his dressing gown, an' he let his best clothes faw intae the bath." Tittering, he covered his mouth with his hand, as children do when suppressing laughter.

Looking towards his mother and without the amusement of his young brother, he asked, "Is that right?"

"Aye, the wet clothes are in a bag behind the kitchen table."

As if doubting his mother's words, Frank left the room to inspect the bag. Just as Mary had said, the bag was filled with his father's sodden clothes.

Some time later, Frank went into the bathroom. He looked round, not really knowing what he was looking for. Things did not add up. It was then he found his father's shoes tucked between the toilet pan and the wall. Pulling them out, he looked down at them. The cold shivers that he felt in the pub returned. He was right, Patrick did have something to do with the earlier incident. The shoes were caked in shale and the tell tale white ring, made by contact with salt water, encircled his father's footwear. Now he was sure his father was involved in something.

Taking the shoes into his own room, he hurriedly wrapped them up in newspaper before hiding them away in the bottom of his wardrobe. Barely sleeping a wink he tried figuring out just what could have occurred down on the cold dark shore that evening.

The following morning, the newspapers carried the story of the mystery man, found battered on the beach. He was said to be fighting for his life and was described as being in his early sixties, five foot eleven in stature and muscular in body. The police were anxious to hear from anyone who might have been on the shore between six and eight thirty that night.

Frank arrived at the bottom of the stair as the paper popped through the letterbox. Pulling it gently from the vice like grip of the box and folding it, he slipped it into the inside pocket of his jacket that hung over the carved ball on the end of the banister, making sure it was well hidden before joining his brother and mother at the breakfast table. He presumed the paper would be full of the story and he wanted to study any speculation before the family heard the news.

With paper in hand, Cissie arrived at Mary's for her morning coffee. "It's still awfull cauld oot there Mary." With a slight shiver she grinned. "'Am a' wrapped up like a grave-digger's *piece (sandwich)," she remarked as she opened her coat and unravelled the huge woollen scarf that was wrapped around her neck three times. "Well, have you seen the news yet?" She pulled the chair from the table and sat down heavily. "Oh ma' knee is fair gien me jip. It's a' this cauld weather," she complained rubbing her badly swollen knee. "Bloomin' artheritis," she called it, no matter how often she was told the right pronunciation.

Pouring the coffee, and sympathising with her friend, Mary sat down at the table. "Our paper is nowhere to be seen. I was thinking the lad was late this morning, but if you have yours, he must have forgot to deliver ours." She bit on her lip thoughtfully. "It's funny our Frank had nothing to say about the paper being late. It's the first thing he lays his hands on in the morning."

"Well, oor toon may be sma', but we dinnae half make the headlines. Last week it wis the pit, noo look, see the latest." Spreading the paper before her friend, Cissie pointed vigorously at the headlines with her podgy index finger. ' BODY ON THE BEACH LEFT FOR DEAD.'

Grabbing at the paper, Mary read the article, then, looking blankly at Cissie, she said quietly. "Poor, poor man, who would do such a thing?"

Stirring the sugar into her coffee, Cissie added, "You dinnae ken yer neebours noo- a -days. Awe them newcomers tae the toon," she gave a sigh. "It could be onybody. There's a lot o' bad buggers goin' roond. Mind, tae happen in this place Mary, it fair makes me feart." Gritting her teeth, her three chins wobbled uncontrollably as she shook her old grey head. "A mind the day ye could leave yer doors open, but no' noo. The buggers wid cut yer throat then steal the bloody knife."

Usually Mary found her friend's philosophy very amusing, but not today as she was now inclined to agree with what she had to say.

"Frank mentioned something about this last night," Mary recalled.

"Aboot the murder?" Cissie's eyes peered though puffy bags.

"Cissie, the man's no' dead," she reminded her. "Naw, he just said that the street was swarming with police."

"Weel," she tutted, "the paur soul wid jist as weel be deid, accordin' tae the paper, he's swinging like a rusty gate. One puff o' wind an' the hinge will jist," she snapped her finger.

This did bring a grin to Mary's lips, "Oh Cissie, you're an awful woman."

The rhythmically swish and clicking sounds made by the ventilator had almost a hypnotic affect on the young policeman that sat at the bedside of Jock McTaggart. Only the constant interruption by the bustling nurse kept him from slipping in to welcome sleep. At his side, the monitor displaying the patient's heart rate bleeped steadily. The emergency operation had gone well but the victim was still unconscious.

The door to the single room swung open and D.C. Walter Taylor lead the nervous woman gently by the arm. Going forward towards the bed, the woman looked down on the distorted features, clutched at her throat and gasped. "Oh my God Jock!"

Turning to the detective, she nodded, distress quivering in her voice.

"That's me man right enough son. Oh my God, is he goin' tae be alright?"

"I'm sure he not ma'am," he assured her. Leading the woman back towards the door, he asked gently. "Have you any idea who would do this to him Mrs. Mc Taggart?"

With a look of hatred in her eyes, Jean McTaggart drew a newspaper cutting from her pocket slapping it into the detective's hand. "Aye a dae. See him," she pointed at the paper, "he's the yin you want tae be talking tae. He's the yin that did it. Aye laddie I am sure! As the Lord is ma' judge I am sure."

Unfolding the cutting, the detective looked upon the face of Patrick Sweeny. Pouting his lip, he returned his attention on Jean. "What makes you think Patrick Sweeny's involved in this?"

Turning round and looking towards her husband, she spoke with tenderness, "He is a good man ma Jock. He has never gone lookin' for trouble, but his blood fair boiled whin he saw that man's face staring from the paper at him." Her neck seemed to push out from under her collar as she held herself straight in a defensive manner.

"An old score was it?" the D.C. asked.

"Eh?" Jean asked, not following Walter's meaning.

"An old score, you know, when...."

"Oh a ken what you mean," Jean interrupted as she caught on. "Aye well, you can say sort of."

"Look ma'am, perhaps we should go for a cup of tea and you can tell me all about it," suggested Walter.

"But but, what aboot?" she glanced in the direction of the bed.

"It's ok, the constable will get word to us when there's any change."

The two men exchanged nods. "Come away now and tell me what you know."

The hospital canteen had quietened down as the lunchtime rush was over.

Walter returned to the table carrying a tray of tea and small sandwich squares. Lifting the plate from the table, Jean remarked, "A dinnae ken why folk cut pieces as wee as that. Kin you imagine a man comin' hame from a hard days graft an' gettin' wee things like that put doon in front o' him. You'd maist likely get them thrown at ye."

Without comment, Walter gave a slight laugh in agreement.

"Well Mrs. McTaggart!"

Interrupting once more she insisted, "Oh please son, call me Jean, everybody else does."

"Well Jean,"

She nodded her approval.

"can you start at the beginning?"

"Oh aye son, a certainly can."

Patrick Sweeny was married to the McTaggart's only daughter Bunty, who by all accounts was a very beautiful and popular girl. The village that they belonged to consisted mainly of miners and their families, so it was inevitable that Bunty's friends were sons and daughters of miner's. Although Patrick lived in a neighbouring village, they met at a fete run by the miners institute. Three months after they started courting they married, much to the disapproval of Bunty's parents. Not long after the marriage the rows started, as Patrick's jealousy reared its ugly head. Bunty could no longer go out without his approval. If she left to go shopping she had to be back at the precise time she stated, which sometimes was rather difficult. His young wife soon changed from being a person with her own identity into a person highly strung with no mind of her own. Her friends soon stopped seeing her, as they were aware of the rows they caused. As the months went by, she saw less and less of her parents as she was subjected to vigorous questioning by both sides. Things came to a head when Patrick arrived home early and found the young insurance man sitting in his kitchen laughing and drinking coffee with his wife. After throwing the bewildered man out onto the street, he set about Bunty, calling her all the foul names he could think of. Having endured this awful humiliation, the now sobbing girl wanted nothing more than to escape her husband's unfounded accusations. Pushing past him, she made for the outside door, only to be grabbed by the hair and hauled back through into the kitchen. Now screaming abuse at her husband, she struggled to get free. Pushing her with force, she landed on the floor. Patrick swore and cursed as he set about her fragile frame with his boots. He would have none of this! No woman would affront him by inviting men into his house. If there was no affair she would have paid the man at the door like any other decent woman.

Bunty yelled back in spite of the dull pain she now felt at her ribs and with short laborious gasps, she protested her innocence. "He goes to my Mother's so I know him well Patrick. I always make him a coffee. There's nothing in it Patrick, I swear."

As Patrick gripped the top of a kitchen chair, with his eyes shut tight he rocked back and forth growling through his teeth. Bunty pulled herself up from the floor holding on to her right side as she did so.

"You have lifted your hands and feet once to often Patrick, I can't take this any more. I don't deserve any of this."

Walking out into the passageway, Patrick followed behind. "You're going nowhere," he called after her, but ignoring his cries, she walked towards the front door. His temper boiled as he realised he was losing control over his wife. "'You hear what I'm sayin'? You are going nowhere!"

Turning, she faced him, brazenly staring him in the eyes, "and what are you going to do Patrick? Another beating?" she taunted.

This was more than he could take. The hatred burning in Bunty's eyes sent him into frenzy. With clenched fist he connected with her jaw knocking her backwards and hitting her head on the outside door. The jealousy burning within engulfed him in evil. The beating Bunty took that day was worse than anything she had endured before. She was found lying unconscious by her mother, as the young insurance man had alerted her knowing of Patrick's reputation.

Bunty survived the beating, but it left her with a dreadful speech impediment. She also is prone to fits and her right arm is now paralysed, but she had no knowledge of the event. Patrick disappeared from the district and as there was no evidence or witnesses as to what did happen, there was never any warrant produced for his detainment.

Walter rubbed his chin. Jean McTaggart sat back in her chair watching and waiting for the detective's comments.

"So this," he waved the cutting in front of him, "this is what led your husband through here."

"Na," Jean said with an air of impudence, "It wisnae the paper that led him through here, it was to get even wi' that big shite what put our lass in hospital. She's never been the same since. A bright bit lassie she was until that-that piece o' shit got a hold o' her. Now she's retarded, thanks tae him!" Taking a piece of tissue from under her sleeve, Jean wiped away the tears that filled her tired looking eyes.

"An' the papers said he wis a married man! Well, a dinnae ken how he could be married if he didnae divorce ma' Bunty."

"Are you sure he's the same man?" Walter asked.

Showing gradual annoyance, Jean snapped. "Dae you think ma' Jock wid be lying in here if it wisnae the same Patrick Sweeny? Aye it's the same man a' right, so you better git oaf your behind and lift him afore he does another runner."

Lowering his head and focusing on his now empty cup, the detective murmured, "It's not that easy Jean. See you just cannot charge anyone without proof."

With a gasp, Jean's body seemed to grow larger, "Awe aye, jist like the last time. You have to have proof. Well mister, take a look at ma' Jock. Is that no' proof enough?"

Shaking his head, Walter tried explaining. "When Jock comes too, we will take his statement, but we will need extra proof. You see Jean, it's only his word against Patrick Sweeny's."

In disgust, Jean rose from the table. "I'll away along an' see ma' man now detective. Maybe if we wait long enough Sweeny might murder someone. Then what'll you dae? Or maybe if Jock snuffs it, God forbid, you'll take heed then."

Mary felt the tension round the table as her three sons and her husband ate in silence. Although there had been many similar occasions, this silence seemed almost deafening. Frank usually had something to say, all be it to irritate his brothers.

The knock on the door came as Mary filled the teacups. As Tony rose from his chair, Mary reprimanded him, "You sit there and finish your dinner, I'll see to the door." Laying the teapot down upon the table, she left the kitchen. The sight of the two burly men and the uniformed officer caused her legs to go weak. Holding on to the edge of the door, Mary regained her balance. "Yes?" she asked with a slight warble in her voice.

"Sorry to bother you ma-am, but does Patrick Sweeny reside hear?"

The word reside almost brought a smile to Mary's lips. "Yes he does," she answered almost barricading the entrance to the house.

"I'm Detective Walter Taylor and this here is Detective Galloway and P.C. Rintoul. We would like to come in and discuss a matter with Patrick Sweeny. In fact there are a few questions I would like to ask the household." Giving Mary a reassuring smile he surmised, "You must be Mrs. Sweeny?"

Mary nodded, and then slowly and reluctantly, she moved to one side and let them in.

As the three men marched through into the living room, she followed on behind.

Patrick felt the colour drain from his face when seeing the three men enter the room. Looking through into the kitchen, Walter smiled at Patrick and the boys. "Oh sorry, I'm afraid I'm going to spoil your meal." With the same introduction he had given Mary, Walter proceeded.

His attention now on Patrick, Walter's face took on a more serious expression.

"Are you Patrick Sweeny?" he enquired.

Laying his cutlery down on his plate, Patrick nodded before rising.

The three boys about to do the same were stopped by Walter.

"No, you lot stay through here until I need you." With the hint of a smile he suggested they finish their meal before it turned cold.

Patrick stood facing his interrogators and although he looked calm and relaxed, his heart pounded heavily in his chest.

"Can you tell me sir where you were last Thursday between the hours off six and eight thirty?"

"Aye a can," replied Patrick brazenly. "I was at the pub, 'The Railway'."

"That would be 'The Railway Tavern' in the High Street I presume?"

Patrick nodded.

"What time did you leave The Railway?" asked Walter, studying Patrick's body langauge.

"I can't say exactly. About eight o'clock, I think." Then as if searching his mind, he altered his statement. "Naw, it was earlier than that. I was hame at eight; see I had a fair drink in me. I was at the mates funeral afore that see." Reaching over to the mantelpiece, he lifted his cigarettes and matches. After lighting the cigarette, he inhaled deeply before blowing the smoke up towards the ceiling.

Walter stood silently watching the defiant antics of the man who was his prime suspect.

"The time you left the pub can be checked sir. Did you at any time have reason to go down onto the shore?"

Mary gasped and held her hand across her chest.

Patrick looked straight into the detective's face. "What are you gettin' at man? No I didn't have any reason to go down to the shore. Why the hell should I?"

Ignoring Patrick's question, Walter glanced at his colleague P.C. Rintoul, who now took over the questioning. "Do you know Jock McTaggart?"

Patrick now showed annoyance. "No. I've never heard of the man."

"I would think twice before denying that sir," remarked Galloway.

"You were at one time married to his daughter, and by all accounts still are," he remarked accusingly.

Mary could not believe what she was hearing. A rushing of blood filled her head and seeing her sway, P.C. Rintoul rushed to her aid. "Come along Mrs. Sweeny and sit down over here." Taking her by the arm, he led her to the safety of the armchair.

The palms of Patrick's hands began to sweat. He wracked his brain trying to think of a way out of the mess.

"Oh aye, a ken Jock Mc Taggart, but I've no' seen him for years. A thought it was someone local you were askin' me about." Then as if developing an interest in the man, Patrick asked, "What are you askin' me about Jock for? How's he doing?"

"I've got to hand it to you Patrick," remarked Walter, "you are a brazen bugger. Fine you know why we are asking about

Jock. You beat him to a pulp and left him for dead last night. Didn't you?"

As Mary watched her husband, she felt nothing but revulsion. The clothes in the bag and the bath last night now made sense. She listened as Detective Taylor gave a summary as to what appeared to have happened. She listened as Patrick's past was laid in front of her like an open book. She also identified her earlier life with that of Patrick's first wife. She too had been trapped by his jealousy, and for years she lived in terror of his temper.

"You wouldn't mind us taking a look round the house then?" Walter asked.

His eyes, still darting from one officer to another, Patrick objected profoundly. "You certainly cannot go charging through my house. Not without a search warrant."

Mary interrupted. "What exactly are you looking for detective?"

Patrick growled through his teeth, "You keep out of this woman."

Without looking at her husband, Mary waited for an answer.

"Oh, anything that could lead us nearer to the truth. Clothes for instance. The person on the beach would surely bring home some evidence."

Patrick smirked as the detective spoke to Mary. He was smart getting rid of the clothes.

"The clothes he wore were collected by the cleaners this morning. He dropped them in the bath last night and they were sodden through."

Walter shook his head wearily, "Charming," he murmured.

At this point, the kitchen door was pushed open and Frank appeared. "I've heard everything and I think I should hear the rest."

Intending to usher him back though the kitchen, P.C. Rintoul laid his hand on Frank's arm. Walter intervened. "Let him stay, I'll be talking to them all before I go anyway."

Turning his attention back to Mary, Walter enquired, "Which cleaners collected the clothes?"

"Whites of Liberton," Mary replied. "They bring them back tomorrow."

"Get on the blower and see if the cleaning has been done yet," Walter instructed the P.C.

There's no need for that, Frank interrupted, "I have his shoes and I saw him coming up the lane from the beach last night." He stared Patrick in the eyes as he spoke.

"You little bastard," Patrick hissed. "You've always been a little bastard."

Frank, still his attention fully on Patrick answered, "Oh well now, as I see it, there's more than one bastard in this family now."

"Frank!" Mary cried. "Enough! I can't stand this." She broke into uncontrollable sobs.

Detective Galloway led Mary into the kitchen where Tony and Allan sat ashen faced. "Sit there a minute." He lowered Mary gently onto the chair. "One of you boys, make your mother a cup of tea!"

"Oh God," cried Mary, "tea is not the answer to this. This is awful! I'll never be able to show my face outside again." Allan pulled his chair over beside his mother's and hugged her tight.

Frank returned from his room carrying his father's shale-caked shoes.

This brought a smile of delight onto Walter's face and a hateful dark look onto Patrick's.

"Bloody Judas," he screamed at Frank. "My ain doin' me in."

"Naw," Frank answered sarcastically, "You let me known often that I wasn't yours, so I feel no guilt. An' besides, my Mother has suffered enough at your hands but you have no hold anymore. I hope you're put away for years."

"Take him away," Walter ordered Detective Galloway. "I have a few more things to do here." Galloway cuffed Patrick and hesitated.

"Go on then, take him to the car. I'll just be a minute. We will read him his rights at the station when he's formally charged."

Walter sat down beside Mary and gently laid his arm around her shoulder. Looking at her sons, he inquired. "Is there someone who could be with her? A sister or neighbour?"

"Tony, go across 'n fetch Cissie. Tell her our Mother needs her right away." Frank instructed. Without hesitation, the young lad ran out of the back door.

Mary turned her tear stained face towards Walter, "I have been married all this time to a bigamist." She tried to control her sobbing. "He told me nothing of his past you know. And that poor poor woman he was, I mean is married to. I can't believe he got away with that so long." Her sobbing eased.

"What will happen now?"

Walter took her hand and looked into her red tear stained eyes. "Now look. Mary is it?" he smiled. "You have nothing to be ashamed of. Do you hear?"

She nodded her head. "What's goin' to happen to him?" she asked.

"He will be charged with grievous bodily harm. That is if we prove it. His shoes and the fact he was seen running from the lane will help, also Mr McTaggart's statement will help."

"Has he come round yet?" Concern etched her face. "That poor man."

"He came round late this afternoon. He's a strong man but he will take a while to recover."

"What about the bigamy thing. What will happen?"

"That will not be dealt with at this stage, but after we convict him on the first charge, that will follow. We will need your marriage certificate and birth certificates, but that will keep for now."

"Are you ready for that strong cup o' tea now Ma?" Frank asked, the tears not far from his own eyes.

"Aye son, Cissie will need one when we tell her what's happened," Mary said. "Oh dear, what will she say about this." The thought of Cissie never ceased to bring a slight smile to her face.

"Come on Auntie Cissie, hurry," urged Tony.

"What's awe the rush laddie? You'd think the hoose wis on fire."

"Ma Mother needs you right away. There's polis and everybody in oor hoose, and ma Da's been taken away with a polis man."

Wobbling hurriedly through to the hall, Cissie threw on her old brown coat. "O' michty me, what's this awe aboot." Resting one hand on the bottom of the banister, she called up to her husband, "'Am away across the road faither, a dinnae ken when I'll be back."

"Right ma hen," came the reply.

Grabbing the excited boy by the arm, she practically pushed him towards the door. "Come away then till a see whit's the matter."

"The polis has Da's shoes, and our Frank says we're awe' bastards," Tony blurted out as he whisked Cissie down the path, her whole body wobbling like a jelly.

Puffing, she reached the gate when she became aware of the police car sitting outside Mary's door. She could see two uniformed men in the front and the figures of two ordinary dressed men in the back.

"That's me Da' in the back, see? They're waitin' on the other detective inside the hoose. Come on Cissie, hurry."

Hardly daring to take a better look, Cissie averted her gaze as she hurried over the road and round the car.

"Michty me laddie, 'am fair oot o' puff," she gasped for breath. "Go an' open the door fur auld Cissie 'till a catch ma' breath."

Noticing two other neighbours standing at the corner, taking in the scene, Cissie raged. Muttering under her breath she commented. "Away an' mind yer ain damn business, you nosey auld buggers." Then to herself she muttered, "You Bessie Broon, you could talk under bloody water."

As she entered the kitchen, Cissie noticed Walter, who still sat, his arm supporting Mary. Frank was sitting head in hands at the other side of the room while Allan stood at the cooker pouring the hot water from the kettle to the pot.

On seeing her old friend, Mary felt comforted.

"What's on the nicht then." Cissie enquired. "What's awe this aboot shoes and bastards."

"Awe Tony, you couldn't keep your mouth shut. Not for a second." Allan spoke in dismay.

"Well, was I no' supposed tae be telt what was wrong?" Cissie jumped to Tony's defence. "In ony case, a didnae' make much sense o' what he was sayin', so could some boady tell me whit's goin' oan?"

Patting Mary gently on the hand, Walter Taylor reassured her, "It will be alright. You'll come through this." Then turning to Cissie he said, "She needs all your support. She'll tell you about it." Then focusing on Frank he added, "Will you make a statement at the station later?"

"Aye" he answered in a whisper, I'll come in tomorrow if that's all right with you.

"Good," remarked Walter, then rising he said, "See you all later."

The other boys followed Walter and Frank through into the hall and retired to their bedrooms.

Alone in the kitchen, the two women sat in silence, Mary, turning her wedding ring round and round on her finger. Observing her friend's nervous gesture, Cissie stretched over cupping her hand over Mary's.

"What's happened luv. What's he gone an' done noo?"

Lifting her tear-streaked face, Mary looked into Cissie's soft kind face. "He's the one that battered the man on the beach Cissie."

"Oh michty me," gasped Cissie, her hand shooting up to her mouth in horror.

"If that's not enough," she rubbed her fingers across her brow, "he married me when he already had a wife."

Cissie's mouth opened and shut emphasising her large pendulous triple chins, but for once in her life she was speechless.

"Fancy that for a laugh," Mary added giving a forced laugh, then with a shake of her head she added, "Thank God my Mother's not here to see this. She saw through him from the start. She said he was a sheep in wolf's clothing once, and she was right." Pleading, she stared at Cissie. "What am I to do now? How can I face folk after he near killed that man Cissie?"

Cissie sat down on the chair the detective had vacated, and pulled Mary to her. "There, there lass, this is terrible richt enough, but it's got bugger all tae dae wi' you. You didnae ken aboot ony o' this, so yer no' accountable fer onything he does. Now are ye?"

"Oh Cissie. Living with a man awe them years and thinking I was married."

"Awe well lass, your no' tae blame fer that either, and just think a meenit, if he's no' wed tae ye, well, he's nothin' tae dae wi ye. You are a free person an' can dae as you like. As I see it, you've been saved frae a maist awful life."

Wiping her eyes and sniffing a few times, Mary sat straight. "I suppose your right Cissie. Oh but this is awful. Supposing the man dies? He'll be charged with his murder." Renewed horror reshaped her face.

"Noo!" Cissie barked, "weel hiv nane o' that. The man will no' dee. Noo, a want you tae keep calm an' tell me exactly whit happened here."

Chapter Fourteen

Patrick stood in the dock looking pale and withdrawn as one by one the witnesses gave their evidence. Freddy the barman testified as to the time Patrick left the bar while Mary was called to identify the bag of soiled clothing the detectives managed to retrieve from the dry cleaners. The shoes were another factor in the case along with Frank's statement. Jock McTaggart related his story to the court and naturally he suggested that it was Patrick who frog marched him to the shore. The cards were well stacked against him. The court heard the story of Patrick's first wife and of how he allegedly left her in the state she was now in. Patrick's lawyer objected to this allegation and although it was to be struck from the record, the jurors could not erase it from their minds. He was sentenced to five years for grievous bodily harm and at a later trial, he pleaded guilty to bigamy and received an additional two years on to his sentence.

Musselburgh Town was busy as the late Christmas shoppers searched for last minute presents. Mary was no exception. Although she had done the bulk of her shopping, she still had odd bits and pieces to buy.

With her bag over her shoulder and three plastic carriers weighing her down, she headed towards the bus stop. As she approached the chemist, she stopped to look in its brightly lit window at their wonderful display of perfumes. As she glanced from one coloured foil box to another, she gave a slight sigh. She would dearly like to treat herself, but she just could not afford such luxuries. She had the boys to think of now and as Patrick was no longer part of her life, she had to manage on her own. At this time of year she had not done too badly as there was the odd catering job due to the Christmas festivities.

Turning sharply away from the window, her body collided with a man who made to enter the shop. As her bags she was carrying connected with his body, the smaller of the three snapped at the handle, sending oranges and apples flying all over the pavement. Crimson with embarrassment, Mary could hardly look the man in the face, her muffled apology almost lost as she clambered after the spilled fruit. Bent awkwardly on her hunkers, she became aware of the man's powerful hand resting on her arm, he too crouched in a similar position. Panic gripped her as she felt his hold grow stronger. Her eyes darted up towards him in utter disapproval, only to soften when recognising the smiling face. With eyes that creased with prominent laughter lines, the strong wide jawbone revealed a slight dimple. Distinguished grey side burns against his rugged looks almost made Mary gasp. Although in his mid forties, Detective Walter Taylor was still a handsome devil of a man.

"Oh Detective Taylor", Mary blushed. She felt her face and neck burn as if on fire. Wrapped up well against the cold chill, she suddenly felt the need to open her coat, as the warmth of her body was so unreal.

Helping her to her feet, Walter relieved her of the torn bag.

"I'm so sorry Mary, I wasn't looking where I was going."

"No," Mary insisted, "It was all my fault. It's me that should be sorry. Really."

"Well then, never mind who's fault it was, it's really nice to bump into you. Excuse the pun."

"Aye well, bump is the operative word right enough." Walter joined her in laughter.

"It's nice to see you all the same Mary." Looking into her laughing eyes, Walter thought how lovely she looked, then on impulse he asked, "You're not in a hurry are you?"

Before she could answer, he once again took her by the arm.

"Come on, put your things in the car and I'll take you for a coffee." Leading her a few yards up the road, they came to Walter's parked car. Taking Mary's bags, he laid them in the trunk.

"I was going for that bus," Mary protested weakly.

"Never mind the bus. I'll run you home after we have had a chat. Come on then." Taking her by the hand, he led her over the road. As his big warm hand gripped hers she was overcome with excitement. She felt so safe as he weaved in and round the slow moving traffic.

The homely little coffee shop had been busy all day with exhausted last minute shoppers. Mary and Walter were lucky enough to arrive, as a couple were about to vacate a small table for two.

"Well that was a piece of luck," Mary remarked. "I looked in here earlier and couldn't get a seat."

"Ah, you see Mary, stick with me and you'll get the best seats."

They ordered coffee for two and while Mary wanted nothing to eat, Walter ordered himself a jam doughnut. "Well then, what have you been doing with yourself these days?"

"Nothing very exciting. I think I've had all the excitement I need in my lifetime."

"I understand what you mean, but life goes on. There are other kinds of excitement you know."

Diverting her eyes from his gaze, Mary ignored his remark.

Noticing discomfort, Walter spoke more cheerily, "Well then, what have you planned for Christmas?"

"Nothing out of the ordinary. I'll be cooking for the boys, oh aye, and Allan's bringing his girl friend for dinner," she frowned mockingly.

"He's serious then?"

"Well, I think he's pretty serious." A warm smile shaped her lips.

"Enough of my plans, what are you doing?"

He thought how radiant she looked, her blonde hair piled on top of her head allowing a few stray strands to fall gently down onto her face. The difference in her since last they met was extraordinary. Cheeks tinted pink gave her face a warm glow, a glow of radiance.

As Mary waited on an answer, Walter's mind seemed to be elsewhere. "Walter," she said, breaking into his thoughts.

"Oh sorry, I was thinking of something else. What was it you said?"

"What are you doing at Christmas?"

"Working I'm afraid."

"On Christmas day?"

"Villains don't take time off for Christmas, I'm afraid. Anyway, Christmas on your own can be a bit of a drag."

Mary looked at him with concerned eyes, "You're on your own? Haven't you any family then?"

"Oh yes, I have family. Two sisters. To be exact, two married sisters with husbands and kids. Six between them." He smiled as he recalled their faces. "Favourite uncle I am."

"And your parents?"

"My Father died when I was fourteen and Mother died with a broken heart six months later. Our Catherine, she was twenty at the time, became the head of the family. Married late in life as she put every thing on hold for my younger sister, Fay and I. Fay's married to a policeman; an old mate of mine. Kate, as we call Catherine, married a farmer she met when visiting the Highland show. We don't half torment her about it. We say her husband went to the show to buy a heifer and came back with her instead." The lines round his dark eyes crinkled with laughter.

"That's cruel," Mary smiled. "I would thump you if I were her."

"Oh don't you worry, she does. And you know you've been thumped. She's built like, like.," he thought of a comparison, "like your friend, the big wife."

"You mean Cissie?"

"Aye. Well that's our Kate."

"Well don't you go to your sisters at Christmas?"

"Aye, I usually do, and I'm always made welcome. George and Kate live down at Selkirk and Fay and her husband are just in Edinburgh, but as I'm working to six, there's no use going at that time."

Walter's easy manner, made Mary feel she had known him all her life. She was so relaxed in his company that her next question was out before she could think.

"Would you like to join us at Christmas for tea?"

Smiling broadly, he said nothing for a few moments.

Mary felt her face flush with embarrassment. She bit her bottom lip as she waited for his rejection.

"Mary, I would really like to come for tea, but, will your boys not mind?"

Smiling and in hurried anxiousness she added, "No, not at all, anyway, you'll be coming as my guest. You will make a change from all the waifs and strays the boys bring home."

Walter frowned.

Mary added quickly, "Oh. I didn't mean you were…"

Catching her waving hand in his, he reassured her, "Mary, I know what you mean. I'm only teasing you." As his gaze met hers he realised she felt embarrassed. He glanced at his watch. "Come on then. If you fancy a lift home we better be making tracks."

The conversation on the way home was light and at no time was Patrick's name mentioned. It was seven months since he was sent to prison, and as far as Mary was concerned, she wanted nothing more to do with him.

Centred in the middle of the room, Mary's table, extended to its full length, groaned with food. Seven colourful place mats, a cracker, serviette tucked inside each wine glass, reserved the places for Mary, her sons, Cissie, Robbie and Allan's girlfriend, whom Mary had still to meet.

Allan had left a few hours ago to fetch Annetta Francittie, whom he had met at a party a few months previous. Frank watched television while Tony's attention was taken up in a book. Meanwhile their mother fussed round the table making sure it look as good as she could get it.

The huge turkey was cooling in the kitchen and Mary had just lit the gas under the vegetables. Cissie would be here any minute and Allan was warned to be no later than three o'clock.

The back door opened and Cissie's voice was heard, "Oh michty me Robbie, what a rare smell. My, wid ye look at the size o' that bird. It could almaist fit intae ma auld coat." She laid a plastic carrier bag, containing a few cans of beer on the kitchen table before following her husband into the living room.

Mary went forward to help Robbie who struggled to walk. "Come on Robbie, sit down at the fire here." Giving Tony a nod, she said, "Shift Tony. Do I have tae tell you?"

"Sorry Ma," the lad said. His attention now on Cissie he chirped, "Hallo Auntie Cissie. Did you like yer present a gave you?"

Pulling a white lace handkerchief from her cuff, she smiled, "Aye it's braw. See, a have it under ma' sleeve. Thank ye very much laddie. It's jist what auld Cissie needs fur her cauld."

A look of horror spread across his face as he gulped, "It's no' for blowin' yer nose wi Auntie Cissie, it's jist for show."

Suppressing her laughter, Cissie teased, "Oh sure a ken that. I wis jist havin' you oan laddie." Winking at Mary, she struggled to get free of her coat. Her attention now turned to the set table. "Oh what a braw spread Mary. My, you've fairly surpassed yersel' this year lass."

"Have to Cissie, It's not every day you meet your son's girlfriend."

"Oh well, you've nae need tae fear, you could entertain royalty nae bother."

"Here Cissie, you sit over there." She led her old friend to the other side of the fire. "Toast your toes down there before the dinner." Turning now to Frank, Mary suggested. "Get a drink for them son, they need thawed out."

"What's you tipple auntie Cissie?" Frank asked smiling broadly.

"A wee whisky son, an' put plenty lemonade in it." She demonstrated the measure using her thumb and index finger.

"An you Rob, what will you have?"

"A can o' pale ale is what a will have son."

Frowning, Frank added, "Lager or heavy is what's on offer uncle Rob."

"A ken fine ye would say that, so I've come well prepared. The bag in the kitchen has ma' cans."

Giving Frank a playful slap, Mary said, "Don't you listen to him Robbie, there's plenty pale ale there for you."

Frank playfully grabbed his mother round her waist and squeezed. Mary laughing hit her foolish son on the head. "You're not too big to be belted you know our Frank. Stop your nonsense and get the drinks."

"Awe Mary lass, it's rare tae see fun in the hoose. An' you lookin' sae happy."

Mary seated Cissie, Robbie and Tony at the table. Frank ladled the soup into the plates. Looking once again at her watch, Mary's became slightly agitated. "I told him three o'clock."

"It's only ten past Mary, an' besides, the buses are runnin' Sunday service, it bein' a holiday. Question how long he's tae wait oan a bus." Cissie informed her.

At that, the front door opened. With a quick glance towards Cissie, Mary patted the side of her hair with her hands before straightening her frilly tea apron, a present from young Tony.

A grim faced Allan walked into the room. Acknowledging Cissie and Robbie with a silent nod, he then removed his jacket.

"Where is she then son?" Mary asked cautiously, sensing the disappointment he was feeling.

"She's not coming."

All eyes fell upon him as they silently waited for an explanation.

"Soups up," Frank called as he carried two bowls from the kitchen. "Well kid, you're just in time," he remarked seeing Allan take his seat. "Where's the bird then?" he asked noticing he was on his own.

"The only bird here is the one we're aboot tae eat," Tony remarked insensitively.

Mary's eyes darted across to her youngest son. Her dark look was enough to caution him.

Seeing his mother's reaction, Allan shrugged. "It's all right Ma, we're still together and all that, it's just difficult for her to get away." Forcing a smile, Tony's remark was directed at Frank. "Well it's good to see him working for a change."

Cissie stretched over and touched Allan's hand, "Eh lad, lets hiv a nice day. It's no' the end o' the wurld, there will be ither times."

With a heavy heart, he managed a cheery smile, "Aye Cissie, you're right." Shrugging his shoulders, he looked at them all in turn, "Come on then, the soup will be gettin' cold. I'm alright, I really am."

The chat round the table was pleasant and entertaining as Frank encouraged Cissie with light hearted banter. Allan, although joining the laughter was not his usual cheery self. Mary knew her son was hurting and there was nothing she could do about it. This made it difficult for her to tell them all her news. She had waited for the right moment but was now beginning to feel as if it would never come.

The meal over, they still sat round the table finishing off their drinks and nibbling at the little chocolate mints. "You'll be able to come with me to Cambell's tonight then brother," Frank remarked to Allan, referring to one of his married friends.

"Why, what's on over there?"

"He's having a few mates over, you know, the usual thing. A couple o' cans and a laugh."

"A don't think so. I'd rather stay here." A look of sadness filled his eyes.

"Oh aye. Do you think she'll call round then?" teased Frank. "Come on man, come and have some fun," he urged.

"Naw, I *said* I'm staying in," A trace of annoyance showing in his tone.

"Well now, you two can do what you like," interrupted Mary, "but I have another guest calling in for tea."

"Oh aye, an' wha's this guest?" asked Cissie. "You haven't let oan tae me."

"It's Santa Clause," Tony sniggered at Cissie.

"wheesht," Cissie reprimanded Tony lightly.

The nerves in Mary's stomach quivered. Tracing her tongue round her dry lips she spoke in a nonchalant manner, "I bumped into Walter Taylor yesterday, and eh... I invited him over."

The boys looked from one to another in silent astonishment. Cissie turned and nodded to Rob. "Did you hear that faither, Mary's finally gettin' a life."

Getting to her feet, Mary was about to clear the table.

"Ma, leave that a second and explain tae me why you invited him *here*." Frank's attitude was apparent. He spoke like a jealous husband.

The expression on Mary's face changed from apprehension to anger. "Are you telling *me*," she prodded her chest in a furious manner, "*me*...who I can ask and who I can't ask into my own house? Look, the lot of you." She traced her three sons with her finger, "I have been told all my *life* what I *should* do and what I *shouldn't* do, and it's *over*. Do you hear? It's *over*. If *you* want to go out, then you do that Frank, but *don't tell me* what *I* should do."

Now standing next to Mary, Cissie rested a hand on her friend's shoulder. "Come on Mary, the lad's only concerned."

Frank looked on in astonishment, he had not expected the reaction he had witnessed and a feeling of shame engulfed him. Rising he went to Mary and pulled her into his arms. "Oh I'm sorry Ma. I didn't mean to upset you. You've been through enough." As he felt his mother's body tremble, it became apparent to him that she was fighting to keep control of her emotions. He had really upset her and now she struggled to keep from breaking down in tears.

Pulling from him, Mary straightened her small apron and without looking him in the face, said in a forced calmness, "Look at us, and on Christmas day an all." Gathering up the plates once more, she headed for the kitchen.

Cissie shook her head in dismay at Frank before lifting a few things from the table and following Mary through, flicking the kitchen door closed with her foot as she went in.

Rob's attention focused on the younger son who watched the situation nervously. "You've no' let me see this train set yer Ma' bocht ye yet son."

The thirteen year old's face changed, almost glad of the diversion. "Uncle Rob, it's no' a train set," he giggled, "it's a scalectrix."

Rob frowned with a puzzled expression.

"Racing cars uncle Rob." Jumping from his chair, Tony pulled at the old man's arm. "Come on then, I'll help you up the stairs and give you a game."

Tottering behind the enthusiastic lad, Rob, puffing and panting, followed him up the stairs leaving Frank and Allan alone in the living room.

Leaning his elbow on the table, Allan spoke critically "That wasn't very smart then big brother, was it?"

An ambiguous expression shaped Franks lips. "Now then, don't tell me you weren't as surprised as I was."

"Aye a was Frank, but not in the same way as you. She's got to get a life you know, and if she wants to invite a man to the house, well, as she said, it's up to her."

"I know that," he said slightly irritated. "It was just out of the blue that's all; Look! I've said I was sorry, so let it go will you!"

Allan answered with a grunt staring at his older brother, trying to figure him out.

"What's this with your girl then?" Frank asked with genuine concern.

Allan's lips tightened, then with a sigh he relaxed back in his chair. "There's nothing wrong with us, it's her bloody parents man. There was hell to pay when she tried to leave for here. They accused her of disloyalty to the family and all that crap."

"Well mate, families can be funny. They usually like to have all the tribe round the table at Christmas. Just like in here. Ma wouldn't have liked it if we went somewhere else for dinner."

"It wouldn't have stopped me if I had somewhere else to go," Allan remarked.

A mocking laugh came from Frank's throat, "Well why didn't you have Christmas with the girl then?" He thumbed towards the kitchen door. "You were scared to upset her, that's why."

Annoyance flashed across Allan's face, "Nothing of the sort." Rejection evident in his voice, "I was never asked. Not being an Italian an all that."

"She's Italian then?"

Allan nodded.

"A' bloody thought so with a name like Francittie." Whistling through his teeth, he teased. "A chip a-shop an' ice a-de-cream parlour an' all?" he asked in broken English.

"You're bloody daft our Frank. Not all Italians are chippies. Mind you, her uncle in Glasgow has one." A silent look passed between them, followed by hearty laughter.

Cissie came back into the living room carrying a large tray. "Crackin' jokes noo, are we," she smiled in approval while filling the tray with leftovers from the table. Noticing Rob and Tony's absence, she lifted her eyes towards the ceiling, "A see he's commandeered the auld man. Aye weel, he'll enjoy that." Then looking back towards the kitchen door, making sure she was not followed through, she said quietly, "She's awe richt noo, so keep it like that." The look she gave Frank was a definite warning, then her tone of voice changed once more to the bright and breezy Cissie, "come away then you twa, the quicker the table's cleared the quicker we git a game o' cairds goin', so get yer coppers oot o' yer pockets ready fur auld Cissie tae take from ye."

"Oh Cissie, for goodness sake, don't mention coppers," Frank joked half-heartedly.

The nerves in Mary's stomach seemed to have started their own celebrations, although on the outside she seemed calm and unconcerned. The day had gone well so far, apart from the scene at the end of the meal. Allan, in spite of his disappointment, had managed to laugh and relax with the family. Cissie as usual, created lots of laughter with her wit and sense of humour.

It was now half past six, and there was no sign of Walter. The knot in Mary's chest grew tighter. She wished she hadn't mentioned Walter to the family as it was becoming obvious to everyone he wasn't coming. No one mentioned him, as if they wanted to spare her embarrassment.

"Well Cissie, I think we better set the table for tea. It's almost twenty to seven an' the lads will be going out shortly."

Frank glanced over, catching Allan's attention. "Ma," Allan said gently, "I know how you feel, remember it also happened to me."

"Don't talk stupid our Allan. It was only a casual invite. I'm not fussy if it wasn't taken up." She laughed nervously. "Come on you three, rise from your hint ends and set the table." Seeing Cissie about to rise, she laid her hand firmly on her shoulder, "You sit where you are, as it's about time the boys did something for a change."

"I like that," Frank remarked. "Who helped serve the dinner eh?"

By nine o'clock, Cissie led Rob, a little unsure on his feet than normal, back over the road. Frank had gone to join his friends while Allan left to phone his girl from the public phone box, saying he might not be back 'till late. The youngest boy retired to his bedroom to catch up on his reading, as he had been given a good few books as presents.

Mary curled herself up on the chair in front of the television, and although she watched the screen, her mind was not on the programme. She was thinking of Walter and how foolish she had been. Reflecting on yesterday, she was aware that it was herself that did the asking and flushed at her boldness. Had he accepted to save her embarrassment? Full of mixed emotions, she felt sorry for herself, but try as she did to put him out of her mind, he just would not go.

The knock at the door brought Mary to her feet. Allan, she thought, he's forgotten his key. Opening the door slightly, her heart quickened. She stood holding on to the side of the door not knowing what to say.

There, Walter Taylor stood, his dark handsome eyes flashing in uncertainty. Although his hair was slightly receding at the front and his sideburns slightly tinged with grey, dark wavy hair was still very evident. "Mary, I'm terribly sorry." Walter looked up at her from the bottom step.

She stood motionless except for a few rapid blinks of her eyelids.

"Aren't I welcome then?"

"Well," she stammered, "I, eh, I." Opening the door she gathered her composure. "Aye, well come on in, but there's only the bairn and myself here now. Everyone else has gone."

Leading the way into the house, Mary felt unsure that she was doing the right thing. Pointing to the sofa she invited him to sit down. Easing his broad manly frame on to the sofa, he undid the buttons of his black wool overcoat as he did so.

"Mary, this is the drawback of the job. I was called out on a case and was delayed. I really am sorry."

Embarrassed at the nervous laugh that came from her own throat, Mary diverted her gaze. "Oh well, I understand. Think nothing of it."

"You'll have to get yourself a phone you know, I could have got in touch if you had one."

"Oh well, I'll have to order one after the holiday," she said quite sarcastically.

Realising he had just said something quite embarrassing, he fumbled inside his pocket, drawing out a neatly wrapped present. "This isn't much as I had no time to shop, but please accept it."

Mary flushed as she reluctantly took the small parcel from him. "You didn't need to do this," she gazed into his handsome face.

"I know, but I wanted to."

Slowly and slightly flustered, Mary undid the paper. Opening the small maroon velvet box, she blinked at its contents. A gold pin with a single pearl in the centre attached itself to the satin lining.

"But this is too much Walter. You should…"

Walter interrupted, "Mary, accept it will you, and change the subject," he smiled. "Come on and get me that much wanted cup of tea."

Clicking the box shut, she laid it on the mantelshelf. "Of course Walter, take your coat off and I'll make some sandwiches."

Drawing a nest of tables forward, Mary set out chicken sandwiches and cake. In no time they were enjoying each other's company in front of the fire.

At eleven o' clock, Walter rose to leave, and although Mary was sad to see him go, she felt a slight relief. She did not want the boys to come in and find her alone with him, not after they thought he had let her down. She would rather explain to them in his absence. As she led him towards the door, he stopped and turned in his tracks.

Mary's heart missed a beat as their bodies touched momentarily.

"Can I take you somewhere tomorrow night Mary?" Smiling he added, "This time I shan't be late. I'm off all day."

She felt her legs go week. The fresh smell of his after-shave filled her nostrils. What if he kissed her? "Well, I suppose you could," she answered with feigned reluctance. "Where were you thinking of going?"

"Oh leave that to me." He looked down at her as if unsure as to what to do. Hesitating, he then turned and walked to the door. "Thanks for a nice evening." Turning on the top step, he laid his finger under her chin. "Right, see you tomorrow." Winking mischievously, he turned up his collar and walked to his car. Mary watched until he was out of sight, disappointed that he made no attempt to kiss her.

Closing the door behind her, she leaned her back against it, dreaming of his touch. Arms crossed over her breasts, she stood with closed eyes imagining her own arms were his.

"What are you standing like that for Ma?"

Startled, she jumped back to reality, flushing as she did. Tony peered over the banister, a cheeky grin on his face.

"Yer no' goin' barmy are ye?"

With a sigh, she reached up as she passed, gently slapping him on the cheek, "No, I'm no' goin' barmy, but I will if you don't get your clothes off and get into bed."

Annetta Francittie, a very beautiful raven-haired girl with eyes that could melt the hardest of hearts, was her father Mario's pride and joy. Heads turned as she passed, men with admiration, women with envy. Straight backed, she carried herself with confidence giving her the look of a catwalk model. The best of clothes draped a figure women would die for. Well educated and a first year student at Aberdeen, he had great plans for his daughter, and Allan Sweeny, a mere panel beater, was not included in those plans.

Mario Francittie and his brother Stephanio were joint owners of the family leather factory in Italy, while Mario also had two warehouses, one in Edinburgh and the other in Glasgow. He had become a very wealthy man and hoped that his son, along with any grandsons he may be blessed with, would take over the firm.

Although her mother had taken a liking to Allan, her father had not.

When the time came, his daughter was marrying another Italian, he would make sure of that! In the meantime, he was as civil as he possibly could to her young man, knowing full well she would soon outgrow him.

As Allan left the phone box, his heart felt lighter. Annetta had been praying he would call, as her twin brother Albert had colluded with her, offering to drive her into Musselburgh where she would meet Allan.

He told his father he was taking her with him to meet his friends. As there were no buses running, it being Christmas night, Allan began walking the four miles into Musselburgh.

Reaching their destination, Albert realised his sister would most likely be hanging round for sometime waiting on Allan, so he drove down the coastal road until Allan came into sight. Picking him up, he then dropped the couple off at the Trotters Hotel, arranging to collect them later.

The atmosphere in the lounge bar was electrifying. Amidst the tinsel and the decorations, the crowd were well into the Christmas spirit. Laughter and light-heartedness swelled the smoke filled air. An accordionist and a fiddler, dressed in full highland dress, had downed their instruments as they swilled back their well-earned pints.

Annetta and Allan stood at the entrance of the lounge, scanning the room for a seat. As usual, Annetta's presence in the frame of the doorway attracted attention. "Looks pretty full, I doubt if there's any seats," she remarked disappointedly.

A voice from the window seats called over, "Come on luv, sit yourselves down here." The middle-aged woman squeezed against her partner making him move along, forcing a chain reaction on the other four bodies spread out along the seat.

"There now," she smiled as Annetta sat down, "Plenty room for you and your man."

Allan returned from the bar placing a vodka and coke in front of his girl, nodding his thanks to the woman.

Sitting alongside Annetta, he gave her arm a tender squeeze. He said nothing but the look in his eyes spoke volumes. It was Annetta who spoke first. With a weary sigh, she shook her head sadly. "I'm sorry about today Allan, they just went berserk when I tried to leave. I knew that would happen. I just knew."

His arm slid along the back of the seat resting on her shoulder, "it's alright. Honest, I understand."

"No you don't Allan. They, they are so domineering, well; it's my Father really. She's not too bad...It's him!"

"He just wanted you all together for Christmas, that's perfectly understandable."

"That's not the case and you know it. He made no objection last week when I said I would not be there for Christmas dinner. No, he had to wait until this morning. It was awful, and to crown it, he had invited the Macari's. Neither he nor Mother mentioned that!" Her hand spread across her forehead, she shook her dark head in despair. "I know what he's trying to do, don't you see. He's trying to push Vincent Macari and me together."

Allan, slightly alarmed widened his eyes. "You're not serious?"

She gave a small disgusted laugh, "I know him. Believe me, it clicked right away. The poor guy twigged as well. How bloody embarrassing."

Allan chewed on his bottom lip. "I'm not good enough for you in his eyes, but believe you me, I'm going to have my own place one of them days. I don't intend working and making someone else rich."

"I know that Allan, but that's not what it's about. I don't care about money."

His mouth opened in disbelief, "Awe, come on pet, you're used to money. You don't know what it's like to go without, so how can you say that?"

Annoyed, she snapped, "Have you gone without Allan? I mean, really gone without? Have you ever felt your belly pain with hunger?"

"Naw, at least I don't think I have, but I can tell you this, my Mother's struggled to make ends meet many a time."

"Then you're all the better for the experience. You see Allan, people with money lead very shallow, and frivolous lives. Just like Marie Antoinette when she said, 'let them eat cake.'"

"Eh?" he responded, screwing up his face.

"The French Revolution!" she prompted, but still the clueless expression remained on his face. " Oh never mind Allan, I'm talking nonsense."

"Naw Annetta, go on. You were trying to say money doesn't matter."

Patting his hand, she lowered her head. "I'm sorry Allan. I can be so stupid at times. Of course money matters, but it's not the main ingredient to a relationship. If you say it is, then you're no better than my father."

"Bloody hell, how is it we end up arguing all the time? What starts as a simple comment finishes up ..."

The musician squeezed a long loud note from his accordion that sounded like a command for attention, interrupting Allan as he spoke. The fiddler ran his bow down the strings, adding his recognition, then in unison, they rattled out a feet tapping tune, filling the ears of the patrons, as the reel caused a few 'yowps' and screams.

"Wid that no' fill yer he'rt wi' pride," Annetta's neighbour nudged.

Answering with a smile, she turned to Allan and grinned. "Not as much as you do. Come on, let's get into the swing of things and enjoy ourselves."

At midnight, Allan and Annetta stood huddled in the cellar doorway of the hotel waiting on Albert to turn up with the car. Shivering, she huddled closer into Allan. He had opened his overcoat and enfolded her inside. The warmth of his body filled her with a sense of security.

Sliding her hand inside his jacket and round to his back, the heat radiated through his crisp white shirt. Taking her other hand, she ran it slowly over his chest. Pulling her to him, he covered her lips with his. Kissing her hungrily he pulled her in closer, the tense overpowering emotion of love engulfing them. It was more than both of them could bear. The passion they felt was cooled by the blast of a horn. Drawing from him, she said dreamily, "Some day very soon Allan, I promise."

Chapter Fifteen

It was well into the afternoon before Frank emerged from his room. In the living room, Allan helped Tony piece together a jigsaw on top of the fold down card table while Mary worked happily in the kitchen. The television in the corner still blazed out Christmas greetings although it was now Boxing Day.

Rubbing his dark tousled hair and looking pathetic, Frank appeared alongside his mother. "Andrews salts Ma?" he asked feeling sorry for himself.

Mary took a long look at him as if in judgment, "Oh aye, and what state did you get home in?" Turning from him, she opened the wall cupboard, shifting a few containers around; she lifted out the welcomed tin. Thrusting it into her son's hands, she remarked, "I've no sympathy for you. I heard you at five this morning trying to mount the stairs quietly. You'd as well sounded the trumpet voluntary and let the rest of the street hear you."

Heaping the white powder from the tin into the glass, he then held it under the running water stirring vigorously. Effervescent bubbles leaped to life spitting and fizzing as they rushed to the rim of the tumbler. Lifting it to his mouth, he drank until all the liquid had disappeared down his throat. Still holding the empty glass, he belched loudly. With a disapproving shake of her head, his mother snatched the glass from her son's hand, slapping him on his broad shoulders as she did so.

The back door opened and in walked Cissie. "Oh michty, whit a sicht tae see my lad. You look awfu'."

"I feel as I look Aunty Cis. It was the last drink that went for me."

Laughing, Cissie caught the joke. "Awe a ken whit you mean, ma' auld man used tae say the same. It wisnae the ten he had in front mind ye, it wis always the last yin that did the damage."

"Cissie, you're encouraging him," Mary chided.

"Well, whit's wrong wi' a skin foo' at this time o' year?"

"Now yer talking Cis," remarked Frank. "Sit doon and I'll make you a brew," he joked half hearted.

Pushing her son towards the nearest wooden chair, Mary remarked, "Sit down yourself Frank, you're as much use as an ash tray on a motor bike."

Allan appeared in the doorway greeting Cissie with a huge grin. "Hi there auntie Cis," then addressing his mother he asked cheerily, "Any spare in the pot?"

"Plenty son. Would you like it here or through the living room?"

The voice from behind called, "Give 'im it through here Ma, he's busy...and get me some juice," Tony added.

Nodding his head in the direction of his young brother, Allan remarked, "nothing like havin' a servant."

Cissie observing the cheeriness of Allan and the perkiness of Mary, nodded her head to sum up a conclusion, "Hem," she murmured.

"Hemm, what?" Mary smiled catching her best friend's contented smile.

"Nought," answered Cissie, "I jist feel somethin' has happened here, particularly in that direction." Her gaze followed Allan as he disappeared into the other room.

"Your right as usual Cissie. I don't know how you don't take up fortune telling as you seem to know everything that takes place."

"Now, a would nae be ony guid tae onybody else, it's just you lot are like ma' very ain. A ken when onything's up, but mind you, it widnae take a great deal o' effort tae see the difference in him."

"Cissie, you deserve a coconut," Frank remarked. "Your observation is spot on see, he met up wi' the girl last night, and by the looks o' things, he scored."

Mary glanced at him with a look of disapproval, "You watch your tongue my lad, or I'll personally skelp your lug."

"What," Frank laughed half-heartedly. "What's wrong wi saying that."

"You know," snapped Mary. "You just watch yourself."

"Well, hark at her," Frank remarked to Cissie lifting his cup and walking into the living room.

"Honestly," Mary sighed, "he gets worse as he gets older."

Their old neighbour sipped her tea without taking her eyes from Mary as she waited to be told the latest bit of gossip.

"Aye your right Cissie, he is a lot cheerier. He met up with his lass. Seemingly she was ready to come here when her folks kicked up a stooshie."

"Puir wee soul." Cissie said sympathetically. "Still, 'am gled things are ok. Noo." There was a moment's silence between the two friends, as if there was more to be told. Cissie watched Mary from over the top of her glasses.

Mary knew she could not fool her for a second and thought, she knows, the old beggar knows. Clearing her throat she remarked casually, "Oh aye, and my friend turned up eventually. Seemingly he was kept late."

As if surprised, Cissie's eyes widened. "Really. And you in here oan yer ain."

"Don't be bloody stupid you old crow, you knew he was here. Didn't you?"

"Aye lass, I saw his car," he laughed.

"Not much passes you, you nosy old tinker."

With a lot of banter, Cissie listened as Mary told her of Walter's visit.

As Cissie and Mary chatted, Frank reappeared at the door of the kitchen. His face was solemn. Held in his hand was the maroon box Mary had left on the mantelpiece. "What's this then?" he enquired.

Mary's chair scraped on the floor as she hurriedly rose to retrieve the box. "That was given to me as a present. Give it here." She took it from her son's hand.

"Aye aye," Frank remarked. "Looks like more than our Allan scored last night."

Through gritted teeth, Mary seethed, "You have been warned Frank, I'll not have that sort of talk in this house. I had enough with Sweeny and I'm certainly not putting up with it from you."

"Well what other reason would a perfect stranger give a woman a gift like that? And another thing, why did he wait until we were all out before he called?"

"FRANK!" Cissie now on her feet, but to late to prevent Mary's hand connecting with her son's cheek.

Holding the side of his face, he looked down at his raging mother.

"How dare you insinuate that I would be anybody's for a stupid brooch. *HOW DARE YOU!* You have lived with insults and smug remarks so long that it seems to have rubbed off on you, so if you have no intelligence or respect, you had better find somewhere else to live as I certainly will not spend the rest of my life in the manner I have been accustomed to. The snide remarks and filthy talk is all in the past and there it will stay, so you'd better think on our Frank before you mark a path for yourself along that line." Mary shook with temper as she stared at her beloved son. She loved him so much, but at this moment in time, she did not like him at all. Frank either ran hot or cold, very seldom displaying a lukewarm temperament.

Turning from his mother, he calmly walked through the living room and out into the lobby.

Mary stood in silence until the slam of the bedroom door jolted her back into action. Her face still visibly angry, she sat down heavily in the seat.

Cissie, still standing, shook her head vigorously. "Now lass, he didnae' mean onything."

With a quick turn of her head, Mary looked straight up at her friend, "You Cissie would cover for that lad if he committed murder."

Cissie held her hand up in protest, "Noo Mary, a ken he's oot o' order, but ye cannae put him oot the hoose. Away up an' talk tae him."

"Listen to yourself Cissie," Mary said in disbelief. "You're taking his side. You heard him. Our Frank is getting as possessive as Patrick was."

"Aye, he's jealous richt enough. But it's his wey o' protecting ye."

Mary stared hard at Cissie, "I can't believe this. You know how I suffered through jealousy. Was that Patrick's way of protecting me too? Was it all right for him to be like that? Oh no Cissie, that'll be the day when I let a son of mine rule my life."

Allan had followed his brother up into the room and found him sitting on the edge of the bed. "Aye mate," he said cautiously, "You really did it this time."

Putting his head in his hands, and without glancing at his younger brother, he swore. "Bugger off Allan. I'm in no mood for your remarks."

Sitting on the small stool opposite, Allan retorted, "Oh aye then big brother, I have to put up with you and your remarks, but it's different when I say anything. Is that how it goes?"

Frank was silent, but the air between them was rapidly becoming unpleasant.

"Answer me big man," demanded Allan. "What gives you the right to order folk around," he goaded. "What gives you the bloody right to talk to our Mother in that way? *YOU!* You're supposed to love her an' awe that. What gives you the right to expect explanations from her?"

Still he gave no response. His head, still resting in his hands, moved from side to side.

"You're no better than our Da'," Allan spat out his words.

This injected life into Frank. His hands dropped onto his knees forming clenched fists, "He's- not- my- Da'," he growled. "He's yours, not mine."

"Well well! Do you think you're any better than him? Do you think you could treat a woman any better than he did, because by the way you behave, I don't think so? You look to me as if you would like to dominate us all. Rule with the iron fist an all that. Oh aye Frank, you're Frank the big man, Frank the laugh a minute, but you're pathetic, bloody pathetic!"

Raising his fist towards Allan, he stopped almost short of his brother's face.

Without flinching, Allan sat still. "Go on then. If it'll make you feel better, take a swipe, take a bloody swipe."

As Allan's expressionless face stared hard into his eyes, he seemed to crumble under his gaze. His hand went back up to his head and tugging his own hair; he spoke as if in torment. "Why. Why do I do it? Why do I want to hurt her, me and my stupid remarks?"

"I don't know brother, but you better get a grip or you're out! Let her get on with things. Be happy for her. You'd think she was flaunting her mutton round town the way you talk. For goodness sake, she has a guy that thinks she's worthy of a nice gift."

Frank looked at his brother suspiciously, "Aye Frank," he continued, "a Christmas gift, that's all it was. She would 'ave let you see it if you'd given her a chance."

"Me an' my bloody temper," he whispered remorsefully.

"Well brother, she's had enough of bad tempered men, enough to last her a lifetime, so get your bloody act together and give her space." Placing his hand on Frank's shoulder, he left it there until his brother lifted his head and made eye contact.

Frank grasped at the outstretched arm, frowning in shame.

Aware of Frank's presence in the doorway, Cissie and Mary stopped their chatter. Frank nodded slightly towards Cissie before moving towards his mother, then for the second time in two days, he hugged her unashamedly. They both stood swaying, entwined in that special love that often outweighs reason. Mary, although softened by her son's actions, broke free from his embrace, her composure and stubbornness returning, "I may as well tell you Frank, I'm going out with him tonight."

Holding his mother by the shoulders, Frank smiled weakly, "Aye," the look in his eyes pleaded for forgiveness. "You have a nice time Ma, and I ...I am so sorry..."

Placing her finger on his lips, the tension in her body relaxed, "Say no more, just let me live."

The excitement in Mary had built up all afternoon like an electric charger. She felt like a teenager about to embark on her first date. Extra time was spent on her hair and particular attention was paid to make up, using a little more than she normally did. Dressed in powder blue jersey wool, the plainness of the dress enhanced by a double row of tiny crystals, hair pinned back loosely with a few loose strands falling gently over her ears, she looked elegant and beautiful. She felt good and it showed. The radiance was within and it reflected in her countenance.

Her three sons were watching television in the living room when she appeared. Tony looked up first his mouth gaping at the sight before him. Allan gave a low whistle dropping the paper that lay on his lap.

"Well I never. Gee Ma, where have you been hiding yourself?"

Walking smartly past, she slapped the side of his head lightly, "Cheeky! Has any one seen ma' navy high heels?" Looking down over the side of the chair, she 'tutted'. Frank's gaze followed her, and as their eyes met he shook his head, then, with a smile he commented, "Ma, you look braw."

"It's easy seen I don't dress very often, you lot have forgotten what I look like. As a matter of fact, so did I," she laughed, then changing her tone to one of irritation, headed towards the hall. "Where did I put my bloomin' navy shoes?"

Allan answered the door and escorted Walter into the living room, calling up the stairs to his mother as he passed the staircase. The lad pointed towards the sofa, and Walter sat down. He was dressed very smartly in a black wool overcoat, immaculate white shirt collar displaying the knot of his blue striped tie. His shoes gleamed, polished to perfection.

Looking towards Frank, Walter greeted him with a friendly nod, "Frank."

"Um," came Frank's reply.

Walter, used to awkward moments took it all in his stride. His attention fell on Tony who sat silent, but who also watched with interest, "Well Tony, did you have a good Christmas?"

Blinking, Tony answered, "Aye, you asked me that last night."

Suppressing his smile, he sucked in his cheek, "Aye, so I did lad. So I did."

It was Allan who broke the ice, " Would you like a wee drink afore you go?"

"A well now, that's extremely generous o' you Allan, but I have the car outside. I better no' have one just yet."

"Where are you takin' our Ma?" asked Tony cheekily and without waiting for an answer, he added, "You should see her, awe man she's braw."

Once more Walter suppressed his smile, "I could well imagine she would be. She's a braw woman."

Sprawling in his chair, Frank scanned his mother's date from head to foot. Although they had encountered each other a good few times lately, albeit in the line of duty, he felt he was meeting this man for the first time, then as if he heard his mother's previous warning, he smiled pleasantly. "Well, where are you both off to," he asked, following up Tony's unanswered question.

Walter rested his huge hands on his knees, rubbing at the surface of his coat. "There's a party at the police club, I thought your Mother would like to meet some of the lads and their wives."

"Well," smiled Frank, "she'll be safe enough there."

Detecting slight sarcasm in Frank's voice, Walter studied him momentarily before answering. "Frank, there is no need to worry about your Mother, I like her a lot, in fact, I'm not one for taking women out, but your Mother's special and I respect her. She'll come to no harm with me. I can assure you of that." He knew the lad's concern for his mother and he respected him for it.

Flushed with embarrassment, Frank lowered his gaze. He was saved further embracement by the entrance of his mother. She walked in, carrying her good navy swagger. As Frank looked at her, his heart swelled with pride.

Walter turned round aware of her presence. Getting to his feet, he stepped to her side. "Well, I know who is going to put the rest of the females in the shade tonight. I will have to guard you closely in case someone else sweeps you of your feet," he teased.

"My, you're not too bad yourself," smiled Mary, no awkwardness in her voice. She felt so at ease with him. Turning to Frank, she gave her final instructions,

"Now remember, if you decide to go out, Cissie is willing to have him," she nodded in Tony's direction.

"I've no plans tonight," he informed her with a sigh.

"I would rather go to aunt Cissie's Ma," Tony pouted. "He gets bored wi' me an' sends me tae bed too early."

Mary's eyebrows raised, "Now don't you start now, or you'll go to bed quicker than that. And you Frank," her attention now on her eldest, "Have a bit o' patience with him."

A look of triumph spread across Tony's face, as he relished the thought of winding his brother up.

Helping with her coat, Walter immediately noticed his gift pinned to her lapel. He held the coat out as Mary wriggled in. Buttoning it up, she took a final look from one son to another, feeling strangely in control. As Walter led her to the door, she called back without turning, "Have a nice time Mother."

A chorus of voices called back in response, "Have a nice time Mother."

"Very civilized my lot." Mary remarked satirically.

The journey to the club alone was enjoyable, as the feeling of being wanted, especially by Walter, overwhelmed her. His whole attention was on her and she found his compliments sincere and very flattering. The feeling of being young again was magical. As she looked up into his handsome face, she had the desire to stretch out and touch it, for by doing so, this would reassure her that this was no dream.

Walter caught her dreamy expression as he too glanced down at her. "What's the matter?" he laughed softly.

Slightly embarrassed by her thoughts, Mary blushed, "Nothing really. I just can't believe I'm doing this."

"Doing what?" he asked with a puzzled expression.

"You know; going out on a date again after all these years."

"Ah," Walter smiled, "then you'll have forgotten what it feels like to have a man who really cares for you eh?"

Shaking her head, Mary added, "I suppose you say that to all your dates."

His attention went back to driving as he steered the car into a small lay-by and stopped, then, without switching off the engine, he turned to Mary, slid his arm behind her back drawing her to him. Looking into her eyes momentarily, he spoke softly, "You my dear, are the only woman I have wanted in years."

Mary's heart almost exploded as she felt his lips softly brush against hers. He gave her lips a few short kisses before resting his lips on hers, moving his head slowly and tenderly in meaningful passion. Her body swamped with desire, something she had forgotten existed. Drawing from her, Walter watched as she slowly opened her eyes. "All right?" he whispered.

Speechless, Mary nodded.

"Then I hope you understand that I intend to keep you, that is if you feel the same."

Blinking a few times, Mary nodded yet again. "I .. I do Walter. It's, it's just."

"Just what?" he questioned.

"Just sudden, that's all."

"Mary, these things happen you know. You have to grab at it when it does, and I don't intend letting you go. Now stop doubting me."

The cheeky twinkle in his eyes made her heart ache. "I hope you mean that," she said.

"I have never been so sure," he smiled lovingly.

Gently breaking free, he put the car into gear and edged his way back onto the road. Mary slid her arm under his, resting her head on his shoulder. "Happy?" Walter asked.

"I certainly am," she replied with feeling.

Walter's friends welcomed Mary with warm sincerity, giving her the feeling that she had known them for years. The slight feeling of apprehension she had felt in the foyer was quickly dispelled. The club itself impressed her, although fairly small, the low stage in the corner was spacious enough for the three-piece band. In the other corner a well stocked bar, glasses, mirrors sparkling to perfection, was run by a retired policeman, his wife and sister-in-law. The fact that everyone knew one another created a friendly, intimate atmosphere.

At each table, there were the appropriate number of party hats for the amount of chairs plus party poppers and crackers. Hundreds of balloons were suspended from the roof, held in place by a huge net, ready to be let down at an appointed time.

Fairy lights beneath the well-tinselled Christmas tree flashed off and on, and to the side of the tree, well-wrapped presents

227

filled a cardboard box ready to be presented the following day to the children at their annual Christmas party.

Mary felt at ease as Walter introduced her to three of his colleagues with pride. The usual comments that went with the slap on the back and the manly know it all winks from his male friends, were taken as they were meant; in good humour. Their wives finally prised Mary from Walter, leading her to the ladies rest room where they hung their coats on the hangers provided.

Fran, who had recently turned thirty, and declared it was the worst day of her life, was a remarkably pretty woman, well proportioned, and had the spirit of a spitfire. Sybil, who because of her pear shaped body, wore loose fitting dresses and tended to be a little heavy on the make up, while Hetty, a fair skinned, heavily set featured woman of thirty six, never used make up in her life. She wore a flowery dress and white cardigan and on her feet, a pair of flat tie shoes. They were an assorted bunch, but the repartee between them was perfect. Their friendly chatter and compliments passed to one another were sincere.

Soon Mary added to the conversation and laughed with them. The door of the rest room opened and in walked a tall well-built woman wearing a half-length fur jacket. She nodded her greetings to the women and as she rested her eyes on Mary, she stared momentarily without speaking.

As none of the others introduced her, Mary felt she was to be avoided.

The woman removed her coat and hung it on the peg, walked towards the mirror where she fixed her short bobbed hair with her fingers, sniffed, had another look at Mary through the mirror before lifting her bosom slightly before walking out. Wearing a mini length polka dot dress, which buttoned up the front, Mary thought she looked so ridiculous.

For a start, the fact that she was very much overweight, made the dress creep up at the back, revealing more of her solid legs beyond decency.

As the door closed behind her, Mary's three companions looked amusingly at one another. Mary frowned and, as Hetty; the elder of the three, but a few years younger than Mary, noticed, she drew Mary over by the arm. "That's notorious Sergeant Tulloch. Big buxom Tully, or sweaty Betty, as her female colleagues named her, who, by the way, has designs on your Walter."

Mary's ears singled out the words '*your* Walter,' filling her with a sense of belonging.

"Aye, she's got a face like a coo's arse an' all," remarked Fran, the young pretty woman, who was now peering into the mirror adding a bit more lipstick to her slightly generous mouth. "Turn milk soor wi' one look an' all."

"Fran, you have a lovely way with words," remarked Sybil. "So well educated."

"Oh aye, and you can come oot wi' some corkers yersel'. I've heard you plenty times."

"Pay no heed to them," laughed Hetty, "They're really the best of friends."

"Well, I noticed she had a good look at you Mary. Just wait 'till she knows your Walter's girl. You'll hear the knife sharpen," remarked Sybil.

"Is Walter aware of her admiration?" asked Mary smiling.

"Oh aye, he gets plenty o' stick about it an all. He feels sorry for her. Imagine anybody feeling sorry for her."

"A right dour faced bitch she is, an' nasty wi' it at times."

The door opened once more and in bounced another two females. "Hi you lot," one said to the three women, obviously knowing them well. "You have tae get a move on, your men are waiting on ye."

"Come on," Hetty ushered them towards the door. "We'll tell them the loo was busy."

Derek, Fran's husband, was dark, of average height, stocky, with a tidy kept moustache, while Sybil's husband Eddie was slightly smaller and had lost his hair a long time ago, although he was still only in his middle thirties. Hetty, in spite of being plain, almost frumpy, had the handsomest of the three when it came to husbands. Jamesie was tall, well built, a fitness freak as she called him, and had the most amazing sense of humour.

During the evening, each of the men in turn, danced with one another's partners. It was obvious they met socially as there was no awkwardness among them. They joked and bantered with one another so freely. Walter was as bad as the others when it came to fun, as he gave as good, as he got. As his eyes met Mary's, they changed. They spoke softly and lovingly, and were filled with a longing, a longing to be alone.

Halfway into the night, the Compeer announced a slow waltz. Grabbing Mary before she was whisked off, Walter led her onto the floor. Holding her tight, his lips brushed gently against her ear. "Enjoying your-self?" he whispered.

Drawing back just enough to look into his face, she smiled, "I don't know when I have enjoyed myself like this before." Pulling her close again, Mary felt the heat radiating from his chest. She felt so safe, so proud. Quivering inwardly, she knew she felt even more and she loved the sensation that flowed through her.

The Compere, with devilment in his voice, announced, "I forgot to say folks, this is an excuse me."

Walter held her even closer. "They daren't. They value their lives too much," he whispered, referring to their company.

From the side of her eye, Mary caught sight of Betty Tulloch. She rose as they danced past her table, her hurried motion almost toppling the drinks.

A finger poked into Mary's shoulder blade, "Eh. I believe this is an excuse me. Well excuse me!" demanded Betty.

Mary hesitated, quite unsure as what to do then, feeling a hand on her arm, Derek pulled her from Walter, leaving him no option but to dance with Sergeant Tulloch.

As Derek whirled Mary in front of the bemused Walter, Fran, who had seconds ago been in her husband's arms, tapped the furious Betty, leaving her standing on her own in the middle of the floor. Now in Walter's arms, Fran led him towards Mary, swapping over once again into her husband's arms.

Walter grinned broadly as he pulled Mary to him once again. "They are well organised our lot. They knew she would do that and they were ready."

"Oh Walter," she rested her head on his shoulders, then lifting it quickly she asked, "What if she does it again?"

"Don't worry, Fran says that it's Sybil's turn to chase her next time." The impish glint in Walter's eyes made her laugh.

"Poor woman, she's obviously besotted with you."

Drawing her tightly into him, he whispered, "not half as much as I am with you."

The night all too soon, came to a close. The men had driven to the dance in their cars with the intention of leaving them in the police compound. This they did, calling a taxi to take them home. They held hands in the taxi, just as young lovers would have done. The contentment Mary felt was beyond belief. As they neared her street, Walter pulled her close, kissing her with the passion of a hungry lover. Mary too felt the hunger, being deprived of love for so long, but there was nothing she could do about it. Breaking free, she searched Walter's eyes. He needed her, she could tell, but dropping her eyes she whispered, "I'm sorry Walter, it's impossible."

His hands enfolded hers, "Nothing is impossible Mary. Some day, when the time is right."

The clock struck 1am as she closed the door behind her. The living room light was still on so she looked in. Frank sat by an almost extinguished fire, paperback in his hand. Like an irate father, he glanced at the clock, then, half smiling he said, "You're late." In the same breath he enquire, "A good dance was it?"

Her head held high and with a satisfied expression, Mary announced, "Brilliant. Bloody brilliant!"

Frank, with gaping mouth, blinked, "Well, good," he uttered.

Turning on her heels she left him standing, then, taking the stairs two at a time, Mary, although feeling tired, could have sung for joy.

The next day was the last of the Christmas holidays and, although the boys lay longer in the morning, Mary was up at her usual time. In the kitchen, awaiting her like an old friend, the dishes piled high. The kitchen table too had not been cleared, butter, still in its open wrapper, a near empty milk bottle, sugar bowl with a used spoon sticking in the middle, sugar lumping round it owing to it's dampness, bread plate with the remaining slices hard, curling up at the ends. Traces of sugar grains had been spilled and left lying on the table among three dirty knives.

Mary stood at the door of the kitchen shaking her head in despair.

"Bloody boys," she murmured, "when will they learn to clear things away after them."

Running the water, she stood a minute with her hand under the tap. The water ran cold between her fingers.

Sighing, she lifted the kettle and filled it with the running water. Usually there was enough hot water in the pipes to allow her to wash the dishes in the morning, but if they all had baths the previous night, the water went cold.

Waiting for the kettle to boil, she cleared the mess on the table. Lifting the butter, she pealed off its wrapper and laid the contents into a glass dish. The hard bread was scooped up and taken outside where Mary broke it into little pieces throwing it onto the drying green to feed the hungry birds. As she turned, Cissie appeared at the edge of the building.

Smiling, Mary remarked, "You couldn't wait. You nosey auld devil."

"Aye yer richt there," Cissie grinned, "but a hiv nae need tae ask if ye enjoyed yersel'. A can tell by the look in yer een (eyes) A hardly slept a wink last nicht thinkin' aboot ye. Noo, come away in an' tell me all aboot it," then with a glint in her eye she added, "weel the decent bits a mean," she added cheekily.

The water, intended for the dirty dishes, was quickly transferred from the kettle to the teapot. Then refilling the vessel, Mary placed it back onto the cooker. "You'd think I had nothin' better to do than sit an' blether to you Cissie. The fire has still to be cleaned, an' look at this place," she moaned casting her eyes round the kitchen. "I could kill Frank. I bet this was deliberately left like this as a sort of penance for enjoying ma' self."

"Awe hen! Frank wid nae' dae that. He's jist a typical man, bloody bone-idle when it comes tae hoose work. He wid maist likely be amusin' the young yin awe nicht."

Almost like a sharp reprimand, Mary chided, "Cissie, behave yoursel'. Our Frank, amusing Tony? You've got to be joking. His backside on the chair goggling at that TV, more like it."

"Weel nae' worry, I'll dae the dishes while you pit oan the fire, but before a go of ma' heid, sit doon an' tell me aboot last night."

A warm smile shaped Mary's lips as she conjured up the feelings of the previous night, then she sat down on the chair opposite her friend. "Ah Cissie, it was grand. I had a great time; and his friends- well, I felt as if I've known them all my life. We danced and danced and laughed all night." Looking into her friend's eyes, she saw the look of concern. Stretching over, she held her hand, then with a note of seriousness, she said, "Don't worry Cissie, I know what I'm doing." Then giving her hand a gentle squeeze, she added, "I really do like him you know, and I'm sure he likes me a lot."

Cissie's mouth raised at one corner in half a smile, "Weel lass, you watch oot an' no' get hurt. You've been there yince too often fer my likin'. When are ye seein, him again then?" she asked cheerily.

With a far away look in her eyes, Mary answered, "At the weekend."

Cissie came out with a sharp reminder, "What. You're supposed tae be waiting at the Co-op tearooms oan Saturday. Ye telt Aggie Purvies ye were."

"Don't get excited Cis, he's picking me up there at nine. I'll be finished by then."

"Yer losing money then? Dis she ken yer no' helpin' in the bar?"

"Well, she'll be told on Saturday. There's others there dying to get behind the bar, so I don't see any problem."

"The problem is ma' lass, there's ithers dyin' tae git yer waitin' joab an all, so be carefu' ye dinnae loose that whin ye're at it."

Mary's features altered none. Not a trace of concern marred the joy in her face.

"Weel he must be worth it tae risk yer wee joab. If ye ask me, I'd say yer feelings fer this bobby is a bit mare than likin'. Still, as long as ye ken whit yer daein', I'm awfu' gled for ye," Cissie held the cup to her mouth almost choking at Mary's next question. The tea spluttered down her chin and over the cup. She could not believe what she was hearing.

"Cissie, would you think I was a hussy if I slept with him?" The expression on her face was almost vacant. "I feel I really want to. He's..he's..so loving and caring."

Cissie wiped her face with the hem of her apron, "Weel lass, that decision is fer you an' you only, but think weel oan it. He micht drop ye efter he's had his wey. Some men dae. He micht no' be sae luving an' carin' efter that." She gave this advice with a shake of her finger as she generally did when a warning was necessary.

Mary knew only too well about that, for didn't Frank's father high tail it when he found out she was pregnant? But this was different. She had been a raw girl of fifteen when she met Ally. Walter was different; in fact, she had never met anyone quite like him before. He almost stamped his claim on her, making her feel wanted in the greatest sense. He was solid and very much down to earth, easy to talk to and very easy to love. Oh yes, Walter was definitely different.

"He wouldn't do that Cissie, I just know he feels the same way as I do." Cissie was looking into the face of someone besotted. She knew that expression; she had seen it before in the eyes of her own sons when they met their wives.

"I love him Cissie. I really think I love him," her eyes softened as she confessed her feelings.

"Aye. A kent that Mary. There's nothin' in the world I, or onybody else can say, fer if ye really love him, things will take their ain course. In the heat o' the moment, yer no' gonnae think, 'oh, a better no, Cissie says this is no' richt,' naw, yer he'rt rules yer heid in them circumstances. A should ken. Ma' auld man wisnae always auld ye ken." Her eyes stared at the ceiling in remembrance. "Naw, he could make the goose pimples rise on ma airms in them days," laughing she added, "The only thing that rises these days is ma arse oot the chair."

Mary laughed and laughed at her friend's reminiscences.

"On dear, oh dear," Cissie wiped tears of laughter from her eyes. "Ye dae what ye think's best ma' hen. Life's too short tae bother aboot what ithers think. You follow yer hert."

The thump of heavy footsteps above, caused the women to exchange knowing glances, "Someone has emerged. Stomach bothering them no doubt." Mary declared.

"Get yoursel' ben the hoose and licht the fire whil'st a get them dishes done. Weel talk later," ordered Cissie as she pushed her great body from the chair with some effort. "This bloomin' arthritis is gettin' me doon. The longer a sit, the stiffer a seem tae get. Auld age disnae come it's sel'."

"Naw Cissie, it certainly doesn't," agreed Mary.

Chapter Sixteen

Kicking her plain black skirt to one side, Mary hurriedly undid the row of pearl buttons before throwing her white blouse onto the small cane chair that stood to her right. Standing in her underskirt, she reached over and slipped the navy dress from the hook on the wall and stepped into it. Without waiting to be asked, her companion twirled her round and zipped her up. Catching the broad belt from both ends, Mary pulled it into place before buckling it up.

"You don't mind taking my things home with you Alice?" she asked the harassed waitress.

"How many times must I tell you Mary, it's no bother to me, only get away with you and don't' keep that fella' waitin'." Throwing Mary's coat at her, the young waitress gently pushed her towards the door. "Come on Mary, get out before old misery guts changes her mind, her face is trippin' her as it is."

Touching the girl's arm and with visual gratitude, Mary thanked her once more for completing her shift.

The old green Austin sat engine purring in waiting for Mary to appear in the doorway. Walter checked his watch. His eyes once more rested on the door. His face crinkled into a warm smile as he saw her appear, coat flying and clutching her shoulder bag. Stretching over, he opened the passenger door from the inside.

"Made it," he laughed.

"Aye, just," she smiled. "She wasn't too pleased with me though, and I suppose she has good reason."

Putting the car into gear while checking the mirror, he asked, "What would you have done if she refused to let you away."

"Quit," she said without hesitation.

Walter turned his head and studied her earnest expression.

"You're serious? You would have walked out?" He frowned.

"Yes. I've done her plenty favours and extra hours, so I believe in coming and going with folk, don't you?"

In mock disappointment, he jested, "And I believed it was just for me!"

"Did you now?" With tongue in cheek she added. "And do you think you're worth it?"

"Of course I am woman. If you don't think so, I will have to turn to sweaty Betty for condolence."

"Oh what a shame. Poor Betty," she sympathised.

"Poor Betty? You don't know the woman. She cracks nuts in her palms!"

Mary laughed heartily.

Turning, he glanced at her with a wicked smile. "Shelled nuts I mean madam, and another thing, she opens bottle tops with her teeth, and that's true! That's why they look like a row of condemned houses."

His impression of his colleague had Mary holding her side with laughter. Wiping the tears from her eyes, she asked, "Where are we going anyway?"

Glancing over once more, he bit at his lip. "I'm taking you home to my abode where I intend cooking you a fabulous meal. Sound alright to you?"

A warm comfortable feeling rushed through Mary's body. He was taking her to his place. Feeling slightly ashamed of her feelings, her face flushed. She could be alone at last with Walter.

As he concentrated on the busy Saturday night traffic, he missed Mary's blushes.

"Fine," she answered. "I can do with putting my feet up." Slipping out of her shoes, she wiggled her toes, her mind not on her feet, but on the excitement of having him all to herself. She was aware of her reckless behaviour, but she didn't care. It was time she thought of herself and her own feelings, and as she was happy being with Walter, he could take her anywhere.

They drove through Mary's hometown, the railway station to her right and the huge red bricked high school to the left.

"Did you go there?" he asked.

"Where? Preston Lodge?" she asked.

"Yeah. Was that your high school?"

Smiling with fond memories she answered, "That was my school right enough, but funny how you hate it when you're there"

Walter lived a few miles from Prestonpans in the historic town of Haddington, a town that through the years managed to retain a sense of architectural unity. As his police headquarters was situated there, he bought a small flat in the High street above one of the many shops. The town's sombre grey courthouse was another dominant feature, and as Mary passed it, she shivered at the ordeal she had encountered not so long ago. Patrick had appeared there before being sent to the High Court in Edinburgh.

The road before them split like a fork, Walter driving to the right. Both streets were lined with shops, flats occupying the two stories on top. The door between the ironmongers and the newsagent led to Walter's flat and as he led the way upstairs that were flanked with whitewashed walls, he held Mary by the hand. Facing the door on the first landing, he turned the key in the lock, pushing the door heavily with his shoulder, "It sticks terribly, but one push." The great lump of wood flew open.

Following him into the long lobby he led the way towards the door that faced them. The first thing Mary noticed was the high ceiling encircled by sweeping cornicing centred by a huge circular ring of embossed splendour surrounding the regency style three shaded glass light fittings. The fireplace was in keeping with the splendour of the great ceiling. Its dark wood carved at each side resembling great pillars holding the equally rich mantelshelf with its carved out acorns and great leaves, their coiling threadlike tendrils entwined with proud Scottish thistles, finished with beige marble back pattern and thick marble hearth. The far corner of the room served as a dining area where a giant oak table was surrounded by six high back-carved chairs.

Books of all shapes and sizes, apparently in no fixed order, filled the groaning bookcases that seemed to be everywhere. The dinning table too was littered with books and the long wooden coffee table in front of the black leather couch also held a scattering of magazines and papers.

Walter was untidy.

"Well this is it Mary, take off your coat and I'll fix you a drink. White wine?"

"Yes Walter, that would be nice," she nodded while slipping off her coat.

Mary smiled to herself. She somehow imagined Walter to be very much with it, tidy beyond the extreme with everything in his life in order, but she was much mistaken. It was obvious to Mary that her man was a keen reader and by the magazines, fond of fly-fishing. She had a lot to learn about Walter and as she thought about him, that warm sensation engulfed her once more.

Walter handed Mary a glass of white wine, "Oh wait till I fix dinner," he grinned. "Do you like Chinese food?"

"Yes. I don't mind."

Going to the phone, Walter grinned, "Only take a second."

A look of misbelieve crossed Mary's face, "You're not ordering a take-a-way?"

Walter grinned.

"I don't believe it," Mary laughed. "I was looking forward to your home cooking and there you are, ordering a take-a-way."

"Home delivery?" Walter spoke into the phone.

The electric fire that stood on the hearth spilled out its warm glow. With one quick sweep of his hand Walter cleared the coffee table and laid two plates of sweet and sour chicken and the opened bottle of wine down before Mary.

"This is better than playing round with pots and pans. Gives me more time to spend with you. See? I'm not so daft." He winked.

"Well it certainly saves on the washing up, but I couldn't help noticing, you gave the order and your name, but you didn't need to give your address." She looked at him with curiosity, "I think you're a regular customer there, and the truth is Walter, you can't cook to save yourself."

He smiled that wicked smile that seemed to melt Mary's heart, "I think you're a better detective than I am. You're right. By the time I get home, I usually bring in something from the chippie or I phone for a Chinese. Pass your glass over for a refill."

She pushed her glass towards him, "Well, Walter Taylor, I do believe you're trying to get me tipsy," she teased theatrically.

Leaning to the side, he whispered in her ear. "Shut up woman, don't spoil my plan."

The meal over, Mary grabbed up the dirty plates. "Where's the kitchen?"

"Come on, I'll show you the flat," Walter suggested.

A small tiled bathroom was situated to the right when leaving the sitting room and down at the end of the lobby, again to the right, was the kitchen, small but compact and a lot tidier than the living room, probably because of its infrequent use. Mary laid the plates on the sink top, and was about to fill the basin.

"Leave that. I will do them later, besides, I haven't finished my tour. Taking her gently by the arm, he led her to the door facing the kitchen, "Walla!" he exclaimed. "This is where I intend seducing you."

The one and only bedroom faced the kitchen door and it was just big enough for a double bed, a single wardrobe and a small bedside table.

Standing at the door of the room, Mary laughed, "You have it all planned. And what if I say no?"

With a look of dejection he moaned, "Then it would have to be sweaty Betty after all."

Pushing him playfully, she headed back along the lobby and into the sitting room. There were two black leather couches in the room, one facing the fireplace, and the other running along the wall to the left. On the wide alcove to the right sat a small portable television which Walter said he hardly ever had on, he was much more interested in his stereo system which at the moment sent the strains of Ray Charles singing 'I can't stop loving you' from the speakers on the wall. At the side of the stereo, Walter's stacking deck was neatly filled with all kinds of tapes, although not in order, there was none scattered round the table, as were his books. It was obvious to Mary; he had great respect for his music.

To the soft consoling music, Mary found it easy to relax in Walter's arms, and soon the small kisses and tender endearments developed into long lingering passionate embraces hardly stopping to take air. His long lingering kisses sent Mary into clouds of mist, her head swimming, not wanting to open her eyes again. She responded to every stroke and caress willingly, giving him back as much loving attention. As she lay under him, they twisted and turned to get comfortable, but the cold shiny surface of the leather felt cold and unyielding.

Walter broke free from Mary, then, studying her reaction he suggested, "This is ridiculous Mary, we ought to move to a more fitting place? I want this to be right and not strained. I want us to look back years from now and remember our first time together as being something wonderful," hurriedly adding, "That is if you want to?"

She did want to. She felt like she had never felt before. As if in a hypnotic trance, all she could do was to nod her approval. Leading her through like a parent would with a child on it's first day at school, Walter stopped inside the room and kissed her tenderly once more before leading her to the bed where they undressed each other slowly enjoying every moment without inhibitions.

As Walter drove her home that night, she held on to his arm as he steered the car, her head lying happily on his shoulder.

"Are you happy?" he murmured.

"What do you think?" She squeezed his arm. For the first time in her life she felt loved, as well as being in love. The unselfish love she had been shown from her father was completely different, and then she smiled at the thought of her Mother. Oh how she would have approved of Walter. She realised that she never had loved Patrick. She had been to young and immature to know the feeling back then, but she definitely knew it now. She now knew how it felt to make love and to give herself freely with out feeling degraded. She longed for more like a child that had just discovered sweets.

Her thoughts were interrupted as Walter drew into her street.

"Here we are my darling," he said softly.

"Coming in?" she asked when they drew up at her gate.

Bending down he kissed her brow. "Not tonight Mary, for if I did, your lad being as smart as he is, my idiotic look and satisfied grin would be a dead give away."

"Give away to what?" she asked teasingly.

"That I had enjoyed the warmth of his Mother's body and I intended to do it over and over again."

Mary now kissed him softly. "I'll think about it Walter Taylor. Don't take too much for granted."

As Walter gripped her arm, Mary felt a slight pressure, "I will never take you for granted Mary. I love you."

Without kissing her, Walter looked in her eyes with genuine sincerity, "I've loved you from the moment I set eyes on you."

Blinking foolishly she tried to answer but was stopped by his finger gently placed onto her soft lips.

"Say nothing Mary. Not yet." As he nodded his head, the cute way he had of raising his lip set an electric charge running through her veins. She longed to shout, I love you too, but she knew she had to wait, as he wanted her to be absolutely sure.

Mary's relationship with Walter flourished. Frank too had slowly learned to accept him and even went with him on fishing trips becoming just as addicted to the sport as he once was. Walter also talked Mary into allowing Frank to buy his first motorbike. Shuddering at the thought, Mary's mind slipped into the past, understanding only too well how her mother once felt about Billy and his bike.

She had thought a lot about her mother in the last few months, the way she had sussed Patrick out, her stubborn temperament and her protective nature towards Billy. Just like Mary's with Frank. She had learned to forgive her mother and longed to tell her she too had been very wrong, but it was too late for that. All Mary could do now was to make sure the rest of her life would be much happier.

Allan had bought himself an old dilapidated mini and spent more time on his back under the worn-out machine than actually driving it. Frank, now a fully-fledged motor mechanic, helped his brother make the vehicle a lot more roadworthy. When it was safe to drive, it disappeared for a week into Allan's work shop, where during his spare time, Allan, along with one of his seniors, hammered, prized, and coaxed the unsightly dents from the body work, replacing a couple of doors from a similar model that had been snatched from the jaws of the grinder that busily chewed up old relics and write off's that lay in wait of their fate in the scrap-yard next door.

A week spent rubbing at the rust preparing for a spray of paint and it was ready. Miraculously it passed its M.O.T, the required documentation for cars that were more than five years of age (at that time). The only thing wrong was the interior. The seats were so badly worn, legs were in danger of being torn apart by the rough jagged edging from the torn vinyl, remedied by the throwing over of tartan plaids.

The car appeared once more in front of the house. Allan had proudly driven it, everything legal, from the workshop on the Friday night.

Mary stood at the window her mouth gaping open with surprise on seeing the car draw up.

"In the name of the wee man. Will you come ben here and have a look at this." She held her hand over her mouth much to suppress her laughter as well as hide her surprise.

Frank joined her; towel in hand, his face and hands being given a quick wash in the kitchen before his meal.

From the upstairs' bedroom, Tony was heard yelling at the top of his voice. Taking the stairs two at a time, he flew out of the door to join his beaming brother on the pavement.

Allan slipped his arm round his young brother's neck, and beamed, "I'll dare you to call her rattling Lizzie now. You'll be wantin' a hurl no doubt?"

"Aye Allan, can we go now?"

Instinct told Mary what was about to happen, so she rapped at the window beckoning them. "Come away in you couple of eejits," she called.

Frank grinned from ear to ear. "Know what they call the mini Ma?"

Looking up at her son in wonder, she gave a puzzled look. "No. What do they call it then?"

Tongue in cheek he grinned, "Your too young and innocent to know."

Mary grabbed at his towel and swiping at him as he made to dive from her reach. "Frank, you have a bad mind. Our Allan's no' like that."

With that, Frank raised his eyebrows in a questioning manner, "Ma, you know nothing."

As Mary stood watching her two youngest admiring the car, she suddenly experienced a terrible sinking feeling. She realised for the first time that her boys were no longer boys but growing men, with the exception of Tony who was still at school and looked younger than most boys at fifteen. He still had his fresh complexion with no sign of facial hair or interests in the opposite sex. She knew Frank had had a few girls, but he was the love them and leave them type, preferring the company of his friends to the company of women, saying once a woman comes on the scene, your money is never your own. Now he had that wretched motorbike. Walter had assured her that bikes were not the cause of accidents; it was bad driving that attributed to that. She would much prefer him to have a woman than the unwanted object that lay under the oilskin hap at the back door.

"What do you think of it now Ma?" called Allan as he flew into the room. "Isn't she lookin' great?" Throwing a kiss towards the ceiling, like an excited Italian waiter, he said lovingly, "And she's purring like a dream."

"Aye aye." Frank glanced over at Mary, the usual impudent grin on his face. His brow lowered in questioning fashion, "See what I mean?"

An agitated shake of the head and Mary sprung into action, "Get through there and have your dinner. Standing here all googly eyed over an old scrap heap."

The weather had been marvellous the last few days and Sunday was no exception. Frank had left after a late breakfast heading towards the borders with fishing tackle he had borrowed from Walter, sandwiches and a flask of tea all strapped on to the rear of the bike. He planned to be gone the whole day.

Tony disappeared with some scrawny youth who had called for him early on. They were last seen heading towards the shore whispering to each other as if they were up to something.

Allan too had left early that morning. He was up and shaved, 'smelling like Nancy boy', as Frank put it. He was off to meet 'the girl' as they had planned a picnic.

It was two in the afternoon before hunger forced Tony back home. He ate a plate of chips and cold meat before fetching an old towel from the cupboard, and then, slipping on his bathing trunks under his shorts he hurriedly made his way back down to the shore.

Stretching the comfortable lounger to its full potential, book in hand, Mary, smeared in sun tan lotion, settled down to soak up the sun. Both sides of the garden were flanked with high hedging giving her the privacy and peace she had craved all week.

The garden was mostly lawn, well cut, with four wash poles to the rear. The area directly from the back door had been paved and to the right stood the coal box. No one in the family was keen on gardening hence the omission of any vegetable plot or flowerbeds.

The book had long fallen from her hand as she slipped into a warm luxurious state of sleep. Her nose twitched to warn off the tickling sensation that started to annoy her. It wouldn't go away despite the flick of her hand. It was back. She jumped with a start realising it could be an insect only to find Walter crouched behind her. He had been playing a long blade of grass along and down her nose.

"Walter!" she exclaimed. "Where did you come from?"

"Finished on time for a change. Well, where's the bikini?"

"Sorry," she grimaced. "Round here the neighbours would be out with a bucket of water. I'm afraid you'll have to settle for a sleeveless top and a pair of long shorts, and that's considered brazened."

Laughing, he scanned his eyes towards the open door of the house. "Where's Tony?" he asked.

"Oh, down the shore. Why? Did you want him?"

"Well, as it happens, I have something to ask him?"

Shielding the sun from her eyes she frowned in question. "What's he been up to? Oh no, I don't think I want to know."

Playfully rubbing her hair, he grinned. "He's not been up to anything." Sitting crouched in front of her, he smiled. "I've been speaking to our Kate on the phone. She has suggested we take him down to their farm in Selkirk during the summer holidays."

Mary's eyes brightened. "That would be great Walter. A day on the farm would be ideal for him."

"No Mary, they mean to give him a proper holiday: A whole fortnight. Sam and Spencer are about the same age as Tony, so, what about it?"

"Oh Walter, I bet he jumps at it." Grabbing him, one hand on each side of his head, she pulled him towards her and kissed him briefly. "You were kind to think of him. Thank you."

Pouting his lips, a look of guilt spread over his face. On seeing his expression change she became concerned. "What is it? What's the matter?"

Shaking his head, he bared his teeth as if his next statement was hard to say.

"I have a terrible confession."

"What?"

He lowered his gaze. "Promise you won't get angry."

"No. I can't promise that. What's the matter? Walter, for goodness sake."

"That holiday arranged for Tony!" He bit his bottom lip.
"Well?"

"I had ulterior motives I'm afraid." Pulling an envelope from his pocket, he handed it to Mary.

"What's this?" She sat bolt upright and pulled out the contents from the envelope. Studying the documents briefly, she looked slightly bewildered as she handed them back.

Walter fanned them in front of her playfully. "Ten days in Spain. What do you say?"

Speechless, she grabbed back the tickets. As she had never seen airline tickets in her life, she examined them a good few times, doubting their authenticity before speaking. "Oh Walter." Then she announced. "But I have no passport. And ...and I ... I don't have that kind of wardrobe. Goodness Walter. I'll have to..."

"Wait a minute. Wait a minute. We'll sort all that out this week. Now, would you like a cup of tea?"

Pushing herself from the lounger she attempted to rise, only to be forced back by him. You just relax. I'll fetch you out a cup. Walking into the back kitchen, he removed his jacket. Throwing it over the nearest chair he rolled up the sleeves of his crisp white shirt before filling the kettle.

Relaxing once more on her lounger, with closed eyes, Mary felt so warm and wonderful. She loved that man to bits and would do everything in her power to make him happy.

At long last Allan proudly presented his girlfriend to his family. It happened without Mary being forewarned. It was almost five o'clock when the mini drew up at the gate. Although it had turned a bit cooler, Mary and Walter still relaxed in the evening sun. He had retrieved an old deck chair from the outhouse and had it propped up alongside Mary's lounger.

They heard Allan call out and turned to find him standing holding the hand of his lady friend.

"Mum, this is Annetta." His face beamed with pride as he gently shepherded his young lady towards his mother. She stood at the side of Mary's lounger, smiling coyly down, her beautiful even teeth made even whiter by her evenly tanned skin. Her shiny raven hair held back loosely with the aid of a pale pink chiffon scarf, the colour matching the cool cotton sun top that revealed the merest hint of perfect cleavage. Her long bare slender legs exposed as she sported the shortest of shorts, beige, with ragged edges, her pink toe nails popping through the strings of her woven string espadrilles. But it was her eyes that made Mary gasp inwardly. They sparkled like brown mischievous imps under her perfectly shaped dark eyebrows.

Mary was suddenly aware of her own appearance and felt slightly self- conscious. She had just thrown on old shorts, ones she had had for several years and were well past their best, as she hadn't expected any visitors. Her hair too was not its usual tidy self, flicked back carelessly behind her ears with loose uncombed strands lying over her now very red brow. Feeling a mess, she jumped from the lounger flicking her fingers through her hair in the hope of tidying it up.

"Pleased to meet you lass," she smiled, taking Annetta by the hand.

Allan, laying his hand on Walter's shoulder added. "And this is Walter."

"Well, pleased to meet you," Walter announced warmly. "Come an' sit yourself down." He rose and offered the girl the deck chair.

Smiling, she declined, looking to Allan for encouragement.

"We're not staying Mum. We only looked in on the passing."

"Nonsense!" Mary insisted, still looking at the girl's bewitching eyes, "You can surely stay a while. I can get tidied up..."

"No really Ma," he insisted. "Annetta has to get back. Her family are expecting her back." A note of disappointment became evident in his voice.

"I can stay half an hour," she hurriedly spoke as if to please him.

"Well then, lets go into the house and have a wee blether." Mary, forgetting her own appearance, offered the girl a welcoming hand.

Taking it, Annetta allowed herself to be led into the house, Allan, shrugging his shoulders as he looked at Walter, followed on behind.

The conversation was a bit strained, as it usually is when meeting for the first time, but Annetta did manage to inform them that she hoped to become a dietician. She was due to start her studies after the summer recess and was quite excited at the prospect.

Allan's face however was a different matter. Masked with a look of gloom, he dreaded the thought of her leaving. Although he intended to drive to Aberdeen as often as possible, she would be meeting new friends, and it worried him that maybe, as her father hoped, she would set her interests elsewhere.

"And where will you be staying up there?" Mary asked with interest.

"The Halls of residence, beside the rest of the students," she informed her.

"That's nice!" Mary remarked, not knowing what else to say.

On seeing Allan's dispirited expression, Walter fully understood how he was feeling and quickly changed the subject. "Your Mother has something to tell you."

Mary looked at him questioningly.

Casting his eyes towards the envelope, "You haven't forgotten already woman?"

"Oh no. I was going to tell him."

"What? Tell me what?" asked Allan, his gaze following Walter's to the mantelpiece.

"Walter's taking me on holiday, to Spain no less."

"You're joking."

"See for yourself." She handed him the envelope. "And before you ask, Tony's holidays are arranged as well."

"He's going too?" Allan asked.

"Yes… No… at least not with us. He's going to the borders. A farm." Mary smiled. "He'll love that."

"Oh aye, so he's got a job frightening the crows from the fields. A real life scarecrow."

"Tattie-bogles," Walter said with an impish grin.

"What?" Mary asked.

"Tattie-bogles. That's what they call scarecrows at the farm."

"Oh well, that'll suit him," laughed Allan, the gloomy look now vanished from his face. "He'll be coming home wantin' us to keep hens in the back green," he laughed.

"Well it would be different," remarked his mother. "I was sick of him wanting a rabbit. That was bad enough."

"Well there's nothing wrong with a lad having a rabbit," Walter sympathised.

"No. I dare say there isn't, but I know who'd be left to look after it."

"Aye Ma. And I ken what Cissie would do with it. Make a rare stew for Robbie an' a muffler from the fur."

"I have heard all about Cissie and Robbie," Annetta laughed. "Allan is very fond of her."

"We all are," informed Mary. "She's very special to us all."

Mary stood at the door with Walter and watched as Allan helped Annetta into the car. They watched silently as they drove off, then turning to Walter, Mary asked, "What do you think?"

Closing the door behind them, Walter nodded slightly. "A nice lass Mary, but I hope she doesn't hurt him."

"That's what I was thinking. She's a bit grand, but he obviously adores her."

"Well that's something we have in common," he grinned. "Not the grand bit I mean," he said teasingly.

"You cheeky monkey," she swiped at him playfully.

Grabbing her arms, Walter pushed her back hurriedly until her back was to the lobby wall. "Gives a quick kiss missus before your young un' appears."

She did. A long, slow, lingering, meaningful kiss.

Two days before Walter and Mary left for Spain, they took the excited Tony to the borders where he was to stay for two weeks. The journey itself was a pleasure. They drove slowly, taking in the magnificent scenery. The golden fields and lush green meadows where herds of cows chewed non-stop at the succulent grass, newly sheared sheep roaming around aimlessly doing the same thing. The rolling hills in the distance grew nearer as they drove further into the country. They were sick of Tony asking every ten minutes,

"Are we nearly there?" The beauty of the surrounding countryside was boring and uninteresting to him. They had turned off the main road and were travelling along a secondary road bordered on each side by thick well-kept hedges. The road twisted and turned for miles, occasionally Mary's heart missing a beat when skilled country drivers raced passed almost forcing them into the ditch. Walter called out, "Road hog!" and laughed when Mary wittily remarked,

"And we were nearly hedge hogs."

The opening to the farm could have almost been missed as only a small wooden sign nailed onto the open gate announced the entrance to "Pendale" farm. The rough track down to the farm tossed them up and down as the car drove into furrows hewn from mud by the constant tyres of the tractor. The large grey stoned farmhouse with its dark green window frames and it's adjoining byres and sheds suddenly came into view. The yard strewn with loose straw where a few single-combed Rhode Island Reds strutted unhurriedly across in front of the oncoming car.

Walter's sister Kate stood at the door wearing a multi coloured criss-cross pinafore, and watched as they drove very slowly into the farmyard. The two boys appeared from the barn when hearing the honking of the horn.

Kate crossed the cobbled yard as soon as the car drew to a standstill; arms wide open and a welcoming smile on her round ruddy face. As soon as he was out the car, his sister had him in a tight bear hug. The two boys, although twins, looked nothing like brothers. One was small and built like his mother while the other was lank and tall, but they both had the same healthy ruddy skin, with blonde, almost white, tousled hair. They stood gaping at Tony who appeared from the other side of the car with his mother.

"Kate," Walter announced proudly, "This is Mary."

Mary felt her face flush as Walter's arm encircled her waist.

"Well. I can see how you took your time in choosing." Although speaking to her brother she looked Mary over as if choosing a prize beast.

"And this must be our guest." She smiled broadly at Tony, emphasising the deep lines sweeping from the corner of her eyes.

Tony returned the smile politely and rather shyly.

"These are my two scallywags here," she turned to her boys. "The short one's Sam an' this yin's oor Spencer." She grabbed the thin one by the ear as she introduced him. Letting the protesting lad free, she spoke directly to Mary.

"Well come away in lass, you're welcome here anytime." With that she turned her attention back to her sons, "Get doon to the big field an' fetch yer faither."

"Is he coming?" Spencer asked throwing a look at the bemused Tony.

"Not at this minute. Git." She shooed them off flapping the skirt of her apron.

The inside of the farmhouse was warm and friendly. It reminded Mary of Cissie's place, cluttered, lived in, and a place of refuge after a long hard day out in the fields.

"Put your wee case on the floor there an' the boy's will see you tae your room in the shake o' a lamb's tail," she said to the beaming boy.

"The big field is just o'er the other side o' the hoose. They'll no' be long."

Turning to Walter, she beamed another welcome. "Its good tae see you again lad, and you're lookin' smashing." She grinned, grinding her teeth with excited pleasure.

"Come then Kate, take us through for a cup." He cast his eyes back across to the door.

"To the kitchen?" she asked with a note of horror. "He's an' awfu' lad this. Has a' fascination fur ma' kitchen." With a heavy sigh, she pushed him roughly, "Come on then," and with a wag of her finger, she gathered her brow into a deep furrow, "But I'm laying the tea table through here, guid china an' all," she warned. Turning to Mary she shook her head complaining. "I very seldom get the chance to show off you know. There's naebody comes here but farm hands and vagabonds." she laughed.

"That's not true Kate. Your known for your wild parties."

"Aye, so a am," She gave him another slap and added, "I wish!"

Mary understood immediately why Walter loved the kitchen for she had never seen any thing like it in her life. She had read about them but not knowing anyone from the country, she had never actually been in one. An old-fashioned farm kitchen. It had been altered very little since her mother-in-law's days, as her husband fell heir to the family farm, except that she had a huge top loading washing machine standing in the corner where once the great double washtubs stood. As far as Mary could see, that was the only modern utility in the kitchen. A double-oven kitchen range, enamel based, with green tiled upper part, sat proudly in the middle of the kitchen wall as if the room belonged to it. The knobs and doors fascinated Mary, as unknown to her Walter studied the amused look on her face.

"See what I mean? Isn't it great?"

"You winnae say that if it was you that had to clean it," his sister remarked.

The high mantelshelf was as cluttered as the room with its fancy patterned tins; an odd unframed family photo, an old oil lamp, one tarnished candlestick and a cheap ornamental highland cow that was minus a horn.

The hooks on the side of the fireplace supported the tongs, fire brush, small silver chrome shovel an oven mitt. A large black enamel pot sat bubbling at one side of the range and a girdle flanked the other while the great black kettle hung maliciously above the open fire spitting the occasional spurt of water into the hot coals. Glancing at her feet, Mary could hardly believe her eyes, for beneath the rag rugs, lay a stunning slab stoned floor, which was in keeping with the old style kitchen. The shelf filled walls held a vast array of plates, tureens, jugs of all sizes, large platters with an occasional ornament here and there. To the right of the fireplace the door to the large walk-in pantry was ajar, allowing Mary a brief look at masses of jars and storing tins. A large barrel of flour jammed against the sidewall prevented the door from closing.

From the beams of the rafters, pots pans and two sides of ham hung lazily.

Various three-legged stools and odd chairs scattered round the kitchen, while a medium sized wooden table stood near the great sink and an even larger table centred the middle of the room.

Kate hurried towards the kettle covering her hand with the skirt of her apron, and then expertly grabbing the handle, she released it from its hook. The awaiting teapot was soon filled and laid to rest by the side of the fire, a well-singed woollen tea cosy placed over it.

Chatting idly, she disappeared into the pantry appearing in a second carrying a large glass bowl. Walter grinned.

"Well sit yourselves down while I throw on a pancake."

As if in a trance, Mary and Tony obeyed.

Turning to her young brother she said sharply, "Hey, not you lad, get the things from the cupboard." Pulling a face at Mary he did as he was told. Going to another cupboard Walter flicked down the latch and pulled out cups and plates, he wasted no time in setting the great wooden table running back and forth from the pantry and the fridge.

Mary watched in amazement at the swiftness of her host as she spooned the ready-made mixture onto the girdle. In seconds a plate of newly made, perfectly shaped pan-cakes (dropped-scones) graced the table as well as thick slices of homemade bread, freshly churned butter and rich strawberry jam. 'A chittery bite' Kate called it, meaning something to keep you going until a proper meal was served (chittering bite, Scottish word meaning-a piece of bread eaten immediately after bathing in the open air.)

The door flew open and the gigantic form of Kate's husband filled its frame. Kate gave the two boys a stern reprimand as they pushed and shoved trying to squeeze past their father.

"Hoy. You two, behave!" Tutting she added, "Away an' wash your hands before you touch onything! Young devils."

Kate's husband George was as warm and friendly as Kate herself. His big cheery grin and responsive nature warmed Mary to him immediately.

"Well a hope you brought yer wellies lad," he said to Tony.

"It's no' rainin'," Tony remarked surprised.

The whole kitchen fell into rapturous laughter and Tony stared mesmerised at their tear stained faces.

"It doesn't need tae rain here lad to warrant wellies, as you'll soon find out. Just take a wander roon the side an intae the pigsty an' you'll find out."

"Pigs!" exclaimed Tony.

"Aye lad. Pigs. What did you expect on a farm eh? Poodle dugs?"

Tony's mouth gaped open to its full extent as Sam, elbows on the table, his chin resting in his cupped hand while he chewed at the crusts of the bread, went through the animals on the farm in a bored know-it-all fashion. "Hens, pigs, coos, sheep, dugs, eh..hens."

"You've already said hens," chipped in Spencer.

"Well then, what else?" he challenged his brother.

"There's the cats, bubblyjock, and...and.. and.. rats."

"RATS!" Tony almost fell from his chair.

"Yer no' feart o' rats," Sam cried.

"Of course no'," snapped Tony indignantly, his face flushing with the lie.

"And de ye ken what a bubblyjock is?" asked Kate in amusement, her big face beaming.

Tony's silent stare told her he didn't. "Why, a bubblyjock is the turkey. That's the sound it makes, bubble bubble bubble."

"Especially when it takes a run and flies at your feet," added Walter leaning towards Tony taunting him. His hands, palms downwards, fingers curled like claws, doing his best to suppress his grin, he sprung at the gaping boy.

A look of shock spread over Tony's face, then, as if aware of the tell tale sign, he straightened up and announced haughtily, "Am no' feart o' anything! See!"

Sam grinned mischievously at his brother, who sat with tongue in cheek, as if to say, "Wait and see!"

When they had finished eating, the boys, along with Tony, who by now was decked in a pair of old shorts and his wellingtons, disappeared from the kitchen. They headed in the direction of the field where a thick rope hung from a tree waiting to be swung on.

The rest of the stay was enjoyable, the lavish tea that was spread before them, Kate's own cured ham from their own pig contributed to the delicious salad. Scones, sponge cake, chocolate cake, tea-bread and creamy melting-moments spread out across the table. Not a bought biscuit or sweetmeat to be found.

Mary rose from the table feeling she had gained half a stone, she had eaten so much, forced of course. Try this. Try that. Are you sure you can't manage a wee bit o' apple pie?

Walter later walked with Mary down the lane behind the farmhouse, heading for his favourite spot. Up on top of the hill, they could see in the distance a small village lying in a far plateau. They walked along past the dry stane dyke till they came to a small wooded area. The trees, mostly conifers, had been planted in deliberate rows and once they both entered the small copse, the sun was hidden from view, dark shadows cast across their faces as Mary looked at him wondering.

"Where on earth are you taking me?"

"A minute and all will be revealed."

They walked on cautiously as the cracking of dry sticks broke beneath their feet, and Mary gasped a few times as hidden ferns brushed over her ankles. As they neared the edge of the wood, the telltale sound of the slow running brook gave the game away as they emerged from the woods, the sun once again beamed down on them like a welcoming friend.

Pulling her along, Walter spoke excitedly, "This is it." He raced towards the edge of the brook throwing him-self down and pulling Mary down beside him. At the other side of the water, the wild meadow swept up and away towards the hills. Trees clumped together here and there like groups of people holding private conversations and wild plants bloomed alongside the river's edge providing sweet nectar for the honey bees that flew tirelessly back and forth. A peewit sounded in the distance as if answering the call from a wild wood pigeon.

"What do you think?" he asked.

"Peaceful," she had to admit.

As they lay, feet dangling in the water, Walter asked, "Mary, are you happy with me?"

"What's made you ask that? You know full well I am," she said surprised at his question.

"But can you love me?"

Her heart leapt. She wasn't ready for his question. She stuttered slightly then hesitated before answering, "Walter. I ..I am sure I love you, but..."

"But?" he asked perplexedly. He rolled from his back onto his side and looked down on her face.

"Walter. I want to make sure before I make a commitment. Things sometimes feel too good to be true." Seeing his brow furrow, she hurriedly added. "Walter, it's not me I'm scared of. It's you."

"Me?" he sounded surprised.

She looked away.

"Mary, look at me!" he almost demanded. "Look at me!"

She turned and looked up into his face.

"You've not heard a thing I've been saying. All those months we have been together...I have tried to convince you. For God sake woman, I love you and want you to marry me."

"Marry!" she gasped in astonishment, her eyes as wide as an alarmed doe. "Oh no Walter, I can't think of marriage. Not yet. Not at this time. It's not been long enough."

"Long enough for what? You're not grieving Mary for heavens sake."

Her expression almost looked hurtful.

Rolling back over onto his back, he lay silently looking up at the slow moving traces of white fluffy clouds. White lines in the sky grew longer as an invisible plane left its mark. The buzzing of a bee grew louder as it neared the side of his head. He gave it an aggravated swipe.

"It's the boys," she admitted. "They would have to get used to the idea."

Walter's heart now gave a thud. Sitting bolt upright, he turned to her, and with a plea filled expression he answered, "It's not them I'm asking Mary. It's you. They are men...an.. They will leave you when the mood takes them without a-bye your leave. Believe me." He smiled knowingly. "I love you. Will you believe me?"

She answered with a nod of the head.

"Well. Do you love me?" His stern solid jaw crumbled as he grinned.

Her eyes moistened as she whispered. "I do love you Walter. I love you like crazy and have done for a long time."

Bending over her, his lips touched her ear. "I'm prepared to give you time. I just wanted you to know what my intentions are. So, now you know."

Brushing his lips over her ear, then up onto her warm brow, he pecked her with small deliberate kisses until his lips had worked their way down finding her willing mouth, then covering it with his, they worked over them slowly, the tip of his tongue brushing slightly on the inside of her mouth. Drawing from her, he brushed the side of her cheek with his, murmuring, "It would be so easy, but..."

"I know," she agreed, knowing exactly what he meant. "It would just take the scallywags to jump from the trees," she laughed.

"Come on then." He jumped to his feet stretching his arms out to help pull her up. "Lets get back and not put temptation in my way, you hussy," he teased.

"It's all this fresh air. It's not good for you. Gives you ideas," she commented rising to her feet and brushing the loose grass from her skirt.

"Come on," he said taking her by the hand. "Lets get back and allow my sister to feed us till we burst."

"Oh not again!" she groaned.

"I could ask her for a doggie bag," he suggested with a smirk.

* * *

They stood in the tunnel awaiting the movement of the queue, the knots of tension gathering in Mary's stomach. Walter gave her a reassuring squeeze and asked, "ok?"

"My stomach! It's churning," she admitted worriedly.

"It's alright. There's nothing to it," he squeezed her once more.

As the bodies in front started to move, Mary was carried along with the flow until they were out on the tarmac, where in front stood the plane.

As they stepped onto the stairs leading to the door, Walter drew her attention to the fuselage. "A few rusty screws here and there, but on the whole, no elastic bands on the propellers."

Knitting her brows together, her face became a mask of fear. "Don't! Please Walter. No more jokes. I feel like turning back."

"Awe', sorry love. I promise, no more jokes. You're worrying unnecessarily though."

"Maybe so, but I can't get rid of the nerves."

Boarding the plane, they were jostled about by passengers going too far back and trying to make their way back along the aisle. The couple in front heaved their hand luggage into the overhead racks, then realising they were at the wrong part of the plane; they pulled it all back out.

Walter and Mary stood waiting until they moved before squeezing down into their seats. "Do you want the window seat?" he asked, preparing to rise and change seats with her, but as quickly as he asked, Mary shook her head vigorously.

"I'm fine here, and I don't want to move 'til we get there," she informed him.

Seat belts fastened, the plane started to taxi along the runway. The stewardesses took their familiar stands in the aisle and gave the usual instructions. Exits here . . .in case of an emergency. . Pillows . . .life- belts under the seats...follow the illuminated lights along the aisle....

"I'm going to be sick!" announced Mary, her knuckles turning white with the grip she had on the armrests.

"You're all right Mary. Relax."

"Why is she telling us all this?" she whispered faintly.

"It's always done before take off, it's routine. Don't worry."

As the plane gathered speed Mary felt her body pull onto the back of her chair, then, as it lifted into the air, she gave a slight cry.

Walter laughed.

At that moment she could have killed him. "How could anyone enjoy this?" she thought. Her eyes still tightly closed, she suddenly felt her body straighten out. A stewardess came to her side. "Are you alright ma-am?" she asked.

"Y.y yes," she stammered, feeling foolish. "I'm alright now thank you."

Although full of apprehension, the rest of the journey was not so bad. She ate very little of the meal but drank two full glasses of lukewarm water; while Walter finished everything he was given, including a glass of Scotch.

Touch down was a very different experience for Mary. Although the dreadful feeling of fear returned, it was taken over by something very much worse- sore ears. The dull excruciating pain in her ears seemed to travel deep down into her jaws while the throbbing of her neck beat out rhythmically. She said nothing to Walter. She had moaned enough she thought. She tried to hide it but it became obvious to him when she ignored his questions.

"Oh no. Poor thing," he sympathised. "Your ears will eventually pop," he assured her.

"Like flying?" Mary thought. "Never!"

The plane landed smoothly bringing Mary's ordeal to an end. As she stepped back on to the tarmac, she had an overwhelming desire to kiss the ground. The aching in her ears had stopped although the dull drumming sound still remained. It was hours before she could hear properly, in fact, she was aware of a slight buzzing all night. It wasn't until she jumped into the pool the next morning that the clarity of her hearing returned.

Their room was in a small family-run hotel that nestled snugly between pine scented headland facing the inviting blue waters of the Mediterranean and although the hotel sported its own well planned swimming-pool, surrounded with lush greenery and exotic plants and flowers, sweeping down from both sides, old, well- worn steps led down to the hotel's own private and secluded beach where the cool clear water of the sea lapped onto the white rippling sands.

Five minutes walk from the hotel brought them to a busy marina, a favourite place of Walter's, where he would stand for ages watching the small rowing boats and local fishing boats bob between the more luxurious yachts. Further on, the area opened out into a vast extensive beach, dotted every few yards with shaded umbrella trees. Its palm fringed promenade stretching for what seemed endless miles.

In the restaurant/bars and quaint pavement cafes, laughing and squealing teenagers, obviously let loose on their first ever unsupervised holiday, drank and sang themselves hoarse, filling the air with the strains of 'Lets all go to sunny Spain'.

The first few days were spent entirely on their own wandering like young lovers hand in hand around the town or lazing by the pool, completely captivated with each other. They spent the warm evenings watching local entertainment and the wonderful nights they lay locked in each other's arms. Walter made her feel vibrant. With all her inhibitions scattered to the wind, she accepted his love as if it was a newly found wonderful thing, as indeed it was, as there was no comparison to Patrick's selfish and degrading lust. She had never given herself to Patrick willingly. He took what he wanted then slept once satisfied. At no time did she ever lie contented in his arms, his hands gently stroking her hair as if every strand was precious.

She could not have explained why it happened. Nothing was said it just happened. All her life, as far as Mary could remember, she felt as if others controlled her. Everything she planned had to be approved and considered. First of all it was her mother. She made all the decisions. The trick was to keep her daughter dependent. Having Frank gave her the ideal weapon. Then as Mary foolishly planned her escape through Patrick, she soon realised that he dished out the same treatment. He kept her short and very much dependent. Even when she did manage to make bit money of her own, it was never enough to give her the feeling of worth. She always had to ask for everything, and not just things or money! Freedom to go where she pleased was something she had never had.

She walked bare-footed; the edge of the water lapping over her toes as they sank into the moist warm sand. Walter paddled on in front, his arm reaching backwards as he held her hand. The sun was sinking on the horizon and the beach itself was by now fairly empty.

For no reason whatsoever, Mary dropped Walters's hand from hers and turned, looking out into the sea. Stopping, Walter turned to wait.

She stood still as if seeing something for the first time.

Gulls soared in the distant sky and as Mary watched, she felt as if she too were soaring. Breathing the air hungrily, her eyes moist like the sand where she now stood. The exhilarating feeling that ran through her veins made her flesh tingle. The air felt fresher. She felt lighter as if something had lifted from her shoulders. She knew at once what she felt and as she stood transfixed, her father's face flashed in to her mind. She was free. For the first time in her life, she was free and it had nothing to do with money. It was her soul that needed its freedom and for some strange reason, standing on a near deserted beach it had happened.

"Are you alright?" he asked, full of concern.

She turned and smiled, "I am now."

Chapter Seventeen

The summer ended quickly that year as rain and gale force winds swept the country. Tony's holiday had changed him for the better. As well as coming back looking taller his face and body puffed fit to burst. All that farm food pushed down his throat had definitely stretched his stomach, as Mary could not fill his new found appetite. To his mother he also seemed older and much wiser, and when she mentioned that to Walter he just laughed knowingly.

"Well if he wasn't educated at a farm, where else would he be," he grinned. "Them two down there would delight in telling him the facts of life."

"The facts of life," she exclaimed in alarm.

"The beasts Mary. Two weeks on a farm, come on. He would be fascinated."

She stood looking with her mouth open.

Allan became moody. Annetta had gone to Aberdeen and had not as yet come home for a weekend. Although they kept in touch by phone, he worried constantly that she would find someone else. Mary suggested that he should take a trip up to Aberdeen, but he refused saying that he would rather wait till he was invited, but the truth was, he knew he would not fit in with her latest friends.

Frank's life was unchanged, except that his fishing trips had become less frequent, due mostly to the weather. His attitude towards his mother and Walter had relaxed to the degree that he questioned Walter's absence rather than his presence. "Walter not coming round tonight?" he enquired before he went out.

Walter had installed the telephone in Mary's house, as his job often demanded extra hours, a nuisance if someone was waiting for you and had no means of communication, so it made a huge difference; Allan for his contact with Annetta, Mary for Walter and Frank for his wide social circle. It wasn't long before they could not imagine life without the black Bakelite object in the corner.

Cissie too had one installed by her family, and constant snatches of news were passed back and forth by 'phone rather than the old pop-in visits Mary had grown to love and expect, but the truth was, her friend was not so able now. She found walking a bit of a pain as 'the auld legs were gien (giving) up. 'The auld man' was failing in health also, so she hated being out of his sight for more than was necessary.

It was the last Sunday in September that year, Mary persuaded Allan to take her and Cissie out for a drive. Frank was going over to give the 'auld man' a hair cut and shave and as he had no plans till evening, didn't mind sitting with him till Cissie came home. It was a nice fresh day, a bit chilly but free from the winds they had been enduring.

As Allan's old car chugged it's way through the neighbouring towns and out into the hills, Cissie sat in the back with Mary, while Tony, pretending he was a tour guide, sat in front with his brother, map spread before him, giving a running commentary on the places they were passing, adding, "To the left is Turnbulls the sweet shop, Whitsons the butchers, and if you's look to the right," pointing to a scattering of sheep), "you can see the morrins (to-morrow's) denner."

Cissie chuckled and Mary reprimanded. "For goodness sake Allan, take that map of him. His tongue has never halted since we left the house."

They drove on through the Moorfoot hills until they reached Innerleithen, a small ancient borders town lying on the edge of Traquair Forest, there they parked at the Tavern and had lunch. Some of the tweed mills in the district had there own small gift shops that were still open, especially on Sundays, as they depended on visitors for their trade, so after lunch, they had a wander before heading for home.

Dropping Cissie off at five o'clock, she returned cheerily into her own house, where she found her husband propped up in bed, waiting for his cup of tea. Frank was in the kitchen buttering him a slice of toast, the warm succulent butter seeping into the golden bread. The tray was ready with the tea, hot black and sweet.

"He had a plate o' soup at one Auntie Cis, and now he fancies a bit o' toast, so here it is all ready to take up."

"Thanks laddie. A'm awful greatfu' fur this. A fair enjoyed ma'sel'. It was good o' you tae sit wi' him." Her eyes darted towards the ceiling.

"Nae bother a taw," he winked affectionately. "He's been fine. Never coughed or wheezed a bit when you were out," he lied, a cheeky grin spreading over his face. "Mind you, it could be doon tae the bit floozy that came in. Chased her round the hoose till he caught her."

Cissie laughed her usual heart warming laugh, her entire body dancing to the sound, "A' wish that wis the cure laddie fur a wid gladly squeeze in tae a fancy pair o, breeks an' let it awe hing oot."

"Noo there's a thought," Frank nodded as if considering the possibility.

"Git away wi' ye." She pushed him playfully almost knocking him off balance, "That's what's wrong wi' him the day," she joked.

Taking the tray from Frank, she nodded towards the door, "I'll take this up, and thanks again." As she smiled, her face folded into the familiar soft creases that was just Cissie.

Robbie sat bolt upright, his head and back supported by a mountain of pillows. His small slight frame was almost comical sitting in the high king-sized bed. The familiar blue and white striped woollen muffler, wrapped twice round his neck, folding over at the front and tucked into his pyjama trousers. His ashen face was almost skeletal with its sunken skin loosely hanging in a hangdog manner. Once bright flashing eyes were replaced by liquid beads of black.

His long bony hands with their dark blue veins risen like swollen rivers, picked at the covers as he lay waiting for his faithful wife to appear.

Cissie called as she mounted the stairs, puffing for breath. "Teas up faither!" Her mountainous frame filled the doorway.

Stopping for a second, she looked from the open door, "Noo dinnae you just look awfu' snug. A tell ye faither, yer in the best place fur it's a nirl oot there. Bright, bit a nirl." (A nirl, meaning an exceptionally cold day.)

Sliding towards the bed, she put the tray in front of her husband, pushing it well down, making a nest for it on top of his legs. "Noo there, eat that up. It'll keep ye goin' till a can rustle up a bite."

Catching her by the arm, he said, "Tae tell you the truth Cis, am no' awfu' hungry. This is jist what a want. Go doon an' make yersel' a bite though."

"A dinnae need a thing", she assured him. "A hud somethin' when we stoapped at Innerleithen."

"Innerleithen!" Rob exclaimed. "You wir at Fife?" A look of surprise crossed his small glazed eyes.

"Naw faither. Innerleithen. The borders. Peebles." She watched as he bit into his toast, his expression one of confusion. Then Cissie drew back satisfied, "You're thinkin' aboot Innverkeithin'." She blew a sigh as she realized his mistake. "They soond the same."

"So a am. I'm a sully auld goat. Well tell me all aboot it," he encouraged, his head nodding.

Cissie sat, her great hips balancing on the edge of the bed as she explained where they went, giving him a laugh by impersonating young Tony. She told him what she had eaten for lunch, and how good Allan had been paying for everything. "An' the price o' things in the shoaps!" she exclaimed disgustedly.

She sat with him as he finished his tea and with non-stop questions from an interested Rob, Cissie, a willing narrator, gladly answered. Taking his tray from him, Cissie walked to a nearby table, placing it down out of the way. "I'll ge ye a wee tuck in afore a go doon," she said turning to him once more.

Robs head was bowed.

"Are ye warm enough?" she asked lifting the covers up to enable her to tuck them in tighter.

His hand fell to the side.

"Faither?" she spoke looking at his bent head. "Faither?" she spoke louder, a slight panic now in her voice.

Rob had passed away as quickly and as peacefully as that, leaving Cissie devastated and lost, the tough facade she had performed all her life shattered. The loss of her 'auld man' or as she called him 'faither,' was hard for her to bear. Although never making a decision in his life and without a clue as to the affairs of the house, he had always been there, either tucked up in bed or propped in a chair, muffler around his neck summer or winter. It had always been a trait of Cissie's to look after folk; her own sons, Mary and her boys, waifs and strays, unwanted animals, and so on. She was never happier unless giving someone a bit of 'seeing too'. Her family grown up and away, Mary settled and the boys independent, her husband had her full and undivided attention. Now he was gone. Her hands were empty.

One of her sons took her away to live with his family after the funeral, but Cissie was adamant, 'she wis no' givin' up hir hoose!' so Mary agreed to look after it until she came back. She was a sore miss to Mary, for at no time could she think of being without Cissie. She had always been there for her. Always. One consolation was, they spoke frequently by phone. Thank heavens for the phone!

Chapter Eighteen

Annetta sat alone in her small bedroom that was located on the first landing of the students' residence. She had cried all evening. Things were getting worse and she had to do something about it. All those weeks of pretending, trying to convince her self that she was doing the right thing. The truth was she couldn't spend another night away from Allan. At first her new surroundings seemed exciting, and her newfound friends were very interesting, but that empty feeling she kept on experiencing was getting worse. She had thought of Allan as she sat in class, her tutor's voice becoming a muted drone in the far distance.

Losing interest in her studies, she had frequently been pulled up for lack of attention. "Miss Francittie, if you are not interested in studying here, think of the poor soul that was refused entry so you could be given a place to sit and dream." Miss Stoddart chided.

Annetta's face fired up into a full-blown blush as the awful feeling of guilt swelled over her.

"If you don't intend listening, I suggest you take yourself out of this class."

Miss Stoddart was right of course; she was not the least bit interested in her studies. All she wanted was to be with Allan. She tried desperately to get on with life without him, but failed miserably. It twisted her inwardly when speaking on the phone to him, for she had managed so far to sound cheery and self-assured, deliberately avoiding her true feelings. It was now too much for her to bear. She had to tell him the truth. She wanted to get back to him, and once she was back, she knew she would never return to Aberdeen.

She had phoned an hour ago and he was out.

She now lay on top of the bed watching the second hand on the clock as it jumped; picking it's way over the small white dots around the edge.

Her eyes swollen with tears, she searched the ceiling. There were one hundred and seventy four polystyrene tiles on the roof, two hanging loosely as if for dear life, two cracked, and a brown watermark almost covering a group of eight. She knew every tile as if they were old friends as she had counted them often enough. The cream paint on the walls of the small room failed miserably to hide the cracks, just like Annetta's pain under the false excitement that was transmitted down through the telephone.

She could wait no longer. The phone hung outside her door as all the students on the landing shared it. Opening her door, she looked along the corridor to make sure she was alone. Lifting the receiver from its rest, she dialled his number once more. The male voice at the other end spoke. It was Walter.

"Hi Walter. It's Annetta again. Is Allan back yet?"

"No he isn't love. Is everything alright?" he asked with concern, detecting a slight break in her voice.

"Oh yes." She lied, but not convincingly. "I just want to talk to him."

"Well I think he shouldn't be too long. He went out in the car, so he won't be drinking." There was a short silence as Walter waited for her to speak. "Are you alright?" he asked again.

Large warm tears ran like rivulets, dropping on her hand as she held the receiver. Taking her other hand, she wiped them quickly from both cheeks.

"Annetta? Talk to me," he coaxed.

"It's nothing really," she sniffed. "I just felt a bit home sick."

"Are you crying?" he asked. "Would you like to talk to Mary?"

"Oh no. Don't bother Mary. It's not all that bad," she tried to sound nonchalant.

Mary, hearing one side of the conversation, strolled over and stood at Walter's side. Catching his eye, she gave a questioning frown.

Walter shook his head as he listened.

"Look, here's Mary now Annetta, talk to her, please".

Taking the phone from Walter's hand, Mary spoke gently, "What's the matter Annetta? Are you all right?"

Feeling foolish and very embarrassed, Annetta struggled to assure her everything was fine, but once again failed as Mary picked up the tension.

"Look Annetta, I'll get Allan to phone you whenever he gets in. You are at the flat?"

"Yes I am Mary. I couldn't be bothered going out tonight."

"Well, you go and make yourself a nice cup of tea and Allan will ring when he gets here. He's not out for the night," she laughed. "I think he might be at the pictures but I'm not really sure. He says very little these days. Missing you too, you know."

She perked up hearing those words. "Is he Mary? Is he really missing me?"

"What do you think now? There's no living with him some days." She waited for an answer but there was only continues silence. "Annetta?"

Annetta's tears now flowed uncontrollably. She sniffed.

"Annetta? Come on love, I know you're missing home, but you must study."

"I can't Mary," she sobbed. "I hate it here and I miss him so much."

"But you'll be home soon," she reminded her.

"Not soon enough," came her reply. "I can't stand it another minute."

"Now, now." Mary's heart sank at the thought of the girl's heartache. "It's probably how you're feeling at the moment. Everyone has days when they feel down," she assured her.

"No Mary, I feel like this all the time. I just can't go on up here."

"Look pet, you hang on there and Allan will call as soon as he gets in, ok?"

She said goodbye to Mary and stood with the receiver still in her hand, the continual burring from the earpiece growing louder in the silence of the corridor. A thud from the ceiling above brought her out of her dream-like trance and she placed the receiver back onto its rest. Returning to her room, she closed the door and stood leaning on its frame. Muted laughter came from the upstairs flat disturbing her silence. She felt anger at someone enjoying them self when she felt so alone, overcome with self-pity, she then threw herself onto the bed and cried herself to sleep.

The phone rang at ten thirty. Annetta, slightly dazed from the depth of her sleep, sat up and looked towards the door. In spite of her earlier anxiousness, she slowly moved from the bed. Going into the hall once more, she lifted the receiver.

"Annetta?" Allan's voice sounded worried.

"Allan!" She sighed before the floodgates opened once more. "Where have you been?" It was almost a demand. "Oh Allan, please come tomorrow. Please come and get me!" Her panic-stricken pleas continued.

"Hoy up lass. Slow down! What on earth has happened?"

"Nothing! Nothing has happened," a trace of agitation crept into her voice. "Nothing's happened Allan. I want you to come and get me."

"But your Father!"

"Bugger my Father!" she screamed. "I want you."

"Alright Annetta. If that's what you want."

"Tomorrow Allan. Tomorrow. Promise!"

"I'll be there. I'll leave here at eight in the morning. I should be there by eleven or twelve."

"And Allan," she said with determination, "I'm not going home!"

He bit his lip as he faced his mother. "She's not going home," he told her.

"Where is she going to stay?" Mary searched her son's anxious face.

"Here!"

"Here? Oh my God," she panicked.

"Ma! We'll manage. We can shift around and manage," he pleaded.

Mary blew a sigh, "Wait till her father finds out! There will be hell to pay."

Annetta stood anxiously waiting at the window, small canvas suitcase and her sports bag at her feet, shoulder bag tucked under her arm. She had been at the window from twelve o'clock and it was now fifteen minutes past one. She shifted weight from one leg to another every few seconds.

"I wish you would sit down," her friend said. "Standing there won't bring him any quicker."

Turning from the window, she smiled nervously. "I know, but he should have *been* here."

Lying on top of Annetta's bed, Penny Scoular picked at the covers, "I hope you know what you're doing Annetta. You'll probably live to regret this."

"No I won't," she murmured. "I want to *be* with him."

Sighing, her friend looked heavenwards, "Oh to be in love!"

The car turned into the campus and stopped directly under the window.

Annetta jumped when the horn blew. "It's him," she announced excitedly. Grabbing her bags, she walked towards the door. "You will hand in those letters?" she asked for the fourth time.

Smiling sadly, Penny assured her, "Of course I will. Leave it to me." Jumping from the bed, she hurried to the door where she hugged her friend tightly. "Good luck to you both, and don't do anything I wouldn't do." They smiled at on another then hugged once more.

As she walked from the building, Allan jumped from the car and hurried towards her. Dropping her luggage, she threw herself into his arms, gripping him as tight as she could, then with quivering lips she asked, "Where have you been?"

Drawing from her, his eyes narrowed. "I got here as quick as I could, getting lost a few times in the process."

"I was frightened you wouldn't come," she said anxiously.

"I said I would. Didn't I?" he said.

Grabbing up her bags from the path, he ushered her towards the open door of the vehicle throwing the luggage carelessly onto the back seats. "I stopped a lass round the corner and luckily she knew exactly where you were, otherwise I would still be going round in circles."

She hurried into the passenger's seat of the car and closed the door.

Allan turned and looked at her before attempting to drive off. "Are you sure of this Annetta?"

"Dead sure", she replied adamantly.

He gave a low whistle. "Dead we will be when this gets out."

They stopped at a small cafe and had a snack before leaving the city, and then they drove without stopping until they reached Edinburgh.

Crossing over the Forth Bridge, Allan turned the car into the service area and parked outside the cafeteria. "Come on," he suggested, "Lets have a coffee and talk this through."

Inside, the cafeteria was almost empty. A family of four sat in the corner, their small child strapped into a high chair screaming for all it was worth, while the parents and their elder child tucked into their meal quite unperturbed. Further up, three elderly ladies drank tea, their frowns and dagger expressions showing utter disapproval at the screaming child.

Frank carried a tray holding two mugs of coffee and a four fingered kit-kat while Annetta followed behind.

They made their way to the back of the room, and sat down near the door. Lifting the mugs, he then slid the tray under the table balancing it against the table leg.

Annetta unwrapped the biscuit and snapped it in two, handing half to Allan.

They sat drinking in silence; Annetta fixing her gaze down the room and onto the child while Allan stared out of the window. Without looking at her, he spoke, "We should really go and confront your Father now," he suggested.

She turned round quickly her dark eyes shifting worriedly, "No!" she rebuked, "he will only force me back."

"If you think he's capable of forcing you back, then you can't be sure you're doing the right thing," he said doubting her.

"I *am* doing the right thing. I want to wait a few days until the principal gets my letter, then there's nothing he can do after that."

"And you know who's going to get the blame of all this. Don't you?" he frowned.

"I'll tell him it was my decision."

"And it was," he reminded her.

"So you think I am wrong to do this."

He sucked in his lips before answering, "I'm glad you've come back. I've been out of my mind without you, but I have no right to deny you a career. You may blame me in the future."

"No! It's what *I* want Allan. I love you and only want to be with you."

Touching her hand, he gazed into her dark pools. Loose strands of hair had broken free from her band, and now lay untidily over her eyes. Reaching over, Frank swept them gently to the side tucking them into the back of her ear. Oh God how he had missed her. He couldn't imagine her being more beautiful than she was now. The anxiety in her eyes gave her a wild Gipsy look. His heart quickened as his very soul was moved. "Come on. Drink up," he said, aware of the yearning that was in his loins. "Lets get home."

Annetta walked into Mary's home unsure of her welcome. She knew she had put Mary in a spot but there was nothing else she could have done.

As she entered the living room, Mary appeared from the kitchen. The two women stood looking at each other both waiting for the other's reaction. Mary, aware of Annetta's uncertainty, made the first move.

With a sigh, she shook her head and opened her arms, "Come 'ere," she beckoned, then Annetta was enfolded in Mary's embrace. As the girl wrapped herself in her arms, Mary looked up at Allan, expression of concern evident in her eyes.

"Frank's away over to Cissies to look after the house, so you can have his room for now," she said breaking gently from the girls hold. "Get your things upstairs and I'll make a bite to eat. Go on Allan, take her up," she nodded towards the door.

Knowing there would be trouble, Mary grew uneasy. Her memory flashed back to her own mother's dominance, and in a way, there were striking similarities. Annetta's father objected vehemently to Allan, as he wasn't up to his standards. He was not good enough for 'his' daughter.

Mary had seen it all before and she knew that there were stormy times ahead for them both.

Walter too felt things were not right. He had called for Mary and taken her out for a few hours on Sunday evening, leaving Allan and Annetta in with Tony. He sat in the corner of the small club- room, a worried expression on his face. "She shouldn't have gone without telling her parents. It's wrong," he frowned.

"Tell me about it," Mary sighed, "but what can I do Walter? She's eighteen and *I* can't tell her what to do," she sounded quite annoyed.

"You've taken her in Mary. That's going to make things worse."

Bending her head, she ran her hands through her hair showing signs of agitation. Then looking at him she suddenly snapped, "What else could I do? I couldn't turn her away."

"Get her to phone tomorrow. She will listen to you," he said rubbing his chin in thought.

When they returned home, Annetta had gone upstairs to bed. Allan was helping Tony with homework, and Frank had retired to Cissie's.

Monday morning, the men had gone to work, Tony had left for school and Mary sat with Annetta relaxing over a cup of coffee. Annetta's long tanned legs, sprawled from beneath the table as she too cradled her mug. As their gaze met, she smiled warmly.

"I think you should phone your Father now Annetta." Mary spoke softly, but the directness of the subject cast a shadow over the young woman's face. Annetta looked from Mary to the floor.

"I will call tonight. Promise." Then looking up once more, she added. "He will have gone to work."

Mary's eyebrows rose, "Your Mother will be at home. Won't she?"

Shifting uneasily in her chair, Annetta did not answer.

"Look Annetta, don't you think it would be better to talk to your Mother first?"

Clicking her tongue, she then gave a tiresome sigh. "Maybe you're right. Maybe I should talk to Mother first," she agreed.

At the phone she nervously dialled the number. As it rang, she shifted her eyes anxiously round the hall. No answer! With welcome relief she replaced the receiver back onto the phone. "I'll try again later," she whispered.

At five thirty, Frank was first to arrive home. Allan was not due back until seven as Monday night was his night for a spot of overtime. Mary had made a pot of vegetable soup and was filling a bowl for Frank, while Annetta sat with Tony on the sofa. At the other end of the table, a similar bowl was cooling.

"Has she contacted her folk?" Frank asked in a whisper as his mother pushed the bowl in front of him. Mary replied by shaking her head her eyes darting worriedly in Annetta's direction. Frank whistled softly through his teeth.

"Are you sure you don't want a wee drop o' soup pet?" Mary called to the girl.

"I'm sure Mary. I'll hold on until Allan gets home," she answered sweetly.

Unseen by Annetta, Frank pulled a face only to be clipped harshly on the ear by his mother making him flinch.

Shaking her head wearily, Mary then called, "Your soup's cooler now Tony. Come now or it won't be worth eatin'."

As the boy rose, the rattle at the front door steered him in the other direction. "Here!" Mary stopped him in his tracks, "Get through there this minute and eat. I'll see to that."

His back to the door, the figure that stood on Mary's step was of a young man, tall dark and very handsome, who turned round as Mary spoke.

The evening light had begun to fade so as the oblong beam of light that filtered from the lobby could trace only the outline of his features.

"Yes?" Mary said, a bit more curtly than she had meant to.

The outside bulb above the door had blown and she had asked Frank as often to renew it, but as usual, he had forgotten.

"Mrs. Sweeny?" the man asked nervously.

Mary squinted. "Do I know you?" she asked thinking he looked familiar.

"No... no. You know my sister Annetta."

"Yes," Mary's heart seemed to quiver slightly. Trouble had come to their door.

"Can I have a word with Annetta?" He shifted nervously from hip to hip, and then turning round, he glanced towards the parked car that stood past the gate. He seemed greatly disturbed. "I know she's here."

Releasing her grip on the door, Mary stood to one side, "You better come in."

On seeing her brother, Annetta sprang to her feet. Rushing to him she tried to throw her arms around his neck, but her expression changed as he caught her arms and held her firmly at a distance.

"You have done it this time. Whatever possessed you to quit college?" he scowled.

"How did you find out so quickly?" she asked looking vacant.

"The principal phoned Father when he was given your letter. He's been trying to find you all day; Mother's in a right state. She's had to go to Aunt Helen's out of the way. He's going berserk."

"Where is he?" she asked, fear evident in her doe like eyes.

"Out in the car. I said I would bring you out." He turned and looked towards Mary who stood at the wall beside the kitchen door. Frank had joined his mother, still unwashed in his working jeans, and stocking feet.

It was then Mary looked into the face of Annetta's brother. She had seen him before somewhere. She was sure. But of course, he's Annetta's twin. There must be some striking similarities, but something about this young man disturbed her, but what?

"I'm not going anywhere." Annetta said defiantly. "I have made up my mind. I'm staying here."

Mary watched Annetta's brother draw back, a mixture of fear and anger sparked from his eyes. Young though he was, he looked weary. "Annetta, you don't know what you're doing."

"I do," she screamed. "Will you stop treating me like a child! I am eighteen, not eight! Go and tell him that I refuse to go back to college and I refuse to stay with them, them and their sanctimonious lifestyle. I am not giving Allan up. He can't do anything to make me."

"He's only doing what's best for you. Come on home Annetta," he pleaded.

"I thought you liked Allan." She looked shocked and hurt.

"I do. There's nothing wrong with him, but you can't stay with him."

"We are going to find a place were we can stay together. We will not be parted again," she was adamant.

"Well Annetta, *you* will have to tell him that for I certainly am not. He's furious at you as it is." Gritting his teeth, his facial muscles quivered. "I've done my best," he shrugged. Turning again to Mary, he said despairingly, "I'm sorry about this, I really am."

Shrugging his shoulders once more, he left dejected.

Annetta stared at Mary and in turn Mary held her gaze. Frank's eyes darted from one to another. Dropping down heavily on the sofa, the now distraught girl buried her head in her hands and cried uncontrollably.

Moving to her side, Mary pulled the weeping lass to her. With Annetta's head resting on Mary's shoulder, both women embraced. Still looking on, Frank scratched his head. Bloody women, he thought, then, as he was about to return to the kitchen, the demanding thump on the door stopped him in his tracks.

Annetta held Mary tight. "It's *him*. It's my Father," she said apprehensively.

Looking round at Frank, Mary said, "Get that," then, gently pushing the frightened girl from her, Mary said sternly,

"If you don't want to go with him, you had better draw yourself together, otherwise he'll break you down."

Nodding in agreement, she wiped her wet cheeks, drew her shoulders back, and with a confident toss of her head, the defiance that had masked her face minutes ago returned.

As Frank made his way up the lobby, the door hammered continually. By the time he reached the latch, he felt a surge of anger. Opening the door, he looked up at the dark figure that filled the door frame, "No need to hammer mister, we hear you!"

"*Get my bloody Daughter out here this instant,*" he demanded.

"*Oye*! Just a tick, who do you think *your* talking too?" Frank barked. "She doesn't want to come out here, so you'd better be off!"

With a sweep of his hand, he took Frank by surprise. As Frank fell heavily onto the half open door, it slammed against the lobby wall causing him to stagger, then before he knew what was happening, the dark figure was charging along the lobby. "*We'll see right now whether she's coming or not!*" he bellowed.

Annetta stood firm beside Mary and as her father's huge frame appeared in the door, her heart pounded from within her ribs, but with her defiant stance, her fear was well hidden.

"What's the meaning of this Annetta!" he demanded. "Get out of here this instant and get your arse back up to that college NOW!" he roared. With narrowing eyes, he peered at his daughter. "Move!"

Although the tone of his voice increased the nervous tension within her, she stood still, drawing herself up to her tallest height she answered without faltering, "I am not going back." Her dark eyes sparked with fire.

"You bloody ungrateful young fool, you'll do as I tell you."
He walked nearer, stopping in front of Mary, his attention still
fully on his daughter.

Rooted to the spot, Mary stared at the man that stood
before her. Blinking rapidly, she couldn't believe her own eyes.
Here in her living room. Here! After all those years.

Frank's voice came to her although it seemed distant.

"Enough of this," he shouted.

Everything seemed to happen in an instant. He was beside
her, beside his daughter. Annetta cried out then Frank jumped
on top of the man knocking him onto the floor.

Mary looked down at the struggle but could do nothing. It
was as though she was watching a film. Then another voice was
added to the fracas. Where he came from, Mary could not tell,
but pulling Frank from the struggling body was Allan. Tony
too had appeared and was screaming for all he was worth.
Still, Mary stood dazed. She felt herself laughing, but only
her stomach muscles were working as no sound came from
her mouth.

"Mother!" Allan called for the fourth time.

Jumping back to reality, Mary became aware of the
situation before her.

"Mother, fetch a towel," Allan ordered.

Running to the kitchen, she pulled the hand towel from
the rail, and then smartly she ran back and threw it to Allan.
Annetta's father was by now trying to sit up, blood spouting
from the gash on his forehead.

Annetta was back on the sofa, her lip bleeding and puffed.
Frank sat beside her, his anger still evident as he punched into
his own hand. "You'll no' strike a woman in this house," he
growled.

Allan tried laying the towel on the bleeding forehead, but the man pushed his arm from him drunkenly. "Leave me be. You bloody bastards!" he said with a struggle.

Annetta's brother appeared back in the room. He had assumed there was something wrong and returned to the house. Seeing his father sitting awkwardly on the floor, he rushed over, "What on earth?"

"Bloody bastards," was all his father managed to say. Pushing Allan to the side, Albert Francittie wrapped his arms round his father, and with an awkward struggle, helped him to his feet. The big man staggered but saved himself by falling down into the near by armchair, Albert almost falling into his lap. "Are you alright father?" he asked concerned.

Nodding and breathing in short gasps was how he answered.

"You had no right lifting your hands to your daughter," Frank said, his voice with less venom.

"You will pay for this. You!" He spat his words at Frank. "I'll have the law on you for this. And as for you *lady*, you think I don't know why you've come here! Quit a good training. Refused to have anything to do with Vincent Marconi? Eh? You're pregnant! Aren't you? That's the way these people work. After my money no doubt, they have no shame."

Annetta, open mouthed, her eyebrows near meeting her hairline, drew in air. All eyes fell on her, all except Allan's.

Looking down on Mario he scowled. "You dirty minded..." he stopped himself from cursing. "You just don't get it, do you? She's not interested in Vincent Marconi, and we don't want your money. She wants to choose her own life. Pregnant?" he shook his head. "She's not pregnant. You filthy minded...". Gritting his teeth, he restrained himself by throwing the towel at Mario.

289

"You better stop the bleeding. Hold that to his head and get him to the hospital. He needs to get that stitched. Get him out of here. I should have let Frank finish him off."

Struggling from the chair with the aid of his son, Mario staggered to the living room door. Clutching his side, he winced. "You'll be hearing from me, I can promise you that." His eyes darted to each face that stood looking on, then as his eyes met Mary's, they rested on her as if seeing her for the first time.

Lowering her gaze, she avoided any further stares.

A solitary grunt and he was gone.

As Frank rose from the sofa, Allan took his place beside Annetta, then, placing his forefinger under her chin, he examined the damage her father had done. "You should put a cold cloth on your lip." Then in a disgusted tone he snarled, "what kind of man would do that to his own Daughter?"

"A bloody idiot," came Frank's reply.

Mary hardly spoke as her mind was in turmoil. She walked from the scene in the living room and busied herself in the kitchen. Her mind could not concentrate on everything at once. She was in shock and could say nothing to anyone. The past had come back to haunt her. She had said nothing in defence of her sons. Bastards he had called them. People without honour! Her normal reaction to such allegations would have been to attack, but she was unable to speak. Even yet her throat was parched.

Gritting her teeth she thought of his honour twenty-four years ago. Twenty-four years ago when she was left carrying his bastard. Her head ached. She had filled the basin with hot soapy water and was furiously stuffing the dishcloth into a cup, turning it round inside with force.

The touch on her shoulder made her jump. "Ma, are you alright?" Frank asked with concern.

Glancing quickly over her shoulder, she nodded, then turning her attention back to the cup, she continued rubbing.

"I'm sorry I went for him Ma. I really only wanted to catch his hand but he struck out at me first."

"I know," she answered, not really knowing what had happened. "Is she alright?" Her hands worked furiously.

"Annetta? Aye. Allan's seeing to her lip." Then with a screwed facial expression, he asked. "Are you sure you're ok?"

With added sharpness, she answered, "Yes. Stop asking me that," then realising she had snapped at him, she turned, her face softening she said, "I'm just upset at what's happened, that's all." With a sigh, she wiped her hands on the dishtowel. "I suppose I'd better speak to her." Touching Frank's arm, she held his gaze momentarily. At that moment she felt the desire to pull him close to her, but refrained from doing so. Sucking in her breath, she walked on past him and joined Annetta and Allan in the other room.

"I am sorry Mary," the distraught girl looked pale and irritable. "I have brought trouble to your family. I truly am sorry."

"Stop it now," Mary chided softly. "It's over and done with. We'll sort something out."

"But he'll not let it go. I know him," she said, her voice almost a whine.

"There's not much more he can do," Allan assured her. "He's been told the situation, besides, you're old enough to make your own mind up."

"And I have." The swelling on her lip distorting her usual beautiful smile. The blow from her father had also caught the side of her face as bruising was now slowly appearing.

"Annetta, can I ask you something?" Mary sounded nonchalant. Without waiting, she asked. "What's your father's name?"

"Mario," she looked puzzled.

"Oh I thought you said he was called Al..something," she lied shrugging her shoulders.

"No Mary. You're thinking of my brother Albert. He has my Father's middle name, Mario Alberto Francittie."

Grinning she remarked as though joking, "It's just so I'll recognise the name when he charges Frank."

Mary was sure now. Ally was what he called himself. Ally, short for Albert.

Walter called in later that night and was given a brief rundown on what had happened. Mary was glad when he suggested he take her for a drive along the coast as she just felt like getting away for a few hours. Driving along the coastal road, he drove into one of the bay car parks taking the car to the edge of the rough where the thinning gorse bushes bordered the sandy shore, there he stopped the car, switched off the engine and turned off the lights. They sat in silence looking over the river Forth that ran out into the North Sea. Over the water the twinkling lights of Fife resembled jewels on black velvet.

The sky above them had clouded over and as they sat, their eyes fixed on the coastal line, spots of rain splashed onto the windscreen. The sea, although calm, looked dark and menacing. They sat in silence; the lapping of the tide on the nearby rocks could be heard faintly.

Mary shivered. Walter slid his arm round her shoulders and pulled her closer to him. Leaning her head against his arm, she sighed wearily.

"Are you cold he asked?"

"A bit" she said softly."

Turning the key in the ignition, he started up the engine, and then with a flick of a switch he turned on the fan. "You'll feel better in a minute," he said.

"You'll flatten the battery," she remarked flatly without taking her eyes from the night scene.

"We won't spend too long here. It's going to be a downpour," he remarked understanding her mood.

"It's so peaceful here though," she said, "I think this has got to be my favourite spot."

"I know. That's why I came here. I thought you could do with the tranquillity."

As she looked up into his face, he stooped his head and kissing her softly on her brow. "You've had a hellish night. You could do without all this worry."

Closing her eyes, Mary pressed her lids tight shut. Her head still hurt despite the codeine she had swallowed earlier and they did nothing to ease the tense knots that still tightened in her stomach.

"Could he charge Frank with assault?" she asked.

"He'd have a nerve, after all, he forced his way into your house and struck his own daughter." Then facing Mary he stated, "and he has no witness. They seem to be all on Frank's side; no, I think he's too smart for that. He'll probably disown Annetta and that will be that."

"Not according to Annetta."

"The best thing they both can do now is to get a place of their own."

Turning her head quickly, she looked a little surprised, "You mean together? Stay together?"

"Aye. What's so wrong with that? They want to marry, so what's the difference?"

Turning her attention back to the night sky, Mary answered with uncertainty, "I don't know. I really hadn't thought--"

"But it's obviously in their minds Mary."

There was a minute's silence before Walter suggested, "Why don't I let them have my flat. I could move in with you."

As quick as he had got the last word from his mouth, Mary turned sharply, "Oh Walter, what would Frank say to that? Oh no. He wouldn't agree--"

"Mary!" he stopped her; "I want to be with you as your husband, not a live-in lover."

Her stare was expressionless. She blinked rapidly.

"You shouldn't be that surprised It's not as if I've never asked you before."

"I know Walter, and it's not that I don't want to---"

"Then what the hell's the matter?" he sounded impatient.

Biting her lip, she looked into the dark night. How could she marry Walter with this dark secret hanging over her? Although Walter knew Patrick was not Frank's father, what would he say to this latest turn around? Feeling confused, Mary ran her hand over the top of her head, and then turning to Walter, she could just make out his handsome features in the dark shadows of the car. Tears welled up in her eyes as she stroked him gently on the cheek. "Walter, there's something I have to tell you." She had to tell him. She needed someone to know.

"What's the matter love?" he said full of concern. "Have I upset you?"

As she shook her head, her fingers moved rapidly under her cuffs. Finding her handkerchief, she quickly wiped her eyes. "Walter, I found something out tonight, something that's troubling me more than that fight."

"Go on. I'm listening," he coaxed her to go on.

"It's about Annetta's father--Mario." She breathed deeply. "I know him...from away back. He...he's Frank's Father."

The silence that ensued was deafening.

Mary looked into Walter's face, and then with bowed head, waited his reply.

She heard him suck in air, and then slowly he exhaled. "Are you sure it was him?"

"Certain," she whispered.

"Do you think he recognised you?"

"No. I'm sure he didn't," Wide eyed, she answered positively.

Sucking more air, he blew. "Well," he shook his head in disbelief. "What are you going to do?"

"About us?" she asked gingerly.

"No. About Frank, Allan and Annetta?"

"What should I do?" she pleaded.

Chewing the inside of his mouth, he thought carefully, and then he advised, "Do nothing!"

"Nothing?" She sounded surprised.

"What they don't know won't hurt them Mary. It'll only cause all kinds of problems with Frank, and besides, Allan's not related. So?"

"And how do you feel about me now?" she asked apprehensively.

"Why? Should it alter things?" he asked surprisingly.

"I don't know. Does it?" she asked with uncertainty.

"Not with me Mary. I think you've had a terrible shock and I'm glad you had the courage to tell me, but it makes no odds to me. I love you. I want what's in the future for us, not the past. If I told you things about me and sweaty Betty!" he joked, trying to raise a smile.

She did more than smile she laughed. Cupping his face in her hands, she reached up kissed him. Walter responded by drawing her tightly to him, the long meaningful kiss answered both their questions.

"Well will you marry me Mary?"

"Why not? I can't think of anything better."

Chapter Nineteen

Because of the happenings of that night, Mary postponed telling the family of her intended marriage, thinking that she had no right to be happy when at that present time there was so much troubling Allan and Annetta however, as there had been no further incidents that week, the following Saturday night was chosen for the announcement.

Allan and Annetta were going out for the evening and were dressed ready to leave after tea. Frank had just arrived home after spending his afternoon at the bookmaker's followed by a few pints at the Railway Tavern.

Setting the table, Mary's eyes darted to the clock on the mantelpiece.

"Walter coming for tea?" Frank asked noticing her glance at the time.

"Aye. He should be here presently."

Standing by the window, Tony announced, "Here he is Ma. I'll let him in."

Settled around the table, the conversation was light. Frank had a post-mortem on the races where he won money, giving no account of the ones that had evened the score.

"You should stop gamblin' my lad. Only brings grief." Mary scorned as she gave a look of disapproval.

"What Ma? A couple of lines on a Saturday? Go on," he scoffed.

"He's not a big time punter. A pound here and there. Our Frank's not that daft." Allan spoke in his defence.

"Maybe so. But it can get a hold of you... Do you want more of this meat?" she asked passing the large plate that lay in front of her over in Frank's direction.

Taking the plate from his mother, he helped himself to another few slices. "Where are you off to the night then?" his question was directed at Walter as he passed the platter on to him.

"Nowhere in particular," he answered, his eyes resting on Mary. "Nothing planned as yet." He gave her a wink of reassurance.

"I'm going with Tommy Baillie Ma, so don't expect me to come with you," piped up Tony.

"An' pray tell me where you both are going?" Mary questioned her youngest son, her narrowing lids and screwed expression warning him of her mistrust.

"His father's taking us to the speedway." He had everyone's attention, all with the same questioning look. "Honest!" he laughed.

"Phone him if you don't believe me," he looked from one to another.

"Don't worry lad, Mum *will*," Frank added.

"Speedway is it?" Allan laughed, "You had better stand right at the back 'cause the spray from the gravel can fair sting your face, and knowing you, you'll be yelling blue murder."

"Don't be daft our Allan, it wouldn't bother me!" he said indignantly.

"Just you mind and stay out of trouble, or there'll be more than your face stinging, that's all I'm saying," warned Mary, pointing a wagging finger. Rising from his chair, the young lad made to leave the table.

"Sit back down Tony, I... we have something to tell you all."

Despite his loud protest, Tony sat back in his chair.

Silence fell as all heads turned to Mary, then prodding Walter's arm, she encouraged him to speak. "Go on. Tell them."

Walter looked at Frank, then over to Allan. Clearing his throat, he then spoke in an earnest fashion, "I have asked your Mother to marry me!"

Frank looked over to Allan before turning to his mother, "Well. What did *you* say?" he asked his mother, his dark eyes flashing.

Sitting straight back in the chair, his mother held his gaze. "I have accepted." Her lips tightened into thin narrow lines waiting for his response.

Allan and Annetta also waited for Frank's reaction. His stern face searched Walter's, who showed no sign of weakness, and then slowly Frank's mouth stretched into a broad grin. "Well it was only a matter of time I suppose, and you know the old saying, take me, take my family."

Mary's heart leapt, as Frank held his hand out towards Walter. She could have cried for joy. Allan and Tony were easy to fathom out, but Frank was another matter. He could just have easily flown into a rage, but here he was, welcoming Walter as her future husband. Allan rose and went to his mother, Annetta behind him. Kissing her on the cheek, he then held his hand out towards Walter, giving his hand a brisk shake while thumping him roughly on the back.

Tony, his arms leaning on the table, his head resting in his hands looked on. "Is that it then. Can I go?" he asked looking bored.

"Thanks for the encouragement son, I knew you would be pleased," Mary remarked laughing. "Go on, before I change my mind."

They planned to wed in three months time fixing a date in January.

The following two months ran like clockwork. Annetta landed a job in a solicitor's office and settled down at Mary's. Cissie returned to her own house, glad to be back as another week at her son's would have suffocated her. Although they had been extremely kind to her, she was not used to being mollycoddled. Frank agreed to stay at Cissie's until things sorted themselves out across the road.

It was seven thirty, Thursday night, Frank left Cissie's heading for the Railway Tavern, the darts night being a regular fixture. It was a particularly mucky night, overcast darkness blotting any natural light from the sky. Very small drops of rain were felt through the air, causing one to feel damp and cold rather than sodden wet. Heading towards the back street, he intended cutting through the vennel and down the narrow high walled lane that ran along side the cemetery, the adjacent wall hemming in a market garden. On top of both walls, broken bottles were encrusted in a bed of cement acting as a warning to anyone wishing to climb on them. The misty atmosphere making the darker shadows even more menacing blurred the beam from the street lighting. Coffin lane, as it was known, ran for over 200 yards, and at various intervals, the high tops of ancient stones loomed up above the wall, looking like great heads, frightening the nervous passers-by. Unfortunately, the only lamp was situated half way down the lane.

As Frank turned into the lane, he was aware of the footsteps behind him. Walking faster, he seemed to gain distance, then laughing to him-self, he thought how stupid he had been to even think of danger, still, every step he took seemed to get faster. He was never so glad to reach the bottom and out into the road, where once out into the open, he turned and looked back up the lane where the shadowy figure behind seemed to loll behind. Carrying on down towards the main street, Frank looked back once more. The man had disappeared. He thought to himself, Frank, you're losing your marbles.

The front street was deserted as all sensible people were in out of the cold. A few cars passed by, the swish of the tyres on the wet road adding to the misery of the night. The black Rover travelling on the other side of the street seemed to slow down as it passed, then picking up speed it moved on. Thinking how mad he was to have ventured out, Frank shivered as he turned his collar further up onto his face. The car that had moments ago passed by drew up behind him, the doors flying open allowing three burly men to spill quickly from the vehicle. Knowing instantaneously that they were after him, Frank tried to run, but was quickly pulled back by his coat. The first out of the car held on to the struggling Frank for dear life, and then with huge soup plate hands, grabbed roughly at his hair. Once in the clutches of this towering monster, Frank had no chance at all. It all happened so fast. Two of the others held him tightly by each arm as the ape-like article delivered the blows. The wind bellowed from Frank's lungs as the second blow hit him full on the stomach, then his head reeled to the side by the force of the great fist that landed on his face, the dull thud causing an inner explosion in his ear. The two goons struggled under the blows to prop Frank up as the power from their mate's punches almost sent them flying. Warm blood trickled down into Frank's mouth and as he tried to draw breath, rivulets of blood finding its way into his nose caused him to cough violently. Frank braced himself for the next blow as his assailant's arm drew back to gather force, then as if by some miracle he saw the ape-like figure hurl around, his arm stretched upwards was locked onto another being. Taking in the situation, the two accomplices that held Frank relaxed their grip, then as if on cue, Frank broke free, jumped back and with a wide sweeping movement with both arms, grabbed both the men's heads banging them together with all the strength he could muster. As they staggered about, Frank jumped onto the back of one forcing him to the ground, there he delivered a few blows from his clenched fist but as the man was much heavier, he soon staggered to his feet with Frank still pounding on his back.

"Get in," screamed a voice from within the car. "Get in you bloody fools!"

The stranger had Frank's assailant in an arm lock over the car bonnet, and as he banged his forehead on the car, the occupant peered out through the steamed up windscreen. The revs of the engine were heard before the car jumped into gear, then despite the doors still flying open, it shot off throwing the sprawling figure to the side, Frank's helper releasing his hold as he jumped clear of the moving car.

Stopping a few yards up the street and at a safe distance, it waited until the three battered thugs picked themselves up and ran panicking behind it.

Doubled up on the payment, Frank struggled to catch his breath. Aware of the man standing beside him, he looked up through hanging strands of loose untidy hair. He gasped at the air.

"You all right mate?" the stranger asked as he helped him straighten.

"I've felt better," Frank remarked groaning.

"Someone doesn't like your face the way it is," the man remarked. "I hope she's worth it?"

"Eh?" Spitting the blood from his mouth, Frank then daubed the side of his face with his handkerchief. His ear had been torn with the violent blow and the ringing he heard from inside seemed to grow louder as he spoke.

"It's got to be a Sheila. Always is," the man laughed.

"Sheila? Oh aye... I mean, no. A woman?" Drawing in more air he blew it back out slowly. "By the way, thanks." Holding his hand out to the man, he introduced himself. "Frank. Frank Fairley." He refused to be known as Sweeny.

"Scotty," came the reply as they shook hands.

Moving to the wall, Frank leaned his tall frame against it, daubing once more at his ear, then as if it just came to him he whispered, "Oh my God- Allan!"

"Allan?" The man asked with interest.

"Aye Allan. My brother. That's what this is about." Working his jawbone back and forward he stroked at his chin in thought.

"Will they go after him?"

Frank, detecting a worried note in the stranger's voice felt that he could trust him. "Maybe. I best get back and warn him."

"Where is he then, at home?" he asked.

"I think so. I hope they're still there. I best get home and warn them," he said anxiously.

"There's no one there to help him if things get rough? I mean, no Father?" he enquired with caution.

"There's just my Mother and his girl... Unless Walter? Naw he's on late shift," he answered himself.

"Walter?" Scotty asked with interest.

"Mum's intended. Look I best be off. Thanks again for your help. Call into the Railway Tavern some night an' I'll pay you back wi' a pint." Holding out his hand he grabbed at Scotty's arm giving it a tight friendly squeeze.

As if the idea had just crossed his mind, Scotty spoke positively, "Look I'll come along, just in case. You'll need a witness anyway."

"Naw man, you've done enough, besides, you don't know what you're getting into."

"Let me be the judge of that, come on before it's too late."

As they hurried on, Frank observed his newfound companion for the first time. He was in his late forties to early fifties, with thick silvery grey hair that complimented his dark leathery skin, an outdoor kind of face, rugged and hardy.

"Your not from around here then?" Frank asked.

"No. Just passing through."

Then Frank announced, "Here. Along here Scotty," he indicated to an adjoining street. "A mate of mine's in that corner house. He has a car."

On approaching the house, Scotty stood by the gate and waited as Frank hurried up the path. He no sooner reached the door than it flew open.

The young man stood as if barring the entrance, a halo of light outlining his burly figure. Dressed in his working jeans and tattered jumper, his toes peeped through the massive holes in his socks. Rubbing his tousled hair he grinned, revealing the absence of several front teeth.

"Oh it's yoursel' Frankie boy. Thought it was Ma's tick man." Grinning wider he asked, "What's up man?"

"Can I borrow the jalopy Muff?" he asked hurriedly.

"Aye. Nae bother. Needs the clutch tightenin'." Becoming aware of Frank's agitation, he pulled a single key from his pocket throwing it into Frank's open palm.

Catching it with a swoop he promised, "Thanks Muff. I'll fix that clutch for you." Running back up the path he left the bemused Muff standing gaping.

Once inside the car Frank turned the key. The starter motor whined but could not catch the engine, then after a few more tries and a couple of oaths, the engine caught, then stalled.

"Oh come on!" his patience exploded. Pulling at the choke he tried again. Caught. Stalled. Caught, then with a shudder threatening to give up once more, he pressed hard against the accelerator playing it up and down gently. The engine roared, then back fired sending a cloud of black smoke billowing from the trailing exhaust. It gave a few heart stopping jumps before moving from the kerb.

"It needs the clutch tightened he said," laughed Frank. "Needs scrappin' if you ask me."

Driving into the street, Frank noticed Allan's car. He groaned with relief, "he's in. Thank God for that." Driving behind it, he brought the old car to a halt. It shuddered as if thankful to be stopping.

"Come on, I owe you a cold beer or something," Frank said his voice more cheery.

Scotty pushed the door open and stood on the road. "No, I best be off. Everything seems all right."

"Come on man." He sounded disappointed.

Waving an objecting hand, Scotty smiled, "No honestly. I'll take a rain check though."

"Any Thursday." Frank cocked his head to the side. "Are you sure you won't come in?"

"Naw I'll give it a miss, but I may see you along at the Tavern."

Leaning on the car's damp roof, Frank watched as his friend disappeared into the mist. He wondered just where he had come from, as his accent certainly was not from around these parts. Shivering, he stooped down and tried locking the car, then smiling he remembered it was an impossible task. "No one in his or her right mind would steal it anyway," he chuckled. "Except the scrap man."

Annetta and Allan lay squeezed side by side along the sofa, her head resting in the crook of his arm, as she watched television. Mary occupied an armchair, her legs curled beneath her as she studied a shopping catalogue. She had thought of calling in on Cissie but decided to leave it until morning, the weather putting her off.

Hearing the key in the latch, she looked questioningly up towards the living room door. Frank was at the pub, Walter on late shift and Tony was in the bath. As she wondered who it could be, Frank pushed open the slightly ajar door. Evidently by his appearance, Mary knew something dreadful had happened. Dropping the catalogue to the floor she rushed towards her bedraggled son. "What in the name?" She pulled him closer and examined the hardened blood that had temporarily sealed the cut on his ear.

"Look at your face man," Allan cried, now sitting bolt upright, his head appearing from over the sofa. Annetta pushed herself up and holding onto Allan to stop herself from sliding to the floor, gave a muted cry.

"Courtesy of a certain gentleman and his thugs." Frank announced. "Lookin' for you or me Allan?"

In shock disbelief, Allan knew whom his brother referred to. "Naw," he said, "he wouldn't."

"Drives a Rover? A black Rover?"

An angry raised voice behind Frank enquired accusingly, "Well Annetta, do you think him capable?"

Annetta nodded, tears welling from her eyes, "Oh yes Mary, that's nothing for him. I thought he had taken things a bit too well. Oh I am sorry Frank."

"He'll be after you both next," warned Frank, "You can bet your boots on that."

Still raging, Mary pulled on Frank's sleeve leading him into the back kitchen where she retrieved a biscuit tin containing bits and pieces of first aid material from the unit under the sink. Removing a dark blue parcel containing cotton wool, she tore off a piece then soaked it in raw Dettol. Patting the tear gently, Frank flinched, "It's bloody nippin'," he complained.

"Hold your tongue," Mary chided. Washing the dried blood had opened up the wound, and as fresh blood began to gush, Mary became alarmed. "That needs stitchin." Calling through to Allan, despite Frank's protests, she insisted that he drive his brother into the accident and emergency to have the wound seen to. The bruising on his face becoming obvious by now, Mary dabbed at the swelling on his lip. "Hold that pad to your ear son." Biting worriedly her own lip she said, "I should have left it. I think I've only made things worse."

"It's all right Ma," Frank assured her, "I'll have it stitched if only to make you happy."

Placing a hand on his shoulder, Mary spoke earnestly, "Do you think he'll go after them Frank. Really?"

"It's for certain. I think they've been watching the house and it so happened to be me who ventured out. No kiddin' Ma, if it wasn't for Scotty I would be in the infirmary by now, and in a worse state than this."

"Scotty?" she frowned questioningly.

"A man who came to my aid. Could handle himsel' an all. You should have seen how he belted hell out o' the big man...."

"Another yobo no doubt," Mary remarked unfairly.

"Awe naw. He was a decent sort of a man, not all that young either. Must be in his fifties, or not a kick in the arse off it."

"Watch your tongue my lad unless you want that other ear matching this one," she warned her usual light humour lacking as she objected to his phrasing.

Allan joined them dressed in his outdoor coat he stood hands in pockets. "Come on then, lets get that ear fixed. Oh hell, it's no' half leaking," he commented as he examined the side of his brother's head. "Get more of them pads and press hard," he suggested. "I don't want me new seat-covers covered in blood."

As the infirmary was unusually quiet, Frank had been taken into the small examination cubicle fairly quickly. Annetta and Allan sat in the waiting room looking out along the corridor towards where Frank had been taken. The waiting room stank of urine and the lingering smells from the down and outs who frequently slipped in for shelter.

Allan looked at his watch. It was now eleven o'clock. They had been waiting for an hour. Frank suddenly appeared from the cubical and was being pushed on a trolley towards the other end of the corridor by a porter. They watched as he disappeared into another room.

"Where are they taking him now?" Annetta spoke thinking aloud.

A small nurse appeared from out of the vacant cubicle making her way towards the waiting room. "Mr Sweeny?" she asked looking directly at Allan who nodded as she spoke. "Your brother has a suspected basal skull fracture I'm afraid and will have to be kept in. Once we arrange a bed we will have him admitted.

Allan blinked unable to take in what was being said. "What's a basal fracture?" he asked.

"The doctor will explain it to you once your brother is in the ward. He'll be alright; if you want you can slip along and see him," she smiled. "Round the corner to your left and you'll find the admissions."

They found Frank lying flat out on the trolley, the side of his head wrapped in bandages.

"What's this?" Allan greeted him with amazement. "What has happened?"

Frank gave a muted groan. "The ear is bloody throbbing brother. Can't hear a thing from it."

"Has that just happened?" Annetta asked vacantly.

"Naw. It's been buzzin' an' that, but since they poked and prodded, man it's awful. Basal skull fracture the guy said. They saw a trickle o' blood in the ear."

"What's that?" Allan asked concerned.

"Oh there's bleeding at the skull and seemingly they're concerned. Got to keep an eye oan me for a few days. The wee nurse has gone tae get a couple o' sand bags to keep my head still. Should be up in the ward in nae time."

"What's to happen now?" Allan thrust his hands in his pockets his temper flaring. "We should dae some thing about this. They shouldn't get away with this."

"Enough!" Frank said in a low but stern voice, "You just watch your back and dae nothing." He watched as his brother's shoulders relaxed, "You hear what I'm saying?"

"Aye. I hear you."

Annetta, feeling responsible for what had happened, felt sick. Every nerve in her body trembled. She knew she had to do something to prevent this going any further. She just had to put a stop to her father's violence.

An hour later, Frank was tucked up in the ward and at ten past mid-night, Allan and Annetta drove home after a brief conversation with the doctor.

Mary sat anxiously by the window, peering out into the darkness, listening for the car. She was giving them another half hour before phoning the hospital to make enquiries. She thought of contacting Walter, but didn't want to get him involved. Her heart leapt with relief when she heard the familiar rattle of the engine as the car drew into the street. Propelling herself from the wooden chair that sat by the window, she was at the door before Allan and Annetta were halfway up the path.

"Where's Frank?" she asked worriedly.

Putting an arm round his mother's waist, Allan led her back along the lobby leaving Annetta to close the door.

"He's all right. He's been kept in just tae see there's nae damage."

"Kept in? For a torn ear?" She looked unconvinced. "Come on?"

Seeing his mother was not going to be fooled, he sighed. "Well...he's got a bad skull fracture."

"Skull fracture?" she repeated. "Oh my God! Is that serious?"

"They're just keeping an eye on him. He's in the best place Ma. They'll sort him out."

"A bad skull fracture you say, how bad?" she shouted in distress.

"There's bleeding Ma. They have to watch him in case it reaches the brain."

"Oh my God!" Mary cried. "It really is serious." She wrung her hands nervously.

"They have to keep checking his pupils and his blood pressure an' that. But they're sure he will be fine Ma."

"We spoke to him before we left Mary. He's o.k." Annetta tried to sound comforting.

Without answering, Mary looked at Annetta with flashing anger in her eyes. At that moment she wanted to shout at the girl who had caused this grief on her family. She wanted to tell her about her father's morality, but as she looked into Annetta's eyes, she saw fear peer through the glistening moisture.

Annetta blinked a few times as she watched Mary struggle to control her thoughts. Then visibly deflated, Mary's shoulders sagged. Annetta threw her arms round Mary's tired frame and hugged her, and with tears running freely from her eyes, she repeated over and over, "I'm sorry Mary. I'm sorry."

As Mary's arms encircled Annetta, the comforter turned into the one now being comforted.

Making sure the last of her family had gone, Mary watched as Tony's bicycle disappeared into the adjoining street. Going into the hall she dialled the hospital number. The ward sister informed her that Frank had a comfortable night. Mary then asked that he be told that his mother rang and would be in later that day, and then sitting on the bottom step she opened the classified directory. Searching through the pages she found the section she was after, 'Leathergoods Importer', then, carefully she ran her finger down the column until she came across M. Francittie and son. Without hesitation, she picked up the receiver and despite her shaking hands, she was driven by necessary determination. She chewed nervously on the wall of her mouth.

"M Francitte, leather importers," the singsong voice of the receptionist informed her. "How can I help you?"

Clearing her throat, Mary answered confidently and in a business like manner, "Can you tell me if Mario Francittie will be in the Edinburgh office today or have I to contact Glasgow?"

"Can I ask who is calling?" came the efficient reply.

"Just a customer who wishes to know where to contact Mr. Francittie. Now can you give me this information or not?"

Sounding a bit put out, the woman's attitude changed, "Well yes, he will be here until twelve thirty but I'm afraid he will be rather busy."

"Thank you," Mary said abruptly before ringing off.

Six shiny brass plaques, three at either side of the open door, informed Mary of the companies that were housed in that particular building. The bottom plaque read, Francittie &

Son, Leather Importers. Their office was on the top floor. She climbed the wide spiral staircase until she reached the landing she was concerned with. Francittie's office was opposite Morris Advertising and as Mary passed, the tapping of a typewriter could be heard from the slightly ajar door. Standing for a few seconds outside the closed door of Francittie's, Mary flicked her hand briefly over her skirt as if removing imaginary lint, and then tugging at the hem of her jacket, she was satisfied with her appearance. With straight back and head held high, she filled her lungs with a deep intake of air before turning the handle of the door.

Inside the narrow lobby, she sidestepped towards the glass-panelled door that was marked reception. The woman who sat head bowed over a ledger, looked up at Mary, studied her with interest without a trace of a smile on her face, then with a voice as disagreeable as her face asked, "Can I help you?"

"I called to have a word with Mr Francittie," Mary said confidently.

"Is he expecting you?" she asked, her lips formed a perfect o shape after her question moving silently as if she was about to whistle...

"No, but if you tell him Mary Sweeny is here to see him, I'm sure he will want to listen to what I have to say." She felt the anger from the previous night rekindle and was glad of it, as her great fear was to mellow with the passing hours.

The woman lifted the telephone and dialled. "Mr. Francittie, there's a Mrs. Mary Sweeny in reception to see you. She..." as her voice trailed off, it was obvious the other end had interrupted her flow of speech. The woman listened tight-lipped, never taking her eyes from Mary. "Yes...Yes...I will." Replacing the receiver, she smiled weakly for the first time. "He is with someone at the moment but he asked if you will wait a few minutes."

Nodding her reply, Mary sat beside the window and looked out into the busy morning traffic.

Mario Francittie smirked as he replaced the receiver. Looking over at his distraught daughter, he felt no compassion for having reduced her to tears.

Like Mary, Annetta had called to try and bring this feuding to an end. She too, like Mary, knew the others would have prevented her approaching her father for fear he would harm her in some way, so she kept the meeting to herself.

Mario Francittie had been able to overpower his daughter by the domineering and authoritarian manner he had ruled with all his life. When she was obedient he was the sweetest, gentlest father who showered everything on her, but her mind and opinions had to be suppressed. Although the family was his prize possession they were moulded and shaped the way he wanted them to be.

"It appears that I have another caller from the Sweeny household," he grinned. "The Mother!"

Alarmed, Annetta's wet eyes widened to there fullest. "Mary? Oh no. She mustn't see me here Father. I - I don't want her to know I've come here."

"Why?" he spoke with mock sympathy. "Is it because they stop you from coming home?"

"No. You know that is not the case. I feel as if I have caused all the bother. I just want you to stop all this. Isn't it enough that you have Frank in hospital? He had nothing to do with it either. It's my choice to be with Allan. Can't you see that?"

"That fellow dared to throw me to the ground. No one does that to *me*," he prodded his chest, the gold link chains hanging from his wrists jingling together. "Get into that room until I get rid of her."

Annetta opened the door and entered what was a tiny box room, used for storing old accounts, ledgers and oddments of office equipment. She knew as she closed the door that what she had done was unbelievably stupid and gave her father an advantage over her. He could easily expose her and make her look deceitful. As she heard her father tell the receptionist to send Mary in she wanted to walk back into the office but she hesitated too long. Her father's voice boomed. "What can I do for you?" as Mary entered his office with out knocking.

"I'll tell you what you can do for me," Mary said angrily, "You can leave our family alone. You have put my Son in hospital with your thuggery and I will not stand around and watch you and your thugs do the same to Allan. If I had anything to do with it, you would be charged!" As she watched him slowly and deliberately open the long silver box that sat on the desk to his right, her face turned red with rage. Ignoring her presence, he selected a cigar and studied it as if looking for an imperfection.

"That's right, go on ignore me, you ignorant stupid man! And you wonder why your Daughter doesn't want to know you!"

His eyes darted to her face. "My Daughter doesn't know what she is doing. Your son has manipulated her. The worst thing we ever did was to allow her to befriend him. He now thinks he's onto a good thing ...well believe you me...he will not get a penny of our money!"

"Can't you get it into your thick head, he doesn't want anything from you! They want each other, but I don't suppose you know about such things."

"I know enough to recognise opportunists, and your son is an opportunist. He may fool you, but that's natural, he's your son, but he doesn't fool me." Pointing the unlit cigar at Mary, his eyes narrowed. "Even if you say he's not after money, do you think I would want Annetta mixed up with a family with the reputation yours have? Oooh I know all about Sweeny. Attempted murder was it, and bigamy? And you knew nothing?" he laughed. "Your sons have bad blood and you expect them to mingle with decent people!" Grinning, pleased with his knowledge, he snipped the end of the cigar.

Mary felt the hairs on the back of her neck rise. Every ounce of blood in her veins boiled as she watched the contentment on Mario Francittie's face. Nothing was going to ruffle this man. Anything she was going to say would make not an ounce of difference. Shaking with anger she watched his mouth spread wide, the gold tooth on his upper front gleamed as it caught the shaft of light from the window. She felt herself struggle to keep from flying at him, the tips of her fingers dug into her palms as she clenched her fists tightly holding her arms stiffly against her sides. She wanted to shock him, knowing that she had the perfect weapon. Through hate-filled eyes, she watched as he sucked on the cigar, the smoke rising making thick white rings as the end glowed menacingly.

"And what about *your* son. Are you including *him* in that statement?" she snapped.

His smug expression change as he now looked annoyed. "What are you ranting about woman? My son has nothing to do with this."

"Oh but I think he has. It will surprise you to know that you put your *own son* in hospital. It was *your own son* you had beaten up."

He frowned questioningly.

"Don't you remember me?" She watched his expressionless eyes. "No I don't suppose you do." With an impatient shake of her head, she gave an uncomfortable laugh. "You probably had so many woman that one was just like the other to you." Her whole body seemed to be thrown forward as she confronted him. "Remember Mary Fairley?" She watched as he screwed his eyes into focus. His jaw dropped as he tried to recognise her from the past. "Surprised! Remember you ran when I told you I was having a baby, your baby!" Shaking her head she grinned. "Isn't it a small world?"

The look of shock on his face told Mary he knew.

"Cat got your tongue?" she taunted. "That baby is lying in the hospital at this very minute. Put there by his very own father. Now there's a turn up for the books."

Annetta stood open mouthed behind the cupboard door. She had heard everything as clear as if she had been by her father's side. Standing in a state of profound shock, her mind could not take in what she had just heard. Numbed by this new revelation her feet seemed rooted to the floor. Frank was her half brother. As she conjured his face to mind, she realised there was a faint resemblance to her own twin.

Mario stared at Mary, and with sudden recollection, he saw the years disappear from her face. The sweat ran from his brow as he realized his daughter was inside the cupboard and would be listening to every word. He had wanted her to hear how he brought this woman down, but he could never have visualised the outcome of the meeting.

"How dare you come in here with your crazy accusations," he fumed.

"They're not crazy. You were told about the baby and you disappeared."

"I have never heard such nonsense." As his brow now perspired profusely he drew a large handkerchief from his trouser pocket, "I will be obliged if you get out of here before I call security. You're mad!" he shouted as he drew his handkerchief across his brow.

"Oh no, I'm not mad, but I bet your wife would be if she found out."

"Are you blackmailing *me*?" He thrust his finger into his chest.

"I don't think you can call it blackmail. I think it's more like righting a wrong."

"You can't prove that I had anything to do with you or your boy."

"Can't I? Can you afford to have me try? No, I think not, because you remember alright." She looked at him in disgust. "You leave my family alone. Leave Annetta alone. That's all I demand."

"Demand?" He laughed nervously.

"Demand!" Mary repeated. She stood a few seconds studying his bull like face before turning to walk from the office.

"Just a minute," he snapped.

Turning to face him, Mary tilted her head in a mischievous fashion.

"You wouldn't dare make this knowledge public. What would your son do? I take it that he knows nothing about this."

Mary nodded.

"Well then, it would damage you as much as it would me."

"You don't know my son. It would make no difference to our relationship." Mary spoke with confidence, although she dreaded to think what really would happen if Frank knew the truth, then as an afterthought she added, "But I dare say, he might want a bit of what is his! That is if he knew who his Father was."

Visibly disturbed, he pulled at the collar of his shirt allowing the swollen veins in his neck more room. "Giving me all this information could be some what dangerous to you."

"In what way?" Mary answered defiantly.

"You could have a very bad accident on your way home. Then who would know all this?"

"I would!" Annetta stood at the door, her face drawn and shocked. I would know Father, just as I know who would be capable of such a thing."

"You'll say nothing of this," he bellowed.

Looking towards Mary, Annetta smiled, "Sorry Mary, I came here to do the same as you, but I didn't have the same ammunition."

"*Go!*" bellowed Mario. "*Go with her, but remember, don't run back to me when things go wrong.*"

"Nothing is going to go wrong Father. Not now," and with impudence, she added, "when will it be convenient for you to send my clothes and personal things to me?"

With a growl, he said reluctantly, "Arrange that with your Mother."

Two steaming mugs of coffee sat in front of the two women. They had said very little on the way towards the bus station, but now both of them wanted to talk but found difficulty in starting. It was Mary who broached the subject.

"I'm sorry you heard all of that Annetta, believe me if I had known you were there, I wouldn't have said anything. I didn't go up there with the intentions of telling him about Frank, but he made me so angry. I just couldn't control my mouth."

"I was shocked Mary. Not because my Father had another son tucked away somewhere, it was it being Frank! What are the odds of that happening I wonder?"

Touching Annetta's hand, Mary's face shaded with worry. "Will you keep it to yourself? Frank thinks his father is dead, I don't think he would thank you for the truth."

With an assured smile she covered Mary's hand with hers, "There's not a chance in the world that I would give him my Father as a legacy. No one deserves that. No Mary, your secret is safe with me."

"Walter knows about it. I had to tell him."

"Well, that's how it should be," smiled the young girl, "You don't keep secrets from your intended." Seeing an anxious look flash across Mary's face, she realised what she had said. "Don't worry Mary, I will never tell Allan. It's nothing to do with us really."

As they sipped their coffee, Annetta suddenly asked, "What was he like?"

"Who?" Mary stared blankly. "You mean your Father?"

She nodded.

As if she had trouble recalling, Mary stared up at the ceiling before answering, "He was very handsome, but as I think back, he had that arrogant nature even then. He was a terrific dancer though!"

"You're joking," Annetta laughed. "He can't dance a step!"

"That's not true. He was a good dancer."

Shaking her head she smiled, "The old devil! He never dances with Mother. Said he couldn't."

"Well that is where I met him. I fell for his style, then, when I told him about the baby, he just disappeared."

"It must have been awful for you." Annetta's sympathy was almost comical.

"There's worse things in life Annetta, believe me. Frank is one of my blessings."

"Well, I will never reveal any of this. I promise Mary."

Smiling, Mary looked into her lovely earnest eyes. "I know you won't."

"Good grief Mary, just think. You could have been my Mother!"

"Oh! Goodness. I think I would've jumped of The Forth Bridge by now! I think I'll stick to being your Mother- in law."

Chapter Twenty

"Frank, if I've to tie you to that bed, and I warn you I will." The pretty Irish nurse lifted him by the legs and swung him back on top of the bed. "Be told and rest!" Her bobbed red hair shone beneath her starched cap and her soft green eyes twinkled as she wagged a warning finger.

"What's all the bloomin' fuss? I'm all right I tell ye!"

"Maybe so, but until the doctor says you're all right, you'll lie flat on your back or get the sharp end of me tongue."

"Really?" Frank grinned. "Come here and give me a hug," he teased.

"I know what I'll give you...a cold bath!" She laughed as she gripped his wrist in readiness to take his pulse.

"How often is this to go on?" Frank asked wearily.

"Every hour, on the hour, pulse, blood pressure and pupil size to be checked. The doctor has already explained all that to you now so don't be going on so. Heavens above, sure, you're like a baby right enough."

Frank lay still, watching as the bright sparkling eyes of the young woman concentrated on her stopwatch. From the first moment Frank had set his sights on her, she triggered something off in his heart. The touch of her hand wrapped round his wrist was enough to give him a feeling of inner warmth. The way her mouth formed when laughing amused him highly. That cheeky independent air and her quick wit he had never known in a woman, except for his Mother, and of course Cissie, who had fed them all on her wittiness.

Yes, nurse Doreen Galloway was what he had been looking for all his young life, although he couldn't have explained his wants to any one, he just knew that he would know is ideal woman when he met her.

As she stared into his eyes, taking note of their condition, Frank gave a cheeky wink.

"Nothing wrong there," she commented. "Nothing that cannot be put right by a cuff round the ear." She pushed her tongue against her cheek as she spoke.

"Very funny," Frank grinned.

"You stay in that bed, you hear? I'll be back later." As she moved away, his eyes followed her. He watched her rounded hips sway beneath the crisp white uniform. Her smart assured walk, and the air of complete control told him that she was nobody's fool. She had sat on the edge of his bed last night and chatted for ages, but no intimate details were exchanged.

As she disappeared out of sight, he looked to the ceiling and closed his eyes. There he lay, his thoughts turning to home.

"Well, how's the wounded warrior?" A coarse whisper filled his ear.

Opening his eyes, he turned his head in the direction of the voice, gazing for a second into the face of the visitor.

"Scotty! What the devil are you doing here?" he asked delighted, pulling himself up on to the pillows by his elbows.

"Oh thanks mate. Is that what I get for bothering about you?"

Laughing, Frank held his hand out allowing Scotty to shake it warmly.

"Grab a seat." Frank said, indicating towards the window where a pile of grey plastic chairs piled on top of each other. "How did you know I was here?"

Dragging a chair behind him, Scotty placed it beside the bed and sat down heavily, "It's all round the town."

Grimacing Frank added, "I should have known. This place has the worlds fastest relay system. Just let one person know and the job's over in an instant."

"I went looking for you at the pub and Freddy told me. I thought they had caught up with you again."

"Naw. It was ma' Mother. Fussin' as usual. I've been lying here flat on my back for three days. I hope to get out in the next two days though or I'll do my nut in. But listen to me. How are you doin'? I never found out where you went."

Scotty shifted uneasily in the chair. He looked into the face of the smiling Frank and knew he had to tell him. Frank was his only chance. Taking his huge tanned hand, he laid it gently on Frank's pyjama covered arm, patting it gently. "I have something to tell you lad and it's something that may not go down well. Certainly not with your Mother."

"My Mother?" Frank screwed his eyes questioningly as he glanced down at Scotty's consoling gesture.

"I was following you that night Frank, you see, I was standing looking towards your house when you left that night from your neighbour's."

"You what? What are you on about?" Then pushing Scotty's hand from his arm, he asked astonishingly, "You were planted by Francittie?"

Giving a half-hearted laugh, Scotty shook his head. "Naw lad, God forbid. Naw. I was trying to pluck up courage. Courage to face your Mother."

"My mother? What has she got to do with you?" He was confused.

Scotty cleared his throat nervously. "Your Mother is my sister." He watched Frank's blank expression. "I'm Billy, your Mother's brother."

"You can't be. Billy's dead. Lost at sea," his tone was defensive.

Finding it hard to explain, Scotty shook his head wearily. His heart pounded under his calm appearance, dreading Frank's rejection. "Naw lad. I jumped ship that morning. It's a long story."

Blowing through puckered lips, Frank stared at Scotty. "Oh my God. I can't believe this." He stared hard. "You're Billy? You've come back from the dead. Oh man, I can see what you mean by plucking up courage."

Both men sat silent studying each other's face, and then with an emotional tear appearing in Scotty's eyes, Frank reached over with welcoming arms and embraced his long lost uncle.

As they broke free from their embrace, Frank held Scotty at arms length. "Why now? Why didn't you get in touch years ago? Why let her think you were dead?"

"Frank, I wrote to her before that happened and got no reply. Sweeny probably turned her against me. He was a pure bastard by all accounts."

"Aye, he was."

"Well I know better now, but at that time, I thought it best to disappear. The longer you take to get in touch, the harder it gets."

"Then why now?"

"I've done well for myself in Australia, but I got thinking; if anything happens to me, who's to inherit my business? No one!"

"You have a business ... in Australia?"

"Aye, and a damn good one at that." He smiled at his nephew's bewildered face, "Four garages. And I hear you have the old monkey grease running through your veins an all."

"Aye. So that's who I take it from." He shook his head in amazement.

"Must be son. In fact, you're a lot like your uncle Billy now I think of it. A confirmed bachelor I am, and it looks like you love them and leave them like I did."

"Freddy! That barman's a lot to answer for." Frank frowned, and then a sudden twinkle appeared in his eye. "I think I'm about to remedy that though Scotty."

"Uncle Billy!" Scotty corrected him gently.

"I better call you Scotty for the time bein'."

"Aye you're right lad, well, who's the lucky girl?" he asked hiding his sudden disappointment.

"She doesn't know it yet, but she will before I leave here. She's a great wee nurse and I intend making her mine," he said with determined conviction. "But what are we to do about you?" Frank bit on his lip as he scoured his brain for a solution. "I think I have an idea, but I will have to get in touch with Walter."

"Aye, who's this Walter? Your Mother's going to marry again?"

"He's alright is Walter. You'll like him. He's great with my Mother. He'll help us break this to her."

Frank and Billy talked for the next hour, filling in the lost years as best they could.

Three days later, Frank was discharged but not before he persuaded his young nurse to have dinner the following

Saturday. Doreen had shrugged and agreed to be taken out, 'only to get rid of him without a fuss,' she said, but secretly, she was as delighted as he was. The hard, no-nonsense attitude she emanated, was part of her charm, mixed with her Irish humour and wild untamed looks. She was the perfect complement to Frank's roguish nature.

Billy stood nervously alongside Frank as he knocked confidently on the door of Walter's flat. Frank had phoned him the previous day arranging the meeting, asking him not to mention anything to Mary. Walter, intrigued by the secrecy, agreed.

As the door opened, Walter acknowledged his future stepson by a sharp nod of his head before turning a quizzical eye towards Billy.

"Come in," Walter beckoned.

As they sat down, Frank held his upturned palm towards his companion, "Walter, I would like you to meet Scotty."

Walter hesitated before offering his hand in friendship. "Oh I know who you are," he smiled.

Billy and Frank looked at each other questioningly.

"Scotty. You helped Frank that night he took the beating. Mary told me about you."

"Oh aye," Frank said nodding his head, "that's right. This is the very same Scotty."

"Well lads, what can I get you, tea, coffee?"

"Naw Walter, not for me." Frank refused with a wave of his hand.

"No thanks," Scotty added.

"Well then, what's this dark secret that has you both here instead of the Tavern."

"Has my Mother ever spoken to you about her brother Billy who drowned a good few years back?"

"Aye she has," Walter smiled broadly.

Scotty shifted uneasily in his chair.

"Well, what would you say if I told you he didn't drown?"

"Go on," Walter urged.

"Well, that's what I came to tell you Walter, he didn't drown."

"How do you know this?" Walter asked rubbing the unshaved stubble on his chin.

Taking a deep breath he prepared to answer but was interrupted by Scotty.

"I'm known in Australia as Scotty, but my name is really Billy Fairley. I wasn't on that ship when it went down. I jumped ship with a mate of mine. We were on the run when we were stricken by malaria. We knew nothing about the ship for years. Finally we made our way to Australia and became illegals, but when the governor declared an amnesty, we gave ourselves up and settled there."

"Good grief!" exclaimed Walter. "She'll get the shock of her life. Why haven't you contacted her before this?"

"That's exactly what everyone asks, but you must remember I was told to stay away by Patrick Sweeny and he was her husband after all. At least, at that time."

"You could have written." Walter persisted.

"I did. Several times. Mind you it was before the ship went down, but I didn't know about that. When we reached Australia, being illegals, we were on the move all the time. You could only stay at the same address for a short period of time in case you were discovered."

"Good God!" Walter exclaimed as he ran his hands through the fallen locks of his hair.

"How are we to break this to her without giving her a terrible shock?" Frank asked.

The two men on the sofa watched as Walter bit hard into his lip.

"We are getting married in two weeks. I think I know what we can do. She'll still get a hellish shock, but we can't prevent that." He looked at Frank, "so, I suggest that you tell her someone has contacted you about this and ...and Billy has arranged to give her a ring from Australia."

"What, from Australia? You mean I have to go back without seeing her?" Scotty protested.

"Let me finish." Walter stretched his lips apart, revealing a row of perfect teeth.

"You will be *here* when you ring. Only Mary will think you are in Australia. Let me tell you what we are about to plan."

The following evening, Mary sat with Cissie going over the last minute details for the wedding. The marriage was to take place in the local church and the reception was to be held in a small family hotel on the outskirts of town.

Cissie insisted on making Mary's outfit and fussed about her like a mother hen. Every detail had to be perfect.

It was ten past ten when Walter and Frank walked in. They had supposedly been out for a pint at the Tavern.

"Want supper?" Mary asked, clearing bits of paper from the table.

"I'll away o'er lass," said Cissie going for her coat.

"Are you not staying for another wee cup?" asked Mary in a tempting tone.

"Naw lass, you see tae the men, I'll get away o'er."

"Cissie," Frank said softly, "I'd like you to stay a bit. There's somethin' a want tae tell ma' Mother."

Mary face fell with the look of expected trouble. She felt that familiar knot tighten in her stomach and the dragging feeling of forthcoming disappointment. "What's happened now? What have you been up to?"

Seeing his mother's worried expression he waved his hand, wiping away her worried thoughts. "Nothing like that Ma', in fact, it's really good news."

"Weel you'd no' think it. Yer face is like a fiddler's elbow." Cissie remarked.

Taking his mother gently by the arm, he swung her round towards the sofa. "Sit down beside Cissie and I'll tell you what I heard."

"Go on then," Mary grinned as she eased Cissie back onto the sofa, "Fire-away. What's all this good news?" She sat by her friend's side and waited for Frank to speak.

Clearing his throat, he looked down on the two women, shuffled his feet and said nothing.

"Fer gidness sake laddie, sit yoursel' doon. Yer standin' there like a waiter at a hoor's weddin'," Cissie said with growing impatience.

He looked round for Walter, hoping for moral support, only to find that he had slipped into the kitchen and the rattle of the kettle told him that he was not about to come out.

"Oh come on Frank, what's this good news that's too terrible to tell?" Mary's too had grown impatient.

Sitting in the chair opposite the waiting woman, Frank, resting his hands on his knees, grinned nervously, "Ma, I met a man in the pub tonight, and he knows your brother Billy."

Mary's smile stayed fixed, "So. He knew Billy. Go on."

"No Ma. He *knows* Billy. Billy's still *alive*."

He watched as his mother's smile slid slowly and painfully from her lips. "Is this some sort of a joke Frank for if it is, it's in poor taste!"

"Go on lad," Cissie urged as she laid her hand on Mary's arm. "What did this man tell you?"

Turning to Cissie, Mary said in annoyance, "Cissie, fine you know Billy's dead."

"Shush lass!" Cissie shook her head, "Let the lad go on."

"Billy was never on the ship Ma. He's in..in Australia."

"Australia?" She glanced swiftly at Cissie before returning her gaze to Frank. "What the.... how does this man know it's Billy?" She wrung her hands with nervous agitation.

"Billy spoke to him...in Australia. He told him about us.... and he's going to phone him and give him our phone number."

Mary shook her head, "Some one's having a sick joke Frank." Then thinking quickly, Mary quizzed. "Why could this man not give you Billy's phone number so we could contact him ourselves, if that's to be believed?" Mary asked.

"He eh, he didn't have it on him," Frank said, trying to sound convincing.

Mary and Cissie sat staring at Frank, waiting for more, then Mary called out to Walter.

Appearing at the kitchen door he smiled warmly.

"Did you see this man Frank's on about?"

"No, he was gone before I arrived." Walter looked directly at Frank, smiling inwardly. He knew by experience that two stories would conflict, so he left Frank to go it alone.

"Aye that's right Ma, Walter just missed him by seconds."

"I don't believe this. Billy is dead." Mary sounded distraught.

Cissie patted Mary's hand, "Lass, there's nothin' in this world cut an' dried. Who's tae say Billy wis oan that ship? Ye never really found oot much, an' it wis as quick as that greedy brother o' yours could sell the lad's flat."

"Do you really think there's a chance he's still alive?" Her eyes, as wide as saucers, stared appealingly at Cissie.

"Well if the chappie that spoke tae Frank gits in touch wi' him, weel find oot."

"Did you ask this man his name, or where he was staying?" She asked Frank.

"He's phoning Australia the night Ma'. It's alright." With outstretched arms, he stroked his mother's hair. "If Sc ..Billy rings," he corrected himself quickly, "it will be early tomorrow, time changes an all that."

Mary's hands covered her face. Her body shook as nerves took over...The warm comfort of Cissie's huge arms enfolded her and held her as the emotion she felt surged out in tears and loud sobs.

Cissie looked over at Frank, warning him with one of her looks. "This better be true lad or yer arse will be kicked up yer back fur a hump." Then looking towards Walter she snapped, "and what're you standing there fur, this is your joab noo. Come away o'er here an' comfort yer wuman. Dear, dear, hiv a tae tell ye whit tae dae next. Michty me, what's this world comin' tae?"

Following a sleepless night, the phone in the hall rang at seven thirty. Her heart thumping against her rib cage, Mary lifted the receiver.

"Hallo," the voice said. "Is that you Mary?"

"Billy?" She asked as her heart beat faster.

"None other," came his reply.

"It's true. It's really you?" The groan that escaped from her throat was followed by nervous laughter. "Oh Billy! Oh Billy!"

Two phone calls followed that week and as Billy had made both, Mary was led to believe he was still in Australia.

The morning of the wedding was bright and fresh. Cissie stood by Mary's window and smiled contentedly at the bright blue sky. She drew in a breath of disbelief, as Tony appeared dressed in a navy blue blazer and dark grey flannels, with shirt and red tie, he looked every inch a young man. At fifteen, Tony had no wish to be grown up, so his discomfort was apparent as he strolled into the room.

"Will ye look at how handsome ye are? It's unbelievable whit a guid wash an' brush up dis. Noo, if there's ony wee lassies aboot, I'll have tae help ficht them oaf."

"Give over Cissie. I look like a prat."

Frank popped his head round the kitchen door and added to the banter, "Where are you goin' son? Your in the wrong hoose." Then as if recognising his brother, he drew his head back in awe, "Well well. I never recognised you our Tony. Going to a wedding or somethin?"

"Shut up Frank. You're used to looking like a prat. I hate this." He drew his hands down his jacket front.

"What would you do if she had insisted upon kilts?" Frank laughed.

"Kilts? She never mentioned kilts. Did she?" His mouth dropped in disbelief.

"Aye. Now then, be grateful wee brother. I persuaded her to change her mind."

"That's the taxis boys." Called Cissie lifting her hat from the chair.

Allan entered the room fixing his carnation to his lapel. "Cissie, can you catch this bleedin' stem with the pin?"

"Oh laddie, I cannae see wi' oot ma ither glesses, but Frank will help ye."

Frank, approaching Allan, grinned. "What are you going to be like on *your* big day brother?"

Blowing, Allan commented, "I hate to think."

"Come on you two," Cissie beckoned, It's time to go." Then going to the hall door, she called on Annetta.

Annetta dressed in pale pink, appeared at the door. "Now boys, be prepared for a wonderful sight." Turning her head to the stairs, Annetta smiled at Mary, "Come see your three sons."

Mary stood in the doorway, dressed in the ivory silk suit Cissie had painstakingly made for her. It was plain, all but the silk embroidered detail on the corner of both pockets. The scalloped edging of the jacket hung expertly round her well-matured hips, the skirt length just ending below her knees. On her head, small clusters of pink roses were entwined through a mass of fair hair, piled high, dropping loosely onto her cheeks. Holding her bouquet of pale pink roses, she smiled demurely at the silent faces.

"Well. Nobody going to comment?" she asked.

Frank broke the silence, "Ma, I think I'll marry you ma' sel'. You look absolutely stunnin'."

Allan took Annetta by the hand. "If you look half as good as that, I'll have no complaints," he said winking.

"Go on then, Cissie pushed Tony roughly on his back, "What have you to say?"

Ignoring Cissie's heavy hand, Tony gulped, "Ma, it's worth gettin' all poshed up fur. Just wait till ma pals see the stotter *I* have fur a Mother."

"You would have worn a kilt then?" asked Frank laughing.

"A' didnae ken about that," Tony answered screwing his nose up till it wrinkled.

"He's a lucky man," Cissie commented, a slight tear emerging from the corner of her eye.

Mary walked towards her, throwing her arms round her neck. "Oh Cissie, thanks for being there when I needed you. Not just now, but all my adult life."

Removing her gently, Cissie joked. "Away wi' ye'. A needed you just as much. Noo dinnae get yer een aw' black wi that miscarriage."

"Mascara Cissie," corrected Allan laughing.

Frank and Mary watched as the others drove off in their taxis. Mary sat down on the wooden chair by the window and Frank stood by her side his hand resting on her shoulder.

"Mum, I'm really happy for you. And there's something I have to tell you before we go."

"Looking dreamily up into Franks face, Mary smiled. "What is it son?"

Crouching down in front of Mary, Frank held her gaze, "Mum,... I love you. We all do. I know I have hurt you many times, I'm sorry."

Mary's lip quivered. "I love you too Frank. I will always love you. I'm a lucky woman. I have three sons to be proud of and now I am adding a wonderful husband.

Bending down, he kissed his mother's cheek.

"Watch out Frank, don't turn all soppy on me, keep it for that young lass of yours," Mary teased. "She is coming to the wedding I hope?"

"Aye that she is Ma. She'll be waiting at the church." His face beamed at the thought.

"I'm glad you have found a nice lass."

The taxi with the familiar broad white ribbons adorning the bonnet, pulled up in front of the house. "I guess it's time for me to give my Mother away," he sighed.

"I'm ready," Mary smiled as she rose and held on to Frank's arm. "Ready to change my life."

A small group of well-wishers stood at the church gates as Frank helped Mary from the taxi. They could hear the muffled strains of organ music as they walked up the path, and as Frank took Mary's arm, she pinched him playfully.

"Excited?" he asked.

"I am now," she fluttered her eyes.

Reaching the door of the church, they stepped into the East wing, where Allan, acting as usher waited. "Walters waiting Ma, and so is someone else."

The vestry door in the corner was slightly open, and the figure of a smartly dressed man stood looking on. As he smiled at Mary, tears filled his eyes. "Hallo sis." His mouth quivered. "I've found you only to be giving you away."

"Billy?" Mary gasped in disbelief. They stood momentarily without moving, and then breaking from Frank, Mary rushed over. "Billy, you came?"

"I was never away Mary. I spoke to you from down the road."

"What?" Mary exclaimed.

"It's a long story that can be told after. The important thing right now is to get you safely down the aisle. That man of yours is waiting."

"Walter knew about this?" she beamed. "And all of you?"

"I'm afraid so Ma," Allan confessed.

The strains of the bridal march filled the church as the two boys left their mother with Billy.

Heads turned as Mary walked up the aisle on the arm of her precious brother. As Walter watched her approach, pride and immense love was evident on his face.

"Who gives this woman to this man?" the minister asked.

"I do," Billy said proudly.

THE END

About the Author

Born in Scotland in the mining town of Prestonpans, Mary was educated at Preston Lodge High School where she went on to work in the editorial department of Macdonald & Son Printers and Publishers. She also spent some time working in retail before moving on into the field as sales representative for Bemrose printers and publishers. Now retired she lives with husband Jim in the beautiful fishing village of Port-Seton, a mile from where she was born.

Printed in the United Kingdom by
Lightning Source UK Ltd., Milton Keynes
142221UK00001BA/3/A